Sunshine and Showers

June Francis' sagas include *Step by Step*, *A Dream To Share*, *When Clouds Go Rolling By*, *Tilly's Story* and *Sunshine and Showers*. She had her first novel published at forty and is married with three sons. She lives in Liverpool.

JUNE FRANCIS

Sunshine and Showers

CANELO

First published in the United Kingdom in 2010 by Allison & Busby

This edition published in the United Kingdom in 2022 by

Canelo
Unit 9, 5th Floor
Cargo Works, 1–2 Hatfields
London SE1 9PG
United Kingdom

Copyright © June Francis 2010

A CIP catalogue record for this book is available from the British Library.

Print ISBN 978 1 80032 799 3
Ebook ISBN 978 1 911591 42 9

Look for more great books at www.canelo.co

Printed and bound in Great Britain by Clays Ltd, Elcograf S.p.A.

1

Dedicated to the memory of my Norwegian-born great-grandfather Martin Nelson and other Mersey Mariners who died at sea.

Chapter One

January 1926

'What are you doing?'

Patsy Doyle started at the sound of her employer's voice and the coal scuttle slipped through her hands, falling with a thud onto the carpet. Lumps of coal spilt out in a cloud of dust. 'Sorry, sir!' She straightened the scuttle and began to pick up the pieces. Her hands in the soiled suede gloves trembled and her damaged finger throbbed painfully.

David Tanner picked up several lumps of coal and limped over to place them in the scuttle. 'I don't know why I agreed to have you here. An older, more experienced woman would have been more sensible.'

Patsy pressed her lips tightly together on the hot words that threatened to spill out. 'I can't help being young, sir, but I'm getting older by the day.'

'Yes, and with a pronounced tendency to answer back,' he said dryly, dropping the hearth brush and shovel beside her. 'Clear up this mess and get the fire going.'

'Yes, sir.' She slanted him a glance and thanked God he wasn't as quick-tempered as his wife.

David Tanner was a tall man with an austere, lean face and floppy light-brown hair. He was in his late twenties but looked older because of the lines that pain had etched about his mouth and eyes. He rested an elbow on the mantelshelf and stared at her moodily. 'What time did my wife go out?'

'Early this morning. She wanted to be at the opening of the Bon Marché sales.'

He frowned. 'But it's half-past five! She should have been back ages ago. Did she say whether she was going on anywhere else? Perhaps to Seaforth to see her mother?'

'She didn't mention it to me but with the lull in the bad weather perhaps she decided to do just that.'

'She really ought to make some effort to be here when I come home from work. Did she say anything more to you? I've heard some wives do make confidantes of their maids.'

'I don't know what a confidante is, sir.'

He sighed. 'Someone to tell things to that she wouldn't tell anyone else, such as her husband.'

Patsy said cautiously, 'Are we talking secrets here, sir?' She gazed at him with wide-eyed innocence.

'Yes! Indeed, we are.'

'Then I'm not one of those thingamabobs yer just mentioned.'

'Never mind,' he said tetchily before changing tack. 'Why didn't you light the fire earlier? It's freezing in here.'

'Orders from the missus, sir. Trouble with the miners, shortage of coal.'

'Well, she may have a point there. Has the evening paper arrived?'

'Yes, sir. Yer'll find it on the occasional table.'

'Don't keep calling me *sir*. I've never been knighted.'

'Then what am I to call you?'

'Mr Tanner.' He moved away from the fireplace and sat on the sofa and picked up the *Liverpool Echo*.

Patsy tended to the fire. Moments later she was conscious of him hovering over her as she performed the task of brushing up the coal dust.

'Did my wife mention what she intended to buy in the sales? Was it a new dance frock? She is fond of dancing as you'll no doubt have realised.'

Patsy straightened up and almost collided with him. 'I doubt she'll get what she's really after in the sales in that case.'

'You mean she mentioned something specific?' He looked alarmed.

'A velvet-lined cloak of silver lame finished with silver fox fur. It's the latest from Paris as seen in the *Echo* last week.'

'Oh my God,' he groaned. 'You mean she planned on buying that as well as a dance frock? Does the woman think I'm made of money? I want her to have what she wants and to be happy, but…' Words seemed to fail him and he perused the pages of the newspaper. 'Would you believe it! They're showing a film called *Ypres* at the cinema. You can bet it'll be a glorified version of what actually happened.' He pushed himself upright and limped over to the window.

Patsy skirted him and made for the door into the lobby.

'Wait!'

She almost jumped out of her skin. 'Yes, sir?'

'Do you happen to recall what Mrs Tanner was wearing when she went out?'

'A beaver hat and a reversible tweed cape over a flared green skirt, a cream blouse and a forest-green cardigan,' listed Patsy. 'She looked very nice.'

'My wife is always excellently turned out.'

Patsy noticed that he was frowning again and wondered if he suspected his wife of meeting someone: a man, for instance. 'Is there anything else, Mr Tanner?'

'No, you can go.' He turned towards the fireplace and took a cheroot case from his pocket. From a jar on the mantelshelf he took a spill and, with a hand that shook slightly, took a light from the fire and lit his cheroot. Then he sat down and picked up the newspaper again.

Patsy considered it was odd that he should ask her not to call him *sir* all of a sudden. In her experience most men liked you to treat them like they were your lord and master. Perhaps he was trying to soften her up for something. She hurried to the kitchen and closed the door behind her. She rested her back against it and let out a long breath. It wasn't that Mr Tanner frightened her but he did make her edgy when she was alone with him. He was another ex-soldier who had experienced more than was good for him in the war.

3

Mrs Tanner had told her that, unlike those men who had lost limbs, the damage to her husband was hidden from the world. She had spoken in a tight-lipped kind of way and fiddled with her engagement and wedding rings as she had done so. Patsy's heart had been touched by this gesture of vulnerability and she had accepted the position of all-purpose maid, not only because she needed the money and a roof over her head, but because she had felt sorry for the woman. There had been times since when Patsy had regretted her decision.

Her previous employer, an old widow woman, had treated her strictly, but kindly as well. A Friend of the Seamen's Orphanage, she had also taught Patsy to speak properly, so that she only lapsed into her native Scouse when under stress. She had provided Patsy with her first job after leaving the orphanage and had trained her to a high standard. Sadly the old woman had died on the same day as the queen mother, Queen Alexandra, last November. Such was the old lady's generosity that she had left five pounds to Patsy in her will. She had been cock-a-hoop about her inheritance and placed most of it in her rainy-day fund.

Within days of losing that position, one of the orphanage's guardians had suggested Patsy apply for the post in the Tanner household in Anfield Road. A large house, with a long front garden, it was close to Liverpool football ground. When the team was playing at home, she could often hear the roar of the crowd when a goal was scored. The house was just over an hour's walking distance from the orphanage where four of her siblings still lived. Sometimes she was able to arrange a Saturday afternoon off so she could visit them. Still, there were times when she felt put upon by Mrs Tanner.

Patsy tossed the soiled gloves into a box in a corner and frowned as she put on the vegetables and checked the steak braising in the oven. While part of her job was preparing the vegetables, she had not been hired as a cook. It wasn't that she did not like cooking, but getting a meal just right was a big responsibility. She would not be sixteen until March. Yet here she was, left in charge of seeing to the evening meal. It wasn't right and she was only paid five shillings a week and cooks earned a lot more than that. Mrs Tanner should have been here overseeing her, not gallivanting. Besides, past experience had made Patsy wary of being left alone in the house with a man.

Her blood still ran cold when she thought of her mother's brother. Not that Mr Tanner was the least bit like Patsy's dead uncle but she was going to be on pins until his wife arrived home. Then you could bet there would be a low-voiced rebuke from Mr Tanner for her being in late, which appeared to irritate Mrs Tanner. She could be really nasty to him at times and on more than one occasion Patsy had received a reprimand that was more severe than the mistake warranted.

She held out her right hand which still hurt. On the first evening of the new year, Mrs Tanner had caught her picking up a couple of sugar lumps that had fallen onto the tablecloth. Absently Patsy had used her fingers instead of the tongs. Mrs Tanner had grabbed her hand and forced her to drop the lumps on the fire. Perhaps she did not know her own strength but the pain had caused Patsy to cry out.

The sound drew Mr Tanner's attention away from his book and he had demanded to know what was going on. The next moment the incident had turned nasty, with Mrs Tanner rounding on her husband and calling him an interfering swine. He had told her not to hurt the girl, before stalking out of the morning room, saying that he would be eating out and Patsy could have the evening off. Mrs Tanner had gone into the hall and used the telephone. Patsy had not been able to overhear the conversation but the upshot was that Mrs Tanner also went out. So Patsy had shared the dinner with the cat.

Later when Mrs Tanner had returned she was all smiles, telling Patsy that she had been with a friend to see *Charley's Aunt* at the Futurist cinema in Lime Street. Then she had mixed herself a vodka Martini before going to bed. Patsy had heard Mr Tanner arrive home just before midnight and go into his bedroom. And that was another odd thing about the Tanners, they had separate bedrooms.

She found the Tanners' behaviour towards each other baffling. They were young, attractive and, what with Mr Tanner being a solicitor, they appeared to have enough money to afford a comfortable lifestyle. So why the separate bedrooms and so many disagreements?

Patsy was roused from her reverie by a hissing noise. 'Oh hell!' She acted swiftly to move the potatoes from the gas ring. Just then she heard the door knocker sound and hurried to answer its summons.

'I forgot my key,' said Mrs Tanner, brushing past Patsy to place several parcels on the hall table. 'Is my husband home?'

'Yes, madam. He's been in at least half an hour and wanted to know where you'd gone.'

'As any caring husband would, Patsy,' said Mrs Tanner, sounding unexpectedly good-humoured. She removed her hat and shook it, scattering raindrops all over the girl.

Patsy wiped her face with the back of her hand and watched her hang up her cape. 'You had a successful shopping trip, madam?' she asked politely.

'Yes, indeedy.' Mrs Tanner fluffed out her blonde hair and gazed at her reflection in the hall mirror. 'Hopefully my husband won't want to know the price of everything I've bought.' Her pale-green eyes narrowed and she touched her mouth where the lipstick was smudged. 'I think I deserve little treats for what I have to put up with.'

'There's no need to say that, Rose.'

She started at the sound of her husband's voice.

'Darling, how softly you creep up on one.' Rose crossed the hall to where David stood and pecked his cheek.

Frowning, he wiped away the lipstick. 'Where've you been all this time?'

Instantly Rose turned on Patsy. 'Didn't you tell my husband that I was meeting my friend, Joan? Really, Patsy, your memory! Did you have the sense to put the casserole in the oven?'

Patsy said, 'Dinner will be ready when you are, madam.'

'Good. I'm starving.' She glanced at her husband. 'You're hungry, aren't you, David?'

'Your concern for my well-being is touching but really you should be here overseeing the girl, not gallivanting round town on shopping sprees. We didn't hire her as a cook.'

'Oh, don't start that again,' snapped Rose. 'Or one day I'll go out and never come back.'

'Hardly the first time you've threatened to do that, dear. Don't try my patience too far.' He took his wife by the arm and ushered her into the drawing room.

Patsy returned to the kitchen. She could not help wondering what was happening in the drawing room and decided to make a pot of tea and put some home-made cheese biscuits on a plate and take them through to the Tanners. After all, there was always the chance that she was mistaken about Mr Tanner not being violent. She prepared a tray and carried it to the drawing room and knocked on the door. 'I've brought a pot of tea,' she called.

'Come in!' shouted David.

Patsy entered the room. Straight away, she noticed that her employer was standing over by the window, gazing out over the darkened garden, but his wife was close to the fire, humming to herself as she held up a dress in front of her. Patsy placed the tray on the occasional table.

David limped over to the sofa and sat down. He took a biscuit and munched on it. A surprised expression came over his face. 'Did you make these?'

'Yes. I had the recipe from Miss Kirk.' She looked at him anxiously. 'I thought they tasted a bit of all right.'

'They taste more than all right. Well done.'

Patsy beamed at him. 'Thank you. Miss Kirk was a real good teacher.'

'Was she someone who taught at the orphanage?'

'Oh, no! It was after my mother died that I met her. Us Doyle children were taken in by a Mr and Mrs Bennett, because there was no room at the Seamen's Orphanage at the time. Mrs

Bennett's dead now but I'll never forget her kindness. Miss Kirk was her housekeeper and she showed me how to cook all sorts of things. We were happy there,' she added softly.

'They were obviously a couple who liked children,' said David Tanner, and a shadow seemed to darken his eyes. 'Did they have any children of their own?'

Patsy shook her head. 'No. Sadly, Mr Bennett is elderly and couldn't cope with us after his wife died. Us kids were put in the orphanage except for my youngest brother who was adopted.' The girl sighed. 'I do miss him because I'd been like a mother to him. Mam never could cope with us even when Dad was alive and on shore leave.'

'But surely you are glad that your little brother has a proper home with people who love him?' said David.

'Of course,' said Patsy. 'Is that all for now, sir?'

Rose placed a dress on the arm of an easy chair. 'Hang on there a minute, Patsy. This Mr Bennett, is he a musician?'

'Yes! Have you heard of him, Mrs Tanner?'

'Yes,' said Rose. 'He really knows his stuff.'

'It's a small world,' said Patsy, remembering Mr Bennett played in a dance band.

'You can go now, Patsy. Thank you for the biscuits,' said David.

'It's a pleasure,' she said, feeling unusually light-hearted after their exchange.

She was on her way out of the room when she was called back. 'I think it'll be more sensible, Patsy, if you serve dinner in here, rather than the dining room,' said David. 'We must conserve our stocks of coal if my wife is not only buying new clothes but dancing the afternoons away.'

'Not every afternoon, David,' said Rose in honeyed tones. 'I went to see Mother the other day. If you'd only take me dancing yourself occasionally I wouldn't need to go with Joan.'

Patsy did not wait to hear his response but hurried out of the room, pulling the door shut behind her. It did not catch properly and she heard him say, 'I don't believe this friend exists.'

8

Rose's penetrating tones drifted towards her. 'You would say that but I'll bring her to meet you one evening. She has a very demanding mother just like mine and the tea dances are her only pleasure. I don't go there to meet other men, if that's what you're thinking. After all, I have you, don't I, *darling*?'

'You don't have to lay it on with a trowel. I'm no fool. Anyway, what do you think about what Patsy told us?'

Patsy's ears pricked up.

'About what?' asked Rose sharply.

'Her brother being adopted. We could adopt a child,' he said with an eagerness that touched Patsy.

'What on earth for?' Rose sounded horrified.

'Wouldn't you even consider it?' he pleaded.

'I've given you my final word and truthfully, David, I don't know how long I can go on like this!'

'People have worse lives. Patsy, for instance. It must have been tough, losing her mother and having to enter the orphanage.'

'Oh, never mind that girl! I wish you wouldn't talk to her as if she was one of us. I don't admire these socialist tendencies of yours. The working classes don't need any encouragement to bring down the structures already in place in society. This is about my life and my needs,' cried Rose.

An angry Patsy moved away, thinking that her mother would have called Rose Tanner *a right bitch*. She seemed to have no idea how the other half lived. She could have told the Tanners just how tough her past had been but Patsy was trying to build herself a new life. As it was, the past still haunted her. Even before her father had been lost at sea, her mother was too fond of the gin, and during the war she'd had a fancy man. By the time hostilities had ended there had been three more Doyles in addition to Patsy, Mick and Kathleen. Anthony had arrived after the news had come about her father being washed overboard and the family had been in dire straits.

Patsy sighed as she remembered how she had struggled to keep the family together. It had been a terrible time but at least they'd had each other. She missed her brothers and sisters and wished that they could all be together again. If she could become a proper cook, one that could live out and earn enough to pay rent on a house, that would be great. She wrote to her siblings once a week but it was not the same as living under the same roof. She wished she could be as free as Rose Tanner to do what she wanted. Her husband might complain about her actions, yet so far he had not stopped her gallivanting. But from what had been said earlier it sounded like there was change in the air, and what would happen to Patsy then?

She removed the casserole from the oven and breathed in the delicious smell of steak in onion gravy. She warmed the plates and served the food. Then she carried the tray to the drawing room, only to pause outside when she heard raised voices.

She knocked loudly and called, 'Dinner!'

The voices stopped and the door was opened by David who took the tray from her. 'That will be all, Patsy.'

'If yer need seconds, sir…?'

'We'll let you know.' He closed the door with his hip. Patsy returned to the kitchen and ate her dinner and fed the cat. No one came and asked for seconds. Half an hour later she returned to the sitting room to clear away. She could hear the strains of music and thought it a nice change from the couple arguing but she needed to knock several times before the door opened.

Rose stood there, half in half out of a dress. Patsy stared at her in surprise and then backed away. 'Sorry, Mrs Tanner, I didn't mean to—'

Rose rolled her eyes. 'Don't be stupid, Patsy! I need help here with these buttons.'

'What about your husband?'

'He's gone for a walk. Come in. See to the gramophone first, will you? It needs winding up.'

'But why are you trying on a dress in here?'

'Use your brains, girl. It'll be bloody freezing upstairs; much warmer down here by the fire. I've a couple of others I want to try on. If any of them need altering, you can sort out what has to be done.'

'If you say so, madam,' muttered Patsy.

She stared at the back of the dress and saw that the buttons started way down at the base of Rose's spine and only half of them were fastened. Patsy did up the rest as far as she could but the dress was a little tight across Rose's shoulder blades.

'I can't fasten the top six, missus,' she said.

'But it's got to fasten,' cried Rose in a panicky voice. 'And don't call me missus! It's madam.'

'Yes, madam,' said Patsy, her voice expressionless.

'I want to wear it on Wednesday afternoon. You can't be doing it properly. It needs pulling round.'

'I'm doing my best, Mrs Tanner, but there isn't a bit of spare material to pull round.'

'This dress was a real bargain. I can't have put on weight.' Rose's fingers inched round her back in an attempt to drag the material together but without success. She swore vehemently, using words that Patsy had heard often enough when the Doyles had lived in the hovel, near Scotty Road, but never from the lips of a woman who was supposed to be her superior.

She was shocked into exclaiming, 'Madam!'

'Oh, shut up, Patsy, I've no doubt you've heard worse. Think of something! I must wear this dress.'

Patsy had to admit that it was a lovely dress, made of cerise georgette, with loosely flowing panels of pink. She checked the label and saw that it was a size smaller than Rose Tanner normally wore. No use telling madam that, though. 'May I make a suggestion?'

'Of course! That's what I've just asked you to do,' snapped Rose.

'If a couple of the panels were removed, it might be possible to unpick the sides of the dress and insert an extra couple of inches where needed. If anyone said anything you could say it's part of the design.'

Rose's face brightened. 'Of course, I'm sure I would have thought of that if I hadn't been so flustered. Help me off with the dress and you can get on with altering it.'

Patsy hoped her idea would work. It was her sister, Kathleen, who was the artistic one with a good eye for colour and pattern. Patsy began the task of unpicking the sides of the dress while Rose tried on the other two dresses.

'These fit perfectly,' she said.

'Couldn't you wear one of them?' asked Patsy.

'No! They're attractive in their way but can't match the cerise one. How are you getting on? I want it fixed before my husband returns.'

'Perhaps I should take it up to my room and sew it there if you don't want him coming in on us,' suggested Patsy.

'Good idea.' Rose's eyes sparkled. 'I'll tell him that I've sent you to bed because you have a blinding headache. I'll even bring you up a cup of cocoa in an hour to see how you're getting on.'

'Thank yer, madam,' said Patsy dryly.

'You not yer, Patsy,' rebuked Rose. 'One good turn deserves another. You have all you need?'

'Yes, madam,' said Patsy.

'Excellent,' said Rose, patting her shoulder.

Patsy left the sitting room with the dress over her arm. It would be freezing up in her attic bedroom but at least she would be left alone to get on with altering the dress. After that she would write a letter to her siblings and her monthly one to her friend Tilly in America.

Patsy thought how life at the orphanage had come as a shock. She and her sisters were segregated from their two brothers and were only allowed to see Mick and Jimmy for a few hours on a Saturday. The food was tasteless and unimaginative and the rules were strict. There was little love to be found in that grim building. They were taught the three Rs and the girls were instructed in knitting, crochet and needlework.

When the time came to leave, Patsy was glad to go out in the world, although it was a wrench being parted from her family.

The year after she had left the orphanage, her brother Mick signed up for the ship *Indefatigable*, to train for a life at sea. This coming Easter, her sister Kathleen would also be leaving the orphanage. No doubt she would also be found a job in service, which meant that only twelve-year-old Jimmy and the eight-year-old twins, Maureen and Mary, would remain there.

Patsy smiled at the thought of the twins: so alike to look at and yet so different. It had become almost second nature to Patsy to unburden herself in her letters to Tilly when there were matters worrying her. The goings-on at the Tanner household were a regular feature.

Unfortunately, by the time Patsy had finished the alterations to the dress, her bruised finger was throbbing more than it had done earlier. Perhaps if she rested it for a while it would be better in an hour or so. Mrs Tanner had not made an appearance despite what she had said about bringing Patsy a drink of cocoa, so the girl decided to take the dress to her.

She was halfway down the attic stairs when she heard the Tanners talking in the hall. Rose was telling her husband about Patsy's fictitious headache and so the girl retreated to her bedroom. She did not have long to wait before her mistress arrived, minus the mug of cocoa.

'You've finished it!' Rose exclaimed. 'Good.'

'I hope it fits.'

'It had better.' Rose gave a slight laugh as she picked up the dress and stroked the material. She inspected the inserts and looked at Patsy. 'They appear to be all right. Goodnight.' Without further word, she left the room, closing the door behind her.

Patsy stared at the door moodily. Selfish madam! She went over to the chest of drawers and paused a moment, gazing at the wooden dolphin on top of it. She picked up the carving and ran a finger over its smooth surface. Her father had whittled away at this graceful creature while at sea. She still missed him and wished her last memory of him was not of his having a terrible row with her mother over a man. He had stormed out saying that he might not be coming back. And he hadn't! She didn't suppose that he had meant that he would die at sea.

Patsy replaced the dolphin and took out her writing materials. She gritted her teeth whilst writing because her finger was still painful and she wished all sorts of nasty things to befall Rose Tanner. When finished, Patsy viewed the pages with dismay. Her handwriting was a terrible scrawl and she could only hope that Tilly would be able to make sense of the words on the page all those miles away across the Atlantic in New York.

Chapter Two

'I've had a letter from Tilly,' said Joy Kirk, settling herself in the corner of a sofa in her sister Hanny's sitting room in Chester. Joy was a plump woman in her early thirties with a pleasant face and lovely brown eyes.

'That's more than I've had in the last month,' said Alice, who was Tilly's sister and Hanny's sister-in-law.

Joy said smoothly, 'It's partly a letter of condolence. Anyway, she has the baby to care for.'

'But I'm her sister and she doesn't write to me as often as I'd like her to,' said Alice, accepting a glass of sherry from Hanny.

'OK! But let's put that aside. I actually came over here to talk to you both about something other than Tilly's letter,' said Joy, pausing to sip her sherry. 'Mother's death has landed me and Robbie Bennett with a problem, so we've decided to get married.'

Alice spilt her drink. 'Look what you've made me do!' she cried, putting down the glass and dabbing at the wet patch on her skirt with a handkerchief. 'I hope you're joking!'

Joy said crossly, 'What's there to joke about?'

'Robbie Bennett is old enough to be your father.'

'Tell me something I don't know.'

Alice stared at her in disbelief. 'I think you're crazy.'

'Not crazy,' protested Hanny. 'Sensible. I could see it coming.'

Joy smiled gratefully at her elder sister. 'I knew you'd understand. Since Mother's no longer there to act as chaperone, I suspect that the neighbours are tittle-tattling about us but I swear we haven't been up to anything.'

Alice brushed her words aside. 'How can you consider marrying him after Chris Griffith?'

'Chris is dead,' said Joy, a shadow crossing her face. She fiddled with a light brown curl and tucked it behind her ear. 'I'll be forty before I know it and if I don't accept Robbie's proposal what will happen to me when he dies? I'd have to find myself another live-in position and I don't fancy that.'

'I don't know why you can't carry on being his housekeeper,' said Alice. 'I bet there're plenty of households like yours.'

'You surprise me, Alice,' said Joy, exasperated. 'I don't like being the subject of gossip. Besides, I love the house and Robbie needs someone to look after him. We're not love's young dream but if I marry him my position will be secure.'

Alice sighed. 'I suppose it makes sense.'

'But he is a bit of a spendthrift and likes a flutter on the gee-gees, so I'm going to have to curb that habit when we get married.' Joy paused to take a sandwich. 'Besides, I'll also be in a better position to help the Doyles when I'm a married woman.'

'I know you've always been keen to support the orphanage but the Doyles aren't your responsibility,' said Alice.

Joy gave a hollow laugh. 'You try telling Tilly that! She still keeps in touch with Patsy Doyle.'

'But it must be two years since Patsy left there… didn't she get a job as a maid?' asked Hanny.

Joy nodded. 'Her first employer died and she's with a couple called Tanner now. According to Tilly, Patsy's not happy.'

'Lots of girls in service aren't happy,' said Alice. 'That's why more and more of them are refusing to work as domestics and going into factories. It's the reason why there's a servant shortage. At least Patsy has a roof over her head and is better off than when she was living with that drunken no-good mother of hers.'

'You are harsh, Alice,' protested Hanny. 'The woman lost her husband at sea and was left with seven children to rear. Where's your heart?'

'In my chest where it belongs,' retorted Alice. 'I try not to allow it to affect my head too much these days. Anyway, what makes Tilly think Patsy is unhappy?'

Joy swallowed the last morsel of egg sandwich. 'Unfortunately, Patsy's handwriting has gone from bad to worse, so Tilly had trouble making out every word, but she's almost certain that Mr Tanner has been mistreating her.'

Hanny started. 'In what way?'

'That's the problem! Tilly couldn't make out that bit,' answered Joy.

'What about Mrs Tanner?' asked Alice.

'Apparently she's a bit of a flibbertigibbet, only interested in clothes and going dancing,' said Joy.

'What do we know about the husband?' asked Hanny, frowning. 'Was he in the army during the war?'

'Yes, he was, but he's a solicitor by occupation,' said Joy.

Alice said, 'Any injuries?'

'He has a limp but Patsy was told he had injuries invisible to the eye or something like that,' said Joy.

'That could mean he was shell-shocked and lives on his nerves,' said Alice, whose own husband had been in the trenches and returned badly scarred, both physically, and mentally. 'Do they have any children?'

'No,' said Joy. 'Apparently they have separate bedrooms. I mean, I'm all for continuing sleeping in my own room and having Mr Bennett remain in his after we're married.'

Alice stared at Joy hard. 'Does Robbie Bennett know that you want to carry on having separate bedrooms after you're married?'

Joy flushed. 'Our marriage is to be one of convenience, so I don't see why he should expect anything else at his age.'

'But he's a man!' cried Alice. 'They're not like us, having to go through the change and no longer being able to have children.'

'Did you actually tell him this?' asked Hanny with a concerned expression.

'You mean did I say *I am not sleeping with you*?' asked Joy.

'Yes!' chorused the other two.

'No. I didn't think it necessary. If he were to start that malarkey I'd soon sort him out,' said Joy, tilting her chin. 'Right now I'm keeping quiet about it.'

'It's a wonder he didn't ask his sister and her family to go and live with him,' said Hanny. 'It's a fair-sized house.'

Joy chuckled. 'Rita would have loved to take over the household but he told me he didn't want her nagging him and complaining about his music. She has one of those voices that grates on you, and to top it all she can't cook the way I can.'

'Are you sure he doesn't want children?' asked Alice, draining her sherry glass.

'Fortunately, the subject has never come up. I mean to say, he's not going to want kids, is he? Not at his age. The man's been spoilt, used to having his own way, although, having said that, he is fond of his nieces and nephews.'

'Perhaps it's for the best, then, that you don't have kids,' said Hanny, looking thoughtful. 'Maybe the Tanners don't want children either? Although… it's possible that they might find it rather exciting sleeping in separate rooms. Maybe… he creeps along the landing and gets into her bed, just like strangers in the night.'

Alice smiled faintly. 'You have too much imagination. Can we be sure that Tilly isn't reading more into what Patsy said in her letter than there is?'

Hanny shrugged. 'I don't see anything wrong with Joy checking out that the girl is all right.'

Alice agreed. 'I wish I could be of some help but I've not only a home to run but the shop as well. And at the moment my daughter is being a real nuisance and a worry. Flora doesn't want to help me in the house or work in the shop. She's persuaded Seb that she has the brains to study for her School Certificate so she is staying on at school. When I think that at her age I was already learning a trade in a milliner's. Which reminds me,' she glanced at the clock and let out a shriek and jumped to her feet, 'I should be opening up. I could be losing valuable customers. Sorry, ladies, but I'm going to have to go.'

'Don't go rushing off just yet,' said Joy hastily. 'I want you to make my wedding outfit for me.'

'When is the wedding?' asked Alice, pulling on a cloche hat.

'We have an appointment with the vicar this week,' said Joy. 'I'll have to let you know the exact date but I'm planning on the Easter weekend.'

'When is Easter this year?' asked Hanny.

'April.'

'We're in February now,' said Alice, frowning. 'What have you in mind to wear?'

'A white wedding gown with a lovely flowery hat to go with it,' said Joy, her expression dreamy. 'I never thought I'd ever get married after Chris went missing, so I want to make a splash.'

Alice and Hanny exchanged glances. 'She's seeing herself as a fairy princess,' said the latter, shaking her head.

'No, I'm not,' said Joy, indignantly, 'because Robbie Bennett is certainly no Prince Charming.'

'No, he's a sugar daddy,' murmured Alice.

Hanny shook her head at her. 'Naughty. Why shouldn't my sister have the best wedding day she can in the circumstances?'

Alice's green eyes narrowed as she scrutinised Joy's stout figure. 'She could do with going on a diet.'

'I know that! I don't need you telling me,' said Joy, getting in a huff.

'Sorry. But don't put it off,' warned Alice. 'Start today. Do you want me to design your outfit?'

Joy nodded.

'I'll get samples of materials for you to choose from. Say I drop by your place in a fortnight's time? By then, if you're very, very good, you might have shed a few pounds. I just wish you could have your own Prince Charming.' Alice fluttered her fingers and left.

'So this wedding…?' said Hanny.

Joy tapped her chin with her fingers. 'I know it won't be a love match like yours but you will be my matron of honour, won't you?'

Hanny smiled. 'Of course. Will you be having bridesmaids as well?'

'I might as well push the boat out because I'm not planning on marrying again. I'll have your Janet and Robbie's two nieces, Wendy and Minnie,' said Joy. 'And perhaps I'll invite Patsy and Kathy Doyle. It'll be a day out for them.'

'That would be kind.' Hanny refilled their sherry glasses. 'Have this one last drink before your diet. To you, little sister!' She raised her glass.

Joy glanced down at her ample proportions and sighed.

'So when will you visit Patsy?' asked Hanny.

Joy wrinkled her nose. 'As soon as I have time. I vow I won't forget.'

'You need to find out as soon as possible if the girl is being mistreated and put a stop to it. Some men can be such swines.'

Joy did not deny it. 'Surely, if there is any funny business going on with Mr Tanner, his wife would be aware of it.'

'She could be one of those who close their eyes to anything unpleasant like Mother did.'

Joy nodded. 'I admire the girl's sense of responsibility, guts and determination. I have to help her.'

Hanny's blue eyes rested on her sister's serious face. 'But you don't want any children of your own to love. It's sad really.'

'If I can't have Chris's children, then I'd rather not bother.'

Hanny understood and said no more, but she could not help worrying that her sister might discover that once she had that gold band on her finger, then Robbie Bennett might demand more from her than she was prepared to give.

Chapter Three

'There's something about churches that makes me uncomfortable,' said Robbie Bennett. He and Joy were crossing Rocky Lane towards the rear gate that opened onto the back garden of his house.

'You should come with me more often.' Joy's smile was strained. 'I really thought with you being a musician that you'd especially enjoy the choir and the organ.'

'I've nothing against them but I'd be just as happy getting married in a registry office.'

'But I wouldn't,' said Joy shortly.

They reached the other side of the road, where Robbie paused to light a cigarette. After the first puff he began coughing. Joy looked at him anxiously and waited until he stopped spitting and spluttering before carrying on walking, and resumed their conversation. 'I wouldn't feel properly married if I wasn't married in church,' she said.

'That's why I decided to let you have your way,' rumbled Robbie. 'Although why you need to make such a big fuss I don't know. I'm sixty-six, Joy, and I'd be happier spending the money going on a cruise for our honeymoon.'

Joy's stomach seemed to flip over. *Honeymoon! A cruise!* It was the first time he had mentioned either. After his last wife died, he had invited himself along on a cruise that Joy had arranged for herself and her mother, who had been living with Hanny at the time. The three of them had got on reasonably well, so he had suggested that Mrs Kirk move in with them. Joy had agreed, thinking her sister had done her share of caring for their mother.

'It's my own money I'll be spending on frocks, flowers and food,' Joy reminded him gently. 'As for a honeymoon, surely we don't need one. We're not love's young dream.'

Robbie took a drag on his cigarette and then puckered his lips and blew out a smoke ring. 'I know, I know. I'm old enough to be your father,' he said testily, 'but I'm not past it.'

Joy's heart sank even further. 'But surely you don't want children?'

Robbie stared at her. 'Children! Hell's bells, I never thought of that.'

Well, think of it now, thought Joy, *and forget any ideas you might suddenly have of sleeping in my bed, Father Bear.*

He puffed frantically and hurried up the path between straggly frosty grass and bare trees towards the back gate. She kept pace with him, but the thought of having him thrashing about on top of her made her feel quite sick. He unlocked the gate and continued to forge ahead of her. She followed him, past the outhouse at the bottom of the garden and up the garden path.

Instinctively she glanced towards the neighbouring house and caught sight of old Miss Parker peering over the fence and guessed she was standing on a box. Joy waved to her and immediately Miss Parker bobbed down out of sight.

Robbie stopped outside the kitchen door and waited for Joy to open up. Only now did she go before him to put on the kettle and make ready a tea tray. He was breathing heavily and bumbled across the room to the rocking chair situated in front of the fire. Neither said a word until the tea was made and both were sitting down with cup in hand. She knew that she had to let him open the conversation. It was obvious that there were things on his mind he was chewing over.

'You might find this embarrassing, Joy,' he burst out. 'But I have to ask.'

She raised her eyebrows. 'Yes, Mr Bennett. What is it you want to know?'

'Don't be so formal all of a sudden for God's sake! We're getting married, aren't we?' He paused, put down his cup and fumbled in a pocket for his cigarette case. 'This soldier, Chris, whom you were in love with and who was killed in the war…' He stopped and lit up.

Joy guessed what he wanted to know but was determined not to make it easy for him because, after all, this wasn't easy for her either.

He swore as he burnt his fingers with a match. 'Damn! Can't you say something?'

'Do you want me to get some butter to put on that burn?'

'I didn't mean that,' he said, exasperated. 'I'm not sure about your… your situation. I mean him and you, did you—?'

'What?' She was not going to say the words for him. *No, Robbie, we never slept together.* Because she would want to add that it was one of the greatest regrets of her life that she had not done so. A memory to comfort her in the long sleepless nights when she had grieved for him. Tears filled her eyes and a sob burst in her throat.

'Now stop that,' said Robbie gruffly, placing his cigarette in his saucer. He leant forward and took her hand and raised it to his lips. 'I didn't mean to upset you. I know it can never be the same for you being married to me but I'm sure we can find some happiness together.'

But not the happiness I yearned for all those years ago wailed Joy inwardly. The tears continued to fall. It was a long time since she had cried. Even when her mother was buried Joy had not wept. When her father had died, she had shed buckets of tears because he had suffered so bravely. She sniffed and wiped her face with the back of her hand.

'I'm sorry, Robbie, I'm sure you're right but please don't let's talk about the past.' She freed her hand and said with a false cheerfulness. 'Now what would you like for supper?'

He looked disappointed. 'If that's what you've decided.'

'Yes. I want to concentrate on the future.'

Impulsively, Joy planted a kiss on his cheek. He eyed her up and down as if he had something completely different on his mind than food. She had seen such lust in men's eyes before and could only hope she was not making a mistake in going through with the wedding. Of course, it was not too late to change her mind but she loved this house and did not want to leave it. Stupid to get herself worked up at the thought of sleeping with this man. She was making him out an ogre and he wasn't. Still, best to think of something else or she would be a nervous wreck by the time Easter Monday arrived. She remembered that she must get invitations printed and make time to visit Patsy Doyle.

Chapter Four

'Patsy, mend this for me,' said Rose Tanner, breezing into the kitchen. She dropped the cerise georgette dress on the girl's lap. 'I caught my heel in the hem and ripped it.'

'Yes, Mrs Tanner.' Patsy stood up with the garment clutched to her. 'When do you want it and have you any other mending you'd like me to do, madam?'

Her employer was already on her way out but now she paused. 'There's a lovely smell of baking in here. What have you been making now?'

'Cherry scones. There was a recipe in your magazine.'

Rose fixed her with a stare. 'You've been reading my magazine?'

'You threw it out, madam.'

'That makes no difference. You should have asked me if you could have it. There's also the matter of your delving into my store cupboard without permission.'

'I'm sorry, madam,' said Patsy, unrepentant. 'But the scones are for you and Mr Tanner.'

Rose shook her head. 'You really have some nerve, my girl, but I've no time to discuss this now. I've a green hat upstairs and the bow at the side has come loose – if you could sew it back on. And I'm also almost certain Mr Tanner has been complaining about having a couple of shirts with buttons missing. If you could see to them.'

'Where are these shirts, madam?'

Mrs Tanner put a hand to her blonde head and pulled a face. 'Probably he's flung them in the corner of his room in disgust.

He still seems to think that I should sew buttons on. I told him that's not in my brief these days.'

'What d'yer…you mean by "brief"?'

'Not part of the job. He wormed his way into my heart and tricked me into marriage,' she said with a dramatic flourish. 'One gives no quarter to a man like that. See you later!'

'Surely you're not going out in this weather, madam?' called Patsy. They'd had rain, hail, snow and gale force winds in the last few days. March had certainly come in like a lion.

Rose ignored her and vanished through the doorway. Patsy wished she knew what her employer meant by *giving no quarter*. And how had Mr Tanner tricked his wife into marriage? How could a man do that? When she had lived near Scotty Road, she had sometimes overheard neighbours talking of a bloke being tricked into marriage by a girl getting herself in the family way, but never the other way round.

She fetched the sewing box and looked for a reel of thread that would exactly match the colour of the frock. Eventually she found one and settled down to repairing the tear. She thought about the lovely clothes belonging to Rose Tanner and wished she had the money to spare to buy even one such frock. It was her birthday on the seventeenth of March and she could easily imagine being led into a tango by Rudolph Valentino, the screen idol, with his Latin good looks, if she was dressed so fine. Not that she was mad about men but she enjoyed imagining that someone good-looking and kind would fancy her one day. But she really did not want any man getting too close to her just yet. Much safer.

She hummed a dance tune as she set tiny stitches and thought how much she enjoyed having the house to herself. She could pretend it belonged to her and that later in the day she would be welcoming home her brothers and sisters.

She finished mending Mrs Tanner's frock and took it upstairs with the sewing box to Rose's bedroom. It did not take much searching to find the hat that needed a few stitches. Once that was done, she went into Mr Tanner's room and found three shirts folded neatly on top of a wicker basket. Not wanting to be found in his room if he should arrive home early – which was not unknown these last two months – she took the garments into his wife's room.

Patsy settled herself in a basket chair by the window over-looking the garden. She had just finished sewing on the buttons when she heard footsteps on the front step, then a key being inserted in the lock. She recognised Mr Tanner's footsteps. Hastily, she reached for the scissors and snipped off the thread and, placing the shirts over her arm, hurried from the bedroom. She caught sight of him at the bottom of the stairs.

He must have seen her at the same time. 'What are you doing up there, Patsy?' he called.

'Sewing buttons on your shirts, Mr Tanner.'

He thanked her and hung his damp overcoat over the newel post.

'Shall I put them in your wardrobe?' asked Patsy.

'No, I'll do that,' he replied, starting up the stairs. 'I presume my wife is out again despite the weather. What kind of woman is it who can't stay in and sew buttons on her husband's shirts and welcome him home?'

Patsy guessed that he did not really expect her to answer, so she kept quiet. She waited until he reached the landing before handing his shirts to him. He inspected her work and said, 'You're a neat stitcher. Now, make me a cup of tea, please.'

'Yes, Mr Tanner,' said Patsy, pleased at his compliment and the *please*.

She was halfway down the stairs when she started feeling suddenly wary of his compliment. Not for the first time she asked herself why he should be nice to a servant girl when he didn't have to be. In her experience most people wanted something when they were nice to you.

She set a tea tray, placing a couple of the cherry scones on a plate. She opened the kitchen door and listened for him on the stairs. When eventually she heard him coming downstairs, she made the tea and carried the tray into the drawing room.

He glanced up from a document he was perusing and then placed it on the sofa beside him. 'You have brothers, Patsy?'

'Yes.'

'Lucky you.'

Involuntarily she glanced up into his face and saw such pain there that it quite upset her. 'You have no brothers?' she asked.

'Not anymore.' He clenched a fist and banged the arm of the sofa.

Patsy almost jumped out of her skin. 'What is it, Mr Tanner? Have I done something to make you angry? Is there something you want?'

'You can't raise the dead, can you?' he rasped.

'No!'

He sighed. 'Of course not. It was a damn fool question. My brothers were killed in the trenches as you've probably guessed. Terribly difficult to accept that I'm the only one alive out of the three of us. I was the youngest and Gerald, my eldest brother, and I were never close. My mother never forgave me for surviving. Gerald was her favourite and was destined to take over the business. I had an altogether different future planned for myself but...' His voice trailed off.

Patsy waited in case he had anything more to say but when he just sat there, gazing into space with a vacant expression, she asked, 'Shall I pour your tea, sir?'

He appeared to come back from somewhere else. 'Yes. I've been trying to get in touch with Rose's brother but he's not answering my letters. Now the last one has been returned not known at this address. It's so frustrating. I wouldn't be having this bother if it weren't for my brothers being killed, and then Rose's other brother was in the navy and his ship was torpedoed. The ship went down with all hands.'

'I see. It's sad.'

With trembling hands Patsy lifted the teapot and somehow managed not to spill any liquid in the saucer. It seemed he was aware of her actions because he reached for the sugar and dropped his customary three lumps into the tea.

'Is there anything else?' she asked.

He blinked and touched one of the cherry scones. 'You baked these?'

'I found a recipe in one of Mrs Tanner's magazines.'

'So not one of your Miss Kirk's recipes?' He smiled faintly.

She returned his smile. 'No.'

'Do you ever visit this paragon?'

Patsy's brow knit. 'What's a paragon?'

'A pattern of perfection.'

Patsy laughed. 'I don't think she'd call herself that but the Bennetts did appreciate her and so did us Doyles.'

'And now Mr Bennett is a widower and she is his housekeeper,' murmured David.

Patsy nodded. 'Her mother moved in after his wife died.'

'You're telling me that Miss Kirk and Mr Bennett were chaperoned by her mother.' He took a large gulp of tea and then added, 'Before you ask me what that means it's—'

'I know what it means,' interrupted Patsy. 'It means that they had company to stop them getting up to something. In my opinion, that was unnecessary because Miss Kirk isn't like that. She has morals.'

David said mildly, 'You really shouldn't interrupt me when I'm speaking. But you obviously have a great admiration for Miss Kirk.'

'I probably took her for granted when we stayed there but I've thought a lot since about how patient she was with us.' Patsy's grey eyes were pensive. 'I didn't have much of an education. Mam kept me home from school to help look after the younger children, you see.'

'Was your mother infirm?'

She screwed up her face. 'You mean crippled, like?'

'Yes, crippled like,' he responded with a twinkle in his eye.

'No. She drank,' said Patsy frankly. 'I don't know how much that was due to Dad being away so much but she shouldn't have been spending the little money we had on gin.' Patsy stopped and shook her head as if trying to get rid of a memory. 'May I go now?'

'If you have to make dinner, then you better had.' He reached for the document he had put aside and muttered, 'Where is that woman?'

Patsy hurried out. She guessed there would be another argument tonight. What was wrong with Rose Tanner that she went looking for trouble? So they didn't have kids! That was no excuse to behave the way she did. Kids weren't all joy.

Back in the kitchen Patsy got on with her preparations. She was not there long when the back door opened and Mrs Tanner poked her head round the jamb.

'Patsy, please tell me that my husband isn't home yet?' she whispered.

'I can't, he is,' said Patsy, thinking that Mrs Tanner didn't look as cold and wet as one would expect, given what the weather was like.

'Damn! He's trying to catch me out,' said Rose, frowning. 'Well, I'll sort him.'

'Perhaps it's only the lousy weather that's brought him home early,' said Patsy conversationally.

Rose nodded. 'Don't tell him you've seen me. I'll be in for dinner and I'll have a guest with me, but not until seven-thirty.'

'He's going to be made up about that,' muttered Patsy.

'What did you say?' asked Rose.

'Nuthin'!'

Rose gave her a hard stare. 'You're lying. I won't forget it.' She closed the door.

Patsy considered walking out and not coming back but decided against it when she heard hailstones battering the window. She hoped Rose Tanner got soaked to the skin. She had no right to call her a liar. Why had she come home, only to go out again? Who was this guest she was bringing to the house? Presumably, whoever it was would be staying for dinner. If she had a fancy man, then it certainly wouldn't be him. Patsy's flesh crept at the thought of what David Tanner might do if he discovered his wife was carrying on with someone else. No, she was not going to dwell on his reacting violently. She had seen little of that in him so far.

The first thing Patsy knew of Rose Tanner's return was when she heard voices in the lobby and her name being called. This meant that Rose Tanner had remembered her front-door key for once. Patsy wiped her hands on a dishcloth before hurrying from the kitchen.

'Patsy, put the kettle on. My friend and I are in desperate need of a cup of tea,' said Rose, shoving a dripping umbrella into the hall stand.

'Yes, madam.'

'Before you go, do help Miss Swift off with her coat and hang it up in the kitchen by the range.'

Patsy glanced quickly at the other woman. She was older than Mrs Tanner and looked ill at ease. Her fingers quivered as she unbuttoned her damp coat. 'I really shouldn't have come, Rose. Mother will be wondering where I am.'

'Heavens, Joan, you're going to have to stand up to your mother some day. I certainly had to. You can't let her run your life,' said Rose loudly. 'Anyway, you can telephone her. I'm sure she'll understand why you're staying here when she looks out of the window. Now, come and say hello to David.'

As Patsy made her way to the kitchen with Miss Swift's coat, she heard the sitting-room door open and Rose say, 'David, I hope you don't mind but I've asked my friend, Joan, to stay the night.'

When Patsy entered the drawing room it was to find that the carpet had been rolled back and Rose and Miss Swift were gliding across the parquet floor to the musical strains of A1 Jolson singing 'April Showers' on the gramophone. David Tanner sat with the newspaper folded on his knee with his eyes on the two women. Joan Swift suddenly stumbled and stood on her partner's toe.

'Ouch! Watch what you're doing,' said Rose, wincing. 'That's the second time you've put in an extra step.'

'It's your stride,' said Joan. 'You should be the man.'

'Don't be silly. You know I always take the woman's part,' replied Rose crossly.

'Well, it's not fair,' said Joan.

'Don't moan. Tea is here now,' said Rose, strolling over to the gramophone and removing the record. She slid it into its sleeve and put it away in the cupboard beneath the turntable. As she straightened, she said, 'We're going to have to put in more time, Joan, if we're to get anywhere in the forthcoming competition.'

'I'm not sure whether Mother will like me being out more often,' said Joan anxiously, glancing about her for a seat.

'Never mind your mother,' drawled Rose. 'We have a strong chance of winning if you put your heart into it.'

'Sit here, Miss Swift,' said David, vacating his chair. 'I need to fetch something from upstairs.' He brushed past Patsy on his way out.

She looked at her mistress. 'Will I pour, madam?'

'No. We'll see to ourselves. You'd better get on. You'll need to make up the bed in the spare room.'

As Patsy left the room, she heard Joan Swift say, 'I don't think I'll stay after all. It must be obvious to your husband that I'm not up to your standard. I'll drink my tea and go...'

'But you can't,' said Rose, closing the door.

Patsy wondered who would win the argument. Perhaps Miss Swift would surprise her by sticking to her guns and going home to her mother.

And so it turned out. She did not even stay for dinner but came into the kitchen and asked for her coat. 'It's still damp,' said Patsy.

'It doesn't matter. Just help me on with it, so I can get out of this house. Such a forceful woman! She really should be the man.' She glanced nervously over her shoulder. 'I told her that I was visiting the lavatory. Now open the door and let me out.'

Patsy obeyed her. 'Are you sure you'll be OK going round the side of the house in the dark, miss?'

Miss Swift did not answer but disappeared into the wet night.

Ten minutes later Rose arrived in the kitchen. 'Patsy, where is Miss Swift?'

'She's gone home, madam. I think she wasn't feeling well.'

'You should have stopped her, encouraged her to stay. I don't know why I put up with you,' said Rose crossly. She turned on her heel and left the kitchen with what Patsy's mother would have called *a face on her*.

Patsy wondered what would be the outcome of what had just happened but to her surprise all was quiet that evening.

Several days later, on a Saturday afternoon that was springlike in its warmth, Patsy was sitting by the open window of her bedroom, attempting to tidy up a jagged fingernail with the sandpaper of a matchbox, when she heard her employers come out onto the patio below. They were talking. Apparently it would soon be their seventh wedding anniversary. Rose had just asked her husband why he had married her when he must have known their union would only result in unhappiness for them both.

'Haven't you ever wanted something badly and been terrified at the same time that you won't get it if you tell the truth?' David's voice reminded Patsy of a saw biting into wood.

'No, I was brought up to tell the truth and shame the devil,' said Rose. 'I received many a clout for that from Mother, I can tell you.'

'I was telling you the truth when I told you I loved you. I would have done so earlier, before I left for France, but you were still Gerald's girl in my thoughts.'

Rose sighed. 'Poor Gerald! I often wonder what he would have thought about us getting married.'

'Our mothers were determined on it. My mother insisted that I needed to make up to you for the loss of Gerald because I survived the hell of war.'

'In other circumstances you might have done so but... oh, why couldn't you have been honest with me?' cried Rose.

'I've already explained,' he said.

'It wasn't an explanation, I was duped. Why don't you go and get us drinks so I can drown my sorrows?' There was a bitter note in her voice.

'You know, if you were in America you wouldn't legally be allowed to drink alcohol.'

She said irritably, 'I know that, but as I'm not planning on going to America why mention it?'

'Because I'll be going there next week.'

'That's a bit of a bombshell! When did you decide it?'

'Yesterday. I'm rather hoping you'll come with me. I thought I'd go to the last place that I heard from your brother.'

'You do surprise me. Why should you think I want Rodney found? He and I never got on.'

'I thought that going over there on the liner would give us a chance to—'

'No, don't say the words *to have a second boneymoon*!' she interrupted. 'The first was a complete shambles.' Patsy heard the sound of a chair being pushed back. 'I'll get my own drink.'

'I was going to say it would be a break for us both. You could do some shopping in New York. I'll make the journey south on my own.'

'You heard what I said,' she said angrily. 'Let go of my arm! You're hurting me!'

Patsy dropped the matchbox and pushed up the lower sash window further. She was about to put her head through the gap and shout *I'm here!* when she heard him say, 'Not as much as you're hurting me. Most wives would jump at the chance of having a holiday in America in the spring.'

'But I'm not an ordinary wife, am I?' Her voice shook. 'Now, let me go before I scream and bring the neighbours running.'

'I'd never do anything to harm you.'

'Wouldn't you? I've had seven years of pretending we're a normal married couple when we're nothing of the sort.'

The silence was longer this time. Then Patsy heard the rapid tap-tap-tap of Rose's high heels on the crazy paving and after that came the sound of a door closing.

If Patsy had not been feeling all of a dither by what she had overheard, she might have thought that what had taken place was just like listening to an act in a play. She wondered when David Tanner would leave for America. It was obvious that he did not wish to leave his wife behind. Was that because he still loved her? Or was it because, despite Miss Swift's visit, he was still suspicious of what his wife might get up to behind his back? Either way, it seemed like he was going to have to risk leaving her behind. Patsy thought of Tilly living in New York and decided it was time to write another letter about the latest goings-on here.

Chapter Five

'This fabric isn't white,' said Joy, peering at the scrap of material in her hand.

Alice had come over from Chester as she had promised, bringing samples of cloth with her. 'I know,' said Alice hesitantly, 'but white and cream are not slimming colours.'

Joy was hurt. 'You came all the way to Liverpool to tell me that.' She tossed aside the scrap of material amongst the various coloured samples on the table.

'I want what's best for you,' said Alice in a soothing voice. 'White might be considered a bit too virginal for a woman of your age.'

Joy flushed to the roots of her hair and put her hands on her hips and said indignantly, 'But I am a virgin! You know, Alice, sometimes you really are too forthright for your own good.'

Alice said, 'I'm sorry. I didn't mean to offend you but you agreed that you needed to go on a diet. But right now, I'm more interested in your being a virgin. I can scarcely believe you and Chris never made love despite his going off to war?'

Joy looked stricken and she walked over to the fire and gazed into the slumbering embers. 'There you go again. You and your big mouth,' she said in a seething voice. 'I can only believe you have no idea how much your words hurt. You had no right to bring that up and also no right to choose what colour I should wear for my wedding.'

'I'm sorry,' said Alice. 'You're right, of course. You believed it was the proper thing to do to save yourself for marriage. So if it is a light colour you want, then…' She reached for her handbag and removed a fold of tissue paper and opened it to reveal a strip of ivory-coloured silk shot through with a silver thread. 'What do you think of this?'

Joy turned and her expression changed. She picked up the material and stroked the silk. 'How much is this? It's lovelier than any material I ever imagined.'

'It's real fairy princess stuff, isn't it?' said Alice, smiling.

'Yes,' said Joy softly, thinking of Robbie's niece, Wendy. The girl wanted to get married but she and Grant Simpson, who was a private detective, were having to wait until she was twenty-one because her mother, Rita, wouldn't give her permission. Their wedding would most likely be a quiet affair because they had little money.

'You're thinking of Wendy, aren't you?' said Alice.

'Yes. How did you guess?' asked Joy, startled.

'I know you're fond of her. What if I buy a few extra yards of this material and it could be your gift to her when she starts planning her own wedding?'

Joy nodded. 'I'll do that and perhaps it will be more sensible if I were to have a suit made of this lovely damask rose material instead of the ivory and silver. After all, this is a marriage of convenience not that of a fairy princess.'

Alice said hesitantly, 'I think you're being wise but it's your decision. I don't want you to feel I'm pressuring you.'

Joy raised her eyebrows in disbelief. 'Of course you are but I think you're right. Make me a dress and jacket of it.'

Alice smiled. 'You always were a sensible girl.'

Joy knew that to be true and blamed her mother. She had insisted that Joy stay at home and help her run the lodging house. That had been Joy's life until her mother went completely off her head.

'I'm going to need Wendy and Minnie's measurements for the bridesmaids' dresses,' said Alice, rousing Joy from her thoughts.

'I'll post them to you.'

Alice nodded and produced a tape measure. 'And now for your measurements.'

Joy whimpered. Despite her conviction that she had shed a few pounds, she wasn't looking forward to having Alice know just how big she was in inches.

'Come on. It won't be as bad as you think,' coaxed Alice.

Joy succumbed and looked gloomy as Alice wrote the figures down. 'I was never this plump years ago,' she muttered.

'Too much good food,' said Alice severely. 'By the way, did you find out anything about Patsy Doyle's employer?'

Joy looked guilty. 'To be honest I haven't visited her yet. I've had so much to do and think about that I'd remember and then forget. But you're not the second one to remind me. Tilly sent a present for Patsy's birthday and suggested I take it to her.'

'I heard from Tilly, too,' said Alice, placing the tape measure and samples back in her bag. 'Have you had the banns read yet?'

Joy nodded. 'The wedding will be upon us before we know it and I've still loads to do but I must make time to visit Patsy.'

Alice agreed, thinking she was going to have to work fast. She really could do with an assistant but business was not so good that she could afford to pay the wages that hiring a woman would entail. If only her daughter, Flora, had been sensible and agreed to Alice training her in millinery and dressmaking. If only Patsy Doyle was not already employed, then no doubt she might have been suitable, too.

—

Patsy was alone in the house. She was sixteen today and she doubted there would be anyone wishing her a happy birthday. She had just finished washing the kitchen floor and was sweeping the patio when she heard the front gate open and footsteps coming up the path. She paused, expecting to hear the rat-tat-tat of the front-door knocker but, instead, the footsteps appeared to be heading round the side of the house. Her grip on the yard brush tightened and her heart began to thud. You heard so much these days about robbery with violence that you just didn't know the minute when it might happen to you. Then a woman hovered into view and Patsy's pulse slowed. She propped the brush against the wall and hurried over to Joy with a smile on her face.

'What are you doing here, Miss Kirk? It's lovely to see you.'

Joy's eyes were warm on the girl. Patsy was no beauty like Alice's daughter, Flora, but she had a lovely smile and a nature to match.

'I meant to get here weeks ago but I've been really busy. I knew today was your birthday because Tilly sent a present for me to give to you.'

Patsy was touched. 'She remembered. It's really kind of you to come, and just at the right time. I've the house to meself and I'm ready to have a break.'

'Good. I've brought some of my home-made fruit cake but I won't be eating any,' she said with a moue of regret, 'I'm on a diet.'

'Why? You're lovely as you are, all nice and motherly,' said Patsy sincerely. 'But come into the kitchen and we'll have a cup of tea.' She led the way inside. Once there she led Joy to a chair and insisted that she rest her feet. 'I can scarcely believe you're here. It seems ages since I've seen you. I suppose Tilly told you that I write to her regularly.'

'Indeed, she did.' Joy sat at the well-scrubbed kitchen table and removed her gloves. She had been almost tempted to say to hell with the diet but that word 'motherly' had caused her to wince inwardly with its connotations of large bosoms and childbearing hips. 'Anyway, happy birthday from me!' She took out a big parcel. 'That's the cake.' Then she took out a slimmer package and placed that on the table too. 'That's from Tilly.'

Patsy picked up the parcel. 'It's very light.'

'Open it and see.'

Patsy carefully unwrapped the parcel to reveal a pair of what appeared to be stockings. But they were not like the thick black ones she normally wore but were beige and felt almost like silk.

'What are they made of?' she asked.

'Rayon. They're the latest fashion in America. Apparently rayon is made from cellulose and the French came up with the idea.'

'Trust the French,' said Patsy, delighted with her gift. 'I'll have to save them for a special occasion.'

'You can hardly wear them to do the cleaning,' teased Joy. 'You'd have holes in them in no time.'

Patsy agreed and parcelled up the stockings. 'Thanks so much for bringing them. I did think that perhaps Tilly mightn't be able to make head nor tail of my writing earlier in the year. I had a sore finger at the time.'

'What was wrong with it?'

'It doesn't matter,' said Patsy, getting to her feet. 'It's better now.'

'Of course it matters. Tilly had the impression that you weren't being treated properly and were unhappy here.'

Patsy paused in the act of pouring milk into cups. 'I can't remember exactly what I wrote in that letter. I suppose I was having a moan about the job.'

'That would probably be it,' said Joy. 'I suppose Mr Tanner is at work right now?'

'No. He's in America. It came as a surprise to me *and* Mrs Tanner that he had decided to toddle off there. He wanted her to go with him but she wasn't having any. I wish you could hear her going on at him when he's at home. With him out of the way she can do what she likes – and that's dancing whenever she wants.'

'What's she like?'

Patsy pursed her lips and looked pensive. 'Wait a mo'. I'll go and get a photograph of her. He keeps one in his bedroom on the side table.'

'They have separate rooms?' asked Joy, making out that she had never heard that before.

'Yes. Odd, isn't it? I thought all married couples shared a bedroom.'

'Depends on their age.'

'I reckon they're nudging thirty,' said Patsy. 'I'll just go and get that picture.'

As soon as Patsy had gone, Joy rose to her feet and warmed the teapot. By the time the girl returned, the tea was made.

Patsy handed a framed photograph to Joy. 'Sorry I took so long but it wasn't where I last saw it. For some reason he'd put it in a drawer.'

Joy stared at the image of a laughing woman. She was wearing a gown that reminded her of the one worn by the Duchess of York for her wedding three years ago. No doubt it was a copy. Round her neck Mrs Tanner was wearing several long strings of beads and the camera had caught her in the act of swinging them round and into the air.

'What do you think of her?' asked Patsy. 'Nice-looking, isn't she?'

'Yes. But there's something about her smile…'

'She likes herself and having her own way,' said Patsy, reaching for the photograph. 'Yet I feel sorry for both of them at times. I'd best return that to where it came from before she gets back. She's gone to the hairdresser's.'

Joy said, 'Why do you feel sorry for them?'

'They're not happy. Anyway, I'd best put this back. I know he's not here but he doesn't like me going into his bedroom.'

'Surely you must go in there to clean the place and make his bed?'

Patsy shook her head. 'No. And she doesn't do it.'

Joy was puzzled. 'I bet his room's a mess.'

'No. Dead tidy.'

'What's he look like? Does she have a photograph of him in her bedroom?'

'No. But there's one in the sitting room of the pair of them on their wedding day. I forgot about it because it's in the book cabinet.'

Patsy hurried out of the kitchen, thinking how good it was to have someone she could talk to face-to-face about her employers.

Having replaced the photograph, she paused a moment before opening a wardrobe door. Some of David Tanner's clothes were still hanging there, so he must plan on coming back. Why should she think he wouldn't when it was the missus who had mentioned leaving? Wasting no more time, Patsy went downstairs to the drawing room. She removed the wedding photograph from its place and carried it to the kitchen.

'There he is. What d'you think?' Patsy placed the photograph on the table.

Joy looked at the couple and had the oddest feeling when she gazed at the groom. 'He doesn't exactly look over the moon to be getting married, does he? In fact, he looks terrified.'

'Terrified?' Patsy peered at the picture. 'I've never really looked at it this close before. You're right, he doesn't look too happy, does he? Nerves probably. She looks OK, though.'

'The blushing bride,' murmured Joy, thinking of her own forthcoming nuptials. She spared Mr Tanner a second look. 'He has good bones, and I suppose if he was smiling, then he would be good-looking. How long have they been married?'

'Seven years. They had their anniversary just before he went away. Not that they were celebrating. She said she'd had seven years of pretending to be a normal married couple.'

Joy put down the photograph. 'I have something to tell you. I'm getting married.'

'Congratulations! Who's the lucky man?'

'Mr Bennett.'

'Oh!' Patsy's face fell.

Joy gave a twisted smile. 'I'm sure Tilly told you that my mother died, and as I like where I'm living and I'm fond of Mr Bennett, I accepted his offer of marriage. I'm sure you can understand my reasoning.'

Patsy understood perfectly. 'Too right, I do. And I'm sure he's fond of you with you being such a good cook. I reckon he's getting the best of the bargain. When are you getting married?'

'Easter Monday. At St Margaret's church.'

'I'll come and watch you get wed if I can get the afternoon off.'

Joy smiled. 'Never you mind you just coming and watching, you can come to the wedding itself.'

Patsy beamed at her. 'Thanks! It'll be a nice change to go to a wedding.'

'I've brought a proper invitation for you to show to your employers,' said Joy, taking a card out of her handbag. 'You can bring Kathleen too if you like,' she added.

Patsy was almost lost for words and clasped her hands together. 'Are you sure you want two of us? What about Mr Bennett? Won't two Doyles be too much for him?'

Joy laughed. 'Of course not. But you'll have to speak to your sister about it. I won't be sending her a separate invitation.'

Patsy nodded. 'We won't let you down.'

'I wouldn't have asked you to come if I believed you would. I'm sure you'll do me proud.'

Patsy felt tears prick the back of her eyes and hastily helped herself to a slice of cake. When she had recovered her equilibrium she told Joy about the day she had baked the cherry scones. 'Although I told Mr Tanner that they weren't to your recipe, he called you a paragon because I'd told him how it came about that you gave me cookery lessons.'

Joy was flattered. 'You must have boosted me up more than I deserved.'

'No. I only told the truth,' said Patsy sincerely. 'His wife never bakes and he likes his stomach, not that you'd know it to look at him. He's as slim as he was in that wedding photograph. She's always out when he comes home in the evening. She loves tea dances and I think he can't get it out of his mind that she might be meeting another man.'

'But he hasn't done anything about finding out if that's true?'

Patsy's brow creased in thought. 'I've no idea. If he did discover she was carrying on perhaps he'd explode and we'd both have to take cover.' She gave a delicate shudder. 'Mrs Tanner actually said to him that their first honeymoon was a shambles.'

Joy was reminded of Robbie's desire for a honeymoon. 'Oh, dear!' she murmured.

Patsy flushed. 'I suppose you're thinking I shouldn't be listening to their conversations but they speak so loudly. Anyway, I've seen and heard worse when Mam was alive. I'm not going to be shocked by anything they say,' she added stoutly.

Joy remembered what she and Hanny had discussed and decided to take the bull by the horns. 'So Mr Tanner hasn't made any advances towards you?' she asked.

'If you mean has he put his hand up my skirt or tried anything else on, then the answer is no. I don't think he's that kind of man. He's told me off a couple of times for being careless but she's done the same. In fact, it was she who hurt my finger. She's got a worse temper than he has.'

'Well, that's a relief,' said Joy, thinking this news would be a load off Tilly and Hanny's minds. 'It's not unknown, you know, for employers to take advantage of servant girls.'

Patsy smiled grimly. 'I've no illusions about the extent some men will go to satisfy their lusts, whether it's for sex, money or power. One of Mam's blokes tried it on with me. I was terrified and kicked up a din. She came running and laid into me!' Her voice cracked. 'I got really angry and ran out of the house. When I went back she made out that she was all sorry. She told me then what blokes could do to a girl and how it could get them into trouble. It knocked me sideways.'

Joy had known something of Patsy's past but never heard this story before. She was shocked and patted the girl's hand. 'Is there anything else you'd like to talk about or any question you'd like to ask me?'

Patsy put all thoughts of the past aside. 'Who are you having for bridesmaids?' she asked eagerly. 'I bet Wendy Wright will be one of them.'

'Of course she will. She's Mr Bennett's niece.'

'Will the famous detective be there, too?' asked Patsy eagerly.

Joy smiled, thinking that the famous detective was how Wendy's mother had cynically referred to Grant Simpson.

'Of course. They're engaged to be married.'

'Wendy will be pleased that you're going to be her aunt but I bet her mother isn't.'

'You're right. She doesn't approve of me at all,' said Joy, considering Patsy perceptive for a girl of her age. 'But let's forget Mrs Wright. I suggest you and your sister come to the house beforehand. My sister will be there with her husband and their twins. They'll be glad of your help with the children. Hanny is to be my matron of honour.'

'I'll be happy to keep an eye on them for her. I know what trouble twins can be.'

Joy smiled. 'I'm glad we can be of help to each other.'

Patsy could not agree more. She believed in favours being returned and Joy Kirk had been generous with her time and again in the past.

Soon after Joy took her leave.

Patsy knew that there were several things she was going to have to do before saying for certain that she and her sister would be able to attend the wedding. Uppermost in her mind was getting permission from Mrs Tanner to have the Easter Monday bank holiday off.

–

'A wedding. You've been invited to a wedding?' said Rose, sounding incredulous. 'I didn't know you had any friends or relatives of marriageable age, Patsy.'

'It's Miss Kirk. The one who helped look after us after my mother was killed. She's really kind.'

'Who is she marrying?'

'Look, here's the invitation,' said Patsy, handing her the printed card.

Rose read it. 'My goodness, she's marrying Mr Bennett!'

'That's right. The one you know who's a musician and has white bushy hair. Remember, I told you that she was his housekeeper?'

'Yes. I believe his second wife was a wealthy widow with property she inherited from her first husband,' said Rose. 'Well, it certainly looks like Mr Bennett knows how to choose his wives and he definitely knows his stuff when it comes to playing the latest dance music from America. Although, that is probably down to an old friend of his, Brendan O'Hara. He's come over from the States and he's a marvellous dancer and has been teaching me – us, I mean, the Charleston. I do so love to dance the latest craze but David won't even try. As you probably have guessed, Patsy, Mr Tanner is an old fuddy-duddy despite being the same age as me.' Rose stopped and looked moody and worried all of a sudden. 'Don't you go telling him what I've just told you,' she added sharply.

'He's not here for me to tell him anything,' reminded Patsy.

'No, of course not.' Rose's smile was back in place once more. 'I will not feel guilty about refusing to go to America with him in search of my selfish, arrogant brother. Although, perhaps I will go there one day if things go my way. You'll keep my secret, won't you, Patsy?'

'What secret is that, Mrs Tanner?'

The woman laughed. 'That's a sensible girl. Now this wedding – it's short notice but you can have your day off because I just might have plans for that weekend myself.'

Patsy thanked her.

'Now I'm going to go into town and buy myself a new dance frock. The competition is this Saturday and there are to be several prizes. I've my eye on winning at least one of them.'

'Good luck to you, Mrs Tanner,' said Patsy, relieved that she had agreed to her having the day off. 'Will you get a big silver cup?'

'Goodness me, I hope not! Where would I put it? A weekend for two in Blackpool, now that would be more welcome,' she said, her eyes gleaming.

Patsy wondered if she would be dancing the prize-winning event with Miss Swift or be partnered by Mr O'Hara. If it was the latter, was he tall, dark and handsome? Mr Bennett would know. She decided to put all that Mrs Tanner had told her out of her mind for now. She had a letter to write to her sister and there was no time to waste.

Chapter Six

'Why did you ask the eldest Doyle girl to the wedding?' demanded Robbie on entering the drawing room a few days later.

A startled Joy glanced up from the list of food she was compiling for the wedding buffet. 'How do you know that when I haven't mentioned it to you?'

He placed his clarinet case on the sofa and sat down. 'Because I know her employer and she told me about it.'

'You're telling me that you know the Tanners?'

'I know Rose Tanner.' He took out a packet of cigarettes and lit up. 'You can stop looking worried. I'm not going to complain that you kept the invitation quiet from me. But you haven't any more secrets up your sleeve, have you?'

'No. But I'm interested in Mrs Tanner. Who does she dance with at the tea dances?'

'I don't know if I should tell you if you've been speaking to that girl.'

'I see. You mean it's a man.'

A laugh rumbled inside Robbie's chest. 'Rosie isn't the kind of lady who enjoys dancing with women.'

'What's his name?'

'Why d'you want to know? You're not going to carry tales back to the Doyle girl, are you?'

Joy was affronted. 'What a thing to say! I'm just curious, that's all.'

'Well, if you must know it's Brendan O'Hara. You'll gather he has Irish blood in him. I know him from way back when he boarded the ship at Cobh the time I set out all those years ago to make my fortune in America. I never did make my fortune but he has his finger in several pies. He's over here for the Grand National amongst other things. He and Rosie make a good couple on the dance floor. Their steps match perfectly.'

'Is he married?'

'He's in the process of getting divorced.'

'Divorced!'

Robbie frowned. 'I know. Shocking, isn't it? But I'm only telling you what he told me. Anyway, what's going on between the pair of them has nothing to do with us or the Doyle girl, so keep quiet about it,' he warned.

'I have no intention of telling her anything,' said Joy, irritated by his warning. 'As you say, it's none of my business.'

'So why did you ask the Doyle girl to the wedding? It's not as if she's family.'

'I felt sorry for her. I've asked her sister to come as well,' said Joy, trying to keep calm. 'They don't get to go anywhere. They're not fortunate enough to have relatives to take them out or buy them presents.'

His bushy white eyebrows shot up. 'I hope you're not hinting that we should take on the roles of aunt and uncle to them? We already have nieces and nephews and we don't need any more to buy presents for. As for taking them out—'

'I didn't mean for us to spend money on them,' said Joy stiffly. 'I just thought that occasionally it would be kind to give them a treat by inviting them to tea.'

'Have you mentioned this to her?'

'Without asking you? Of course not.'

'Then don't,' he growled. 'If I want children hanging around the house, then I'd consider having my own. Now I'd like a coffee if you don't mind getting up and making me one?'

'I don't mind at all,' said Joy. 'Isn't that what I'm here for? I'll not invite the girls here once the wedding is over. Although, they're hardly children. Patsy is sixteen.'

He reached for her hand and squeezed it gently. 'You're here for more than waiting on me, hand and foot. I count myself a lucky man that I'm marrying an attractive younger woman who is an excellent housekeeper and cook and will bring me comfort in my old age.'

She knew what he expected her to say. 'You're not old. You're still an attractive man with your own hair and your own teeth.'

He beamed at her. 'You certainly know how to flatter a man. Now give us a kiss.' He drew her towards him.

Joy resisted only for a second but then allowed herself to be pulled onto his knee. She did not want to antagonise him at this stage. He planted a spanking kiss on her lips and she did not find it too distasteful. As long as the comfort he sought did not go further than a few kisses and cuddles she thought she could cope. But it did worry her that he might read into these little signs of affection an invitation to more intimate behaviour. It could be the thin end of the wedge but she could not see what she could do about it at the moment.

'We'll have some champagne when I get back later,' he said, releasing her.

'What for?' she asked, startled. 'What are you celebrating?'

'Do I need to be celebrating anything special? I like champagne. As it is, you're right in thinking I have something to celebrate. I've been asked to be the accompanist for one of the turns in a variety show at the Hippodrome next week. Their usual man has been taken into hospital with appendicitis. I'm due for a rehearsal this evening. I'll bring the champagne home with me,' he wheezed against her ear.

Joy would much rather forgo the champagne. A couple of glasses and she became really woozy and it wasn't as if she liked the taste. Goodness knows where it might lead if she were to have one glass too many. She decided not to wait up for him. Her mind drifted to what he had told her about Rosie Tanner and Brendan O'Hara. Of course, it could be that the relationship between the two dancers was kept strictly to the dance floor. Or were they having an affair? If so, what would Mr Tanner do if he were to find out?

Patsy entered the drawing room to find that yet again the carpet was rolled up and the furniture shoved against the wall. Rose Tanner was dancing alone to the strains of a tune Patsy recognised as being popular a couple of years ago. 'California, Here I Come' had been whistled by every delivery boy who had called at her previous employer's house. She stood, clutching the telegram and tapping her foot to the music. Her mistress was oblivious to her presence, so Patsy allowed herself a few moments to think about the letter she had received from the guardians about Kathleen.

Apparently they had found a position for her at the home of two elderly spinster sisters and she would be starting work there as a domestic within days of leaving the orphanage. Patsy did not know whether to feel glad or sorry. It was good news that there wouldn't be a man in the house for her sister to want to fuss over her but, on the other hand, Kathleen did not like old women. Patsy could imagine her getting discontented within days. She would not settle and might end up doing something stupid to get out of there.

A sigh escaped Patsy and she wondered how she could help her sister to be happy. Then she became aware that the music was getting slower and slower. She rushed across the room and wound up the gramophone and the tempo returned to normal.

'Thank you, Patsy!' called Rose in a breathless voice. 'I do so love this song.'

'It's very catchy, madam.'

'Millions agree with you.' She glanced in Patsy's direction and the girl waved the telegram.

'Oh hell! I hope that isn't what I think it is,' said Rose, her steps faltering. 'Open it and tell me it's not from my husband.'

Patsy did as asked and saw that it was as Mrs Tanner feared. 'Mr Tanner says that his liner is expected to dock in Liverpool tomorrow morning.'

'Well, at least he's given me some warning,' said Rose, going over to the gramophone and removing the record. 'I don't suppose

I'll be playing this in here again.' She placed the record in its sleeve and then sat on the sofa. 'Fix the carpet and then run me a bath. I want to look and feel my best this evening.'

'You're feeling better now, then, madam?' asked Patsy, unrolling the carpet and smoothing it flat. Rose had been bilious every morning for the last few days.

'Yes. Much better. It must have been something I ate the other day. Maybe the oysters?' she said brightly. 'You'll need to make up Mr Tanner's bed and give the room a clean. It's the final of the competition this afternoon. You'll have to wish me luck, Patsy.'

'I do, madam. You'll be wearing your new frock?'

Rose smiled. 'Naturally. But not new shoes. I'll be wearing the ones that have carried me through this far.'

'Will you be having dinner at home afterwards?'

'No. Hopefully we'll be celebrating, so I won't be in until late. You can have a few hours off but be back here by nine at the latest.'

'Yes, madam. Thank you.' Patsy hesitated. 'Is it possible, madam, for me to use the telephone? I've received a letter from the orphanage and I must visit there but I need to find out if it's convenient first.'

Rose frowned and appeared to give it much thought before saying, 'All right. Just this once. But run the bath for me first.'

Patsy thanked her and hurried out of the room. The bathroom was in a converted small back bedroom and the bath was large and white and stood on claw-shaped feet. The hot water came from a heater on the wall. She put in the plug and turned on the taps and took a jar from a shelf and threw a handful of Attar of Roses bath crystals into the water. Then she put out a couple of thick fluffy towels on the rail. When she judged the water was just as Rose liked it, she turned off the taps and hurried downstairs.

While her employer was having her bath, Patsy used the telephone and was delighted to be given permission to take her sisters and brother out for a couple of hours. She could not wait to see them.

One of the twins was the first to reach Patsy. She flung her arms about her eldest sister's waist and beamed up at her. 'It seems ages since you were last here.'

Patsy returned her hug and planted a kiss on the top of her head. 'You must have behaved yourself if they're letting you out.'

'I've been as good as gold,' she said earnestly. 'Ask our Mary!'

'She'd say yes even if you hadn't.' Patsy stared at the other twin. 'How have you been?'

'I'ff losth a tooth,' said Mary, opening her mouth and showing the gap. 'I'ff goth a new one comith fru.'

Patsy made a suitable comment and smoothed back a strand of hair that had come loose from one of Mary's plaits. The twins were carrot tops with a sprinkling of freckles across the bridge of their noses. At times like this she was reminded of the night that they were born. She had thought her mother was dying the way she had carried on screaming and swearing. The woman who had tended her at the birth had not been a registered midwife but one of the neighbours who had ten children of her own. Patsy had overheard her saying that, with their red hair and dimpled chins, the twins were as unlike the older children as cheese and chalk. She might as well have said that the twins did not share the same father as the other Doyle children. Patsy was aware such things happened during the war, with so many husbands away and the possibility of their never coming back. Whether they shared the same father or not made no difference to the way she felt about the twins. She loved them.

Jimmy touched her arm and she smiled at him. 'You OK?'

This brother had her light brown hair and grey eyes and strong chin. 'I'd like to discuss with yer a couple of matters that are bothering me,' he said seriously.

'OK! But first I need to talk to Kathleen.'

Patsy hoped Jimmy was not getting bullied. He did not mix easily and no doubt missed his older brother, Mick, who had always looked out for him. She turned to Kathleen and immediately her heart sank because she just knew that her sister had a mood on her. Blonde and blue-eyed, Kathleen was already showing feminine curves in the right places beneath her navy-blue coat and skirt.

'All right, what's eating you?' asked Patsy.

'Let's get out of here. I've had enough of this place,' muttered Kathleen. 'Thank God, I'll be able to walk out next week and not come back.'

Patsy slipped a hand through her sister's arm. 'Don't say that in front of the twins,' she asked in a low voice. 'They've still years ahead of them. Anyway, what about the position with the two spinsters? How d'you feel about that?'

'Two right old miseries dressed in black crêpe from head to toe. They're still mourning their father who was killed in the Boer War. They have photographs of him in uniform on the sideboard.' Kathleen rolled her eyes. 'And if yer could see the house! It sent a shiver up me spine I can tell yer. Narrow passages and steep stairs – and dark! I could break me blinkin' neck going up and down them. They don't even have gas but use oil lamps and candles. I don't know what the guardians are thinking of, wanting to send me there. In my opinion they just want to get rid of me.' Her mouth tightened. 'Well, I'm making me own plans and it won't be working for those two. The guardians can't force me to do what they want.'

'It does sound pretty gruesome, just like in a horror flick,' said Patsy worriedly. 'But what else do you have in mind?'

'Fellas! They're what's on her mind,' said Jimmy, who had been listening. 'She gets herself into trouble because she thinks she knows it all when she doesn't have a halfpennyworth of common sense. She won't listen to anyone. Yer'd think she had cloth ears.'

'Shut up, shrimp!' snapped Kathleen. 'Yer a boy and boys get away with murder compared to girls.'

'That's not true,' he said indignantly. 'I bet you've never had six of the best. I have and I don't want whacking again. So now

I take notice of what I'm told and do it. I aim to get somewhere in the world and I've enough nous to realise that the only way to do that is by getting myself noticed for the right reasons. Not like you, making eyes at the workmen and not looking where yer going.'

'Shut up, you!' Kathleen poked her elbow viciously in his side. He gasped and called her a bitch.

'Stop it, the pair of you,' cried Patsy, annoyed with both of them. 'I didn't come here to listen to you two argue. Anyway, what's this about workmen?'

'She walked into a pile of bricks and almost knocked herself out,' said Jimmy, rubbing his side and glaring at Kathleen. 'Talk about stupid.'

'Did you hurt yourself, Kath?' asked Patsy with concern.

Kathleen hunched her shoulders. 'I only split me lip and scraped me elbow, so whoever told our Jimmy about the accident got it all wrong. Anyway, *he* helped me up and escorted me to Matron's office.'

'Who's *he*?'

Kathleen barely hesitated. 'Billy the apprentice. He quite fancied me.'

Patsy frowned. 'What did Matron say?'

'She put iodine on it and that really stung but I didn't whinge,' said Kathleen smugly.

'Good. So you haven't seen any more of this Billy?'

'No. The builders finished the job and left.'

'That's a relief. I don't want you flirting with anyone at your age. Remember what I told you about you know what.'

Kathleen looked amused. 'Oh that! I'm not interested in that! I just want a fella who'll treat me to the flicks.'

'If a fella spends money on you, then he'll expect something in return and it won't be a cup of tea and a bun,' warned Patsy. 'You stay away from the opposite sex. Now, let's get across this road.' She grabbed hold of the twins' hands and hurried them past a couple of cyclists and a horse-drawn van. 'Anyway, I've something to tell you that should cheer you up, Kath,' she called over her shoulder.

'That'll be a change,' muttered Kathleen.

'You bet it will,' said Patsy.

She turned to Jimmy and handed him a paper bag. 'Here's some stale crusts. Take the twins and feed the ducks.'

'OK! But after yer've told our Kathy what yer don't want us to hear, I want to tell you what I want to do when I leave the orphanage – and it's not joining the navy,' said Jimmy.

'All right! Later,' said Patsy, shooing him and the twins away.

For a moment she watched the three head for the bridge overlooking the boating lake and then she faced her sister.

'So what's this big secret?' asked Kathleen.

'A wedding on Easter Monday,' replied Patsy with a pleasurable glow. 'We've been invited to Miss Kirk's wedding.'

Kathleen looked surprised. 'You mean Miss Kirk who worked for the Bennetts?'

'I'm glad you haven't forgotten her.'

'She was good to us and showed us how to make gingerbread men and jam tarts. But why should Miss Kirk want us at her wedding? Who's she marrying?'

'Mr Bennett. And why does she want us? Because she thought it would be a treat for us. We're almost grown up. There'll be good food and other young people you'll remember meeting at Tilly's wedding.'

'Tilly and her husband still send money to the orphanage at Christmas for presents for us.'

'Trust you to remember them for their money and presents,' said Patsy.

Kathleen smiled. 'Why shouldn't I? It isn't as if I don't appreciate what they do. Anyway, if the wedding is on Easter Monday, I won't need the guardians' permission to go—'

'So you've decided to accept the invitation?'

'Yeah! Yer never know what might happen.' Her blue eyes gleamed.

'That's true. But I don't think you'll find a job there. You've got to think seriously whether you're doing the right thing about not taking this position with the spinsters. You need somewhere to live, and for girls in our position the only option is a living-in job. It would be different if I was older and we could rent a house. A house where we could all be together. I'm sure Mick would be willing to put something in the kitty to help out with Jimmy and the twins.'

Kathy stared at her in disbelief. 'Yer talking about something that's of no benefit to me right now. Anyway, some of us might have other plans than to play at happy families.'

Patsy was annoyed by her sister's reaction. 'You mean you!'

Kathleen laughed. 'I can bloody imagine a better future than living with the twins and our Jimmy! Out of all of yer I prefer our Mick, but with him in the navy he'll be useless to me.'

'He'll still need a place to come home to,' pointed out Patsy, hanging on to her temper.

Kathleen said, 'He can put up at the Seamen's Home and then in a few years time he'll be casting around for a wife. It's not me that doesn't have any common sense, it's you. Yer should be doing what you told me not to do and look out for a fella to walk out with. One who has a trade and will want to marry yer one day.' She paused for breath but did not give Patsy a chance to interrupt. 'Unless yer find yourself a sugar daddy. Perhaps you'll be lucky and he'll be prepared to put up with our Jimmy and the twins.'

'What the hell do you know about sugar daddies?' asked Patsy angrily.

'I've heard a couple of the kitchen staff talking.' Kathleen smirked.

'What did they say?'

Kathleen did not reply but instead said, 'I could do with a new frock. Now, if I had some decent material I could make one. I'm pretty nifty with me needle.'

'But you haven't the time and you haven't the material,' cried an exasperated Patsy.

'Then I just mightn't go.'

'Please yourself. I'm going to catch up with Jimmy and the twins. You can look after the girls while I have a word with him.'

'What are you going to talk to him about?' asked Kathleen, looking suspicious. 'Me and the apprentice?'

'With him gone why should I bother?' Patsy left her sister and hurried in the direction of the boating lake bridge. 'Come on, don't hang about there,' she called over her shoulder.

Kathleen stuck out her tongue at Patsy's retreating figure and slowly followed her. She knew there was a lot of truth in what her sister said but she'd be damned if she would go and work in that dark miserable house with those prune-faced spinsters. She guessed there'd be no fellas worth looking at who might come visiting the old girls. But even if there were she just knew those two women wouldn't give her the opportunity to speak to them. She was just hoping that something would happen so she could do something else.

'Is our Kathy moaning about us again?' asked Maureen, looking up at Patsy.

'No.' Patsy thought Kathleen was too wrapped up in herself to spare much thought for the twins. 'Why should she?'

'Because she thinks we're nuisances.'

'She probably doesn't mean to give that impression. She's a lot on her mind with leaving the orphanage.'

'No, she means it,' said Maureen firmly. 'She'd much rather giggle in corners with girls her own age than be with us.'

Patsy said easily, 'Did you hear what they said?'

Maureen's cheeks reddened. 'Don't want to talk about it. It was rude.'

Patsy said, 'You really shouldn't be listening, then.'

'I didn't mean to but our Kathy has a loud voice. Anyway, I'm glad she's leaving. She gave me a Chinese burn and I didn't like that.'

'I'll speak to her about it,' said Patsy, thinking she would like to give Kathleen a Chinese burn in way of punishment.

Maureen shrugged. 'No point. Anyway, our Jimmy is wanting a word with you.' She grabbed her twin's hand and ran with her in the direction of the paddling pool.

Patsy called to Kathleen and shouted at her to keep her eye on the twins. Then she turned to her brother. 'So what is it you want to do?'

'Work on the railways,' he blurted out. 'I want to be an engine driver.'

She remembered that a railway line ran behind the orphanage. 'So do hundreds if not thousands of other boys, Jimmy,' she pointed out. 'Think of something else.'

He jutted out his chin. 'I don't want to do anything else. I want to be an engine driver and I thought you would help me. So what if there are loads of other boys wanting the same job? There's plenty of engine drivers needed. Why shouldn't it be me that makes it?'

'I wouldn't argue with what you say,' said Patsy, not wishing to discourage him. 'Do you know how to go about becoming an engine driver? I would think you'd have to serve an apprenticeship and that would take a few years. It's a very responsible job.'

His face brightened. 'I reckon I'd have to be a fireman first. Yer know, shovelling coal to heat up the water to make steam.'

'Yes, I know. So how do you become a fireman?'

'I probably have to get an ordinary job on the railway, like be a porter. It would build up me muscles. Yer have to be strong to shovel coal.'

'I suppose building up your muscles is a good start.'

Jimmy frowned. 'I have to start somewhere. I just want yer to make sure the guardians don't send me to a training ship, like they do most of the boys.'

Patsy thought that in two years time she would be eighteen. Hopefully, the guardians would be prepared to take notice of what she had to say by then. If not, she was going to have to find a man to speak for her. If only her father had still been alive. But, of course, she was wishing for the moon.

She ruffled Jimmy's hair. 'You keep on hoping and we'll see what can be done. In the meantime…' Her voice broke off as she noticed Kathleen signalling frantically to her.

Jimmy had noticed her as well. 'I bet our Mo has fallen into the paddling pool.'

Patsy had almost forgotten how accident prone she was and began to run. It was as Jimmy had guessed and they were confronted by a weeping and extremely wet Maureen.

'Why does it always happen to you?' cried Patsy, removing her sister's sodden coat and wrapping her own about her shivering form. 'Now this has happened the orphanage might think twice about allowing you to come out with me again.'

'I was trying to float a lollipop stick on the water,' grizzled Maureen.

'I only took my eyes off her for a moment and in she goes,' said Kathleen. 'It wasn't my fault.'

Patsy snapped, 'You should have known better than to take your eyes off her, even for a second.'

She ushered them in the direction of the orphanage and as soon as they arrived there, a huffy Kathleen made herself scarce. It was left to Patsy to explain to Matron what had happened. She received a scolding but managed to make her escape with her own damp coat without being told that she needn't bother coming back for the next few months.

There was no time for her to go in search of Kathleen to arrange where they were to meet before the wedding, always assuming she would come, so Patsy decided she would have to write her a short note when she returned to the Tanners and post it as soon as she could.

Chapter Seven

Patsy let herself into the kitchen and hung up her damp coat. She was just lighting the gas ring when she heard a noise upstairs. Could Mrs Tanner have come home earlier than she had planned? Perhaps she had not won the competition after all.

Patsy left the kitchen and walked along the passage to the foot of the stairs. 'Is that you, Mrs Tanner?' she called up.

For a moment there was silence and then she heard footsteps overhead.

'No, it's me, Patsy. Where have you been?'

Patsy received such a fright that she put a hand to her breast as if to steady her heartbeat. 'Mr Tanner! I thought your ship wasn't due in until tomorrow morning!'

'We made up for some lost time,' he said, coming downstairs. 'Do you know where my wife is?'

He had a bundle of envelopes under his arm and she thought that he looked sad and weary. 'Mrs Tanner gave me permission to visit my sisters and brother at the orphanage. She was performing in a dance competition this afternoon, but I honestly don't know where it's taking place.'

He nodded. 'How has she been while I've been away?'

Patsy hesitated. 'She's had a bit of an upset tummy.'

'I see. Obviously she's feeling better now if she's gone out.'

'It's this competition, Mr Tanner. She's dead keen.'

'So I believe but I'll say no more on that score. Can you poach me a couple of eggs on toast and bring me a pot of tea? I'll be in the drawing room.'

'Yes, Mr Tanner.'

Patsy wondered if he had spoken to one of the neighbours who had complained that his wife had played dance music almost constantly when she was not gadding about and coming in all hours of the night. She felt apprehensive about what might happen when Mrs Tanner arrived home.

She prepared his supper and carried it in to the sitting room. He was gazing into space and there was a typewritten letter open on his knee. What was it about its contents that caused him to look so drawn and unhappy?

'Your supper, Mr Tanner,' said Patsy.

David folded the letter and put it in an envelope. 'Thank you.'

'Is there anything else you need?'

'No.'

She was on her way out of the room when he called her back. 'Wait, Patsy. You mentioned seeing your sisters and brother – did you have a good time together?'

She was pleased that he should take an interest. 'It was lovely seeing them but our Maureen went and fell in the paddling pool and Jimmy was telling me he wants to be an engine driver. I'd like to do my best to help him get the job he wants but I'm sure it's not going to be easy. As for our Kathleen, she'll be leaving the orphanage in the next few days and she's a bit of a rebel and is kicking up about the job the guardians have found her.'

He smiled faintly. 'What is it she wants to do?'

'God only knows! I doubt she knows herself. But I'm hoping she'll be sensible and stop complaining.'

'So a lot for you to worry about,' he said.

'Yes! Fortunately, I've something to look forward to,' she said, smiling.

'And what is that?'

'A wedding next Saturday. Mrs Tanner has given me permission to go. I hope that's all right with you, Mr Tanner?'

'Whose wedding is it?'

'Miss Kirk's. She's marrying Mr Bennett.'

He looked surprised. 'The paragon is marrying her boss! I hope she'll be happy.'

'He's old enough to be her father,' blurted out Patsy.

'One presumes she knows what she's doing,' said David.

'Well, she's got a head on her shoulders, if that's what you mean,' said Patsy. 'She came and wished me a happy sixteenth birthday and brought me some cake, as well as a present from my friend, Tilly, in America. They're related by marriage. I've still got a bit of the cake if you'd like a taste?'

'A taste of the paragon's cake,' he mused. 'Why not? So you're now sixteen, Patsy?'

'Yes, Mr Tanner. Be seventeen next year and soon be an old woman.'

He smiled. 'You've cheered me up. Go and get me a slice of that cake.'

Patsy had never seen him smile in such a way before and thought it made him look quite attractive. It's a pity he couldn't look happy more often. 'Rightio,' she said, hastening away.

When she returned he looked grim-faced again and had another envelope open with a letter sticking out. 'Your cake,' she said, placing the plate on the table.

He nodded, without looking up.

She stood a moment, waiting, but when he did not speak she crept out. What were the letters he was reading? They hadn't come through the letter box here, that was for sure. Perhaps they had been sent to his office and he had called in there before coming home.

She made herself some supper and then settled in a chair by the fire with a novel. She was engrossed in the story when David Tanner entered the kitchen with the tray. He placed it on the draining board. 'Did my wife give you any idea when she would be home?'

Patsy tore herself away from the page. 'Sorry, Mr Tanner. What did you say?' She put aside the book and got to her feet.

He leant against the sink. 'I asked if my wife said when she would be back.'

'No. But she did say that if she won the competition, then she would be celebrating.'

'With whom?'

'She didn't say.'

He left the kitchen without saying another word.

Patsy carried on reading. After a while her eyes began to droop so she placed a marker between the pages. She visited the outside lavatory, washed her hands and cleaned her teeth in the kitchen before going to bed. Rose was still out and Patsy wondered if she planned on staying out all night. She tried to stay awake and listen out for her but she was too tired and soon drifted into sleep.

Patsy was roused by the sound of a car stopping outside. There was laughter and a male voice mingling with a feminine one that she recognised as Rose Tanner's. Patsy's heart seemed to bounce in her chest. She glanced at the alarm clock beside her bed and saw that it was one o'clock in the morning. Heck! What if Mr Tanner was still awake and heard the noise? Hopefully the car was a taxi and the man's voice that of the driver.

She climbed out of bed and padded over to the window. But if she had wanted to warn her mistress, then it was too late. She heard the front door open and David asking, 'Do you know what time this is, Rose?'

The silence that followed those words felt heavy and ominous. 'Please, God, let the man be a taxi driver,' whispered Patsy.

Rose smothered a nervous giggle. 'Brendan, can you tell my husband the time, seeing that he doesn't know it himself?'

'Don't try and be smart with me, Rose,' thundered her husband. 'You're drunk!'

'No, not drunk,' said Rose, 'just a little tipsy! And you would be, David, if you'd had an evening like mine. We won, we won!'

'Perhaps I'd better explain, Mr Tanner, what's been happening,' said the man accompanying Rose. 'It's not what you might think.'

'I'd rather you didn't waste your time and mine by lying to me,' said David coldly. 'I know what you and my wife have been up to and I think you'd best go. I need to talk to her, alone.'

'But you can't know,' cried Rose. 'You've been away.'

'Can't I? The pair of you should have shown more discretion. Now, Mr O'Hara, I'd appreciate it if you were to leave,' said David.

'No, Brendan,' cried Rose, panic in her voice. 'He'll hurt me. You have to stay. You know what a terrible temper he has!'

'You lying bitch,' rasped David. 'It's you who has the temper. I swear, by God, I won't lay a finger on you if you come inside quietly. We have matters to discuss.'

'Don't believe a word he says, Brendan, he's out to destroy me,' said Rose in a quivering voice. 'Please, Brendan, take me with you!'

'He's not going to take you anywhere,' said David, a sneering note in his voice. 'Definitely not to America.'

'Brendan?' pleaded Rose.

There was the noise of a sash window going up. 'Will you three shut up down there,' shouted a man's voice.

'Fred, don't,' called a woman's voice. 'Come back to bed.'

Patsy could imagine Mr Tanner's embarrassment and anger at the thought of half the road listening to what was going on. She heard a scuffle and then the sound of a door slamming. There was a noise of a fist hitting wood and then the murmur of voices. After that a car door opened and shut, an engine accelerated and the car moved off.

Her curiosity intensified. Should she go downstairs and see what was going on? Had Brendan and Rose driven away or had Mr Tanner persuaded his wife to come inside and finally given in to a violent impulse. Unexpectedly Patsy heard her name being called from outside. She poked her head out of the window and, to her amazement, saw Rose Tanner standing on the front path.

'Madam, what are you doing down there?' she called.

'Mr Tanner has shut me out. I've tried the back door but it's locked. Will you open it for me?'

Patsy was surprised. 'You want to come inside? What about that man – that Brendan O'Hara?'

'He's none of your business! Now... now get down here and let me in!'

'Mr Tanner might stop me,' said Patsy.

'He won't hurt you. Besides, this is all his fault. If only he'd been honest with me in the first place, none of this would have happened.' Her voice broke on a sob. 'I'm going round the back.'

Patsy put on a frock and crept down to the first-floor landing. She almost jumped out of her skin when she saw a shadowy figure. David Tanner was standing outside his bedroom. She waited for him to say something but, instead, he went inside his room and closed the door. She let out a pent-up breath and hurried to the kitchen. As soon as she unlocked the back door, Rose Tanner fell inside.

Patsy picked her up and heaved her onto a chair. Then she fumbled in the dark for the matches and felt her way to the stove. She lit a gas ring and turned it full on before facing Rose. 'Are you all right, madam?' she asked.

'What a stupid question! Of course I'm not all right.' Rose buried her head in her hands and added in a muffled voice, 'Everything's gone wrong, and it was such a lovely evening.'

Patsy felt her ire rising. 'What do you want me to do, madam?' she asked in a cool voice.

'Put a hot-water bottle in my bed.'

The request was so prosaic that Patsy thought she must have misheard her. 'I beg your pardon?'

'You heard me! I want a hot-water bottle. I'm going to bed and they'll both regret what they've done to me!' She placed her hands on the back of the chair and pushed herself up. Patsy stared at her. Tears had caused Rose's mascara to run, her lipstick was smeared and her features were twisted in an ugly grimace. 'Never trust a man,' she said, tears filling her eyes. She staggered away from the chair and made for the door.

Patsy paused to put the kettle on before hurrying after her, concerned that she might fall down the stairs. She followed her all the way up, placing a hand to the small of her back when she seemed in danger of toppling over. At last they reached the landing and Patsy saw her mistress inside her bedroom and helped her undress. She seemed dozy and Patsy drew back the bedcovers and dragged her onto the bed and covered her up. Then she went downstairs and filled a hot-water bottle.

When she returned Rose appeared to have passed out, so Patsy took the hot bottle upstairs and put it in her own bed. She undressed and crept beneath the bedcovers and hugged the hot-water bottle to her. She longed to have someone to talk to about what had just taken place. Joy Kirk? But how could Patsy possibly bother her right now when she was up to her eyes in wedding preparations? She was just going to have to stick it out here and cope with the aftermath of what had happened on her own. It appeared that Mr Tanner had known about the man called Brendan O'Hara all along.

–

'You'll never guess who I saw at the tea dance competitions last night,' said Robbie, picking up his knife and fork.

Joy paused on her way out of the dining room. 'Who?'

'The great detective.'

'Grant Simpson! Was he with Wendy?'

'Yes. But they weren't dancing but keeping a keen eye on the competitors.' He cut into a fried egg and forked it into his mouth. 'You might like to know,' he added, 'that Brendan and Rose Tanner won the Charleston and the foxtrot competition.'

'How nice for them,' said Joy dryly. 'Did you manage to speak to Wendy?'

Robbie nodded. 'She came over and said hello and ever so casually asked me how well I knew Brendan.'

Joy's eyes sharpened. 'What did you tell her?'

'I told her the truth and she told me to tell you that she'd be here today with Minnie.'

'I haven't forgotten,' said Joy. 'Alice is coming over with my wedding outfit and the girls' dresses. Fingers crossed they'll fit without any alterations being needed.'

'I suppose you'll want me out of the way,' said Robbie, wiping yolk from his chin with a finger and licking it.

'If you don't mind.'

'No. I thought I'd go and spend my winnings.'

Joy looked surprised. 'You mean you won on the Grand National yesterday?'

He grinned. 'Aye. Jack Horner. It was an American-owned horse and I had a tip-off from Brendan. He sure knows his horses.'

She hesitated. 'Do you want to invite him to the wedding?'

'I already have. Didn't think you'd mind,' said Robbie. 'As I told you, we go way back.'

'I presume he won't be bringing Mrs Tanner.'

'No. Apparently Mr Tanner is due home today.'

'That will stop their gallop,' murmured Joy. 'Did Mr O'Hara say he would definitely be coming to the wedding?'

'He said he would let me know.'

'That's all right, then. Anyway, I hope you enjoy spending your winnings.'

'You bet I will.' He smiled to himself.

Joy closed the door, glad to be away from the tempting smells of bacon and eggs. It had been a terrible struggle sticking to her diet but she had lost weight and felt the better for it. She felt bad, though, about not offering Alice and the girls some of her delicious home-made scones or cake when they arrived. Still, they needed to fit into their wedding outfits so none of them would want to put on an ounce.

–

'This is lovely material,' said Joy, fingering the pale-pink taffeta skirt of Wendy's bridesmaid's dress. 'You do like it, don't you?'

'Of course!' replied Wendy, flicking back her mousy hair and regarding herself in the mirror.

'So do I,' said Minnie, nudging her elder sister out of the way so she could get a better look at her own reflection. She was a blonde, voluptuous eighteen-year-old, who normally had plenty to say for herself.

'Hanny has opted to wear a deeper pink as matron of honour,' said Alice. 'You're both happy with the design and the fit?'

'Oh, yes,' said Wendy, her face breaking into a delighted smile. 'I can't wait to see Grant's face when he sees me looking so… so…' She was lost for words and turned to Joy. 'I'm sure Uncle Robbie will be knocked for six when he sees you walking down the aisle.'

Joy gave a faint smile. 'He's convinced I'm making too much of a fuss and that the money could be better spent elsewhere.'

'It's probably Mam who said that to him,' said Minnie. 'She's spitting nails about it all. I won't repeat her words.'

'I can imagine,' said Joy.

'Never mind what Mam thinks,' said Wendy, placing an arm around Joy's shoulders and hugging her. 'We're made up you're going to be our aunt. She's just jealous that you're going to have more influence over Uncle Robbie than she will.'

Joy patted the hand resting on her arm. 'It's really nice of you to say so. I couldn't ask for two nicer young ladies for nieces.'

'All this work, though, has made up my mind that when I get married I'm only having the one bridesmaid and that'll be our Minnie,' said Wendy. 'It'll be simpler and less expensive.'

'Have you set a date yet, love?' asked Joy.

'No! But I'll sort Mam out, don't you worry.' Wendy's eyes gleamed with determination. 'We'll definitely be tying the knot this year, whether she likes it or not. We'll probably have to have Grant's widowed sister living with us but I'll cope with that. We just need to find the right place for the three of us to doss down together in comfort.'

Minnie said, 'The trouble with Mam is that she doesn't want to lose the money you hand over. It's the same with Uncle Robbie getting hitched again. She had her eye on this house and the money Aunt Eudora left him when he pops off.' She gasped and put a hand to her mouth. 'Sorry, sorry, Joy, I shouldn't have said that.'

'No, you shouldn't have,' rebuked Wendy, scowling at her. 'You've got no tact.'

'Stop worrying,' said Joy firmly. 'What Minnie said is nothing new to me. I know how your mother's mind works where money is concerned.'

'She just doesn't appreciate how generous Uncle Robbie's already been to our family,' said Wendy earnestly. 'After Dad was killed, Uncle Robbie saved our skins when he came back from America to help us out.'

Joy knew the story and thought Rita Wright just did not know how to be grateful for her good fortune in possessing four decent children and a brother who had been prepared to shoulder some of her responsibilities. 'I don't know how your mother would have coped if she were in Patsy Doyle's shoes with no money, no home and five younger brothers and sisters to worry about,' murmured Joy.

'How is Patsy?' asked Wendy, easing the bridesmaid's dress over her head. 'I heard that she was working as an all-purpose maid to a Mr and Mrs Tanner.'

'Now, who mentioned that name to you?' mused Joy. 'It wouldn't be the great detective, would it?'

Placing her bridesmaid's dress on a hanger, Wendy avoided Joy's gaze. 'Why should you think that?'

'From something your Uncle Robbie told me this morning about you and Grant being at the tea dance yesterday,' said Joy. 'I believe her husband is back from America today. What's he going to think when he hears that a Mr O'Hara has been her regular dancing partner?'

Wendy sighed. 'You know, you'd make a good detective.'

'Did Mr Tanner hire Grant to keep an eye on his wife?' asked Joy.

Wendy gazed at her woodenly. 'I'm not at liberty to say.'

'That means I'm right,' said Joy.

Wendy mimed buttoning her mouth.

'Understood,' said Joy, inspecting her own reflection. 'But I am concerned about Patsy. I visited her at the Tanners' house the other week. She's worried about them. Is a divorce on the cards, would you say?'

Wendy said, 'I can't discuss the case but I can tell you that Mr Tanner is back home. He phoned the office this morning. Now, I think I'd better go and make an appointment to have my hair done for the wedding. You coming, Minnie?'

'Yeah, OK,' said her sister.

'I've asked Patsy to come to the wedding,' said Joy. 'I haven't heard back from her as to whether she can make it, so I just might drop by at the Tanners' house. I don't want Mr Tanner putting the kibosh on her having the day off.'

'I don't see why he should,' said Wendy. 'He seemed a decent bloke to me. See you soon.' She made for the back door and Minnie followed her out.

Alice looked at Joy. 'Are you really going to go to the Tanners' house? You could walk straight into a row if Grant has told Mr Tanner about his wife and this man, O'Hara.'

'That's true but I want to make sure that Patsy is OK. It would be upsetting for the girl if she was caught up in a nasty divorce case and called upon to be a witness in court. Even worse if she gets hurt because no one was there to take her side and protect her.'

Chapter Eight

Patsy stared in disbelief at the alarm clock and flung back the bedcovers and slid out of bed. She could scarcely believe that she had slept past her normal waking time and that it was ten o'clock. Mrs Tanner would be having a fit if she was waiting for her to bring her breakfast in bed. Then the memory of what happened during the night came flooding back. She dressed quickly and tiptoed downstairs to the first-floor landing but the house seemed as silent as the grave. She wished that she hadn't thought of the word *grave* with its connotations of death. Suddenly she heard a groan. The sound caused her to freeze. There came another groan and then a noise of someone throwing up.

David's door opened and for a moment he and Patsy stared at each other. Then he said, 'There's no need to creep about the place as if you were a burglar. Tell my wife I want to talk to her.'

'I doubt she's in a fit state to talk to anyone right now,' said Patsy bluntly. 'It sounds like she's being sick again.'

The muscles of his face tightened. 'You'd best go and see if she needs help. No doubt she'll be expecting someone else to mop up the mess.'

'Yes, Mr Tanner.'

Patsy supposed that it had not occurred to him that his wife could be suffering from morning sickness. She did not bother knocking on Rose's bedroom door but went straight in, only to baulk at the smell of vomit. She pinched her nose and hurried over to the window and opened it and took several deep breaths before facing her mistress.

A wan-faced Rose lay back against the pillows, having placed the chamber pot on the bedside table. She waved a hand in its direction. 'Empty that,' she ordered.

'Yes, madam. Obviously, you aren't feeling any better this morning.'

Rose muttered, 'Did I dream my husband was here last night?'

'It was no dream,' said Patsy. 'He wants to talk to you.'

'I don't want to see him,' groaned Rose. 'I'm feeling dreadful.'

'That's not surprising given the state you were in last night,' said David, appearing in the doorway. 'We've got to talk.'

'Not now,' said his wife in a faint voice.

'No. In an hour's time. I expect you to be dressed by then.'

Patsy picked up the chamber pot and followed him downstairs. How she hated chamber pots. After she had emptied it in the outside lavatory and cleaned up afterwards, she returned to the kitchen. To her surprise, she found David putting on the kettle.

Without looking at her, he said, 'If I remember rightly you told me that my wife had been sick several times. She should see a doctor.'

Patsy nodded, wondering what would happen if the result of such a visit was the news that she was pregnant. Would he be overcome with delight? Or fury if he suspected that the child might not be his? He made no move to leave the kitchen and ring for the doctor but opened several cupboards before removing a packet of grape-nuts. He found a bowl and filled it with cereal before asking for milk.

Patsy found the morning newspaper pushed halfway through the letter box and a couple of envelopes on the doormat. She picked up both letters and the newspaper before opening the front door. Outside it felt like a normal day and she took several deep breaths. The sun was shining and a couple of sparrows were chirping in the privet hedge. All might have been well with her world if last night hadn't happened but she was convinced more than ever that change was on its way. She picked up the milk bottle from the step and went back inside and closed the door.

73

She found David sitting at the kitchen table with his head in his hands and remembered Rose sitting in a similar position in the kitchen in the middle of the night. 'Are you all right, Mr Tanner?' she asked solicitously, placing the milk, newspaper and envelopes on the table.

'I'll never be all right,' he answered in a muffled voice. 'I don't know what to do.'

'Eat your breakfast?'

She thought she caught the sound of a laugh. He lowered his hands and looked at her. 'You're a tonic. What do you think is best to make my wife less queasy?'

'A cup of tea and an arrowroot biscuit,' said Patsy firmly. 'That's what I've heard some woman swear by.'

'See to it.' He reached for the milk but then changed his mind and picked up one of the envelopes instead and slit it open with a knife.

Patsy watched him out of the corner of her eye as she reached for the biscuit tin. She heard him swear and turned round. 'Did you say something?' she asked.

He did not answer but left the kitchen in a hurry. She heard his feet thudding on the stairs. She switched off the kettle and crept up after him. He burst into Rose's bedroom and did not bother closing the door. Patsy's heart was beating fast as she sat on the stairs where she could see through the open door.

'What do you want? The hour's not up yet,' said Rose angrily.

'He's married! Did you know that?' asked David.

Rose gasped. 'I don't believe you. You're lying. Anyway, how can you know that?'

'I've been having you watched while I've been away. The detective's reports were waiting for me at the office but the very latest one was pushed through the letter box this morning. How do you feel about Mr O'Hara being married?'

'How *dare* you have me watched!'

Patsy heard the sound of a slap and then that of a struggle. She stood up and moved towards the bedroom.

Rose Tanner cried, 'It's not true, it's not true!'

'According to Mr Simpson it is! No, don't you try and hit me again. A man can only take so much.'

'I'll go and ask him,' said Rose in a seething voice. 'You're a freak! He's a proper man.'

There was the hiss of an indrawn breath and then he roared, 'And you are an adulteress!'

'You've driven me to it. Now let me past,' screamed Rose. 'I'm going to prove you wrong.'

'You won't, you know!' David came out of his wife's bedroom and went into his own.

Rose appeared in the doorway. Patsy shrank back against the banisters but there was no hiding place. Rose came towards her, dressed but not looking her immaculate self. 'You're a witness, Patsy, that my husband is a liar and a bully.' She brushed past her and ran down the stairs. Making straight for the front door, she opened it and then slammed it shut behind her.

'Oh dear,' murmured Patsy, walking slowly downstairs. 'Should I leave now?'

She went to the kitchen and a few moments later the door opened and David stood there. With his fists clenching and unclenching, he looked so wild. Patsy panicked. She lunged for the bread knife and held it in front of her. 'None of what happened is my fault. Please, don't hurt me.'

'Bloody hell, Patsy, what do you think you're going to do with that?' asked David, his expression altering. 'I'm not looking to hurt you! I assume you heard all that went on.'

'I couldn't help it,' said Patsy in a trembling voice. 'I don't blame you for being cross but some men are inclined to take their anger out on the nearest person to hand.'

'Well, you don't have to be scared of me. If I were a violent man I would have beaten Rose by now for the way she has spoken to me in the past. I might have made mistakes but I tried to make up for them.' He snatched up the other letter from the table and left the kitchen.

Patsy put down the knife and sat on a chair. She caught sight of the bowl of grape-nuts and poured milk over the cereal. She began to eat, concentrating on each mouthful. She had only eaten half of it when she pushed the bowl away, unable to eat anymore.

What a mess! She felt all of a dither. What was she to do? She could not think straight. Suddenly she decided to do what she often did when she was in a bit of a state. She got up and opened cupboards and took out ingredients. As she beat the cake mixture she began to feel much better. When the cake was in the oven, she felt better still. The house was so silent that it was difficult to believe that Mr Tanner was still there. Perhaps he wasn't. Maybe he had left by the front door. She decided to go and see if he was in the house. First, she went to the drawing room. The door was open and there was nobody inside. Perhaps he was upstairs. She hurried up and stood on the landing, listening. The sound of a drawer slamming and then footsteps convinced her that he was all right.

She hurried downstairs and decided to scrub the front step. She was still feeling a little twitchy and that was another task that always calmed her. After heating up the water, she carried the steaming bucket with cloths and a scrubbing brush around to the front of the house. She was halfway done when she heard the front gate open. She glanced up and could scarcely believe her eyes when she saw Joy Kirk standing there, watching her.

'You all right?' asked Joy. 'I thought you might need someone to talk to.'

'How did you know?' Patsy clambered to her feet and stumbled towards her. 'Mrs Tanner came here with another man and all hell was let loose,' she whispered.

Joy put an arm around her. 'She's a fool, that woman. Shall we go into the kitchen?'

Patsy nodded.

They went round the side of the house and into the kitchen and sat down. 'A little dicky bird told me that Grant Simpson has been keeping his eye on Mrs Tanner,' said Joy.

Patsy's eyes widened. 'The great detective is involved in this?'

'Yes. I suppose it's not surprising. I presume Mr Tanner has an office in town and so does Grant.'

'I think Mr Tanner's is near Fenwick Street.'

Joy nodded. 'So close to Grant's office which is in Fenwick Street. So what happened?'

'There was a terrible row in the middle of the night and a letter came this morning. Apparently Mr O'Hara is married.'

'I know. Mr Bennett has known him for years, and when Wendy asked him about Brendan O'Hara, he told her what he knew.'

'Mrs Tanner went out in a rush to find out whether it was true.' Patsy brought her head close to Joy's. 'I think Mrs Tanner is having a baby and I'm wondering whose baby it is.'

Joy's jaw dropped. 'That'll make things awkward. Are you sure?'

'Mam had six kids after me. I mightn't have been aware what was going on with the first three but I remember she had morning sickness over the twins and Anthony.'

A door opened and there was the sound of footsteps coming downstairs. 'Patsy!' called David. 'Are you there?' Before she could answer, he had pushed open the kitchen door and walked in. He stopped in his tracks and stared at Joy. 'Who are you?' he asked.

She stood up. 'I'm Miss Joy Kirk. I've come to see if it's all right for Patsy to come to my wedding on Easter Monday.'

'I thought my wife had already decided that Patsy could have the day off.'

'So she might have done but I hadn't heard from Patsy and I needed to know for definite that she and her sister were coming.'

'Well, now you do,' he said shortly, tapping his fingernails against the door jamb.

'You want me to leave?' asked Joy.

'Did I say that? I just hope Patsy hasn't been telling you I'm a danger to her.'

'No, she hasn't. But are you?' asked Joy boldly.

His austere features darkened. 'You've got a nerve asking me such a question.'

'It was you that mentioned your being dangerous. I know something of your situation and I don't want Patsy getting caught up in anything nasty.'

'Please, Miss Kirk…' Patsy shifted uncomfortably on her chair. 'I didn't say that he—'

'No, you didn't,' said Joy, staring at David. 'I will explain, Mr Tanner, why I know something of your situation. Not only does my future husband play in the dance band at the tea dances your wife attends but my future niece is engaged to the detective, Grant Simpson. Not that she has betrayed any confidences. Rather, I put two and two together when I was told that she and Grant were at the dance and asking my fiancé questions about Mr O'Hara.'

'Is what you have to say supposed to make me feel better?' rasped David, his grey eyes glinting. 'How many more people know what's going on? I can't afford a scandal in my line of work. I understand your concern for Patsy, Miss Kirk, so perhaps you should take her with you when you leave!'

'No!' Patsy was aghast and sprang to her feet. 'I don't want to leave. I don't believe I'm in danger. I admit I was feeling upset and scared earlier because I was thinking of my uncle who killed my mother. But you're not like him at all, Mr Tanner. I want to stay.'

David could only stare at her. 'Your uncle killed your mother?'

'Yes! He also killed Mr Bennett's dog when he broke into the house. He was a burglar and in cahoots with their neighbour.'

'Good lord!' David Tanner's eyebrows nearly shot through the top of his head at this latest revelation regarding Patsy's family history. 'You have had a tough life, Patsy. You can stay. I have business in Seaforth. I'll see you later.' He nodded stiffly in Joy's direction and left the kitchen.

'Ooof!' exclaimed Joy, sitting down. 'So that's your Mr Tanner. He's different than I imagined.'

'He's had a bad night and an even worse morning,' said Patsy. 'Mrs Tanner has gone to see Mr O'Hara.

'She claimed that he was a real man, not a freak like Mr Tanner.'

'My goodness, what a thing to say to your husband.' Joy was aghast. 'I wonder what will happen when she discovers that Mr O'Hara is getting a divorce. Mr Tanner could use those words against her if he decided to divorce her but, of course, that would mean involving you.'

'I don't want to be involved in any divorce case,' said Patsy hastily. 'Although, you heard what he said about not wanting a scandal.'

'She could still leave him and he might have no choice in the matter,' said Joy, tapping her fingers on the table. 'Well, if the Tanners' marriage does break up, Patsy, you won't be able to stay here alone with him. However much you would like to do so. You must come and stay with me.'

'Thanks,' she gave a relieved smile. 'You know, little as I like to admit it, I might have been annoyed, shocked and frightened at times but living here has been as good as one of Tilly's stories,' said Patsy. 'I'm desperate to know how it'll end.'

Joy felt the same. It was all such a mess and Mr Tanner was going to have to cope with something that was surely not of his making. It made planning her wedding seem a simple matter. She looked out of the window at the garden and was suddenly aware of a restlessness that was unfamiliar. Obviously Mr and Mrs Tanner were not right for each other. Maybe their marriage was one of those that would never have happened if it had not been for the war. Hers to Robbie would not be happening if it was not for the war taking away the man she had loved. Was she doing the right thing marrying him? How well did she know him? She toyed with the belt round her waist. Then she told herself that she probably knew him better than many a bride knew her future husband. There was no changing her mind now just because the sight of Mr Tanner had unsettled her.

Chapter Nine

'Where's my husband?' Rose Tanner carefully closed the back door and stared at Patsy.

The girl thought, how many more times is she going to ask me that question? If she had been here the last few months when he arrived home, then she wouldn't be in this mess. 'He's gone to Seaforth,' she replied.

'Not to see his private detective, then,' she said vehemently, placing her handbag on the table and sitting down. Then she frowned. 'Why Seaforth? I hope to God he's not gone to tell my mother what's going on. But perhaps he'll tell Greg.' Rose drummed her fingers on the table.

Patsy did not speak but carried on polishing the silver cande-labra as if her life depended on it. She wondered if Greg was another of her brothers. Rose surprised Patsy by going over to the larder and peering inside. 'Did the butcher boy deliver the weekend order?'

'Yes, madam. I put the meat in the safe.'

'And we've vegetables?'

'Yes.'

'Good. Perhaps I should cook dinner. You know what they say – the way to a man's heart is through his stomach. I'll go upstairs now and have a lie down.' Rose picked up her handbag and walked out of the kitchen.

Patsy was longing to know whether she had visited Mr O'Hara and if she now knew he was getting a divorce. It didn't appear likely that she was about to walk out on her husband when she was talking about cooking his dinner. She was obviously going to try and get round him. Patsy wondered when Mr Tanner would arrive back and visualised how he might react to being summoned to his wife's bedroom.

Six o'clock and still David Tanner had not returned. Rose was sitting on the drawing-room floor listening to music. It seemed to have slipped her mind that she was supposed to be cooking the dinner. It was over an hour and a half later when David finally entered the house. Immediately he asked for the music to go off and dinner to be served.

'I'll be with you shortly, Rose,' he said, not giving her a chance to speak. 'I need a quick wash and to change.'

'Why did you go to Seaforth?' demanded Rose. 'I hope you haven't told Mother and Greg about this business.'

'Why should that worry you? You don't seem to care that half the neighbourhood knows you were brought home by another man, believing I was still away.' He left the room.

When he returned Rose pounced on him. 'Well?' she cried. 'Weren't you worried about me leaving the house the way I did?'

'You're here, aren't you?' David went over to the cabinet and poured himself a whisky. 'Do you want a drink?' he asked.

Rose shook her head. 'I just want you to tell me what your business was in Seaforth.'

'I went to see how your mother is coping with the children. Greg is worried about them. They're a bit wild but that's not surprising given the circumstances. Your mother is starting to go senile and it won't be long before she can't manage them at all.' He sat down and sipped his whisky.

'What do you expect me to do? I'm not taking on Grenville's children.' She squeezed her hands tightly together. 'So you didn't mention to Mother the difficulties we are having with our marriage?'

'I discussed your mother and the children with Greg. He does his best but he has to go out to work. I reckon that the time is coming when we are going to have to accept responsibility for your mother and the children.'

Rose's face set stubbornly. 'The boys were always her favourites. She'll only complain about me whatever I do. There is no way I'll help her and those brats.'

David stared at her in disbelief. 'I can't understand how it is you don't want to help the children. They're your own flesh and blood.'

'I have explained. I'll go and see Mother when it's needful but I'll not have her or the children living under our roof.'

'That wasn't my plan,' said David. 'I put it to her and Greg that we could go and live there.' He removed the lid of a tureen and helped himself to a couple of mutton chops.

Rose clenched her fists. 'I know what your game is. You think that once you get me there, you'll have Mother to keep her eye on me.'

David shook his head. 'Didn't you hear a word I said? Your mother is going senile. She needs an eye keeping on her.'

'I don't want to discuss this anymore. I think I will have a drink,' said Rose, hurrying over to the cocktail cabinet and taking out a bottle.

Suddenly David seemed to realise that Patsy had brought in the vegetables. 'Put them down, Patsy, and go.'

'Yes, Mr Tanner.'

'And close the door properly,' ordered Rose.

'Of course, madam.'

Patsy left the room and made a great show of carefully closing the door. Even so she was still able to catch part of their conversation before she moved away.

'You didn't tell me that Brendan was in the process of divorcing his wife,' said Rose. 'You know what that means, don't you?'

'That you want a divorce, too?'

'I'm considering it,' she replied.

Patsy's heart sank. So they were going to break up. She wished that she was a fly on the wall so she could hear what David Tanner said next. Perhaps he would refuse to give his wife a divorce. What would Rose do then?

Maundy Thursday: Patsy was summoned by Rose to fetch her a cup of tea and a couple of arrowroot biscuits. She wasted no time in doing so. 'Is there anything else I can do for you, madam?' she asked.

'You can tell me what kind of mood my husband is in. Is he agitated?'

'He's reading the morning paper and eating his breakfast.'

'Well, that sounds civilised.' Rose smiled. 'You can get out my green and cream linen suit, the eau-de-Nil blouse and cream shoes. It's possible that my husband will want you to take some of his clothes to the cleaners. Do ask him.'

'Yes, madam.'

Patsy did as Rose ordered and then went downstairs. She repeated his wife's words about the cleaners to Mr Tanner.

He nodded. 'I'll leave the clothes outside my bedroom door. While you're out, Patsy, you can go to the post office and get me a dozen postage stamps if you would.' He reached into a pocket and produced a ten-shilling note and handed it to her. 'I'm going to the office. I'll see you this evening.' He got up and left the house.

She collected his cleaning and hurried out. When she arrived back it was to find Mrs Tanner dressed and putting on her gloves.

'Patsy, I'm going away for the weekend. You'll be able to manage what needs to be done without my being here, won't you?'

'Yes, madam. May I ask where you're going?'

'Blackpool. I'm going to see a friend who is appearing onstage there.'

Patsy thought this an unlikely story but wisely kept quiet. 'I hope you have a nice time,' she said coolly.

'Thank you, Patsy. I hope all goes well with Mr Bennett's wedding. Now open the door for me.'

Patsy watched her go down the path with her suitcase to the car waiting at the kerb. She closed the door and listened to the silence for a moment and then she wasted no time in dialling the orphanage number, hoping she would find her sister still there. Kathleen had not responded to her note and she was worried about her. To her dismay she was informed that they had no idea of Kathleen's whereabouts. Apparently she had not turned up at the house where she was supposed to be starting work. Remembering what her sister had said when last she had seen her, Patsy was worried. Where could Kathleen be?

Chapter Ten

'You'll have to go back, Kathy,' said Joy. 'I've explained to you what this show of blood means, although I can't believe that Patsy hasn't done so already. If she didn't, surely Matron—'

'If Patsy did, then I wasn't listening,' interrupted Kathleen, twirling her feet and admiring her slim ankles. 'As for Matron, I bet she thinks we're better off not knowing about such things. D'yer think I've pretty ankles?'

'Yes, but show a little modesty. I'll bring this matter up with Matron when I return with you to the orphanage.'

'I've left there now, Miss Kirk. They've chucked me out into the big, wide world. I was thinking that perhaps Mr Bennett could speak up for me at the Palladium? I know he once played in the orchestra there and I wouldn't mind being an usherette.'

'You're too young to be an usherette, and besides, he left the cinema years ago. You'd be better off going into service, the same as Patsy. At least you'll have a roof over your head.'

'I don't want to go into service,' said Kathleen with a shrug, 'but if I have to, then perhaps you can take me on? Surely when you marry Mr Bennett on Monday, he's not going to expect you to do all what you do now?'

Joy knew Robbie expected exactly that from her. He'd been quite frank about it, saying he would save himself some money not having to pay her wages. Perhaps she should suggest that he sell the automobile because he did not use it as often as he used to do and, although he had given her a few driving lessons in the past, he did not really like her going out in it alone. But she was not going to say any of this to Kathleen. She had to confess the girl was irritating her, but as Joy did not want her to be a burden on Patsy, she decided to try and help Kathleen in another way.

'I'll tell you what, Kathy, you can stay in the outhouse until after the wedding. Then I can ask around to see if anyone local needs a maid. Your only other option is to sign on at the Servants' Employment Bureau.'

Kathleen was not keen at all to sign on but knew she had best act as if she was willing to work. 'That's really kind of you, Miss Kirk. I know in the past Mr Bennett wasn't keen on having us Doyles here but I'm older now and I'm sure, once he knows me better, he could get to like me.'

Alarm bells rang in Joy's head and it struck her that, just like Patsy, Kathleen was probably in need of a father figure or, in Robbie's case, a grandfather figure. Well, Joy was certainly not going to encourage her in that notion. It was true that she was no longer a child and older men could sometimes act very foolishly where adolescent girls were concerned.

'I think we had better let Patsy know where you are,' said Joy abruptly. 'I'll put through a call to the Tanners' house and hopefully they won't mind passing a message on to your sister.'

'There's no need for you to do that,' said Kathleen hastily. 'Patsy sent me a letter saying I was to meet her here the morning of the wedding. I can tell her everything on Monday.'

'Did you reply to her letter?'

'No, but she'll know I've got it.'

'How?'

Kathleen did not have an answer to that and Joy was just about to telephone when the instrument rang. She hurried to answer it and had to wait a few moments before a familiar voice asked, 'Miss Kirk, is that you?'

Joy felt a rush of relief. 'Patsy, I was just thinking of you.'

'How strange. Is it because you know something about Mr O'Hara? Has he gone to Blackpool for the weekend?'

'I wouldn't have thought so because he's been invited to the wedding.'

'Oh, in that case he can't be with Mrs Tanner. So why were you thinking of me?'

'Wait, hold on! What's this about Mrs Tanner going to Black-pool?'

'She said she was going to see a friend who's appearing on the stage. I didn't believe her. I thought she was going away with him.'

'How does Mr Tanner feel about that?'

'I don't think he knows. He's gone into the office. Anyway, I was telephoning you about our Kath. She's gone missing.'

'She's here,' Joy explained.

'Oh, that is a weight off my mind,' said Patsy. 'She'll get a flea in her ear from me when I see her. I'd best ring off now because Mr Tanner doesn't know I'm using his telephone.'

'Wait!' cried Joy. 'So you are going to be alone in the house with Mr Tanner?'

'I'll be fine.'

'Probably! But perhaps it's best if you leave a note telling Mr Tanner there's been a bit of trouble with your sister and that you'll be back in the morning.'

'If you feel I must, then I'll do it,' said Patsy. 'But what is Mr Bennett going to say?'

'You and Kathy can sleep in the outhouse so you won't be a bother to him. Have you enough money for your fare?'

'I'll walk.' There was a click as Patsy rang off.

Joy decided to telephone the orphanage to let them know Kathleen was with her and that she would take responsibility for the girl. They thanked her and sounded relieved to have her off their hands.

Joy managed to resist scolding Kathleen as she told her about Patsy's telephone call but her voice was chilly. She ordered her up to the attic. Kathleen appeared subdued as Joy rooted out a couple of the spare mattresses that had been stored there from the time the children had stayed at the house. But at least she showed willing to help her carry them downstairs.

There was enough space on the floor of the outhouse to unfold the mattresses. Then they returned to the house for bedding. It was only when they were making up the beds that Kathleen said, 'I really do appreciate you helping me like this, Miss Kirk. I know you came from a good home with decent parents who looked after you. I also accept that you are aware of the kind of place where I was brought up and how different it must have been from your upbringing. You might think I should be really grateful for my life at the orphanage because of the dump I came from. Life was really bleak then. Worse for me than our Patsy. At least she'd spent time with Dad and knew that he loved her. I had none of that except from me uncle. But it's no use me talking about him to you because you only saw the worst of him.'

'Your uncle was a brutal man. He murdered your mother, he killed Mr Bennett's dog and he broke into this house,' said Joy, her eyes sparkling. 'If you think I'm going to be touched by this sob story of yours, then you're mistaken.'

Kathleen said meekly, 'I'm sorry about the dog but you should feel sorry for me. I had a drunken mam who went with men and there were times when I could have starved to death.'

Joy took a deep breath. 'When I was just a little bit younger than you, my girl, my mother fell down a flight of stairs. She was never the same again. She lay in bed and didn't speak for months. My sister, Hanny, took over the running of the house and my younger sister and I did our best to help her. Eventually Mother was able to speak and walk again but when my younger sister drowned in the canal, Mother never recovered from the shock of it. We all have our problems, Kathy. We have to work to overcome them. You and I are the same in one way. We're lucky to have an older sister who cares about us.' Joy's voice softened. 'My sister, Hanny, has always been a good friend to me. Stop complaining and don't take Patsy for granted.' Joy made for the door.

Kathleen was stunned by Joy's tirade. 'Perhaps yer'd like me to leave?' she said in a shaky voice.

Joy said sharply, 'Did I say that?'

'No, but—'

'Come on, then!' Joy led the way out. 'Patsy will be here soon.'

They hurried up the garden together, only to pause when a tremulous voice from the direction of the fence asked, 'What's going on?'

Joy and Kathleen looked in the direction of the old woman. 'This is a friend who is coming to stay because I'm getting married soon,' said Joy.

'That's nice. Hope you'll be happy,' said Miss Parker and disappeared.

They carried on up to the house and half an hour later there came a knock at the door. 'It's Patsy here. Can I come in?'

'Of course you can, love,' shouted Joy. 'Kathy, open the door for your sister.'

Kathleen hastened to do so and almost fell over herself to apologise. 'I'm really sorry to have caused yer worry, Patsy, but I just couldn't handle going to that house.'

'OK! You've said your piece but you're still going to have to get a job. Now can I get in?'

'Of course.' Kathleen stepped aside.

Patsy wiped her feet on the mat and flashed Joy a serious little smile. 'Thanks for taking her in. I really appreciate it.'

'You sit down and relax,' said Joy, smiling. 'Mr Bennett's gone out.'

Patsy placed her coat over the back of the rocking chair and sat down. 'I left Mr Tanner a note and I hope you don't mind but I wrote your address and telephone number on it in case he needs to get in touch with me this evening.'

'OK.' Joy sat opposite her. 'I've been thinking that perhaps you and Kathy could stay at the outhouse until after the wedding. It would be more convenient for the pair of you.'

'It might be but…' Patsy frowned and absently twisted a lock of her hair around a finger. 'Mr Tanner might need me and I don't want to get the sack from my job, and the second thing is that I haven't brought my dress with me.'

'I don't have a dress that properly fits me,' interrupted Kathleen, 'because I've developed.'

'Is that a hint that you need a new frock?' asked Joy.

'She can't have a new frock,' said Patsy firmly. 'But I'll tell you what, Kath, maybe we could go to Paddy's Market on Saturday if Mr Tanner will let me have the time off. We'll go to the second-hand stall where Mam used to take us and I'll buy you a frock for your birthday.'

Kathleen wrinkled her nose. 'Second-hand?'

'There's no need to look like that,' protested Patsy. 'You'd think you'd never worn hand-me-downs in your life. Take it or leave it. If you don't want it, I'll keep me money.'

'I'll take it,' said Kathleen hastily.

Joy made an impatient noise in her throat which drew the sisters' attention to her. Immediately Kathleen said, 'Thanks, Patsy. I don't mean to sound ungrateful.'

Patsy shook her head at her. 'I know you don't but that's how you sound. We'd both like new frocks but I need to have some rainy-day money so I'm not spending for the sake of it.'

'Now that's out of the way,' said Joy, 'I was thinking that with tomorrow being Good Friday you can both—' She was interrupted by the ringing of the telephone and hurried out of the kitchen.

'I wonder who it is on the telephone?' whispered Kathleen.

'What made you come here?' asked Patsy.

'Because of being invited to the wedding. I thought if Miss Kirk was taking an interest in you, then she might do the same for me,' said Kathleen.

'What have you said to her?'

'Didn't she tell you?'

'Yes, but I doubt she told me all of it.'

'I talked about Dad and how I missed out spending time in his company. Unlike you. You were definitely his blue eye.'

'I wasn't!'

'You was! When he died I thought I'll never get any hugs from him now.'

Patsy got up and put an arm around her sister and hugged her. 'There's nothing I can do about it now, Kath. But the day will come when you'll probably have a husband to give you lots of hugs.'

'Not if I have to stay away from fellas like you told me,' said Kathleen bluntly. 'Anyway, we're sleeping at the bottom of the garden, yer know, so we won't bother Mr Bennett. I wonder if we'll see any fairies,' she added, with a giggle.

Patsy smiled. 'I wonder what he'll say when he knows we're sleeping there.'

'If we're out of earshot, I doubt he'll ever be told,' said Kathleen.

A few moments later Joy entered the kitchen. Her colour was high. 'You'll never guess who that was.'

'Mr Tanner?' hazarded Patsy.

'Yes. He found your note and asked if his wife had mentioned to you where she was staying. I said no and asked was he going to join his wife in Blackpool.'

'You didn't!' exclaimed Patsy.

Joy bit on her lower lip. 'It just slipped out. I expected him to tell me to mind my own business but he asked whether Mr Bennett knew if Mr O'Hara was going away for the weekend. I told him that he'd been invited to the wedding on Monday.'

'What did he say to that?' asked Patsy.

'He just rang off.'

'Oh hell! He'll know I've told you that Mrs Tanner's gone to Blackpool.'

'I don't see what's wrong with you telling Miss Kirk,' said Kathleen.

'If Mrs Tanner meant it to be a secret she shouldn't have told Patsy,' said Joy. 'In fact, she must have wanted him to know where she was going, once she was out of the way.'

'I wonder if she expects him to go chasing after her,' said Kathleen.

'She would have told me the name of the hotel if she wanted him to do that,' said Patsy.

'Not if she wants to put him off the scent and hasn't gone to Blackpool but somewhere else and she wanted him to waste time looking for her,' said Joy.

There was silence while the three of them thought about that and then Joy said, 'Let's have supper and then you two girls can skedaddle. Go for a walk in the park or down to the outhouse. I don't want you here when Mr Bennett comes in.'

Patsy said, 'We'll go for a walk and then slip round the back and down the garden without bothering you.'

Joy said, 'What a good idea!'

Later Joy had to wait until Robbie came in before putting the question to him whether he knew where Brendan was and if he had gone away for the weekend, say until Easter Sunday evening.

'Yes. He told me that he had some business up north. He'd hired a car so he could get around easier.'

Joy frowned. 'What kind of business?'

Robbie shrugged and avoided meeting her eyes. 'He doesn't tell me everything he's up to and I didn't ask.'

'But he's planning to be back for the wedding?'

'He hopes to be there. Why are you so interested?'

'Because Mrs Tanner has gone to Blackpool for the weekend without Mr Tanner,' answered Joy.

Robbie reached for his cigarettes. 'I suppose you have this information from the Doyle girl?'

'Yes. I hope you don't mind but she and her sister are staying in the outhouse.' Joy steeled herself for his reaction.

When it came it was not what she expected. 'As long as they stay out of my way that's OK. I suppose they're only staying here until the wedding?'

'Yes.'

He asked if the evening paper had come. She went and fetched it for him and left him to read it while she washed the dishes. She mulled over what he had said and came to the conclusion that he was keeping something from her and this business he mentioned was in Blackpool and involved Mrs Tanner.

The following day Robbie cried off from going to the Good Friday service at St Margaret's. Joy made up some tinned-salmon sandwiches for lunch and then took the girls to church with her. By the time they returned to the house the afternoon was almost over and she was planning on toasting hot cross buns and making a fish pie for supper.

But she had no sooner cut the buns in half and handed the girls toasting forks than Robbie appeared in the kitchen. His face was ashen.

'What is it? What's wrong?' she asked.

'It's Brendan,' he said heavily. 'He's dead.'

Joy could scarcely believe it. 'Dead! What do you mean, dead?'

'Dead dead,' he muttered, lowering himself into a chair.

Joy went and put an arm around his shoulders. 'It wasn't Mr Tanner who killed him?' she asked, aware of the Doyle girls listening.

'No. But it was him on the telephone. It was a car accident. The police reckon he skidded in a patch of horse muck and hit a lamp post. Mr Tanner didn't give me all the details but apparently the police got in touch with him. He rang to speak to you about Patsy and said that he wants her to return to the house tomorrow and look after the house and the cat. He said her sister could stay with her if she doesn't want to be alone. He'll leave the key under the stone outside the back door. He's taking the train to Blackpool.'

'You mean Mrs Tanner was with Brendan?' asked Joy. 'Is she dead, too?'

'No. But she's badly injured and is in hospital. He'll be staying in Blackpool until…' Robbie's voice broke off and he puffed on his cigarette. 'What a mess! I suppose the police will get in touch with Brendan's sister. I'll need to get in touch with her as well as soon as I can.'

'What a terrible thing to happen,' said Patsy, who had heard every word. 'It's–it's like a punishment.'

Joy glanced across at her and saw that she was looking pale, too. 'Yes. But it doesn't say that Mrs Tanner is going to die. Now get on with toasting those buns,' she said bracingly.

'I'm going to have to do some shopping,' said Patsy.

'Will you be all right for money?' asked Joy.

'I've some,' said Patsy. 'I'll shop in Great Homer Street when Kathy and I go to Paddy's Market. I presume your wedding will still go ahead?'

Joy glanced at Robbie. He nodded. 'It's not as if he was family. I'm upset but…' His voice broke off.

'Well, that's settled,' said Joy, squaring her shoulders. 'You'd best go first thing in the morning, girls.'

Chapter Eleven

'I wonder if Mrs Tanner has died,' said Kathleen.

'You don't have to sound so cheerful about it,' said Patsy.

The sisters were on a tram going along Oakfield Road in the direction of Liverpool football ground.

'Well, why should I be upset? It's not as if I know the woman,' said Kathleen with a shrug.

'I know that!' Patsy had not slept well and was tired. 'Hopefully Mr Tanner will telephone today with news. I have been wondering whether to go to the house first before going on to the market in case he telephones early.'

Kathleen said, 'We've paid for our tickets to Scotty Road. It would cost more if we were to get off and on again.'

'I only said *I'd been wondering*. I'm not doing it because I'd worked that out for meself. I think I've enough money on me to buy you a frock. I just hope I don't miss his telephone call.'

'If yer ask me he's not going to worry about you when his wife could be dying,' said Kathleen frankly.

Patsy knew that her sister was probably right and changed the subject. 'Have you heard from Mick?'

'No. But then I haven't written to him either.'

'I hope he's getting on all right,' said Patsy.

'He'll be fine. Our Mick gets on with everyone and doesn't let life get him down. You should know that.'

'I do, but it's different once you're away from your family. Anyway, what are you going to do about a job?'

Kathleen rolled her eyes. 'I wondered when you were going to ask me that again. I'll sign on at the Servants' Bureau on Tuesday. Satisfied?'

Patsy wondered if her sister was just saying that to keep her quiet but decided to say no more on the subject and instead gazed out of the window at passers-by. She thought about Mrs Tanner laying in hospital, still and silent, while Mr Tanner sat patiently by her side.

As they left the tram on Scotland Road, Patsy transferred the money from her pocket to inside one of her gloves for safe keeping. The streets were thronged with people and there were bound to be pickpockets about. She led the way to Paddy's market where it was even more crowded.

'So where is this stall, then?' asked Kathleen, turning her head this way and that. 'Gosh, look at them!'

Patsy's eyes followed her sister's to where there was a line of men all following one another. She chuckled. 'Don't you remember seeing the coolies off the ships before? They really know how to haggle with the stall owners.'

'But there's about a dozen of them and all carrying stuff on their heads.'

'That's how they carry their loads in their own country. I remember Dad telling me,' said Patsy. 'And he should know, he'd travelled to lots of places.'

'See! He used to talk to you!' The corners of Kathleen's mouth drooped. 'He told you things.'

'I was the eldest, that was the only reason. You were too young to take in such information,' said Patsy patiently. 'Use your nous.'

'OK! I'll take your word for it. Yer know, Patsy, I'd forgotten Scotty Road was this busy and noisy.'

'How could you forget?' asked Patsy, gazing about her at the shawlies selling fruit and flowers and other stuff from handcarts. There was a street musician and vendors selling birds in cages and second-hand books for sale, crockery and oddments that would be useful to someone and stall owners offering bread, cakes, pies and meat for sale. For a moment she was overcome by nostalgia for the days when her parents were alive and her mother hadn't hit the bottle so much and they didn't quarrel.

Then she pulled herself together and made a beeline for the second-hand clothes stall that she remembered occupying the same pitch as it did years ago. All about her she could hear the nasal twang of her fellow Liverpudlians mingling with Irish and Welsh, as well as the broken English of the cosmopolitan mix of people that frequented the port. She burrowed her way through the masses until she managed to wriggle into a space near a trestle table spread with all kinds of clothing.

Unfortunately black appeared to be the dominant colour; most likely this was due to the fashion pages declaring it was now out of fashion and that it was time people discarded their mourning clothes. She guessed that it was going to be a real job finding a suitable frock for Kathleen. As she searched through the garments on display, she felt a poke in the ribs and, twisting round, saw her sister.

'Bloody hell! What a crush,' said Kathleen. 'I lost yer for a while because I stopped to have a look at some puppies.'

'Why on earth were you looking at puppies?'

'Because of something Miss Kirk said about Mr Bennett's dog that died.'

'You mean got killed by our uncle,' said Patsy grimly, continuing with her task.

'Here, let me have a look,' said Kathleen, managing to squeeze in beside Patsy and beginning to riffle through the clothes. 'There was this little puppy,' she added, 'I think he must be the runt of the litter and I'm sure wouldn't cost much.'

Patsy stopped what she was doing and stared at her. 'What are you suggesting? That I buy it for Mr Bennett?'

'For both of them! A wedding present.'

'I'm pretty sure they wouldn't be expecting a wedding present from us because they know how we're fixed for money,' said Patsy frankly. 'But I must admit it's a lovely thought.'

Kathleen's face lit up. 'Thanks. Why don't you go and have a look at the puppies and see what it costs? I can carry on looking here.'

Patsy thought a moment and then she felt inside her glove and removed a couple of thrupenny bits and two pennies. 'That's all I can afford for the frock if I'm going to buy a puppy.'

'Yer don't have to buy it,' said Kathleen hastily.

'Don't spoil a good thought.'

Patsy began to make her way through the throng. She found the puppies with no trouble. They were inside a hutch squatting or lying on sheets of newspaper. A couple of them were asleep and another was sniffing around the perimeter of the cage. The one that appeared to be the smallest approached the wire netting. It gave a yelp and attempted to poke its nose through one of the holes. It had the brightest eyes she had ever seen and one of its ears was folded over giving its head a lopsided appearance. She decided this was the one for her.

She counted the coins in her glove and went over to the elderly man sitting on a chair. 'I'd like the smallest puppy but I can only afford to pay tuppence,' she said boldly.

'Thrupence,' he said.

'Tuppence farthing.'

'Tuppence three farthings.'

'Tuppence halfpenny.'

He sighed heavily and got to his feet. 'Yer drive a hard bargain, girl, but I want them off me hands, so I'll let yer have him dirt cheap.'

Patsy grinned and waited until he handed over the puppy before giving him her tuppence halfpenny and then she walked away. The dog snuggled against her and licked her chin. It tickled and she laughed. It yelped and she thought it was laughing back at her. Hopefully it wouldn't wee on her on the way home. She stood on tiptoe on the edge of the crowd surrounding the second-hand clothing stall, trying to catch sight of her sister. Then she spotted Kathleen's hat and was glad that it was bobbing towards her. Within minutes she had reached Patsy, who saw that she had a frock clutched against her chest.

'I got it for next to nothing because the stitching had come undone on one side,' said Kathleen, her blue eyes sparkling.

'Good.'

'I see you got the puppy.'

'Mmm! How much change have you got?'

'A penny ha'penny!'

'Good, that will pay for the tram fare.'

'Come on, then, let's go. You said you didn't want to miss a telephone call from Mr Tanner.'

Once on the tram Kathleen showed Patsy the frock which was supposedly a mixture of cotton and silk. It had a mandarin collar and long sleeves. 'I really like the collar,' said Kathleen, 'but I do think a few embroidered flowers about the collar, bodice and cuffs will make it that little bit more special, seeing as how it's for a wedding.'

Patsy agreed, thinking that she should be able to find a few remnants of embroidery silks in the sewing box.

Fortunately the puppy behaved itself on the tram by not making a mess or too much noise. Even so Patsy was glad when they reached their destination. She bought a couple of halfpenny buns at Edmond's bakery and headed for the house. It was only when they went round to the back and the cat came running that Patsy remembered that cats and dogs were supposed to fight like, well, cats and dogs. The cat stopped in its tracks, hissed and bristled. The puppy struggled to get down and slid out of Kathleen's arms. Tail wagging he approached the cat. Immediately it swiped a paw at the puppy. The dog backed off and was about to make another approach when Patsy swept the cat up into her arms.

'I should have thought about you before I bought the puppy,' she said, carrying the cat into the house. 'Kath, make sure the gate clicked shut properly, so the puppy can't get out into the front,' she called over her shoulder. 'Then give him a saucer of water.'

'OK!' Kathleen checked the gate and then watched the puppy as it wandered around the back area. Then she went inside and sat down at the table and gazed about the deserted kitchen, wondering where her sister had gone. The next moment Patsy reappeared, carrying a bottle of milk.

'So where will I sleep?' asked Kathleen.

'Up in the attic with me. I doubt Mr Tanner intended you to sleep in the guest room.' Patsy shook the bottle before removing the cardboard top and pouring milk into a saucer. 'I'm wondering what to do about the puppy. I don't think I should keep it here. What about you taking it to Joy Kirk this afternoon? You can use a bit of rope for a lead, so you won't have to carry it.'

Kathleen did not look too pleased with the idea. 'I don't know about that.'

'It's a straightforward walk from here to Mr Bennett's house. We did most of it on the tram earlier. It was your idea to buy the puppy, so I think it should be you that hands it over.'

'OK! But am I allowed a rest first and have something to eat?'

'You can have a rest while I go to the shed and find the rope. I'll put the kettle on first, so we can have a cuppa and you can butter the buns. Then I'll need to see what's in the larder and telephone the shops to see if I should be expecting any deliveries.'

'OK! Do I come straight back?'

'Yes, unless you've a good reason for hanging around there. You'll want to get the embroidery to the frock done.'

'That's true. I'll need to try it on first and sew up the side.' Kathleen suddenly put a hand to her mouth. 'It's a good job I am going back to Mr Bennett's. Yer know what I've left there?'

'What?'

'My bag from the orphanage with me things in.'

Patsy smiled. 'Joy Kirk will probably have found it by now and might even be expecting you.'

–

Joy had found Kathleen's bag and was debating whether to telephone the number Patsy had given her when there was a knock at the back door. 'Come in!' she called.

The door opened and in the doorway stood a smiling Kathleen. 'I've brought you a present,' she said.

'I was just thinking of you. I found your bag.'

'Sorry about that but, what with all that was going on, I clean forgot about it. Anyway, did you hear what I said, Miss Kirk? I've brought you a wedding present.' Kathleen turned and bent down and straightened up with the puppy in her arms. 'I thought you and Mr Bennett might like this in place of the one that he lost,' she explained.

For a moment Joy could not speak and then she moved forward and took the dog out of Kathleen's arms. She held it at arm's length and inspected it and then a smile warmed her face. 'Fancy you thinking of doing this. You surprise me, Kathy.'

Kathleen laughed with pure pleasure. 'I knew it was a good idea. Even our Patsy admitted it. D'yer think Mr Bennett will like it?'

'Oh, I'm sure he will,' said Joy without hesitation, stroking the puppy's head. 'It mightn't have a pedigree but how could he resist such a little charmer. I reckon he's half collie.' She tugged gently on the folded black and white ear.

'I bought a second-hand frock from the market, so I won't stop,' said Kathleen. 'I want to dolly it up with a touch of embroidery here and there.'

'You're good at embroidery, are you?'

'Yeah. I like making things pretty. I'll see yer, then.'

Joy's smile deepened. 'Yes. Monday. Don't forget your bag.'

Kathleen picked it up. 'Tarrah,' she said and left.

Joy was just debating what she should do first to provide for her unusual wedding present when there came another knock on the door and a voice called, 'Are you in, Joy?' She recognised Wendy's voice and went and opened the door.

Immediately the girl asked, 'What have you got there?'

'It's a wedding present from the Doyle girls. You could have knocked me down with a feather when Kathy gave it to me.'

Wendy stroked the puppy's head. 'It's a little sweetie. I wonder what Uncle Robbie will say. There's only one thing for you to worry about. Who'll take care of it when you go on your honeymoon? Mam hates dogs.'

Joy stiffened. 'What honeymoon? We're supposed to be staying at home.'

'Oops! It seems I've let the cat out of the bag.' Wendy pulled a face. 'I heard Mam and Uncle Robbie talking and he asked her to come and look after the house while you're away.'

'I bet she jumped at the chance,' said Joy, an edge to her voice.

Wendy hesitated. 'You don't really believe that she'll be poking in all the corners and seeing what skeletons you've got in your cupboards, do you?'

'She'll be wasting her time if she does,' said Joy grimly. 'Anyway, the puppy's staying here so you'd better come and look after the house if I agree to go away. Although, a dog this young shouldn't be left alone all day in a strange house.'

Wendy pursed her lips. 'I suppose I could work from here. There is a telephone, or if Grant really needs me in the office for clients I don't suppose he'll kick up too much of a fuss if I take the puppy in with me.'

'I wouldn't be too sure of that but it's good of you to offer,' said Joy. 'Where's Grant now?'

'He's doing something for Uncle Robbie.'

'You're not going to tell me what it is? Client confidentiality and all that?'

'I can't even hint because I don't know anything. Grant's keeping mum about this one,' said Wendy. 'You're looking tired. Uncle Robbie looks tired, too. It was a terrible shock to him hearing about Mr O'Hara.'

'Terrible. I presume you haven't heard anything more about Mrs Tanner?'

Wendy shook her head.

'Let's change the subject.'

'OK. By the way, I don't think Uncle Robbie plans to leave until Tuesday.'

Joy was relieved about that.

'Another thing I've been thinking about,' said Wendy. 'Who's going to give you away?'

'My brother, Freddie. He and his wife and my nephew are coming over tomorrow and staying the night.'

'Uncle Robbie made no mention of it,' said Wendy, wrinkling her nose.

Joy said dryly, 'No, I don't think it's even occurred to him that I need someone to give me away in a proper wedding ceremony. I'll remind him when he comes in and also ask him about this honeymoon he's arranged without telling me.'

Wendy looked crestfallen. 'I'm sorry for betraying his surprise. Is there anything I can do to make amends?'

'I'm not cross with you so there's no need,' said Joy. 'But there is something you can do. We never got rid of Nanki Poo's basket and paraphernalia. It's all upstairs in one of the attics. Could you fetch the lot down for me?'

'No trouble.' Wendy left the kitchen.

While she was gone Joy pondered on what to do about Robbie's proposed honeymoon. She supposed it would seem unreasonable and ungrateful if she asked him to cancel it at such late notice. Perhaps if she looked upon it as a holiday and trusted to his good sense for everything else, then there would be no need for her to worry about it. Even as she told herself this, she had a feeling she was kidding herself. It was the thin end of the wedge.

When Robbie arrived home he did not immediately realise there was an extra member to the household. He entered the house by the front door, bringing with him the smell of cigarette smoke and beer.

'I don't think I need to ask where you've been,' said Joy, putting a light to the oven.

'No, sweet Joy, you don't,' he said, waiting until she straightened up before kissing her cheek. She reminded him that Freddie, Clara and little Nicholas would be staying tomorrow night.

'I hadn't forgotten. Nicholas is a nice little lad and I'm fond of Clara. If it wasn't for her, then I might never have married Eudora or met you, of course.' He planted a kiss on her lips this time. 'I've lots to be thankful for. I would have been in a right sticky mess if she hadn't. Eudora left me well provided for.' He sat down and gazed about him. 'She left you a few bob, too, didn't she, love?'

You're just a little drunk if you're being so honest about Eudora's money, thought Joy, wondering what he meant by *a right sticky mess*.

Suddenly Robbie sat up straight and stared at the sleeping puppy in the dog basket. 'What's that?'

'It's a wedding present from the Doyle girls,' said Joy, smiling. She had fed the puppy some best beef mince and with a full belly it had gone almost immediately to sleep. 'We're going to have to come up with a name for him.'

Robbie pushed himself out of the chair and managed to get down on his hands and knees to have a closer look at the dog. 'I'm touched, Joy. Fancy the girls thinking of such a welcome present. There's only one problem, who's going to look after him while we're on our honeymoon?'

She was tempted to say *What honeymoon?* but decided not to tease him. 'Wendy was here earlier and she offered to stay and take care of him. As we know, Rita doesn't like dogs and we don't want the puppy nipping her ankles. Dogs sense when people don't like them, don't you think?'

He agreed. 'Wendy's a good girl. When she gets married, you'll have to choose a nice present for her and Grant.'

'Of course. Any more news about Mr O'Hara? I don't suppose you've heard when the funeral will be?'

'No.' He staggered to his feet and fumbled for his cigarettes. 'You haven't heard any news from the Doyle girl about Rose Tanner?'

Joy shook her head.

Robbie sank into a chair and rested his head against the back of it. He lit his cigarette and inhaled deeply. Joy waited a few moments before saying, 'So where are we going for this honeymoon?'

He cocked a snowy brow at her. 'I knew you weren't in favour of a cruise, so I thought you might like a trip to London. I was thinking of taking the car and stopping at different places on the way.'

Joy did not instantly respond with enthusiasm but thought about the plan and decided she could go along with it. 'I quite like that idea.'

'Trouble is, after hearing about poor old Brendan crashing his car, I'm not so sure about motoring down.'

'Why not? You're a steady driver.'

Robbie pursed his lips. 'That's true,' he wheezed. 'And it'll make a longer holiday of it. We could spend a few days in the capital and take in a few shows.'

Joy began to feel really enthusiastic about the idea. 'I've never been south. It'll be exciting seeing Buckingham Palace and Hyde Park where Mrs Pankhurst and the suffragettes gathered for the big rally in nineteen-eight. Alice was there, you know?'

'I didn't know,' he said, looking surprised.

'My sister and I used to go along to meetings in Chester. We were all for getting the vote and equal wages for women,' reminisced Joy.

'Didn't know that either.' He looked disgruntled. 'You weren't one of them that smashed windows and tied yourself to railings, were you?'

'Goodness, no. My parents would never have allowed it. At least it got the women's cause noticed but there are still thousands of widows or wives with crippled husbands struggling on insufficient income trying to keep themselves, and some have children. It just isn't right!'

'I know, I know,' said Robbie, reaching out and taking her hand. 'Don't get yourself all worked up. You're not in that position. Now, think about what you're going to pack for our honeymoon.'

'I've very little new.'

'Doesn't matter. You've got money of your own to buy stuff in London.'

Joy decided what he meant was that he wasn't going to fork out for a new wardrobe for her. Disappointing as that was she could not help but still feel excited about going to London and came to the conclusion that Robbie knew her better than she had realised.

'We need to decide what to call our dog,' she said.

'Our dog.' Robbie beamed at her. 'How about George Rex after the king?'

She decided that probably the George would soon be dropped and the puppy would be answering to Rex. What the king would say if he knew he had a dog named after him! Excitement charged through her. She might see the king and queen for herself in London. What could be more thrilling than that?

But at what price? Her excitement receded to be replaced by trepidation. Most likely Robbie would expect them to share a bedroom on the journey down and with them being married it would mean a double bed. She guessed that maybe all along he had wanted the marriage to be in more than name only. It seemed that unless she cancelled the wedding and moved out, she might have to give way to his wishes and share his bed.

Chapter Twelve

'So what did Joy Kirk say about the puppy?' asked Patsy, glancing up as her sister walked in.

'She was really pleased. I wish you could have seen her face.' Kathleen placed her bag on the floor and sat down at the kitchen table. She eased off her shoes and wriggled her toes.

'Well, I'm glad about that,' said Patsy, smiling.

Kathleen glanced up at her sister. 'Did you get out any embroidery silks?'

'Yes, although there're no full skeins.'

Kathleen's smooth brow knitted. 'What colours are there?'

'Red, green, yellow, blue, lilac, black and brown. I think Mrs Tanner probably went through a phase when she embroidered cushion covers. Unless someone else did the ones in the drawing room.'

'I must look at them. Yer've never seen her doing any sewing yourself?'

'No. She doesn't even sew on buttons.'

'Not even her husband's?'

'No. You'll find the silks over there,' said Patsy, indicating a shelf with a jerk of the head.

The bell rang in the telephone box as Kathleen padded across the floor in her stocking feet. Patsy wiped her hands on her apron before hurrying out of the kitchen. She held the black Bakelite receiver to her ear. The operator told her that there was a call for her from Blackpool. Patsy clutched the receiver with tense fingers.

David Tanner's voice crackled down the line. 'Patsy, just to inform you that Mrs Tanner has regained consciousness, and although she is still in a critical condition, she has managed to speak to me. I'll be staying in Blackpool until I can bring her home.'

'Yes, Mr Tanner,' said Patsy loudly. 'Can you tell me what her injuries are in case anyone asks about her?'

'She has concussion and facial injuries as well as a broken shoulder and a cracked kneecap,' he replied. 'It's a miracle she survived. There's something I want you to do for me. I can't telephone the news through to Rose's mother or Greg because they're not on the telephone, so I want you to go to the house in Seaforth and let them know what's happened. You'll find some change in the top drawer of my desk that you can use for the fare. Have you a pencil and paper to hand, so I can give you the Seaforth address as well as that of the hospital?'

There was a notepad and pencil handy. 'Yes, Mr Tanner,' she replied. 'Fire away!'

As he spoke Patsy laboriously wrote on the pad and then there was a click as the call was terminated. She headed back to the kitchen.

Her sister looked up from sorting out the silks. 'Well, was it him?'

'Yes! And Mrs Tanner has regained consciousness.'

'Is he bringing her home?'

'Not just yet. She's still critically ill, has facial injuries and broken bones.'

Kathleen gave a little shiver. 'Facial injuries sound nasty. I bet her nose is broken and she looks a mess.'

'He didn't say. What he did say was that he wants me to go to Seaforth and let her mother or Greg know about the accident.'

'Who's Greg?'

'I presume he's another of Mrs Tanner's brothers.'

Kathleen's face brightened. 'I'm all for having a day out at Seaforth.'

'Me too. We could take a picnic and have it on the sands. It might be crowded with it being the Easter weekend but what the heck! It'll be a nice relaxing break and you should still have enough time to sort out your frock.'

'I'll make time even if I have to stay up until after midnight,' said Kathleen happily. 'This beats working for those two old spinsters.'

'Yes, but don't forget you've still got to sign on at the Servants' Registry on Tuesday,' warned Patsy.

Kathleen pulled a face. 'Obviously you're not going to let me forget,' she complained.

Patsy gave her a look. 'Get on with sorting out those silks. I don't want to hear another word out of you until supper's ready.'

The kitchen fell silent. As Patsy prepared their evening meal she was wondering what Rose Tanner had felt when she was told Brendan O'Hara was dead. Of course, she mightn't have been told yet in case she took a turn for the worse. For the moment, at least she still had a job, unless Rose Tanner went and had a relapse and died. She wondered what Mr Tanner would do then.

It was a while since she had spent an evening with her sister, so Patsy allowed herself to be persuaded to play some of Rose's records. Neither of them got up and danced but they did sing along to several of the popular songs of the last decade.

The following day, Patsy was wakened by the joyful ringing of church bells. She decided that they should skip church and set out early before the crowds were out making the most of this Easter morning. 'Maybe if we have time we could go to the evening service at St Simon and Jude's,' she suggested.

'*If* we have time,' said Kathleen, pulling a face. 'I still have work to do on my frock and there's no one here to make us go. I would have enjoyed a chocolate egg, though,' she added with a sigh.

'Me, too,' said Patsy. 'I thought we'd take the overhead railway, seeing as how it stops at Seaforth Sands. I remember Dad taking me on it. You get a really good view of the docks and the river.'

'There you go again about Dad,' said Kathleen, rolling her eyes.

'Don't start moaning! I'll try never to speak of him again.' Patsy put on her jacket and dropped a handful of change in her pocket before pulling on a plain blue felt hat. She grabbed the shopping bag with the sandwiches, water and a couple of slices of cake. 'Come on, Kath!' she called, opening the back door.

They caught a tram into town and then went to the overhead station near the Pier Head. There were already plenty of people out and about, making for the ferries or other transport to take them to the seaside. Patsy could almost hear her father's voice explaining to her why it was best to try and get a seat well away from the carriage door, so you were not always getting disturbed by people going in and out.

'The carriages are really dull,' said Kathleen, gazing about her.

Patsy did not argue that the varnished brown interior was a bit gloomy. 'Don't start complaining. Once we're out of the station, it'll be lovely and bright, you'll see.'

'The seats are hard, too,' muttered Kathleen.

'What do you expect of wood?' said Patsy. 'This is a third-class carriage. If you ever get rich, then we can go first class.'

'I'd like to be rich,' said Kathleen, her eyes gleaming. She clutched Patsy's arm as the train started to move. Both were silent for a while and it was not until they had passed several of the dockyards and had a clear view of the river that Kathleen said, 'Look at that liner! Wouldn't yer just love to go on that ship and sail across to America in luxury?'

Patsy smiled. 'There you go, dreaming again.'

'Nothing wrong with that, is there?'

'No. It's just like window shopping and imagining yourself being dressed in the latest fashions.'

'I don't want to just dream,' said Kathleen, her nose pressed against the glass. 'I want it all for real.'

'You and me both, but be realistic,' murmured Patsy. 'There's little chance of us becoming rich.'

Kathleen fell silent and Patsy enjoyed gazing out of the window for the rest of the journey undisturbed. It did not take long, due to the train not stopping at every station as it would weekdays, when men were going to their workplaces along the dock road. Eventually the train swung slowly round a curve, the line passing over a main road, where woodyards and the unfinished Gladstone Dock Complex gave way to a view of sands stretching northwards. It noisily passed over points and several intricate rail tracks before drawing up at Seaforth Sands station.

Patsy took several deep breaths of the sea air before leading the way to the exit. After having their return tickets clipped, the girls descended the steep stairway to the street where, adjacent to the station, there was a tram terminal. Patsy stood on the pavement, perusing the piece of paper on which she had written Mrs Tanner's mother's address and tried to remember the instructions he had given her.

'So which way do we go?' asked Kathleen, tapping her foot impatiently. 'Are we getting a tram?'

'No. We walk,' said Patsy firmly, pocketing the piece of paper. 'Come on! Let's get across the road.'

It proved to be a bit of a walk to Beaconsfield Road and Kathleen was complaining that her feet were hurting after all the walking she had done yesterday. Patsy expressed sympathy but most of her attention was taken up looking at numbers of houses. There were plenty of children playing in the street and so she asked one of them where Mrs Smith lived and the girl pointed the house out to her.

A young man wearing leather trousers and a leather jerkin was tinkering with a motorcycle on the pavement. He did not appear to notice Patsy as she walked up the short path to the front door until she lifted the knocker and banged it.

'Hoy! Don't do that!' he called. 'Can I help you?'

Patsy turned. 'I'm looking for Mrs Smith.'

'She's gone out with the children. Can I help?' He wiped his hands on a greasy rag and walked towards her.

Patsy stared at the wiry, dark-haired figure and noticed that he had a smear of oil on his cheek. 'You wouldn't be Greg, would you? Mr Tanner has sent me with a message.'

'David sent you?' He screwed up his face. 'What's so important on an Easter Sunday that he should send a messenger? It isn't about Rodney, is it?'

'No!'

'Then, why are you here? Who are you?'

'I'm Patsy Doyle and this is my sister, Kathleen. I work for Mr Tanner. He asked me to let you and Mrs Smith know that his wife was involved in a motor accident and is in hospital in Blackpool.'

Sooty eyebrows hooded blue eyes. 'Is Rosie seriously hurt?'

'She's in a critical condition.'

'But not on an urgent note?'

'He didn't say.'

'He would have said if she were,' he muttered, looking thoughtful. 'Is he staying in Blackpool?'

'Yes.'

'What is it he wants me to do?'

'He didn't say. I was just to let you know.'

Absent-mindedly, Greg wiped his cheek with the rag and left another smear of oil on his face. 'Were they there for the weekend? Was she run over?'

'No. She was in a motor car. I was told that it skidded and hit a lamp post.'

'Nasty! Surely David wasn't driving? He hates anything with an engine that runs on wheels these days. Completely disapproves of my having a motorbike,' he added with a wry smile.

That smile caused Patsy a fluttering in the region of her heart. 'No. He wasn't,' she replied.

'I thought not. What happened to the driver?'

'He was killed.'

'He? Was she in a taxi?'

Patsy hesitated. 'Not to my knowledge.'

Greg frowned. 'You don't have to answer. I know Rosie of old. Awkward for David. If he telephones you again tell him I'll try and get up to Blackpool but I can't guarantee it, not with the way things are. Do you have the address of the hospital?' She gave it to him and he thanked her.

'It was no trouble. Goodbye.' Patsy thought he seemed to know what was what with the Tanners. She seized her sister's arm and walked away.

'Is that it?' asked Kathleen. 'We're not even getting invited into the house and offered a cup of tea?'

'You heard him say that Mrs Smith is out.'

'Yes, but...' Kathleen scrutinised Patsy's flushed face. 'You've taken a shine to him.'

'Don't be daft,' she said fiercely. 'I've only just met him, and besides, I've no room in my life for fellas even if he wasn't out of my class.'

'He didn't look out of your reach. Not tinkering with that motorbike and wearing leathers and what with oil on his face. Doing a labouring job,' said Kathleen.

'The fact that he can afford a motorbike says that he's no simple labourer,' said Patsy.

'Perhaps not. How old, d'you reckon?'

Patsy shrugged. 'Nineteen, twenty maybe. Now, let's forget about him.'

'If you say so,' said Kathleen, smiling. 'But we're just as good as anyone else.'

'So you might think but you'll still find plenty of snobbery around,' warned Patsy. 'Now, let's go and have our picnic.'

'OK! Now, which way do we go?'

Patsy sniffed the salty breeze and began to walk towards the Mersey. She told herself that just because she had felt a bit peculiar when Greg had smiled at her it didn't mean anything. She was not about to fall in love with anyone. It was more sensible to forget about him and think of the wedding tomorrow. It dawned on her that Joy Kirk was going up in the world by marrying her employer. Perhaps there was nothing stopping Patsy from winning herself a husband with a bit of money. Hadn't Rose Tanner said the way to a man's heart was through his stomach? Patsy had plenty of time to reach Joy's high standards, so it could really pay off if she were to improve her cooking skills. In the meantime she had plenty of other things to think about.

Chapter Thirteen

'Where's my tie?'

'It's here, Robbie,' said Freddie Kirk, handing it to him. 'Where's your best man? He should be doing this.' Freddie was a handsome, dark-haired man in his mid twenties.

'Grant will be here shortly, I'm sure of it,' said Robbie, fastening his tie with trembling fingers. 'He's doing a bit of investigating for me in connection with a long-time friend of mine who was killed the other day.'

'The Irish–American?' said Freddie.

Robbie's hands stilled. 'Joy told you about him?'

'Yes. She said you were upset. Understandable if you'd known him since you were young.'

'Aye. But it's a bit more than that. I haven't mentioned this to Joy and I want you to keep mum about it because I don't want her worrying. She doesn't understand investment and the risk involved to accumulate money.'

Freddie stilled. 'This friend of yours wasn't in the motor business, was he?'

'No, mining.'

'That's a relief,' said Freddie, who worked for the family motoring business. 'We don't need any more competition over here.'

There was a knock at the bedroom door. 'Grant's here, Uncle Robbie,' called Wendy.

'You can go now, lad,' said Robbie. 'Thanks for the calming influence. This will definitely be the last time I tie the knot. I intend making your sister happy and I want to make certain she wants for nothing.'

Freddie made no comment but left the room. As he went downstairs, he passed Grant on the way. They nodded at each other and then Freddie continued leisurely to the kitchen. There he found his wife, Clara, with Wendy and Minnie. They were already dressed in their wedding finery but were also wearing pinnies while they made sandwiches for the buffet. 'How are things going?' he asked.

'Nearly finished,' said Clara, smiling at him. 'We've managed without the older women. They're all upstairs fussing over Joy and talking about their own weddings. If you want to know where the men are, they're in the garden keeping the kids out of mischief and talking about the transport strike and the miners. The older kids are in the music room which has been cleared for dancing.'

'So there's nothing for me to do, except wait for the blushing bride to appear,' said Freddie, relaxing. At that moment the door bell jangled and the three women looked at him. 'OK! I'll go.'

He hurried to open the front door. On the step stood two girls. 'You are...?' he asked.

'Don't you remember us, Mr Kirk?' asked Patsy, smiling. 'We're the Doyle girls and we have been invited.'

Freddie grinned. 'Of course, I remember. Come on in.'

Patsy was aware that her sister was staring at Mr Kirk as if she had never seen anyone quite like him. He led them to the music room and flung open the door. 'The Doyle girls,' he announced. 'Be nice to them.'

Several pairs of eyes turned in Patsy and Kathleen's direction.

'Do come in,' said a red-headed girl, who was the spitting image of her mother, Alice. 'I'm Flora and this is my brother, James.'

'Nice to meet you all again,' said Patsy, determined not to be self-effacing. After all, it wasn't her fault that she was a poor orphan. 'Perhaps I'd better reintroduce us. I'm Patsy.' The boys got up and shook hands. 'And this is my sister, Kathleen.'

Kathleen flashed a smile around the circle and suddenly noticed a tall, flaxen-haired, strong-looking youth sitting on a piano stool, facing away from the piano. 'I've not seen you before,' she said boldly. 'Who are you?'

'I'm Daffyd Christopher Davies but most people call me Chris because my dah is a Daffyd, too,' he replied, glancing across at her.

Kathleen's smile deepened. 'You've Welsh blood.'

'Aye. And Irish.'

'I've Irish blood, too. We're both Celts.'

'That's right. I gather from your accent that you were born here,' he said.

'Yes. But you know what they say. Liverpool is not only the real capital of Ireland because there's so many Irish here but also Wales because the Welsh have built so many houses in the city,' said Kathleen.

He smiled faintly. 'I haven't heard that.'

'Well, now you have.'

Flora glanced at Chris and then at Kathleen before going over to him. She perched herself on the edge of the piano stool. 'Chris's uncle would have married Aunt Joy if he hadn't been killed in the war,' she said. 'His mother is a friend of the family.'

'Is your mother here, too, Chris?' asked Kathleen.

'Yes, and my dah. Ma understands that Miss Kirk can't mourn for ever.'

Flora gave him a nudge. 'Never mind all that, Chris. Why don't we play a duet?'

'I'd rather not.'

Flora slipped her hand through his arm. 'Why not?'

Chris removed Flora's hand from his arm. 'If you want to play you can give us a demonstration of your skills on your own.'

Kathleen said hastily, 'I wish I could play but I don't have the talent. I've never had lessons. Perhaps if my dad hadn't been lost at sea, then I might have learnt the piano.'

'That's tough,' said Chris.

Kathleen sighed. 'Yes, but I scarcely knew him because he was away most of the time and then Mam was murdered.'

'Kathy,' whispered Patsy. 'Not the time or the place.'

'Are you telling tales?' asked Chris, gazing down at Kathleen.

'Cross my heart and hope to die if I dare to tell a lie!' She sketched an invisible cross on her bosom with a finger.

'How?'

Kathleen moistened her lips. 'Smothered.'

'Was her killer brought to justice?'

'Oh, yes, he's dead.'

'So who looked after you? Did you have a gran?'

Kathleen sighed. 'I wish! No, we had no grannies or aunts. There were seven of us and we were put in an orphanage.'

'Dear God! I think I've heard something of this story,' said Chris.

Before Kathleen could ask who had told him about them, the door opened and a woman, who was a stranger to Kathleen, poked her head round the jamb. 'Just to let you know that it'll be time to get moving in a few minutes. We'll be walking to the church.'

There was a groan from Flora. The woman smiled. 'No need to look put out, me girl. You're young with lovely strong legs, not like us older ones. You'll be there in no time.' She withdrew her head and closed the door.

'Who was that?' asked Kathleen.

'My mam,' said Chris, looking relieved. 'I was worried she might get upset but she looks happy enough.'

'Come on, Chris,' said Flora. 'It's time we were going.'

He said to Kathleen, 'You coming, too?'

She nodded but before she could make a move to accompany him, Patsy took hold of her arm. 'Come on, Kath, you stick with me.' Before Kathleen could protest, Patsy dragged her away.

'What did you do that for?' asked Kathleen. 'He was interested in me.'

'Forget him. He lives on the other side so it's a waste of time your flirting with him,' said Patsy. 'Flora obviously has her eye on him so leave well alone. Now, let's get to the church before the bride arrives there.'

Joy was alone in the house with Freddie and taking a final look at her reflection in the hall mirror. It was as if she was staring at a stranger. 'I don't look like myself,' she said.

'Of course you do,' responded her brother, hovering in the doorway. 'It's just that you've never had much opportunity to dress up and go out on the town. You've spent too much time wearing a pinny and looking after other people.'

'I don't think that's going to change much once I'm married.' Her voice was strained.

He scrutinised her face. 'You're not having second thoughts?'

'No. Once I made up my mind I knew I had to go through with it,' she murmured, 'but seeing young Chris here with his mother brought back so many memories of his uncle. You remember him. He was so bold and had such a twinkle. Within days of our meeting he had swept me off my feet.' Tears filled her eyes.

Freddie hastened to remove a handkerchief from his breast pocket and carefully wiped away Joy's tears. 'He'd have approved of what you're doing. Chris had no illusions about life and would want you to have a kind husband and a decent roof over your head, so no more regrets.'

She nodded, picked up her bouquet of spring flowers and forced a smile. Freddie laughed. 'Now you look like a gargoyle. Be natural.'

'I find that difficult.'

'Of course you do,' said Freddie softly, 'but you're not going to the scaffold, big sister.'

That made her smile. 'You!' She punched him lightly on the arm.

'Now, that's more like it. You do look lovely.' He kissed her rosy cheek. 'That pink colour suits you.'

'Thanks.'

He pocketed his handkerchief. 'Ready?'

'As ready as I'll ever be.'

Joy thought she might not be a fairy princess but she looked a bit of all right for her age. No more thinking of Chris if she was to get through the service without breaking down. She must not think of her father either but count her blessings. As she left the house, she thought she heard a whispering voice and what it said caused her steps to falter.

'Have you forgotten something?' asked Freddie.

'No. I just imagined I heard a voice.'

'Eudora's?'

Joy stared at him. 'Are you psychic?'

Freddie grinned. 'This was her house and she was a medium and you're marrying her husband. It wouldn't surprise me if she had a thing or two to tell you about him.' He closed the door behind them and ushered her to the waiting car.

The church was fragrant with the smell of incense and the perfume of white lilies and narcissi. As Joy walked down the aisle on Freddie's arm, she kept telling herself she had imagined that voice. Eudora was dead and foretelling the future was a gift she had never used.

—

Afterwards, when they were all gathered back at the house Joy came face-to-face with Robbie's sister. Rita's expression was as sour as if she had been sucking lemons. 'So you got him as you planned from the moment Eudora died,' she said.

'You're wrong,' said Joy, determined not to allow Rita to rile her into losing her temper. 'I'd have been content to carry on as we were if it had not been for my mother's death. Why can't you be happy that your brother has me to continue to look after him? He isn't in the best of health and at least I've had experience of nursing the sick and elderly.'

Rita gasped. 'You're really upfront, aren't you? You're saying that you don't expect my brother to live for much longer. That's why you've married him, so that you'll have this house and his money.'

'I'm not saying anything that Robbie hasn't said himself,' said Joy, flicking back her hair. 'And you do know that Wendy will be staying here to look after the house and our puppy while we're away?'

'Yes! She told me.' Rita's mouth thinned. 'I think you asked for that dog deliberately, so I wouldn't stay here.'

Joy stared at her incredulously. 'Believe what you like. It's not true. It was a gift from the Doyles.'

'Those common Doyle girls. You'll rue the day you kept in touch with them, mark my words.' Rita turned on her heel and walked away.

'Oh dear, Mam still in a mood?' said Wendy, coming up behind Joy.

'You could say that. She's just told me I'll rue the day I kept in touch with the Doyles.'

'Take no notice of her. She's probably wishing that she was going to London with Uncle Robbie instead of you.'

Joy was surprised. 'I've never heard her express a wish to go to London.'

'I'm a bit envious meself, actually. I'd love to have fun in London, shopping and going to the theatre,' said Wendy, her expression instantly dreamy.

'I wish you and Grant could come with us,' said Joy impulsively.

Wendy looked startled. 'Don't be daft, Aunt Joy, it's your honeymoon.'

Joy's spirits plummeted. 'Yes. Of course, it was just a joke.' She fiddled with her new shiny wedding ring. 'I suppose I should go and have a word with Patsy. I wonder if she's heard any more news about Mrs Tanner.'

'She has,' said Wendy. 'But you go and find out for yourself.'

Joy made her way over to the french windows where Patsy was standing, talking to Grant. 'Hello, you two,' she greeted. 'I hope you don't mind my interrupting?'

'Of course not, Mrs Bennett,' said Patsy, smiling. 'You look really lovely.'

'Thanks. I just wanted to ask you how Mrs Tanner is?'

'I was going to come and tell you when you didn't have people round you. She's woken up and has facial injuries and some broken bones. Mr Tanner is staying in Blackpool for now. Mr Simpson reckons she probably hit the windscreen.'

Joy shivered. 'Nasty!'

'Are you all right?' asked Patsy, looking concerned.

'Of course I am.' Joy smiled brightly. 'It's just that someone walked over my grave, that's all.'

'I've never understood why people say that,' said Patsy.

Joy said, 'Neither do I, frankly. I'd better circulate.'

She moved away.

Grant said, 'They're going away in the morning, driving down to London.'

Patsy's eyes widened. 'It's a long way, isn't it?'

'Nearly two hundred miles.'

'Perhaps that's why she had that shiver, worrying about the journey, knowing about the crash.' Patsy felt trembly all of a sudden and could only pray that they would be all right. 'I must find our Kathleen and make sure she's not making eyes at that Chris Davies,' she said.

'Don't be a spoilsport,' said Grant. 'You're only young once.'

'You don't have to tell me,' said Patsy, leaving him to go in search of her sister.

To her surprise she found Kathleen not amongst the young ones but with Alice. Patsy wondered what possible interest she could have in her sister but decided not to interrupt them. She was not to find out about Kathleen's business with Alice until they were rattling along on the tram to the Tanners' house.

'You're never going to believe this but Flora's mother told me how much she liked the embroidery on me frock,' said Kathleen smugly. 'I told her that I designed the pattern myself and she offered to teach me all that she knows about dressmaking and millinery if I went and worked for her.'

Patsy was delighted. 'I'm glad to be proved wrong about you're not finding a job at the wedding. You know she made all the dresses?'

'Of course I know that,' said Kathleen scornfully. 'But did you know that she has her own shop in Chester?'

'Go'way!'

Kathleen nodded. 'As soon as I knew that I was keen to speak to her. I had everything crossed that there might be an opening for me. Trouble is that she suggested in payment for her teaching me I could work in the shop for no wages.'

'What did you say to her?'

'I asked her what I was supposed to live on. I said that however much I would like to accept her offer, I couldn't in the circumstances.'

'It's a shame,' said Patsy. 'I wish you could do it.'

Kathleen chuckled. 'I thought yer might if it meant you could stop worrying about me. She came up with an answer but I can't say that it made me happy.'

'What was it?'

'Working part-time in the shop and part-time as an all-purpose maid at her house.'

Patsy laughed. 'You lucky duck! You'll be living in with the Chester Bennetts! I believe they have a lovely house right by the River Dee.'

'Oh yeah, great! I could be working for hours for nothing and then cleaning and washing and stuff for a whole two shillings a week in the house.'

'That's good! Just think how much you're going to learn and I bet you'll have a lovely room and all the food you can eat.'

'I'll also have Flora looking down her nose at me and trying to boss me around. She stayed on at school to study for some certificate or other. Mrs Bennett wanted her to do what she asked me to do but working in a shop and being a dressmaker isn't good enough for her.' Kathleen glanced out of the window. 'Isn't this our stop?'

'Yes!' Patsy rose and hurried along the aisle and jumped off the tram, followed by Kathleen.

As they began to walk in the direction of the Tanners' house, Patsy was about to suggest that her sister give Alice Bennett's offer some more thought, but one look at Kathleen's face made her decide to keep quiet on the subject for now. It was possible that Flora's mother had already told Kathleen to take a little while to consider the matter. If so, she could continue to stay at the Tanners' house during that time.

At least today had ended on a positive note. The wedding had gone off well. The bride had looked lovely and even the bridegroom hadn't looked half bad for his age. He had thanked her for the puppy and that had pleased her. She wished the three of them happy.

Chapter Fourteen

'Do you mind if the puppy sleeps in my room, Robbie?' Joy was standing on the landing cuddling the puppy.

'Why not? I heard it whining last night,' wheezed Robbie, executing a few dance steps on the landing.

'So did I,' said Joy, 'so I brought his basket upstairs and made him comfortable on a bit of blanket and he settled down after a while. I didn't want him disturbing our guests.'

'Well, I'd rather he didn't disturb us.' Robbie cocked a bushy eyebrow at her. 'You know what I mean? It is our wedding night and I could do with a bit of tender loving care myself, never mind Rex getting all the cuddles.'

Joy's hand stilled on the puppy's head. 'I thought we had an agreement?'

'Yes, but...' He rubbed the back of his neck. 'Brendan's death really shook me up. I haven't been sleeping well. I'm sure I'd feel better if I had your company through the *small hours* when everything seems darkest. A man needs his wife then.'

Joy knew she should not feel resentful and angry. It was natural that he would want the comfort and pleasure that asserting his marital rights would bring him in the aftermath of his old friend's death.

'All right, if that's how you feel,' she said, trying her best to sound amenable. 'But perhaps we should take Rex into your bedroom.'

'No, leave him in yours,' said Robbie firmly.

Joy decided not to argue. Without another word, she went to her bedroom and settled the puppy. Then she picked up the plain white cotton nightgown she had bought last week. She held it to her for a moment and then dropped it onto the bed. She undressed and put on the nightgown before quietly leaving her bedroom. She knocked on the door of Robbie's bedroom and waited for his summons.

'Come on in, Joy. There's no need to stand on ceremony,' he said heartily, flinging the door open. He was wearing paisley-patterned pyjamas.

'Thank you,' said Joy.

She hesitated for a second before walking past him. She told herself that it was not as if she had not been in this bedroom numerous times to change the bedding and pick up his dirty clothing, to dust, polish and sweep.

'You're all ready for bed,' he said.

She wondered if that was disappointment in his voice.

'I thought it would save time,' she murmured, drawing back the bedclothes from the opposite side to where he normally slept. Strange that he hadn't taken to sleeping in the middle after Eudora died. She climbed into bed, lay down and drew the bedclothes up to her chin.

Robbie got in the other side. She felt the bed dip with his weight and tossed up a prayer that he would not suffocate her when he crawled on top of her. He had left on the light and so she closed her eyes. Perhaps if she imagined he was someone else. Chris! No! Chris had been sturdy and muscular with a young man's skin and smell. Mr Tanner? No, he was a married man, and besides, he had a lean and wiry body.

As Robbie pushed up her nightgown and heaved himself on top of her, the smell of tobacco that overlaid that of soap, hair oil and alcohol threatened to make her throw up. She felt a rising panic as he fumbled down below. When it happened the pain was intense for a short while and then it was just a matter of enduring while he gasped and wheezed as he flopped up and down on her. It was a relief when it was all over and he rolled off her.

Propping up his pillows he rested against them, getting his breath back before lighting a cigarette and saying, 'You were a virgin,' in a pleased voice.

Joy waited for him to say something more. Perhaps thank her for agreeing to do what he asked but he continued to puff on his cigarette. Joy felt so angry that she could not speak. She slid off her side of the bed and, clutching her nightgown to her, made her way to the lavatory. She did not return to his bed but to her own where she put on her old nightgown. Then she lay with the puppy beside her on the coverlet, stroking him and thinking of Eudora's voice before she had left for the church, saying *It won't be for long.*

Robbie visited Joy in her bedroom some time later that night and she endured his attentions without a word. When he returned to his own bedroom she rose and visited the bathroom before dressing and going downstairs to prepare a picnic for the journey tomorrow.

–

Joy was having trouble breathing as she tried again to rouse Robbie but her attentions were to no avail. She was aware of sparrows chirruping under the eaves and it seemed impossible that Robbie's death could have come so swiftly and on such a lovely spring day. At least he had a smile on his face so he must have slipped away quite quickly after he returned to his own room. For what felt like an age she sat on the side of the bed, staring down at him. Then she drew the sheet over her husband's face before going downstairs and ringing the doctor.

–

'Auntie Joy, aren't you ready to go yet?' asked Wendy, entering the kitchen.

Joy was feeding Rex and did not immediately answer. 'No, I'm afraid not.' She sighed and lifted her face to that of her niece by marriage.

'You've been crying,' said Wendy. 'Have you and Uncle Robbie had a row?'

Joy realised how difficult the next few hours were going to be. 'No, love. I'm terribly sorry to have to tell you but he-he's dead.'

Wendy stared at her in disbelief. 'It can't be true. You were only married yesterday.'

'I know.'

'You've made a mistake.' Wendy's face was pinched about the nose and mouth.

'No, love.' Joy's eyes filled with tears. She had been able to forgive Robbie for his thoughtlessness once he was dead and remember his good points. Now she felt deeply sorry for Wendy who had truly loved her uncle. 'He passed away in his sleep.'

'Oh no!' Wendy's voice broke on a sob. 'I'd best fetch Mam!'

'No!' Joy could not bear having to face Rita just yet. She placed her arm around Wendy's shoulders. 'Let's have these few moments alone.'

'I don't understand!' Wendy was shivering in Joy's hold. 'How could he die? He was so pleased with himself yesterday.'

'A heart attack. I've had the doctor and that's what he's written on the death certificate. Or something in more medical language. When your uncle had bronchitis last winter the doctor told him that he should give up smoking and take things easy. But what did he do? He joined a dance band. I don't know why he had to put himself under such pressure.'

Wendy said wretchedly, 'He loved his music.'

'I know that and he could have carried on giving music lessons here at the house. His health should have come first,' said Joy.

'Playing in bands had been his life, Aunt Joy.' Tears trickled down Wendy's cheeks. 'I should go and tell Mam, although I dread doing so.'

'I know.' Joy's voice quivered. 'She's going to blame me.'

Wendy squeezed her hand. 'She has no reason to but he was her only brother and she wanted to be the centre of his life. She might realise now that he meant more to her than just as a financial prop.'

'I think you're right and that will make matters worse.' Joy took a deep breath and made a real effort to keep calm. 'He was really looking forward to going to London, you know? Now we'll never get there.'

'Oh, Aunt Joy, please, don't talk like that!' A sob broke from Wendy and she hugged her. 'You'll upset yourself even worse.'

Joy rocked the girl in her arms and then she released her. 'Do you want to see him? He's upstairs.'

Wendy wiped her face on her sleeve. 'No. I'd best go and tell Mam. We'll see him together.' She squeezed Joy's hand and left.

Joy sat there a moment and then went and asked the operator to put a call through to the family motor engineering business in Chester. When her sister answered the telephone, Joy said, 'Hanny, I need you.'

'Joy, is that you? Where are you? What's happened?'

'At home. Robbie's dead and Rita is bound to blame me.'

There was a shocked silence at the other end of the line. Then Hanny said, 'I'm coming. Get someone to make you a cup of hot, sweet tea and I'll be there before you know it.'

Joy replaced the receiver and returned to the kitchen. Rex was sniffing at the outside door. She let him out and sank into a chair. Suddenly she began to shake. She felt as if she was falling to pieces and could not understand why. It was not as if she had loved Robbie in that heart-wrenching way she had felt when the news had come that Chris was missing. She wrapped her arms around her, thinking that she had to hold herself together or she would fall apart.

She remembered that smile on Robbie's face when she had found him dead. It had been totally unexpected.

There was a sound at the door and Joy braced herself as she saw her sister-in-law standing in the doorway. 'What did you do to him, you bitch?' yelled Rita.

Joy did not answer.

'Cat got your tongue? No excuses ready?' shrilled Rita.

Joy found her voice. 'You know what his health was like. I'm sure Wendy told you the doctor's diagnosis.'

'I want a second opinion,' gulped Rita.

She rushed out of the kitchen and Joy was tempted to follow her but decided it was best to leave her to have these moments alone with her brother's body. It was not long before Joy heard Rita descending the stairs.

She burst into the kitchen and there were tears on her cheeks. 'You killed my brother! You were determined to get your hands on this house and his money,' she accused.

'You can believe what you like,' said Joy. 'But I know Robbie wanted to marry me.'

'You led him on. You waited until your mother was out of the way and you made a play for him.'

'That's not true.' Joy tried to set aside her dislike of Rita. 'Can't we mourn together?'

'No thanks,' spat out Rita. 'I'll do my grieving with my family, so you just keep away from them.'

She turned to go but at that moment the door opened and Wendy came in. She paused in the doorway and looked at the two women. 'I could hear you outside, Mam. Can't you be friends?' she asked.

'I'm willing,' said Joy.

Rita looked at her with loathing and seized her daughter's arm. 'You're coming with me. I want you to have nothing to do with this woman.'

'Don't be daft, Mam. Joy's Uncle Robbie's widow and my aunt now.' Wendy tugged herself free. 'Don't you even want to see him? I thought we could go upstairs together.'

'I've already seen him,' said Rita, her lips trembling. 'You always were one for sucking up to her. She killed your Uncle Robbie as sure as I'm standing here. We should phone the police.'

'By all means do, I've nothing to hide,' said Joy, starting to get really annoyed with her sister-in-law.

Wendy said, 'Mam, I've no time for this. I know it's been a shock for you but Aunt Joy's no murderess.'

'You don't know her.'

'I know her better than you.'

Rita's face was set like stone. 'I'm going to tell the police what I think.'

'More fool you,' said Wendy.

Rita's face twisted with rage. 'You'd never have spoken to me like that in the past. It's her influence and your working in that detective agency mixing with the lowest of the low. I won't stand for it!' She raised her hand.

'Don't try it, Mam,' said Wendy in a low voice.

Rita gazed at her and then, instead of trying to get past her daughter to go out the back way, she turned and went through the other door into the main part of the house.

Wendy exchanged glances with Joy. 'I'm sorry.'

'So am I, love, but you don't need to feel that you have to choose between us. Your first loyalty is to your mother. I've telephoned my sister and she's coming over from Chester to be with me.'

Wendy heaved a sigh. 'I'm glad. Our Minnie and the lads are going to be really upset when they hear the news.'

'You go after your mother. I'll be all right.'

Wendy gave her a hug and then made her way to the front door but paused when she thought she heard a noise in the dining room. There it was again. It sounded like a drawer being opened. Cautiously, she pushed open the dining-room door and to her amazement saw Rita rifling through the sideboard. 'What do you think you're doing, Mam?' she asked.

Rita started and turned a ravaged face on her daughter. 'None of your business. Go away!'

'You've no right to be in here.'

Rita turned and faced her with her arms folded across her bosom. 'I've every right! You meet all sorts serving behind a counter and I've met Joy's sort before. They seem lovely and kind on the surface but underneath they're sly and selfish.'

'I'd rather not think the worst of people,' said Wendy, tilting her chin. 'Uncle Robbie knew what he was getting when he asked Joy to marry him.'

Pain flickered across Rita's face. 'He was only a man and we all know what fools they can be. Well, he told me something and I was just checking it out. I suppose you'll only give me hassle if I carry on here, so I'm going home.'

Wendy said, 'OK. I'll come with you. You know, this is a time, Mam, when we should be being kind to each other.' Her voice wobbled.

Rita's eyes were suddenly shiny with tears and she rushed from the room. Wendy followed her not knowing what her mother might do next. Hopefully Grant would call at the house before returning to the apartment where he lived with his widowed sister, Elspeth. At that moment Wendy was in need of a bit of tender loving care herself.

Joy heard the front door close and went out into the garden to check on Rex and wait for her sister. She so desperately needed her.

When Hanny arrived, she enveloped Joy in a bear hug. 'I can scarcely believe it,' she said.

'That's how everyone is going to feel,' said Joy, dabbing at her eyes. 'I can imagine their faces and it hurts me to think about how upset they're going to be when they find out.'

'You have a list of the names of Robbie's friends?'

Joy nodded. 'I don't expect the young ones of our family to come to the funeral.'

Hanny agreed. 'Shall we have a coffee and have you any whisky? I think you could do with something to relax you.'

'Robbie enjoyed his whisky.' Joy swallowed the lump in her throat.

Neither sister spoke until they had their mugs of coffee and whisky and sugar and were sitting down by the fire in the drawing room. It was Joy that broke the silence. 'To think that only the other day Robbie was grieving for Brendan O'Hara. They say things come in threes, I hope to God that doesn't mean another death.'

'What of the woman that Patsy works for? The one who was in the car accident?' asked Hanny.

'Mrs Tanner. According to Patsy she's regained consciousness.' Joy sipped her coffee in silence and then said abruptly, 'You're the only one I can share this with. I feel I'll burst if I don't say what's on my mind.'

'Go on,' said Hanny, gazing at her intently.

Joy took a deep breath. 'It started with the puppy. He'd whined the night before and so I took his basket up into my bedroom last night. Robbie saw me hugging Rex and...'

'He wanted some hugs?'

Joy reached for the whisky bottle. 'You can imagine what happened next. I let him take what he wanted. What made me angry was that all he said afterwards was that I was a virgin. He seemed so pleased with himself about it that I wanted to hit him but I told myself that I wouldn't have to put up with him for long. I'd had this voice in my head telling me that he'd die soon.' Joy paused and with a trembling hand poured a little more whisky in their mugs. 'I went back to my own bed but he came into me later and did it again. Now I'm wondering if that's what killed him.'

'If it did, then it's not your fault but his own. I'm amazed at his age that he managed it twice in a night,' said Hanny frankly.

Embarrassed, Joy moaned and took a large gulp of the whisky and coffee. She rested her head against the back of the chair. 'You know, I still feel angry with him. If he'd stuck to our bargain he'd still be alive now.'

'You don't know that but I admit it's likely and very sad,' said Hanny.

'You will stay, won't you? I'd appreciate your help with all the arrangements.'

'Of course! I wouldn't leave you on your own.' Hanny sighed. 'It's not as if it's the first time we've had to lay out the dead and make their final passing a memorable one.' Hanny leant towards Joy. 'Whatever you do, don't go blaming yourself. Robbie was old enough to know the risks he took marrying a much younger woman.'

Joy took another gulp of her drink. 'I wanted to call off the wedding not so long ago. I felt something briefly for someone and it made me restless and question what I was doing marrying someone I didn't love.'

'Why didn't you?'

'He was married. Besides it was nothing like love at first sight or what I felt for Chris,' said Joy, 'but I tell you, if Rita knew what I'm telling you, then she would have another reason to believe that I wanted Robbie dead.'

Hanny reached out and put a hand over her sister's. 'But you didn't and she's not ever going to know. Robbie's time had come. Better he went the way he did than coughing his heart out for months and dying of some horrible lung disease. Neither of us will ever forget the way Dah suffered.'

Joy nodded. 'Will you write and tell Tilly? She was fond of Robbie.'

'Of course I will,' said Hanny softly. 'She'll want to send her condolences to Wendy, too. You know what friends they were. His death won't make that much difference to their lives. It will to you, though. He's bound to have left you the house and the income from the properties that Eudora left him, so you should be all right financially.'

'Yes,' murmured Joy. 'Whatever Rita says I have a right to this house. But I'll need to give myself some time to get over his death before I decide what I'm going to do with the rest of my life now he's gone.'

Chapter Fifteen

'It seems odd not having a grown-up breathing down my neck,' said Kathleen, sitting on the garden seat and watching Patsy peg out the washing.

'Make the most of it.' Patsy pushed in the last peg before sitting beside her sister. 'You can't stay here much longer. Have you made up your mind yet what you're going to do about Alice Bennett's offer? You don't want to leave it too late. If you're not going to accept it, go and sign on.'

'I thought with you being here all on yer own there was no rush.' Kathleen held her face up to the sun. 'I had a dream last night that, if I accepted her offer, she just might make me manageress of her shop one day.'

Patsy smiled. 'You know my dream. Us Doyles living together in a house like this.'

Kathleen snorted. 'You've got a hope. Leave me out of your plans!'

'OK! But I'm hoping to provide a home for Jimmy and the twins in a few years time. At least if you do take up Alice Bennett's offer, she'll be there if you need advice about anything.'

Kathleen folded her arms and closed her eyes against the sun and made no comment. Patsy shut her eyes and was just relaxing when the telephone rang. Immediately she got up and went indoors, wondering if it was David Tanner with news of his wife.

She was surprised to hear Wendy's voice on the other end of the line after the operator's. 'Hello, Wendy,' cried Patsy. 'It's nice to hear your voice. What can I do for you? If it's Mr Tanner you want, he's still in Blackpool.'

'No, it's you I want to speak to,' said Wendy, her voice sounding strained. 'I've some sad news, Patsy. My Uncle Robbie has died.'

Patsy was stunned and for a moment could not speak, and then she managed to say, 'Was it a motor accident? Is Miss Kirk… I mean Mrs Bennett all right?'

'No, it wasn't an accident. He had a heart attack.'

'I'm so sorry, Wendy.'

'Thanks.'

'How is Miss Kirk… I mean Mrs Bennett coping?'

'It was a terrible shock as you can imagine. I don't want to say anymore now, Patsy, it's all so upsetting. We just wanted to let you know,' said Wendy, a tremor in her voice.

Patsy heard the click as the call was terminated. For a moment she just stood there and then she put down the receiver and hurried into the garden. She blurted out, 'You'll never guess what's happened!'

Kathleen opened her eyes and held up a hand to shade her face from the sun. 'What?'

'Robbie Bennett's dead!'

Kathleen gasped. 'But he only got married the other day. How can he be dead?'

'Apparently he had a heart attack.'

'Bloody hell!'

'I know!' Patsy sat down and stared into space, thinking of Joy and how she must be feeling.

'He was old, though,' said Kathleen after several moments. 'It was bound to happen sooner or later. Better him than her. She's still reasonably young and will have the house and everything. Not bad.'

'You are hard. I wonder when the funeral is; Wendy didn't say.'

At that moment the telephone bell rang again and Patsy got up and went inside, wondering if it would be Wendy telling her the date of the funeral.

'Patsy?'

Immediately she recognised David Tanner's voice. 'Yes, Mr Tanner.'

'My wife is coming home. She says there's no sense in her staying here any longer when she can rest at home, so we'll be on our way soon.'

'You mean today?'

'Yes. Do you have trouble with that?'

'No, Mr Tanner.'

'Besides, I must get back to the office. The work is piling up. There's something I need you to do before we arrive.'

'What is it?'

'Remove all the mirrors in the house.'

'All of them! Why?'

'Don't ask questions, Patsy. Just do as I say. You'll have your answer soon enough. Now, make sure there's a meal ready for us. We should arrive back about four o'clock.' He rang off.

Patsy put down the receiver and turned to see Kathleen standing in the doorway. 'Mr and Mrs Tanner are coming home today,' said Patsy.

'Then I'd better go,' said Kathleen.

'Where will you go?'

'To Chester. Can you lend me the fare?'

Patsy sighed. 'OK. But first you can help me take down all the mirrors.'

Kathleen looked incredulous. 'Why are you doing that?'

'It can only be because Rose Tanner can't bear the sight of herself,' said Patsy. 'I can't help feeling sorry for her.'

'Yeah. Well, let's not waste time on sympathy but get the mirrors down. I want to be on my way.'

The removal of the mirrors meant there were patches of clean wallpaper on the walls. Patsy was certain Mrs Tanner would have something to say about that. Her heart sank as she realised just how much she was dreading Rose Tanner's return. No doubt she would be even more inclined to fly off the handle than before and Patsy could easily be the target for her moods.

As soon as the mirrors were stowed in the attic, Kathleen was set on leaving. Patsy handed her a florin and asked, 'Did Mrs Bennett tell you how to get there?'

'Yeah! I can either take the ferry or the underground train from Central. Either way I need to catch the Chester train in Birkenhead,' said Kathleen, picking up her bag.

'Right you are, then,' said Patsy brightly. 'I hope all goes the way you want.'

'Thanks!' Kathleen pecked Patsy's cheek. 'I'll see yer when I see yer.'

'Write to me and let me know how you're getting on,' said Patsy, returning her kiss.

'I'll do me best.' Kathleen twiddled her fingers and walked jauntily down the path.

Patsy watched her until she was out of sight and then went back inside the house. She set about making up the beds, thinking about what to cook for the Tanners' evening meal. She just hoped that whatever she did would be to Mrs Tanner's taste.

—

'Careful, careful, mind my knee!' screamed Rose through the black lace veil dangling from the brim of her hat. She clung to David's lapel as he carried her inside the house. Her other arm was strapped to her chest and one leg was bound to a metal splint and stuck out at an angle.

'I am being careful,' he protested.

'Not careful enough. This is all your fault.'

'Don't start blaming me all over again,' warned David. 'I didn't get you into this state – this is down to your lover!'

'Don't say that in front of Patsy,' she hissed.

'Why? She knows all about Brendan O'Hara. She was here when you brought him to the house, remember?'

'Trust you to remind me of that,' said Rose through gritted teeth.

Patsy hovered in the background as David swung his wife round and gazed at the various closed doors. 'Where do you want to go?' he asked.

'To my bedroom, of course! I'm exhausted and I need to rest.' Rose turned her head in Patsy's direction. 'I hope there're clean sheets on the bed.'

'Of course, madam!' Patsy's voice was stiff with outrage. 'As if I'd leave the soiled ones on.'

'Don't answer back, Patsy,' said Rose. 'Or you'll be out on your ear. What I really need is a nurse.'

'You can forget that,' said David icily. 'I can't afford a nurse and a maid after the money you've wasted. Now behave yourself, Rose.' He turned to Patsy. 'Run upstairs and make certain Mrs Tanner's bedroom door is open, there's a good girl.'

'Yes, Mr Tanner.'

Patsy took the stairs two at a time and flung open Rose's bedroom door. The scent of the spring flowers she had picked from the garden mingled with that of furniture polish. She stood aside whilst David placed Rose on the bed.

'How is that?' he asked, stepping back and gazing down at his wife.

'I need to be further up and I can't shift myself,' said Rose. 'You've no idea of the pain I'm in,' she added on a sob.

'Trust you to believe you're the only one who knows what pain is.' He hoisted her up higher so that she was sitting almost bolt upright against the pillows. 'Is that better?'

'I need more pillows and a glass of water to take my pills.'

David looked at Patsy. 'I'll fetch the pillows,' she said.

As she left the bedroom, David said, 'Do you want me to help you undress, Rose?'

'Good God, no! Patsy can do that when I'm ready. What I need is my handbag.'

'A please wouldn't go amiss,' he said, his grey eyes angry.

Patsy returned with the pillows and, at Rose's direction, managed to place them to her satisfaction. 'That's better,' she said, closing her eyes. 'Now, if you'll remove my shoes.'

Patsy did so. 'Is there anything else you want me to do, madam?'

'Yes! But allow me a few moments just to lie here. It's such a relief to be back in my own room. You've no idea what I've been through. The horror of it all,' moaned Rose. 'Poor, poor Brendan!'

Patsy's sympathy evaporated. If Rose had not lied and gone away with Mr O'Hara, then he would still be alive today. 'Shall I bring you something to eat, madam?' she asked coolly.

'Not yet.'

David re-entered the bedroom, carrying a black patent leather handbag and a glass of water. 'Is there anything else you need?'

'No. You can go now. I'll send Patsy if I need you,' she said, reaching for the handbag.

David's lips tightened. 'I'll be in my study, Patsy,' he said in clipped tones. 'You can bring my meal to me there in half an hour.'

'Yes, Mr Tanner.'

As soon as her husband had gone, Rose took her pills and leant back against the pillows. 'So how did the wedding go?' she asked.

Patsy was surprised that she should be interested after all that had happened to her. 'Lovely! But I've had bad news today.'

Rose's shoulders stiffened. 'What do you mean bad news?'

'Mr Bennett has had a heart attack and died.'

The veil was sucked against Rose's face as she drew in a rasping breath. 'I can't believe it,' she mumbled, pulling away the veil with an unsteady hand.

'I know. I felt like that, too.'

'He was such a friendly, cheerful person. So gifted.' Rose dabbed at her eyes with the veil. 'The poor man! Who'll be next? Me?' Her voice broke on a sob. 'I had such plans and now they're shattered! I want a gin and tonic.'

'I'll tell Mr Tanner.'

'No. Give me some time,' muttered Rose. 'Serve the master of the house first and then you can bring my supper with that G and T.'

'Yes, madam.' Patsy was glad to escape to the kitchen.

Half an hour later, when she carried casseroled chicken into Mr Tanner's study, she noticed papers all over his desk. He looked up. 'I hope you'll be staying on with us, Patsy. I know my wife will cause you more work, but the next few months are not going to be easy for any of us. If you feel that you'll be able to cope with extra duties, then I intend to increase your wages to ten shillings a week.'

Patsy blinked at him. 'But that's double what you pay me now!'

His eyes twinkled. 'I can add up, Patsy. I have no doubt you'll earn every penny.'

Patsy hesitated. 'Is Mrs Tanner's face cut very badly?'

He nodded. 'Her broken nose has been fixed and hopefully, as time goes by, the scars will fade and she'll feel that she can dispense with the veil.' He fiddled with the fountain pen on his desk. 'There is another important matter which I suspect you might already be aware of and that is that my wife is having a baby. I did think that with the accident that she might have miscarried – but no.'

'Congratulations, sir,' she said politely.

'Quite. I am hoping the baby will help to put the recent upset behind us and that we can take up the threads of our life together again. The child is due in October.'

Patsy thought he was a hero to have his wife back. She wondered if he suspected the baby might not be his but he seemed prepared to accept it as his own. 'A baby needs a lot of love and attention, Mr Tanner, but it can bring people together.'

'That is my hope,' said David. 'Can I take it that you will stay?'

'Oh yes, Mr Tanner.'

'So how did the wedding go?'

Patsy hesitated and then said in hushed tones, 'The wedding was lovely but since then we've had news that Mr Bennett has died of a heart attack.'

'So your Miss Kirk – Mrs Bennett, I mean, is a widow! Good Lord, how is she coping?'

'I don't know. I spoke to Mr Bennett's niece, Wendy. You've met her.'

'Terrible shock for her, too.' David looked thoughtful. 'I must send them both my condolences.' Absently, he placed the tray on the papers on his desk and picked up his knife and fork.

'Is there anything else you need?' asked Patsy.

'No. See if Mrs Tanner is ready for her meal.'

'She said that she'd like a gin and tonic.'

'Did she, indeed?' he said dryly. 'Leave it to me.'

Patsy left the study and ran upstairs to knock on Mrs Tanner's bedroom door to see if she was ready to eat. As she entered the bedroom, Patsy spared a thought for Kathleen, hoping that she had not got lost in Chester but even now was being welcomed into the Bennetts' home.

Chapter Sixteen

Kathleen paused on Queen's Park footbridge. Her feet were aching after walking down into the city from the railway station and through the park. She had gazed in shop windows, wishing she had known where Mrs Bennett's shop was, but she had only been given the address of the house. She liked what she had seen of the city. It was smaller than Liverpool but teeming with life. The people looked prosperous and the shops were filled with all kinds of goods. The ancient cathedral and the town hall were right in the city centre but the river was outside the old city walls. The Dee was very different from the Mersey and easily crossed by bridge. It was prettier, too, with trees bordering its banks and tea rooms and bandstands set a little back from the water's edge.

She gazed down at the top of a youth's head. He was rowing a girl in a small boat. Kathleen did not rate the girl's dress, much too drab. She had read in the *Echo* that Paris had decided that skirts were to be sixteen inches from the floor and the fashionable cape that was normally a separate fashion item was to be part of a frock from now on.

Kathleen continued on her way to the other side of the bridge and toiled up the path to Victoria Crescent. On reaching the crescent, she glanced at the slip of paper in her hand and then at the house opposite her. She wasted no time in opening the gate and hurrying up the drive.

Hearing children's voices, she decided to go round the back. There she found Flora hitting a ball with a wooden mallet through a hoop on the lawn. She was wearing a frilled pink blouse and a floral skirt in shades of mauve and blue. It was a pretty ensemble.

Her brother, George, was watching her and so were the Moran twins, Allan and Janet.

Flora straightened her back. 'You do understand what you have to do now, children?' she asked.

'Of course, it's simple,' said George, swinging his mallet in an arc. It slipped through his fingers and flew through the air, narrowly missing Kathleen.

'Hey, watch it,' she said.

They all turned and stared at her.

Flora's eyes narrowed. 'So you've turned up,' she said in an unfriendly voice. 'Mother told me that she had offered you a position. You're a bit late in coming.'

'Mrs Bennett did say I could take a few days to think about her offer,' said Kathleen, bristling slightly. 'Is Mrs Bennett home?'

'As it happens she came in an hour ago. Not much going on at the shop due to a number of customers going to London tomorrow. They're taking part in the Stop the Strikes Crusade.'

'What's that?' asked Kathleen.

Flora raised her eyebrows in a supercilious manner. 'Where have you been living? There have been strikes happening for ages. The engineers, transport workers and the miners are forever clashing with the owners and the government. I hear now that over in Liverpool there's been a shortage of meat because the slaughter men at the abattoir are on strike. There's a fear that the TUC will have the whole country laying down its tools in support of the miners.'

'I haven't heard a thing,' said Kathleen. 'But that's what life's like when you live in an orphanage. But why is someone like you so interested?'

Flora drew herself up to her full height. 'Because there are more women than men in this country since the war and there'll come a time when women will need to be involved in how this country is run.'

Kathleen gave her an incredulous stare. 'Women haven't got a hope of getting into Parliament. Anyway, what have the miners and the rest of them to do with you, living in this lovely place?'

Flora's eyes flashed. 'Whatever class one is, one needs to get involved. The owners want the miners to work longer hours for less pay because during the war they lost sales. Britain used to export coal to Europe but now Poland, Russia and even Germany have taken over those markets. To get them back our mine owners will have to sell their coal for less.'

Kathleen tried to get her head around what Flora had said and murmured, 'That doesn't seem fair.'

'No, it isn't. As well as that some of our precious seams of coal were used up for the war effort, so we actually have less coal to sell in Britain.'

'It still doesn't seem fair that the miners should work longer hours for less pay. It sounds to me as if it's the rich profiting by making the poor suffer again,' said Kathleen.

Flora frowned. 'That might be true but you can't allow anarchy to rule and tip the country into revolution the way it happened in Russia.'

'Britain's not Russia,' said Kathleen in a voice that suggested she knew all about that far country. 'We're much smaller, so easier for the government to keep control. Anyway, I didn't come here to discuss the state of Britain but to see your mother. Can I go in through the kitchen?'

Flora said impatiently, 'If you must. You'll probably find her with my Aunt Hanny. Mother might send you away with a flea in your ear for not responding to her offer sooner.' Flora turned away and picking up the mallet she whacked a ball through another hoop.

Kathleen headed for the house and knocked on the open kitchen door. 'Mrs Bennett, are you there?' she called. 'It's Kathy Doyle.'

There was no answer, so she stepped inside. Immediately she became aware of the hum of voices and so followed the sound. She knocked on a door and called, 'Mrs Bennett, it's Kathleen Doyle. I've come about the job.'

'Come in.'

Kathleen entered the room and her heart began to hammer. What if she had left it too late? 'Good afternoon, Mrs Bennett.' She almost bobbed a curtsey.

Alice's expression was severe. 'So you've come at last. It's been almost a week. I feel like saying *Well, you're too late. You can turn on your heels and go back to where you came from.* What kept you?'

Kathleen placed her bag on the floor and hastened into speech. 'I was keeping our Patsy company. I didn't like leaving her alone when she needed me, worried as she was about the Tanners. Then we heard about the other Mr Bennett. We're both very fond of Mrs Joy Bennett and it upset us. Anyway, on top of all that Mr Tanner rang to say that he was bringing Mrs Tanner home today, so I knew I could leave Patsy in Mr Tanner's charge and make myself scarce.'

Alice glanced at Hanny. 'Should I forgive her?'

Hanny smiled. 'Of course. At a time when there's been so much upset in Patsy's life, it was good for her to have her sister staying with her.'

'I agree,' said Alice. 'But, Kathleen, you should have written to me explaining your reasons for the delay.'

Kathleen said, 'I'm better with my needle than letter writing.'

Alice raised her eyebrows in much the way her daughter had done earlier when Kathleen had said her piece. 'I should hope so, seeing as that is the reason you're here. Now tell us, how is Mrs Tanner?'

'I didn't see her, meself,' replied Kathleen, 'but Mr Tanner asked our Patsy to take down all the mirrors in the house.'

'Oh dear!' exclaimed Alice, biting on her lip.

Kathleen waited for her to speculate on Mrs Tanner's injuries but Alice changed the subject. 'I know you have some skill with your embroidery needle, Kathy, but how are you with button-holes and the simple task of sewing on buttons?'

'They were part of the course that they taught us girls at the orphanage. I can also do crochet work and knit.'

Alice's green eyes brightened. 'I do so love crochet but it's a skill I've never acquired. Now, what about the sewing machine?'

Kathleen stuck her tongue in her cheek and ran it round her mouth and then she said firmly, 'I can learn.'

Hanny laughed. 'You've a willing horse here, Alice.'

'Just what I want,' said Alice, smiling. 'You're hired, Kathleen Doyle. I'd appreciate your help with washing the supper dishes later. Tomorrow the shop will be closed because I'll be attending the funeral, so you can stay here and I'll give you some tasks to do.'

Kathleen thanked her and was glad she was not expected to attend the funeral. The last one she had attended had been the former Mrs Robbie Bennett and it had brought back memories of her mother and she'd rather not go to another. She would be perfectly happy having the house to herself.

–

'Gosh, I'm really glad Mam's come but I hope she behaves herself,' whispered Wendy to her sister. They were proceeding down the aisle behind Joy, Hanny and Freddie towards the choir and sanctuary ahead.

'Where is Mam?' asked Minnie in a low voice.

'In the middle of the front pew on the left,' replied Wendy out of the corner of her mouth.

'She's such a liar, saying she wasn't coming,' murmured Minnie. 'What do we do? Are we going to sit with her or stay with Aunt Joy?'

As the coffin bearers laid down their burden in front of the communion rail, both girls kept their eyes on the high altar which was constructed of elaborately carved wood. 'Sit with her.' Wendy's voice was barely above a whisper. 'Aunt Joy has her close family to support her.'

'Hush, you two,' whispered the girls' youngest brother. 'Aunt Joy will hear you.'

Joy had not caught what the girls had said but she was aware of Rita's black-clad figure sitting bolt upright in one of the front pews. Joy made for the pew on the other side and Rita's children joined their mother. Hanny slipped her hand into Joy's and gripped it tightly. Freddie on the other side of her put his arm about her shoulders. Joy raised her eyes to the stained-glass window depicting the crucifixion and other scenes from the Bible and suddenly the scenes blurred as tears filled her eyes. It seemed unbelievable that only a short while ago she had stared up at those images after reciting her wedding vows. Now what was she going to do with the rest of her life?

It was a relief when the funeral was over, although the service had not been the ordeal that Joy had dreaded, but interments were always stressful and Joy was just glad that Rita must have decided not to attend the actual burial. She had dreaded that Robbie's sister might do something dramatic like throw herself on his coffin before it was lowered into the ground.

Back at the house, Joy was able to cope with mingling with Robbie's friends over drinks and food but fortunately no one stayed for long. By three in the afternoon, the only people that remained were her close family, Wendy and Grant and Robbie's solicitor. Not that his will should contain any surprises, thought Joy. Robbie had told her that he was leaving everything to her but for small sums of money to his nieces and nephews. As for his sister, he intended to instruct his solicitor that there was need for her to pay the debt she owed him.

As the solicitor finished speaking, Joy remained in her chair. Her legs had turned to mush. She did not want to believe that Robbie could have behaved not only so secretively but so stupidly as well.

'I am so sorry to have given you such a shock, Mrs Bennett,' said the solicitor. 'At least you can be thankful that Mr Bennett did not mortgage the house or cash in his insurance policy.'

'But the insurance money won't amount to much once the funeral is paid for,' said Joy, clearing her throat. 'I find it almost impossible to believe that he would sell all the properties that his last wife had left him. What has he done with the money?'

'I wish I knew,' said the solicitor, shaking his head.

Joy felt sick, wondering how she was going to support herself. Fortunately there were no bills outstanding except for the funeral expenses but she needed an income. She would have to find work. Not so easy when there were so many women already looking for jobs.

It was not until the solicitor had left that Freddie surprised Joy by saying, 'I can shed light on what Robbie spent the money on.'

Joy stared at him. 'What? You?'

'Aye, me.' Freddie looked uncomfortable. 'On the morning of your wedding he spoke of having invested money in a mining project.'

'I can add to that,' said Grant, surprising her even further.

'You know something about this, too?' said Joy, turning to him.

'Yes. It was after we heard the news that Brendan O'Hara had been killed. Apparently Robbie had invested money in a scheme of O'Hara's. He said something about needing to get in touch with Brendan's sister in New York but not having her address. He asked me to see if I could trace O'Hara's family in Ireland and see if they could help with finding her.'

'And…?' asked Joy, clenching her fists.

'I managed to get the name of a town in Ireland from a horse trainer who had been at the Grand National and that's as far as I got,' said Grant.

Freddie said, 'If Robbie invested money in a mining project, then surely he should have a share certificate somewhere.'

'I'll have to search for it,' said Joy, frowning. 'But I'd have thought he would have kept it with the insurance policy and the deeds of the house but he obviously didn't.' She could scarcely conceal her anger.

Silence.

Joy looked at her close family who were exchanging glances. 'I know. You're going to have to go.' She forced a smile. 'Thanks so much for coming. I've appreciated your support but now I'm going to have to get used to being on my own.'

'At least you have Rex,' said her brother, picking up the puppy and handing him to his sister.

Joy cuddled the dog against her bosom. 'Robbie was so pleased when he found out the Doyle girls had given us a dog for a wedding present.' Her voice cracked.

Wendy had kept quiet until then but now she said, 'Perhaps Mam might know something about Uncle Robbie's shares.'

Joy looked at her. 'I don't see why, love. If he didn't mention them to me, why should he have told your mother about them?'

'It was just a thought.' Wendy glanced at Grant. 'Do you have anything else to say?'

'I could go to this village in Ireland if Joy wants me to,' he answered.

She stroked Rex's head. 'It would cost money and besides I'm not sure it would help.' She sighed.

Hanny asked, 'Will you be all right?'

Joy nodded, thinking that she had suffered loss before and survived. Surely she would this time.

Chapter Seventeen

'Patsy, where are you?' shouted Rose. She rapped on the floor with her stick.

Patsy hurried inside the house, leaving the front door ajar. 'Coming, Mrs Tanner,' she called, going to the foot of the stairs. 'Is there something you want from down here?'

'Yes! I want something to read. Go to the newsagent's and collect my magazine.'

'This week's won't be in until tomorrow,' said Patsy.

Rose sighed heavily. 'What am I going to read? There are no newspapers because of this stupid general strike.'

'There's last night's single-page bulletin of the *Echo*,' said Patsy. 'Have you read that?'

'What does it say?'

'It's about the general strike. The prime minister is appealing to the nation to go back to work and hopes for a peace move today.'

Rose yawned. 'Anything else?'

'It's snowing up north.'

'Snow in May! David will have something to say about that if it comes down here – what with him having to walk to the office. I can see you're going to have to join the library for me. Oh! Someone has just come up the path. See who it is, Patsy,' ordered Rose.

Patsy turned as she heard a crash and the next moment a leather-clad figure entered the house, looking slightly guilty. A smile welled up inside her. 'Is it Greg?' she asked.

He wiped the grime from his face and gazed at her. 'Is it Miss Doyle?'

'Yes.' She was pleased that he had remembered her name.

'Someone's left a bucket of water on the step. I'm afraid I knocked it over.'

'Sorry. It was my fault. I was washing the step when Mrs Tanner called.'

'Is that part of your job?'

'I'm afraid so,' said Patsy ruefully. 'I do a bit of this, a bit of that and I cook as well.'

Greg removed his helmet and gloves and smiled. 'You sound like a useful person to have around. How is Rosie?'

'I'll just run up and tell her you're here and you can see for yourself.'

Rose called down, 'I heard, Patsy. Come up, Greg. It's about time my family showed some interest in me. Mother didn't come, of course.'

'That's because she'd get lost,' said Greg. 'At least she hasn't forgotten about you.'

Rose sniffed. 'Most likely because she wants something from me. If it's Nelson and Helen she's worried about, tell her that there's nothing I can do. I'm having a baby and I won't risk losing it.'

'She's going senile. If you don't come in the next few months it's possible she might not recognise you.'

'Then it doesn't matter if I go or not, does it?'

'You really are hard-hearted,' said Greg, pausing at the top of the stairs and staring at the veiled Rose standing in the bedroom doorway.

'Don't look at me like that!' she said savagely. 'You've no idea how much I've suffered and am still suffering.'

'I didn't realise the scarring was that bad you felt a need to hide your face,' said Greg, his voice softening. 'I'll try and explain to your mother.'

'You don't have to make excuses for me.'

'No. But I think it'll be in your interest if I do so.'

Rose sighed and the veil fluttered. 'I suppose you'd like a cup of tea?'

'I am a bit thirsty. You get all sorts flying in your face on a motorbike.'

'You should get rid of that contraption. David could tell you how dangerous they are.' Rose paused to call down to Patsy to bring some tea to her bedroom.

It did not take Patsy long to prepare a tray and take it upstairs. The bedroom door was open so she popped her head round and said, 'I've brought the tea and a plate of buttered scones.'

'Thanks,' said Greg, turning away from the window. 'Could you put that down on the table, please? She'll be back in a minute.'

'Mrs Tanner has improved a lot since she came home from Blackpool.'

'I'm glad to hear it. Have you seen her scars?' he asked, dropping his voice.

'No! I do quite a bit for her but she's really careful to keep her face hidden,' whispered Patsy. 'It's a blinking shame. She was a good-looking woman.'

Greg agreed. 'Has she been out at all since she came home?'

'No. She's had the doctor and a nurse here a few times.'

'It must have been a really bad accident.'

'She was lucky to survive,' said Patsy. 'Do you want me to pour?'

'Thanks.'

She poured milk into the cups. There came the sound of Rose's stick tap-tapping. 'I'd best go,' whispered Patsy. 'She'll have heard me come up.'

'A bit sharp, is she? I'll speak up for you,' said Greg, smiling.

'No! But thank you for the thought.' She left the bedroom, stepping aside to allow her employer to pass. As Patsy went along the landing, she overheard Rose say, 'How long was she here? I thought I heard the two of you talking.'

'Only briefly.'

'That's as maybe but you shouldn't have kept her talking. These girls' heads can be so easily turned.'

'You're a snob, Rose. I haven't forgotten where we came from even if you have,' drawled Greg.

'You make it sound as if we were the lowest of the low when we weren't,' said Rose angrily. 'My father was a decent hard-working man and pulled himself up by his boot straps and that makes me middle class.'

'Don't let's get started on the class system,' said Greg. 'I'm not saying anything against him. But I don't remember having servants living in when we were growing up. Just a woman who came in daily for a couple of hours to do the rough work.'

'OK, OK! I've had enough of this conversation. I'd rather you thought of something to cheer me up.'

'You're lucky to be alive,' said Greg. 'Who was this friend who was killed?'

'I suppose Mother wants to know but his death upset me dreadfully. He was a good friend. I feel dreadfully low at times.'

'How fond were you of him?'

Rose's head shot up. 'What has Patsy been saying to you about him?'

'She hasn't told me anything.'

'David then?'

'Not a dicky bird.' Greg bit into a scone and the pastry seemed to melt in his mouth. 'These are good.'

'Yes. I can't cook or bake at all now. I have to leave it all to her. My main complaint is that Patsy has no sense of her position in this household.'

Greg said, 'Maybe, but useful to have someone who does a bit of everything.' Rose made no comment but lifted her veil slightly, so she could eat and drink. 'Tell me, do you stay up here most of the time?' he continued.

'Yes. I find the stairs difficult and I can't risk falling.'

'I'm sure David would carry you down.'

'And what if he stumbled and dropped me and I lost the baby?'

Greg sat up straight. 'So I did hear you mention having a baby. I thought I'd misheard.'

'If you're going to say Mother will be pleased I don't believe you. She only ever cared about her boys.'

Greg did not deny it. 'How does David feel about this miracle?'

'Thrilled to bits,' said Rose with a trill of laughter. 'He can't wait for it to be born. I'm hoping for a boy just like his father. Perhaps you could tell Mother all this. It will help her to understand why I haven't visited in ages and why I can't help with Grenville's children.'

'I'll explain to her that you're still using a stick and having trouble going downstairs. She's not completely lost her wits so she'll understand.'

Rose hesitated. 'I suppose she's made her will.'

'You'd be best asking David about that,' said Greg in a colourless voice. 'Is there anything else you'd like me to tell her before I go?' he asked politely.

'Don't tell her about the veil,' she blurted out. 'I don't want her laughing at me.'

Greg frowned. 'Why the hell should your mother laugh at your misfortune? Have you looked at yourself lately?'

'No! Now, go away. You don't have to come again. If you need to let me know anything about Mother you can speak to David.'

'If that's what you want,' said Greg, tight-lipped.

He left the bedroom and went downstairs. Hearing a girl singing he went outside and saw Patsy sweeping water from the step with a yard brush.

'You're busy,' he said.

She stopped and smiled at him. 'Mind you don't get your feet wet.'

'Bit difficult not to,' he responded, setting aside his irritation with Rose. 'Those scones melted in the mouth. You could make a living as a pastry cook.'

Patsy's eyes shone. 'You think so? I'd like a full-time job as a cook. I really enjoy food, preparing it and generally following a recipe. But I also like to experiment when I don't have the right ingredients. Like now with the strike on there's stuff I can't get.'

'I'm sure you'll come up with something tasty for their supper,' said Greg. 'See you around, Miss Doyle.'

'Tarrah!' Patsy waved as he went down the path to where his motorcycle was parked. 'You look after yourself on that contraption now,' she called.

Whether he heard her or not she did not know but he waved a gloved hand before roaring off along Anfield Road. Patsy sighed, wondering when she would see him again.

–

Bang, bang, bang, bang!

Patsy looked up at the ceiling. Here we go again! Carefully she flattened the one-page bulletin of the *Echo* and placed it on the hall table before running upstairs. It was two days since Greg's visit and Rose had been in a right mood since. Patsy could not help being curious about what they had discussed which had resulted in her mistress's prolonged and, even more than usual, demanding behaviour. Perhaps it had nothing to do with him but was down to the continuing strike.

So far there was no sign of a peaceful agreement. Instead there was every indication of a tightening up of the strike organisation. The transport men were obstructing supplies of food, although a boat from Cork had arrived in Liverpool with food supplies and another eighteen ships were expected to dock soon. Two thousand men were expected to help discharge the food. The strike had extended to Liverpool's postmen, who were neither collecting nor delivering post. There was also a network of charabancs going from Liverpool to London to support the miners' demonstration.

'What were you doing?' asked Rose.

Patsy detected a suspicious note in her voice. 'I was in the kitchen. I'm thinking we'll be eating from tins today. Maybe tomorrow we'll get some fresh meat.'

'Why tomorrow? Why not today?' demanded Rose, shifting restlessly on the bed.

'Because, although ships are coming in with food supplies, the transport workers are determined to prevent carts and wagons from leaving the docks.'

Rose was silent for what seemed a long time and then she said, 'I want you to help me downstairs.'

'What!'

'You heard me,' said Rose, reaching for her stick and pushing herself upright. 'It's time I saw what was happening downstairs. How do I know you're not stealing from me?'

Patsy bristled. 'I'm no thief. I've a good mind to go on blinking strike myself.'

'Don't be silly! You don't belong to a union.' Rose made for the door.

Patsy hurried after her. 'How are you going to climb downstairs?'

'I'll slide down.'

'That's stupid. You mightn't be able to stop yourself at the bottom and hurt yourself further.'

'Don't you call me stupid,' said Rose angrily. 'You'll get in front of me, so that if I start sliding you'll break my fall.'

'Ha! D'you think I'm an idiot? I could end up toppling over and possibly breaking my neck,' cried Patsy.

Rose glared at her through her veil. 'Think of the baby. If you have a good grip on the banister while going backwards you won't lose your footing.'

'If you come sliding down on me, I could do. Better to wait until Mr Tanner comes home,' said Patsy.

'No, I want to go down now and when I get there I'm going to have an enormous G and T.'

'Well, you're doing it on your own, madam,' said Patsy tartly. 'I've had enough. I'm giving notice.'

She made for the stairs and was halfway down when she heard a slithering noise behind her. She only had seconds to grab hold of the banister before Rose slammed into her. Patsy swung round and her shoulder thudded into the wood. She felt sick with pain and could not move. Rose screamed and the sound vibrated inside Patsy's head.

The next moment she felt a hand on her shoulder and let out a cry. She glanced up to see David Tanner gazing down at her. 'What the hell has been happening here?' he demanded.

'You ask the missus,' gasped Patsy. 'I can't blinkin' move. We're stuck.'

'Ignore her, David. Help me up,' groaned Rose.

'I'll have to move Patsy out of the way first,' he retorted.

David managed to extricate Patsy from her position and helped her to her feet. She staggered to one side and leant against the wall, nursing her shoulder. She watched him lift his wife to her feet.

Rose leant against him. 'It's her fault,' she said, attempting to adjust her veil with trembling fingers. 'She refused to do what I asked and then was bloody impudent.'

'You've forgotten to add that I also gave notice,' said Patsy, catching a glimpse of Rose's scarred face. She almost felt sorry for her. 'Mrs Tanner decided she was going to slide down the stairs, sir, and I was to go in front to break her fall if she lost control. Which she did! She could have broken my neck.'

David stared at his wife with such a look on his face that Rose shrank back. 'I'm fed up with being upstairs all the time,' she cried. 'Besides, I don't trust *her*. She could be stealing from us and giving stuff to a fence.'

'What are you talking about?' demanded David.

'I've been reading a book from the library. She could have been an orphan leader who stole fruit from handcarts and bread from bakeries.'

Patsy's head shot up and she lifted her arm painfully. 'Can't you tell the difference from what's real and what's not? It sounds like you've been reading Tilly Pearce's book. Anyway, I'm packing my bags and leaving.'

David looked alarmed. 'Don't be too hasty, Patsy. We need you here.'

'Let her go,' muttered Rose. 'You didn't hear the way she spoke to me. She threatened to go on strike. Give her the sack. We're bound to find someone else who doesn't have so much to say for herself.'

'Be quiet, Rose!' snapped David. 'Patsy would never steal from us and we're lucky to have her. We wouldn't get another maid who would do all that she does for the money we give her.'

Patsy said, 'That's true. Anyway, I need to sit down.' She moved away, still nursing her shoulder, and headed along the lobby.

'The arrogance of the girl,' cried Rose.

David clapped a hand over her mouth. 'No more, Rose,' he said softly. 'I have only so much patience. Where were you intending going when you came downstairs?'

'The drawing room,' she muttered. 'I thought I'd have a G and T and play some music.'

Patsy did not hear what he said in response because she was out of earshot. She went into the kitchen and sat down in the rocking chair. The cat sprang on to her knee and she stroked it absently with her left hand. Annoyingly it was her right shoulder that she had damaged. She began to calm down and felt amazed and shocked that she had lost her temper and spoken to Mrs Tanner the way she had. Should she leave or should she stay? Mr Tanner wanted her to stay and so perhaps she should. But she was definitely in need of a day off. She tried to remember when last she'd had any time off and realised that it was not since Mrs Tanner's return. Well, that needed to be rectified.

There was a noise at the door and Patsy turned her head and saw David Tanner standing there. 'How is your shoulder?' he asked.

Patsy noticed the lines of weariness and pain on his face and struggled to her feet. 'Still a bit sore, Mr Tanner. I'm sorry I lost my temper and said what I did to Mrs Tanner. The thing is that I haven't had any time off since she came home.'

'Then you must have a day off. Take Sunday off and then let me know what your decision is about staying on here.'

'Mrs Tanner doesn't want me here. Not since Greg's visit.'

David froze. 'When was he here?'

'A couple of days ago.'

'She didn't mention it.' He was silent for several moments before saying, 'My wife does not pay your wages, Patsy. I do. You've proved yourself hard-working, trustworthy and patient. I want you to stay but you can give me a definite answer, as I said, after your day off. I'll be here to see to my wife's needs.'

Patsy felt much happier after those words. 'Rightio, Mr Tanner. I'll visit the twins and Jimmy. Hopefully I'll be allowed to take them out for a couple of hours. I could pop in on Mrs Bennett and see how she's doing as well. She might just have heard something about my sister, Kathleen.'

David smiled. 'Good idea. Do give Mrs Bennett my regards.'

Chapter Eighteen

Joy's mouth felt dry and her heart was beating faster than normal as she gazed at the calendar and counted yet again the weeks since her wedding. She had missed her monthlies and had felt nauseous for the last few mornings. She did not want to believe that she was pregnant. She had still not found herself a job but was living sparingly on what was left of Robbie's insurance money. She had searched the house but had not found anything that resembled a share certificate. Grant had gone to Ireland busy with a case and had promised to see if he could find out anything from Brendan O'Hara's kin whilst he was there, but she did not hold out much hope.

At least there were several items she could pawn and, if she was very careful with the money, then she should manage until January when she reckoned the baby would be born. But what then? She did not want to use up the small nest egg she was saving for her old age.

She clenched her fists and fought back the waves of differing emotions that still threatened to swamp her at times: guilt, anger, grief and a deep anxiety. The latter made worse by the thought of enduring the discomfort of pregnancy and the pains of childbirth alone.

She had yet to mention her fears to Hanny and was reluctant to do so, guessing that her sister would suggest that she sell the house and move back to Chester and share her home. As much as she loved her family, Joy was determined to stand on her own two feet. Besides, she did not want to leave her lovely home and live elsewhere. She and Rex were settled here.

She bent and stroked the dog, who was of great comfort to her. If she really was pregnant, then she was going to have to find a way to support the three of them which meant still being able to stay in this house.

There was a knock on the back door. 'Come in!' she called.

The door opened and to her surprise Patsy stood on the step flanked by her twin sisters and brother. 'I hope you don't mind us visiting you on a Sunday, Mrs Bennett?' asked Patsy. 'But I felt I had to come.'

'Of course not! How are you all?'

'Never mind us,' said Patsy, gazing at her anxiously. 'How are you? You look thinner and your face is all pale. I was so sorry I couldn't come to Mr Bennett's funeral but Mr Tanner brought Mrs Tanner home and I haven't had any time off since.'

'I understand,' said Joy, looking concerned. 'I hope that they're not working you too hard, love.'

'I've coped so far and Mr Tanner doubled my wages,' said Patsy. 'But she's difficult and I can't see that changing even when the baby's born.'

'So Mrs Tanner is definitely having a baby,' said Joy, thinking of her own situation and how fortunate the other woman was to still have her husband after her misbehaviour. He must really love her to be prepared to forgive her and be a support to her. She felt envious. 'How is she recovering from her injuries?'

Patsy began to tell her about Rose wearing a veil to conceal her facial scars but was distracted by the twins and Jimmy edging closer to Rex. 'Gosh, is that the puppy? He has grown,' said Patsy. 'I bet he's good company.'

Joy smiled. 'I wouldn't be without him. He was the best present I could have had in the circumstances. Why don't the twins and Jimmy take his ball and play in the garden with him?'

The children did as she suggested.

'It was a good idea of our Kathy's,' said Patsy, seizing the opportunity to ask, 'Have you been in touch with your sister or brother at all recently? I presume you know that Kathy's working for Alice Bennett in Chester?'

'Yes, I do know,' said Joy.

'You wouldn't know how Kathy's getting on?'

'I haven't heard anything negative so she must be doing all right,' said Joy. 'Hasn't she written to you?'

'Only a brief note saying she'd got the job but after what you've said I'll take it no more letters means no news is good news,' said Patsy cheerfully.

'So tell me, when is Mrs Tanner's baby due?' asked Joy.

'October. That's if she doesn't do something else stupid.'

'What do you mean?'

Patsy was happy to be able to tell Joy all about the incident on the stairs. 'She gave me all kinds of abuse, so I was going to hand in my notice because she as good as called me a thief. Fortunately Mr Tanner arrived and sorted everything out. He asked me to stay. I told him that I'd think about it and that's why I've got the day off.'

'So what are you going to do?' asked Joy. 'If you were thinking, Patsy, I could give you a job here, it's out of the question, love. I just couldn't afford to pay your wages.'

'Gosh, Mrs Bennett, it never occurred to me to ask you for a job,' said Patsy hastily. 'I'll be staying on at the Tanners. I don't want to let Mr Tanner down. He appreciates me.'

'Well, I'm glad to hear it,' said Joy, getting up and putting on the kettle. 'But what's the woman thinking about accusing you of being a thief?'

'Maybe she's not thinking straight because of what happened to Mr O'Hara and her face being a real mess. I got a glimpse of it yesterday for the first time. At the moment she won't go out because she doesn't want people looking at her.'

'Understandable, I suppose,' said Joy. 'She's fortunate to have you to run errands for her and a husband who can afford to have groceries and other food stuffs delivered. I confess after the terrible shock of Robbie's death, I often didn't feel like going out but I had no choice. I also decided to start work on the vegetable patch to save money.'

'You must miss having a gardener. I see Miss Parker is still living next door. I remember how she would gaze over the fence while we played.' Patsy paused. 'Has Mr Parker ever been in touch with her?'

'She's never said. I don't know how things work out so she can stay on there but I presume some kind of arrangement was made with his solicitor before Leonard Parker disappeared.'

'I wonder what will happen when she dies,' mused Patsy.

'I really don't know,' said Joy.

Before Joy could say anymore there was the sound of footsteps outside and then Wendy and Grant made an appearance.

'Hello, you two,' said Joy, her brown eyes lighting up. 'When did you get back, Grant? Did you have any luck?'

'Some,' he said. 'But to make use of the information I'd need to go to America and I can't see either of us being able to afford the cost of the journey.'

'So what have you to tell me?' asked Joy.

'First of all,' said Grant. 'Did you know that there are mines in Ireland?'

'Mines?' Joy looked puzzled. 'Are you saying that Robbie invested in a coal mine in Ireland?'

Grant shook his head. 'I used to think that Ireland was just a country of peat bogs, churches, cattle, mushrooms, leprechauns and would-be republicans, but I've discovered not only do they have coal mines but silver-lead, zinc and copper ones as well.'

'So what has this to do with Brendan O'Hara?' asked Joy.

'I met O'Hara's cousin who told me that two of his uncles were miners who went over to America in the 1890s in the hope of making their fortunes. They staked a claim in a silver mine over there.'

'And?'

'They kept in touch with the family over here for a while but then their letters petered off until they stopped altogether.'

Joy frowned. 'Are you saying that Brendan O'Hara knew about this mine and saw it as a way of making money by selling shares in it?'

'It's a possibility.'

'Where is it exactly?'

'That's the rub! The cousin didn't know. His father's dead and he was only a boy when his uncles went to America. He still lives in the same shack as his grandfather did, so-o-o… may be the letters are there somewhere collecting dust amongst years of clutter. He did say he would try and find them but it's possible he forgot about doing that as soon as I left.'

'Presumably Brendan O'Hara didn't ask his cousin to buy shares in this silver mine,' said Joy.

'He doesn't have money to invest.'

'So what next?' asked Joy. 'So far all this is guesswork and not getting me any money. As you say, we can't afford for any of us to go to America even if we knew where this silver mine was.'

'I could ask Mam did Uncle Robbie ever mention a silver mine to her,' suggested Wendy.

'No, love,' said Joy firmly. 'Most likely she'll only go on about my only caring about Robbie's money. I can't rely on anything to do with his investments. I have to think up another scheme to bring in some money.'

There was a long silence.

'I've an idea,' said Grant. 'What about taking in paying guests, Joy?' Grant reached out a hand to Wendy. 'We could be your first ones.'

Joy felt a lifting of her heart. Wendy was looking at Grant as if he had offered her the moon. 'We're going to get married as soon as you're twenty-one,' he said.

Wendy took a deep breath. 'Of course, the perfect solution.'

Joy smiled. 'I know it's not long since Robbie died but I'm sure he'd be in favour of the idea.'

'Mam won't like it,' said Wendy, 'but I'll be twenty-one in August and she won't be able to stop me then.'

'My sister can come, too, and she'll pay her whack,' said Grant.

Joy's eyes glistened. 'I don't know why I didn't think of it myself! After all, I used to help my mother run a lodging house.

And if you and your sister would like to move in sooner, then you can, Grant. All the rooms are furnished and the bedrooms have washstands. I need to consider what you'd do about cooking if you wanted to cook for yourselves in your rooms.'

'A couple of gas rings would be good enough to start with,' said Wendy.

'But you can use the kitchen if necessary,' said Joy.

Grant looked pleased with himself. 'I'm glad you two women know a brilliant notion when you hear it and appreciate me. I'll speak to Elspeth.'

'Then we'll go and see the vicar this week and book the church,' said Wendy.

'And if you want you can have your wedding breakfast here,' suggested Joy.

Wendy hesitated. 'You wouldn't find that painful?'

'If I do I'll just have to cope with it and so will you,' said Joy firmly. 'Although I suppose your mother will be against the idea.'

'Yes, but she doesn't want me to get married and leave home, anyway,' said Wendy.

'Then it's settled,' said Grant. 'We'll be married in August.' He kissed Wendy and then leant forward and kissed Joy's cheek. Then, realising Patsy was still there, he kissed her too. 'You'll have some news to tell Mr Tanner when you go back to the house. How are they getting on now Mrs Tanner is home?'

'Pretty much the same as they used to do except she doesn't go gallivanting anymore,' said Patsy, smiling. 'Perhaps that's just as well now we know for definite she's having a baby.'

'They've had a long wait for this baby,' said Wendy. 'It does make me wonder whether—'

'We know,' said Grant.

It was on the tip of Joy's tongue to say that she thought she was having a baby, too, but she decided to wait a while longer until she was absolutely sure. Besides, she would want to break the news to Hanny before anyone else. After all, it was possible that her missed period could be due to all the upset she had endured since

Robbie died. She thought how pleased he would have been to see his niece married to Grant.

Suddenly Joy remembered the ivory and silver material Alice had suggested would suit Wendy for a wedding gown. She had paid for a suitable length of the fabric at the time and Alice had it stored away over in Chester. She mentioned it now to Wendy. The price Joy had paid for the material was worth every penny when she saw the pleasure in her niece's face.

'Alice is so clever at designing clothes that I can't wait to get in touch with her about the kind of wedding gown I want,' said Wendy, wriggling with excitement.

'You'll look like a fairy princess,' said Patsy.

Wendy looked at Grant. 'Do you think you can manage being Prince Charming?'

'Of course he can,' said Joy. 'So, what if we take a visit to Chester as soon as these strikes are over?' She glanced at Patsy. 'Perhaps I could also have a word with your Kathy at the same time and tell her to drop you a line.'

'I'd appreciate that,' said Patsy, looking pleased.

All the talk about Brendan O'Hara and silver mines had given Patsy an idea but she was not going to say anything about that right now. So she kept quiet and soon after collected her sisters and brother and they took their leave.

Once her visitors had gone, Joy attached Rex's lead to his collar and took him for a walk in the park. She thought how much good it would have done Robbie, if he had still been alive, to walk the dog every day. Too late now. She thought instead of Wendy and the coming trip to Chester. She wanted her to be happy, and although Joy knew that the girl still mourned the loss of her uncle, she also knew that the young were resilient and Wendy had much to look forward to that would ease her grief.

Chapter Nineteen

Kathleen stood in the doorway of Alice's shop on Foregate Street, enjoying the fresh air whilst she crocheted a lace collar in a two-ply beige cotton and wool mix thread. If she saw any prospective customers looking in the window she planned on encouraging them in. Trade had been terrible since the beginning of the general strike. No women or girls tootling round the shops in search of that special outfit for the Whit bank holiday coming up but hopefully things were about to improve.

The strike had officially ended on the twelfth of May but here it was, Tuesday the eighteenth, and some of the men were still refusing to return to work. Fortunately the railway unions and owners had at last come to an agreement, so hopefully the trains would now return to normal and bring in the day trippers.

Suddenly Kathleen noticed two women walking along the pavement on the other side of the street. They looked familiar and every now and again they paused to gaze in a shop window. It was only as they drew level that Kathleen realised who they were and immediately she waved and called, 'Mrs Bennett, over here!'

Joy glanced across the road. Kathleen could see that she was frowning and it occurred to her that she and Wendy might not have recognised her and that made Kathleen feel good about herself.

'It's Kathy Doyle!' she shouted.

Joy and Wendy both stared at her in astonishment and then, waiting only for a horse and cart and a cyclist to pass, they hurried towards her.

'Kathy, it is you,' said Joy, eyeing her up and down. 'I wouldn't have believed someone could change so much in such a short time.'

Kathleen chuckled. 'I'm really something, aren't I?'

'Give us a twirl,' said Wendy, smiling.

Kathleen twirled and the scalloped hem of the shapeless shift dress in a cream and navy soft jersey fabric fluttered about shapely knees encased in flesh-coloured rayon stockings.

'That is the shortest dress I have ever seen,' said Joy, a hint of disapproval in her voice. 'And where has your chest gone?'

'I'm wearing a Symington Side Lacer,' said Kathleen in a confidential whisper. 'Mrs Alice Bennett says my wearing the latest fashion is a good advertisement for the shop. You pull on the laces at the sides and it flattens your breasts.'

'So having a flat chest and showing your knees is fashionable now, is it?' asked Joy, shaking her head in disbelief.

'Yeah. In Paris they call it the *garçonne* look and the best-known designer is Coco Chanel.'

'Well, you are knowledgeable,' said Wendy, her eyes dancing.

'The word means boyish according to Mr Bennett. He was in France, yer know, during the war.' Kathleen touched the crown of her head. 'And what d'you think of me hair?'

'Definitely boyish,' said Wendy, surveying the girl's blonde crop. 'I'm pretty sure that Grant wouldn't approve of me having mine that short.'

'I suppose you don't have to,' said Kathleen. 'You only need it this short if you want to wear the latest tight-fitting cloche hat.'

'Hmm!' Joy looked doubtful. 'I've never been one for taking much notice of what's fashionable. Anyway, what are you doing out here?'

'Enjoying the fresh air and looking for customers. Trade is slow and rather than just stand behind the counter waiting for one to appear, I thought I'd be a better advertisement for business outside. Mrs Bennett has taken Georgie to the dentist and told me to mind the shop. Normally I'm in the workroom at the back if there's any dressmaking or alterations to be done.' Kathleen smiled. 'She shouldn't be much longer. She's been gone for nearly two hours.'

'We'll wait for her inside,' said Joy. 'It's ages since I've been here.'

'She's got plenty of new stock in,' said Kathleen, leading the way.

Joy and Wendy gazed around the interior. There were dresses, skirts and blouses, as well as a couple of bathing costumes, hanging on racks. Behind the polished oak counter was a cabinet with drawers upon drawers with glass fronts containing underwear and stockings.

'Do you have a changing room?' asked Wendy.

'We have to make do with two curtained-off alcoves at the back of the shop right close to the workroom. We have a couple of workbenches, the sewing machine, store cupboards and shelves for materials in there,' explained Kathleen. 'You reach it by going up these two steps,' she added, leading the way beneath an arched opening to where there were coats, jackets and mackintoshes, as well as the odd hat on a stand.

'I never thought it would be this big,' said Wendy, following Kathleen through a door into the workroom. Here it was a lot lighter than the interior of the shop because an uncurtained sash window reached from ceiling to floor.

'I like working in here,' said Kathleen. 'But we've only orders in for a couple of dresses and a costume for a wedding at the moment.'

Wendy leant over the table and picked up a couple of samples of material on a cord ring. 'I've come about Mrs Bennett making my wedding gown. I believe she already has the material for it.'

Kathleen's face lit up. 'If it's the ivory and silver material I can get it out for you.'

'I'd appreciate that,' said Wendy, smiling.

Kathleen put down her crochet on a sheet of tissue paper and went in search of the material. Joy went back into the shop and was just in time to see a girl lifting a blouse from a hanger.

'Hey, what are you doing with that?'

The girl jumped and turned round. Joy saw that it was Alice's daughter. 'Hello, Flora! Shouldn't you be in school?'

'Hello, Aunt Joy. Mum didn't say you were coming.'

'No. I'm here with Wendy Wright. She had a few spare hours so we came on the spur of the moment. That's a pretty blouse.'

'Yes, isn't it. I'm hoping Mummy will let me have it. I'm seldom allowed factory-made clothes. Is she in the back?'

'No. Apparently she's taken Georgie to the dentist.'

'Oh, I'd forgotten about that,' said Flora casually. She held the blouse against her in front of a mirror. 'I could have been a shoplifter. Kathy should have been keeping an eye on the place. You've no idea, Aunt Joy, how thoughtless she is.'

'You're misjudging her. She was looking out for customers when we arrived. She and Wendy are in the back looking at material for a wedding gown.'

'Oh!' Flora's pretty face flushed. 'But she is thoughtless and she's a flirt. Mummy doesn't seem to notice but I do. She flirts with James and teases Georgie, as well as buttering up to Daddy, making out that he's the handsomest and cleverest man in the whole world. When you'd have to be blind not to see his scar. She asks him this and that. I don't know why Mummy has to have her living in the house. I'm prepared to help with the housework. We don't need extra help.'

Joy felt uneasy listening to what Flora had to say about Kathy's flirtatious ways, but was she telling the truth? It was obvious Flora resented there being another pretty girl in the house. Having two brothers and a father who had spoilt her because she was the only daughter could have that effect. It was possible, too, that Seb might be flattered by Kathy's attention but she felt certain that he loved Alice too much to behave foolishly with an adolescent girl.

'I think you have to remember that Kathy has no father, and even when he was alive, she seldom saw him,' said Joy. 'It's not surprising that she should admire yours. She does have an older brother but he's at sea. She must miss him.'

'Well, she's not having *my* brother or any of my friends,' said Flora, with a toss of her gold-red hair.

'Who's not having your brother?' said a voice behind her.

Flora's cheeks flushed a bright pink and she turned and said, 'Hello, Mummy.'

Joy smiled at Alice. 'Is Georgie OK?'

Alice shuddered. 'He's been a brave little soldier but he needs the rest of the day off, so I've left him with Clara. I was wondering when I would see you. What brings you over here?'

But before Joy could answer, Alice had switched her attention to her daughter. 'What are you doing here and with that blouse?'

'We finish at twelve for lunch at school and you don't close until one,' answered Flora. 'As for the blouse, I'd like it. I mean you have Kathy dressed out in the height of fashion. Why shouldn't I have this?' She flourished the blouse.

Alice said mildly, 'The style is too old for you. Now, put it back. As for Kathy, she is an advertisement for the shop.'

'You're not going to let me forget that I didn't want to work in this pokey shop, are you?' snapped Flora, colour flaring afresh in her cheeks.

'No, I'm not,' retorted Alice, her green eyes glinting. 'And I don't want any more impudence from you.'

Flora threw down the blouse and stormed out of the shop.

'Oh lor', I didn't handle that very well, did I?' said Alice, bending to pick up the blouse. 'It's just that her attitude to everything at the moment, and me in particular, is driving me mad.'

'She's jealous,' said Joy. 'Quite normal, really.'

'Flora has no need to be jealous. Anyway, let's not talk about my daughter right now. Instead, tell me why you're here.'

Joy explained and Alice's expression lightened. 'I'll just turn the sign round to "closed" and we'll go in the back. I'm really looking forward to making this wedding dress for Wendy. It'll lift my spirits like nothing else will at the moment.'

'Business bad?'

Alice shrugged. 'I'm sure it'll buck up now the railway strike is over. Putting the wedding aside, how are you?' She turned the sign round on the door and was about to bolt it top and bottom when Joy stayed her hand.

'I'll answer that after I've seen our Hanny. I'll slip out now and I'll be back in about an hour.'

'But...' began Alice.

She was too late. Joy had already slipped out and closed the door behind her.

—

Joy stood beside her sister on the balcony of the house over-looking the River Dee. 'I still find it difficult to believe that it's really happened to me,' she said.

'I know. You getting pregnant so quickly does seem a bit of a miracle,' said Hanny. 'I'm delighted for you.'

Joy said grimly, 'I could do without this kind of miracle. The thought of supporting a child — that's if something doesn't go wrong — I mean it's early days yet.'

'You'll be fine,' said Hanny bracingly. 'And what with Wendy getting married and she and Grant living with you, I don't know what you're worrying about. They'll be there to support you. The child will be a consolation to you in your old age.'

Joy rolled her eyes. 'Thanks a lot! Getting old is the last thing I want to think about right now.'

'Sorry, but you know what I mean. If you're worrying about baby clothes, pram, cot, playpen, I can help you out there. I haven't thrown anything of the twins away,' said Hanny. 'I thought if I did, then I might immediately fall pregnant again.'

Joy said, 'I'll be glad of them. I just need to let Wendy and the family know now.'

'I wonder how Rita will take the news,' said Hanny, glancing at her sister. 'I suppose she'll be as mad as can be that Wendy will be living with Grant under your roof.'

'You can say that again. Perhaps I won't mention it yet. If all goes well, then I'll announce it after the wedding.'

'Is it all right if I tell Tilly in my next letter?' asked Hanny.

Joy thought about that and nodded. What harm could it do?

Chapter Twenty

'What are you doing, Patsy?'

Patsy lifted her head and looked towards where Rose Tanner was sitting in a deckchair with her hands folded across her swollen belly. Her face was almost concealed by a huge floppy sun hat but Patsy would bet a penny to a shilling that she wore a discontented expression. Recently she had started dispensing with the veil and experimenting with cosmetics.

'I'm bringing in the washing, madam,' said Patsy.

After the kerfuffle on the stairs Rose had been very cool towards Patsy but since the girl did almost everything for her, she had to speak to her. Rose was still refusing to go out and mix with people and was often lonely. She was now over six months pregnant and was getting crabbier by the minute. Patsy had overheard her discussing her confinement with the midwife. Rose wanted both a midwife and a doctor in attendance.

'But the sun's lovely and hot after it being dull for days,' said Rose.

'The washing is dry and I could iron it today and put it away. It's my afternoon off tomorrow and I'm going to see a wedding.'

'Whose wedding is it this time?' asked Rose in pettish tones.

'Robbie Bennett's niece. My sister helped make her wedding dress.'

Rose's head jerked up. 'Oh, poor Robbie Bennett! To die so suddenly just like poor Brendan.' She drew in a shuddering breath. 'Life can be so bloody. How is Robbie's wife?'

'She's pregnant. My friend wrote and told me.'

'Good God! I suppose that's why they married.'

Patsy did not like this slur on Joy's morals and thought Rose had a cheek to say that about her friend. 'I'm sure that's not true. The baby's not due until January.'

'Don't be impudent,' snapped Rose. 'And don't be back late. I need you here. I had hopes of Greg paying me a visit. I feel I'm being neglected. I haven't had word from my family in Seaforth since just after the Duchess of York gave birth to the little princess. You'd think that Greg would have made an effort but I bet he's cross with me because of Mother; he just doesn't understand how I've suffered.'

Patsy remained silent, thinking what a selfish madam Rose was, but she wished Greg would visit. He hadn't been snobby at all and she had enjoyed talking to him.

'I rather like the name Elizabeth. If my baby is a girl I might just name her after the princess,' said Rose. 'Although, I'm hoping for a boy just like his father.'

'Well, Mr Tanner is good-looking,' said Patsy.

Rose made no comment but asked, 'What else does your friend have to say?'

'There was a lot in the letter and I read it in a rush. I do remember a mention of a silver mine,' lied Patsy casually.

'A silver mine? What does she know about silver mines?'

'Not much. But her American husband has bought shares in one.'

'I believe there are plenty of working silver mines in America. I remember Brendan saying his American cousins owned one out west somewhere.'

So the O'Hara silver mine was out west, thought Patsy. If she got the opportunity tomorrow, then she would pass on that snippet of information to Joy.

-

'Are you sure you're all right?' asked Elspeth, hovering in the lavatory doorway.

'Yes!' Joy wished Grant's sister would go away and leave her to throw up in peace. It was three hours to the wedding, and if all the other days when she had suffered morning sickness were anything to go by, then she would be fine within the hour and able to change into her wedding outfit. She would then put on a pinny and take her place in the kitchen to make sure the buffet would be ready in time. There were to be no more than twenty guests. She felt a lump in her throat, thinking about how Robbie would have enjoyed throwing a party for his niece's wedding. What would he have said about the baby? Probably boasted of his prowess as a lover.

'Would you like me to make you a cup of weak tea?' asked Elspeth.

'Kind of you but not right now,' muttered Joy, wiping her mouth as she straightened up and leant against the wall.

She found Elspeth difficult. A fluttery, clingy kind of woman, she was so different from her brother. From the moment she had arrived at the house, it was obvious that she believed that because she and Joy were widows they were going to be company for each other and the best of friends. Her husband had been killed in the war and the woman had suffered nervous debility. She had told Joy that if it had not been for Grant, then she would have expired from grief. She was driving Joy mad but she could not rebuke her too strongly when they had to live under the same roof. What Joy needed was a widow whom Elspeth could latch onto, so she would leave Joy to her own devices.

'Better now?' Elspeth patted Joy's arm and gave her an encouraging smile.

Joy nodded. 'Yes, thank you. Now I need to get ready.'

'Perhaps I can help you?'

'No, I'm fine. You go and get yourself ready.'

'I am ready,' said Elspeth.

Joy stared at the skinny figure in the black frock that dipped at the hem an inch or two above her ankles and was almost lost for words. Then she said gently, 'Don't you think it's time to put off your mourning? I'm sure your husband would want you to look bright and happy for your only brother's wedding. I know that's what Robbie would have wanted me to do.'

Elspeth looked dismayed. 'Are you saying you won't be wearing black?'

Joy said, 'No! I'm certain Robbie would want bright colours and happy faces at Wendy and Grant's wedding.'

Grant's sister pursed her lips. 'Did he tell you that?'

'What do you mean?' asked Joy, surprised by her tone of voice.

'Wendy's mother was saying that your husband's other wife was a medium and you helped her during séances. I just wondered if you'd been in touch with your husband.'

Joy was annoyed with Rita for gossiping to this woman about her. 'Certainly not! Robbie was a non-believer. He would never attempt to get in touch with me nor I with him. Now, if you'll excuse me, Elspeth.'

Joy brushed past her and went into the bathroom to wash her hands and face. The door she locked behind her because she believed that otherwise Grant's sister would follow her in. As she turned on the tap, Joy gazed at her reflection in the mirror above the sink. She looked peaky and had lost weight. Perhaps she might manage to fit into the outfit she had bought off the peg a few years ago. Suddenly she thought how helpful it would be if Robbie could get in touch with her and tell her where those blinking shares were but she was certain it would never happen.

She went into her bedroom and riffled through her clothes until she found the outfit that she wanted. Memories flooded back of the day when the champagne had flowed and they had danced to the music played by some of Robbie's friends from the Palladium cinema orchestra. Neighbour Leonard Parker had been a welcome guest then, although she had always been a bit suspicious of the man's polished manner. She shook her head in an attempt to rid herself of the disturbing memories and began to get dressed.

It was a relief to discover that the dress and jacket still fitted her and she reckoned the russet-brown shade with dark-brown piping about the neck and cuffs was just right for a woman in her circumstances. The matching brown hat decorated with a cream artificial flower flattered her face. She smiled at her reflection before removing the hat. After she had dealt with the catering, she must remember to come back for it.

-

As Patsy watched Wendy float down the aisle on her brother's arm, she wondered, if she were ever to get married, whether her brother, Micky, would be available to give her away. If only her father had not been swept overboard, she would have loved him to do it. Still, she would have to put up with Mick, although it was almost a year since she had last seen him. She was concerned that they might lose touch altogether. Where was he now? She prayed for him and her other siblings.

Afterwards when she came out into the sunshine it came as a surprise to be hailed by Kathleen. 'What are you doing here?' asked Patsy, delighted to see her sister.

'I helped make the wedding gown, didn't I?' said Kathleen, her manner as proud as Punch. 'What do you think of it? Doesn't Wendy look lovely?'

Patsy agreed. 'What part of the gown is your handiwork?'

'Some of the plain sewing and the embroidery on the bodice and round the hem, of course,' said Kathleen. 'My reward was being invited to the wedding. I'm really looking forward to the buffet. Pity my favourite man isn't here, but Peter is and I won't have you there watching me from the sidelines, ready to spoil my fun.'

Patsy pounced. 'Who is this favourite man? I hope you haven't been silly.'

Kathleen's smile faded. 'I wish you'd have some faith in me. I'm not stupid, you know.'

'When you talk about a favourite man and then mention Peter Wright in the same breath, is it any wonder I worry about you? I wish you wouldn't say such things.'

'Have you ever thought I might do it to get you going?'

'Do you?'

Kathleen smiled.

Patsy said, 'I only worry about you because I care.' She sighed. 'Let's change the subject. How are you getting on with Flora Bennett?'

'She hates me,' said Kathleen cheerfully. 'But I'm determined not to let her get my goat. It's almost as much fun teasing her as it is my working in the shop. But not quite. I enjoy talking to the customers about the latest fashions and there's several who are always wanting to know whether Mrs Bennett can copy the new styles for a tenth of the price.' Kathy struck a pose. 'Do you like my latest ensemble?'

'Yes,' said Patsy, thinking the beige and white dress and jacket suited her sister's colouring. The neckline of the jacket was unusual in being shaped like a horse's collar. Also she appeared flat-chested and altogether slimmer. 'You're as lean as a lamp post and you look older.'

Kathy grinned. 'Thanks, that's the effect I'm after.' She glanced about her. 'I'd best go. My Mrs Bennett is waving to me. We must be leaving for the house. Take care.'

She blew Patsy a kiss and skipped across the churchyard towards Alice.

Suddenly Patsy spotted Joy and sped across the churchyard to catch her up just as she went through the gate onto Belmont Road. 'Mrs Bennett,' she called.

Joy turned and smiled. 'Patsy! I didn't see you in church. How nice of you to come and watch Wendy's wedding. I suppose Kathy wrote and told you the date.'

'No. I had a letter from Tilly.' She hesitated. 'I just want to say congratulations on the baby.'

Joy flushed and she laid a hand on Patsy's sleeve. 'Sshh! I haven't told Wendy and her mother yet. It came as a bit of a shock. How's Mrs Tanner?'

'She's keeping well but she gets really fed up because she won't go out.' Patsy hesitated. 'Remember last time I called at your house you were talking about shares and a silver mine?'

Joy stared at her intently. 'Go on!'

'I decided to see what I could find out from Mrs Tanner. She said that there were plenty of working silver mines in America and that Brendan had American cousins who owned one out west.'

Joy smiled. 'Clever you! Did she say where?'

'No,' said Patsy apologetically. 'So I don't think Brendan O'Hara sold her some shares.'

'I suppose not. I'll have to go, Patsy. Your Kathy made a lovely job of the embroidery on the wedding dress, by the way.'

Patsy beamed at Joy. 'I'm glad she seems to be fitting in all right over there.'

Joy appeared to be about to say something else when Rita came up behind her. 'What's this I've just been hearing about you having a baby?' she asked bluntly.

Joy said a hurried goodbye to Patsy before facing her sister-in-law. 'Who told you?' she asked.

'That Alice Bennett mentioned it and I had to pretend that I knew already,' said Rita harshly. 'I suppose this baby is the reason why Robbie married you?'

'Trust you to think that,' said Joy. 'I was going to tell you today. As for Alice already knowing, she's one of my oldest friends and her brother is married to my sister and I told Hanny first.'

'All right, keep your hair on,' said Rita, calming down. 'Does Wendy know? If she does and she hasn't told me there's going to be trouble.'

'Surely not on her wedding day?' asked Joy, annoyed that Rita should make such threats. 'Anyway, I haven't told her.'

Rita looked slightly mollified. 'All right. I'm sorry if I accused you unjustly but I'd like to have been told earlier.'

'I didn't want to tell you in case something went wrong.'

'All right. I accept your apology. I just wish our Robbie was here to hear the news.'

'He mightn't have been pleased,' said Joy.

'Of course he would!' exclaimed Rita, looking shocked. 'Hopefully it will be a boy and the image of him.'

Joy realised that she had given no thought to whom the baby might look like but now she did. 'He was a goodlooking man, Robbie.'

'Yeah, he was.' Rita sighed. 'The lad won't go far wrong if he looks like his dad. But one thing is for sure, I don't want him growing up and wandering the world and doing damn stupid things like playing music and never settled down until he was in his bloody dotage. Fancy him being tricked into buying shares in a silver mine!'

Joy stiffened. 'I suppose Wendy told you about that?'

'Who else?'

'I don't suppose you know anything about the shares he bought?'

Rita's eyes widened. 'Why should I?'

'I thought that maybe—'

'No, he didn't.'

'Right. Now, if you don't mind, Rita, I want to reach the house before the bride and groom do. Wendy looks lovely, doesn't she?'

'She's not half as pretty as our Minnie and I'll miss her money,' said Rita grudgingly. 'But I suppose she's doing the sensible thing living with you.'

Joy was about to say *Is money all you ever think about?* but then remembered she was forever thinking about money lately.

Despite all their best efforts to make the wedding breakfast a happy occasion, it was an emotional time, especially when Grant proposed a toast to absent loved ones. Joy hugged them both before they left for a honeymoon in London. They were both delighted about the baby and she was pleased by their reaction because she felt their support would be vital to her in the coming months. Grant suggested that it wouldn't be a bad idea if she got in touch with Rose Tanner after Joy mentioned what Patsy had told her. She said that she would think about it and waved them off.

When she turned round and saw Elspeth standing behind her, Joy's heart sank at the thought of having to cope with Grant's sister during the coming week. But she need not have worried as Elspeth was at work during the day and went out soon after supper most evenings. Joy did not ask where she went and Elspeth did not tell her. Even so, she was glad when Wendy and Grant returned home and she had their company again.

However, Joy was not looking forward to the winter. Despite most of the miners having returned to work at the end of August, coal was still rationed so she had not been able to build up a stock to see them through the colder months. She had Grant chop down one of the trees in the garden, thinking that, after it had dried out, then they could have log fires. According to the *Echo*, there were a couple of good things about the strike: there were less deaths from respiratory trouble in Liverpool due to the cleaner air.

Joy was thrilled when she felt the baby quicken. Hanny had told her what to expect, saying it was like a fluttering, as if tiny fingers and toes were exploring the safety of the womb. The baby became real to her in a way that it had not done so before. She knew that she must look after herself and the little one and eat properly and exercise by taking Rex for long walks.

It was an article in the *Echo* that reminded Joy of the silver mine share certificate. Apparently a large number of people on Merseyside had invested in oil but the shares had slumped and it was estimated that six million pounds had been lost. It made her doubt whether there was any possible chance of her ever getting Robbie's money back. Even so, she made up her mind to go and visit Patsy and hopefully she would get a chance to talk to Rose Tanner about Brendan O'Hara and shares in the silver mine. She needed that money.

Chapter Twenty-One

'Have you seen this?' Rose was lying on a chaise longue in the drawing room.

Patsy glanced up from polishing the sideboard. 'What is it, madam?'

'A dance frock for the winter. The new silhouette from Paris. Apparently fringes are in fashion,' she murmured. 'Now, that I quite fancy. Imagine all the fringes shaking when one does the Charleston.'

'Yes, madam.' Patsy knew that Rose had been experimenting with facial cosmetics and she had been out a couple of times recently. She had no idea what had suddenly prompted her to take steps to make a conscious effort to improve her looks. There were now mirrors in her bedroom, the bathroom and the hall.

Rose flung the newspaper on the floor. 'As soon as I have the baby and get my figure back I'll send off for some mail order catalogues and I'll have a spending spree.' She pushed aside the blanket and eased herself up into a sitting position. 'Hell, look at that rain. Won't it ever stop?'

Patsy knew that Rose was not expecting an answer. She was forever asking such questions.

'Goodness! Would you believe there's someone out there? Hurry, Patsy, and open the door!'

Patsy put down her duster and went to the front door. She was surprised but pleased to see that it was Joy Bennett on the step.

'Hello, Mrs Bennett! Come in quickly. You're getting soaked.'

'Thanks! What a day!' exclaimed Joy, wiping her feet on the mat.

Patsy took her dripping umbrella and placed it in the hall-stand. 'What are you doing here? Has something happened to our Kathy?'

'Not that I know of,' said Joy, removing a sodden glove. 'Is Mrs Tanner in?'

'Yes. Have you come to see her?'

Joy smiled. 'I wanted to know how you were but I wouldn't mind having a few minutes of her time. Do you think she'll see me?'

'I'll ask her.' Patsy headed for the drawing room, only to collide into Rose who was standing just inside the doorway.

'I heard,' she said, her eyes alight. 'Show her in and then go and make some coffee.'

Patsy turned to Joy. 'Mrs Tanner will see you. Here, let me take your coat. I'll put it in the kitchen to dry.'

Joy thanked her. Patsy showed her to the drawing room and hurried with the damp garment to the kitchen. Joy took a deep breath and rapped lightly on the drawing room door before entering. She saw a blonde woman lying on a chaise longue with a blanket thrown over her legs.

'Do sit down, Mrs Bennett,' said Rose, stretching out a hand to her. 'I hope you don't mind my not getting up, but once I'm down, it takes a real effort to get up again. You'll understand when you're further on in your pregnancy.'

'I see Patsy told you about that,' said Joy, sitting in an armchair close to the fire. Her feet were freezing in her damp shoes. She slipped them off and hoped that Mrs Tanner would not notice.

'Patsy, yes. So what can I do for you?' asked Rose.

Joy attempted not to look as if she was staring at her and plunged straight in to what she wanted to say. 'I hope you don't mind my calling but I need to ask you a couple of questions about Brendan O'Hara.'

Rose stiffened. 'It would depend on what you have to say.'

'It's to do with Mr O'Hara having been such a close friend to my dead husband. I believe it must be over forty years they'd known each other,' said Joy in a quiet voice. 'Mr O'Hara's death came as a terrible shock to him. I believe it could have even contributed to Robbie's heart attack.'

Rose's eyes were bright with unshed tears. 'I was so sorry to hear of Mr Bennett's death. He was such a lovely man and so talented musically. You must miss him.'

'Naturally, I was very fond of him and coming so soon after we were married was terribly upsetting.'

'Of course. So what is it I can do for you?' asked Rose.

Joy cleared her throat. 'It's to do with some shares in a silver mine that my husband bought from Mr O'Hara. I can't find the share certificate so I need to get in touch with the owners in America. I wondered if you had a name and address.'

'You'd need to get in touch with Brendan's sister,' said Rose. 'She's a widow in her fifties and lives in New York. I don't know her address but her married name is McIntyre.'

Joy could not conceal her disappointment. What use was a name without an address to write to? Although, she supposed it was possible that Tilly might be able to trace the woman through a directory, but surely it would be difficult in a city the size of New York?

'I'm sorry I can't be of more help,' said Rose. 'Was it a lot of money your husband invested?'

'Yes,' said Joy with a grim smile. 'But at least I can be thankful that he didn't mortgage the house.'

Rose agreed. 'But, of course, you'll need money to live on. When is your baby due?'

'January,' said Joy.

'Mine's this month. I'll be glad when it's over. I feel like I've been pregnant for ever.' She glanced towards the door. 'I think I hear Patsy.'

Patsy arrived bearing a tray. 'Mr Tanner's just arrived home,' she announced.

'I didn't hear him come in,' said Rose, looking surprised.

'He came in the back way because he's soaking wet,' said Patsy. 'When I told him that Mrs Bennett was here, he asked me to bring a fresh pot of coffee and a cup for him in ten minutes. He's gone up to change.'

'Thank you, Patsy. You may go,' said Rose before turning to Joy. 'I don't think you've ever met my husband, have you, Mrs Bennett?'

Joy presumed Mr Tanner had never mentioned her visit to the house, so chose not to answer the question. 'I believe Mr Tanner is a solicitor?'

'Yes. I was engaged to his eldest brother but he was killed in the war. Their father was my father's solicitor. When he died, just after the war, David was persuaded by his mother to take over the family firm. It did not come easy to him as he'd originally wanted to be an architect.'

'Talking about me, Rose?'

Both women started and turned to look at David who had quietly entered the room.

'Darling, how you startled me!' Rose held out a hand to him. 'Come and sit down. This is Mrs Bennett. Do you remember her husband died almost as soon as they were married?'

David turned to Joy. Their eyes met and held. 'How are you managing, Mrs Bennett?'

Joy's cheeks were suddenly hot. Hastily she reached for her coffee cup. 'I'm coping, thank you, Mr Tanner. My husband's niece and her husband are living with me. It's a great comfort having their company now the nights are drawing in.'

David said gravely, 'I'm glad to hear it.' He limped over to the cabinet and removed a bottle of whisky. 'Something to keep the cold out in your coffee, Mrs Bennett?'

Joy wondered if he had noticed that she had slipped off her shoes. 'Thank you. That would be welcome.' As he poured a cap of whisky in her coffee she wondered about those wounds invisible to the world that Patsy had mentioned.

'So to what do we owe the pleasure of your company, Mrs Bennett?' he asked. 'Is it something to do with Patsy?'

Joy hesitated and glanced in his wife's direction.

'What other reason would she have for coming, David?' said Rose lightly. 'Anyway, Mrs Bennett and I got talking. That film on at the Trocadero? Have you seen it, Mrs Bennett?'

Joy said readily, 'My niece told me that it's set in Russia during the time of the late tsar. Apparently there's a ladykilling grand duke, a handsome hero, and a powerful but thoroughly bad hat, who sails away with the girl on his yacht at the very moment her dearly beloved is to be shot at dawn.'

'It sounds like perfect escapism,' said David.

There was a discreet knock on the door.

David opened it and took the tray from Patsy. He poured his own coffee and asked the women would they like their cups topping up.

Both nodded.

'So what was your niece's opinion of the film?' asked David, sitting down.

'Wendy said it was fun but Grant said it was predictable. He only agreed to go to the cinema because they were showing the Dempsey-Tunney fight as well.'

'You mean the big boxing match?' said Rose. 'I adore seeing two strong men fight. Trouble is, it's ages since I've been anywhere to see anything.'

'You'll get out and about once the baby arrives,' said David. 'You'll be able to wheel him out in his pram.'

'I didn't mean that kind of *out*,' said Rose, frowning. 'Fun out! I need cheering up. I'd like to watch Maxwell Stewart, the champion ballroom dancer, performing the Charleston.'

David said mildly, 'Haven't you had enough of dancing?'

Rose did not answer. Joy felt uncomfortable and wondered how soon she could make her excuses to leave. David drained his cup and said, 'If you'll excuse me, Mrs Bennett, there are some documents I have to read.' He left the room.

Rose said in an exasperated voice, 'He just doesn't understand a woman's needs. You have no idea, Mrs Bennett. See what I have to put up with just because of my interest in dancing? I used to love it and so miss Mr O'Hara. Our steps matched perfectly.'

Joy could feel her heart racing and wanted to leave. 'We all have to give up some of our interests at certain times in our lives,' she said, easing her feet into her shoes. 'I'm sure when you have your baby, you'll find a lot of pleasure in taking him out.'

Rose nodded. 'You're right. This baby is what keeps me going. Without the thought of having a part of Brendan to love I'd want to die. If people only knew what I've had to put up with since David and I married. He's impotent, you know. It happened during the war. He loved motorcycles and was a messenger. His machine caught fire with him still on it.'

Joy felt the colour rush to her face. 'How dreadful for him! But, really, Mrs Tanner. I didn't need to know that!' she stood up, abruptly. 'Thank you for the information about the mine, and the coffee. I hope all goes well with the birth.'

'But you don't understand! I didn't discover this until after we were married,' cried Rose. 'He should have told me.'

Joy did not know what to say and she hurried out before Rose could say anything else that was inappropriate and embarrassing. She entered the kitchen. 'Can I have my coat?' she asked.

Patsy stared at her flushed face. 'Are you all right? What's been going on in there? They haven't been arguing in front of you?'

'Nothing for you to worry about, love,' said Joy, taking her coat from the back of a chair in front of the range. It was still slightly damp but at least it was warm. 'Thanks, Patsy. Call in and see me sometime.'

'What about your umbrella?' called Patsy, watching Joy open the back door. 'I'll get it for you.' She rushed to do so and returned swiftly and handed the umbrella to her. 'You'll be OK, won't you?' she asked anxiously.

'I'll be fine. Bye!' called Joy, splashing towards the gate through the pouring rain.

Patsy watched her go, hoping she would get home safely and wondering what had happened in the drawing room that had upset her.

As Joy made her way to the tram stop she could not get Rose Tanner's words out of her head. Fancy telling a woman who was a stranger to her that she was not only carrying another man's child but that her husband was impotent. Poor David Tanner! Had he kept quiet about his condition because he had loved Rose so much? He shouldn't have done so, of course. She remembered the expression on his face in the wedding photograph that Patsy had shown to her. No wonder he had looked half scared to death. Joy could imagine his mortification if he knew that his wife had revealed such a personal piece of information to her. And what must he be feeling about his wife's pregnancy in the circumstances? Was he prepared to put up with her behaviour because he wanted a child whatever the injury to his pride and pocket? She thought of the baby she was carrying and the ageing Robbie who had made her pregnant and then died. How unpredictable and unfair life could be. She could only pray that all would go well for both children.

Chapter Twenty-Two

Patsy's heart sank as she reached the Tanners' house. She'd had an enjoyable few hours in town watching the pageant parade for Civic Week. It had been a wonderful sight with people wearing all kinds of costumes, many to do with the city's seafaring past. David Tanner had given her permission to go and watch the parade this Saturday morning, saying it was a sight she might not get to see again for a while. He was working from home as the baby was due any day now. Rose Tanner had been as tense as a violin string ever since Joy Bennett's visit. Patsy could not help wondering, once more, what had happened that had caused Joy to leave in such a hurry.

She entered the house and was immediately seized by her employer. 'Rose's pains have started,' said David. 'I've telephoned the doctor but his wife told me that he was out attending a seriously ill patient. I'm not sure what to do next.'

'What about the midwife?'

'She's not on the telephone. I would have fetched her but Rose does not want to be left alone in the house.'

'I'll go,' said Patsy immediately. 'How long is it since Mrs Tanner started labour?'

'A couple of hours.'

'I wouldn't worry too much if I were you.' Patsy smiled. 'I remember Mam and the neighbour who delivered her last baby saying first babies always take their time.'

She left the house and hurried to the midwife's home, only to discover that she was in attendance at another birth. Patsy left a message for the woman with her daughter and ran back to the house to inform Mr Tanner of the news.

'But this is crazy,' said David, clutching his hair. 'What am I supposed to do?'

'Don't panic. Go and sit with her and keep her calm,' ordered Patsy. 'I'll put the kettle on. The midwife and doctor will need hot water.'

David went upstairs but it was not long before he was down again. 'She says she doesn't want me and suggested that I ask Mrs Kelly next door to come and sit with her. As you know, she has several children.'

'I'll go and fetch her,' said Patsy.

At that moment there was a scream from overhead and he headed for the stairs. 'Hurry up, Patsy! I can't cope with this.'

Patsy left the house and went up next door's path and banged on the door. 'Who is it? What do you want?' shouted a voice.

'It's Patsy from next door. Mrs Tanner's started in labour and the doctor and midwife are out on cases. She wants you to come and sit with her until they arrive.'

The door opened and Mrs Kelly stood there with her hair in pipe cleaners. 'I thought the baby wasn't due for another week.'

'No, any day now.'

'How close are her contractions?'

'I don't know.'

'Tell her I'll be around as soon as I've taken my curlers out.' She closed the door.

Patsy returned to the house and discovered David Tanner sitting on the top stair. 'Isn't Mrs Kelly coming?' he called down.

'Yes. She'll be here as soon as she can.'

The words were scarcely out of Patsy's mouth when there came a banging at the front door. She went to open it and found the midwife on the step.

Patsy smiled her relief. 'Are we glad to see you. Come on in.'

'Take me up to her,' said the midwife.

Patsy only got as far as the foot of the stairs when Mr Tanner took charge of the midwife and escorted her to Rose's bedroom. He opened the door for the woman but was ordered to stay outside. Patsy put the kettle on for more hot water in case it was needed.

When David entered the kitchen he looked a little less fraught. 'The midwife would like a cup of tea. She said it could be some time before the baby arrives. Apparently it's in the wrong position and she's hoping it will turn itself.'

Patsy's heart sank. 'Did she say whether it was a breech?'

He frowned. 'I can't remember. Rose was carrying on something terrible in the background, so I couldn't hear everything that was said.'

'Our Maureen was a breech but fortunately it wasn't a long labour and Mary, who came first, made it easier for her twin to be born.'

'Well, let's hope this baby will do what's needed,' he said, looking harassed.

The next visitor was Mrs Kelly. 'Thanks for coming but no doubt you'll be glad to hear that the midwife has arrived,' said Patsy.

The neighbour looked relieved. 'That's good. How's Mrs Tanner getting on?'

'The baby is the wrong way round. I know that can cause problems.'

'Oh dear,' muttered Mrs Kelly. 'Well, I'll be thinking about her. Let me know what it is when it comes.'

Two hours later there was a telephone call from the doctor's wife saying that her husband was on his way. Patsy had answered the telephone and she informed her employer. He thanked her for the news and raised his eyes to the ceiling as another scream pierced the air.

Just then the doorbell rang and David went to open it. 'Doctor Morgan, am I glad to see you,' he said. 'According to the midwife, my wife doesn't seem to be making much progress.'

'Well, let's see what we can do,' said the doctor in comforting tones.

The two men went upstairs.

Time seemed to pass dreadfully slowly and Patsy could not keep still. Mr Tanner had come downstairs twice and asked for coffee and the second time he had fetched the whisky from the drawing room and poured a tot into his own cup. She kept going to the bottom of the stairs and listening but the sounds issuing from Rose's bedroom were still those of suffering. Patsy prayed that soon she would hear a baby's cry.

After doing this for about the twentieth time, she decided to tidy the kitchen cupboards and set about doing so. She was wiping out the last one when she heard heavy footsteps coming downstairs. She dropped the cloth and climbed down off the chair and went to the door and opened it.

David Tanner stood there. He did not need to speak for her to realise something was dreadfully wrong. He looked so sad. 'The baby was stillborn, Patsy,' he said in a low voice.

'Oh, I'm so sorry, Mr Tanner!' Patsy placed a hand on his arm. 'And Mrs Tanner?'

'The doctor said that she will be all right but she'll need looking after. She's been through a lot. He was a perfect little boy but apparently the head got stuck with him being the wrong way and it—' His voice broke off and he swallowed. 'You can imagine how broken-hearted Rose is.'

Indeed, Patsy could. She guessed there were difficult times ahead for all of them.

An hour later the doctor left the house but the midwife stayed on for a while longer, making several trips up and down the stairs. When she finally left the house David came into the kitchen. 'What an excellent woman that midwife is, Patsy. She saw to everything and seems to have calmed Rose down. The doctor has left her some pills to help her sleep.'

'Poor Mrs Tanner. Will she be wanting supper, sir?' asked Patsy.

'Not at the moment. She just wants to sleep.'

Patsy went outside into the garden and cut some chrysan-themums, removed the bottom leaves and trimmed the stems before placing them in a vase of water. Then she took them upstairs. She could hear David Tanner's voice but not what he was saying. She waited until there was a silence and then she knocked on the door. He opened it and she held out the vase of flowers to him.

'That is thoughtful of you, Patsy,' he said, taking them from her.

'Is there anything else I can do, sir?'

He shook his head.

Patsy went downstairs and walked round the garden, wishing herself anywhere than where she was at that moment. She wondered what difference the loss of the baby was going to make to the Tanners' marriage.

Mrs Kelly called over the fence to her. 'So what was it?'

'A boy, but he was stillborn, I'm afraid,' answered Patsy.

The woman's face fell. 'What a shame! After such a long wait for the pair of them, too.'

Patsy agreed but wondered if the woman suspected at all that the baby might not have been Mr Tanner's. Surely she would not have forgotten the kerfuffle the night that Mr O'Hara had brought Rose home to be greeted by Mr Tanner, newly returned from America. Patsy went back inside the house. So far she had not had a chance to speak to Rose Tanner and in one way perhaps that was a good thing. What could she say that would be of any help to her?

So Patsy went to bed without seeing her mistress. Despite all that had happened that day, she slept better than she had thought she would and woke about eight in the morning. She should have been up by now, lighting the fires, but she lay a moment longer with her hands behind her head, watching a shaft of sunlight shining on the wall opposite the window. She thought of the poor baby and how much Rose Tanner had suffered to bring him into the world, only for him to die. A tear trickled down her cheek. Poor little lamb. She wiped her face with the back of her hand and threw back the bedclothes.

She padded across the chilly linoleum and washed her face and hands in cold water at the washstand. After getting dressed, she crept down the top flight of stairs and stood on the first-floor landing. All was unusually still and silent. Generally there were some sounds coming from the Tanners' bedrooms at this time of day: one of them shifting in bed causing it to creak, coughs or sighs. On this sad morning, she half expected to hear Rose Tanner weeping for the loss of her child.

Suddenly, Patsy had the oddest feeling and the hair on the back of her head prickled her skin. She tiptoed over to Rose's bedroom and placed her ear to the panel of the door and rapped her knuckles gently on the wood and called, 'Mrs Tanner, would you like some breakfast?'

No response.

She knocked and called to Mrs Tanner again and still there was no reply. Then David Tanner's bedroom door opened and he stood in the doorway in pyjamas and dressing gown. His hair was a mess and he had dark circles under his eyes. 'What's all the noise, Patsy?'

'I've knocked and knocked on Mrs Tanner's door and she's not answering.'

'She's probably still asleep.'

David walked over to Rose's room and opened the door. He remained motionless, gazing at the bed where his wife lay curled up beneath the eiderdown. Then he took a deep breath and hurried over to her.

There was a smell in the room that caused Patsy to baulk but she followed him, noticing that there was not just one but two empty pill bottles on the bedside table. She had seen one of the bottles before when the doctor had prescribed the pills for Rose after the accident and thought they had all been used up. She watched as David fumbled for his wife's pulse.

Patsy was filled with apprehension. 'Is she…?'

David turned a strained face towards her. 'I think so. But stay with her, Patsy, while I telephone the doctor.' Patsy moved out of the way to let him past. She would much rather have gone with him. She sank onto a chair, staring at the face of the woman in the bed. She looked so peaceful, much more so than she had ever seen her in life. Suddenly Patsy noticed a sheet of paper half under the bed. She was about to pick it up when David reappeared.

'I'm wondering if that's a note, Mr Tanner,' she said, pointing at the sheet of paper.

He reached for it and she watched him read it and then tear it into tiny pieces. 'This note never existed, Patsy. I'm sure it was an accident. What do you say?'

'If that's what you want me to say, sir, then yes, I agree,' she said stoutly.

'Right. Good girl!' He patted her on the shoulder and limped out of the room.

Patsy lowered herself to her knees and slowly began to pick up every scrap of paper.

Chapter Twenty-Three

'Now here's a shock,' said Wendy, lifting her eyes from the *Echo* and staring across at Joy.

'What is it? What's wrong?' Joy moved away from the kitchen sink and peered over Wendy's shoulder.

'Mrs Tanner. She's dead.'

Joy snatched the newspaper from her and began to read the article beneath the headline that blazoned *City Solicitor's Tragedy: Wife Found Dead after Overdose of Sleeping Tablets*. When she finished reading it, she sank onto a chair and gazed into space, remembering her conversation with Rose Tanner.

'What must he be feeling after forgiving her for betraying him?' muttered Joy. 'He must have loved her to do so. He *must* have hoped that this baby could have healed and given fresh meaning to their marriage. Then for it to die. Poor tot.' Joy pressed her hand against her abdomen as if to protect her own baby from harm.

'I wonder what he'll do now,' said Wendy.

'What can he do but get on with his life?' said Joy. 'The question is whether he'll want to continue living in that house with the memory of such a double tragedy taking place there.'

'What about Patsy?' asked Wendy. 'I wonder how she feels.'

Joy glanced at the article again. 'There's been an inquest and the verdict was accidental death.'

'Do you think it was an accident?' asked Wendy.

'I wonder,' murmured Joy. 'I think I might go and visit tomorrow. If he's back at his office, I should be able to speak to Patsy. Poor girl, I hope she's not in a state. It could have brought back memories of her mother's death.' Wendy folded the newspaper. 'Do you want me to go with you? Only Grant has asked me to go into the office today. We were going to attend one of the Armistice services in remembrance of my dad and Grant's cousins. Did you know that they're having two minutes silence in the new tunnel they're digging under the Mersey?'

'No, I didn't read about that,' said Joy. 'But you and Grant stick to your arrangements. I'll be fine. I'll walk to the house and take Rex with me. We both need the exercise.'

Wendy looked at her anxiously. 'Are you sure about this? I mean, walking all that way in your condition after having such a shock.'

Joy smiled. 'I'm not an invalid and I'm feeling really well.'

'I'm surprised Patsy didn't ask Mr Tanner's permission to telephone you. I'm sure she'll have known that you'd want to know about the baby and Mrs Tanner.'

Joy shook her head. 'Patsy's not daft. She'll have considered that the news of Mrs Tanner giving birth to a stillborn baby might upset me in my condition.'

Wendy bit her lip. 'Sorry. You're right. It's me that's not thinking straight.'

Joy assured Wendy that she understood. It was true that she did feel upset by the news of the dead child but these things happened and it did not mean that it was going to happen to her baby. She could only hope and pray that everything would go well when it came time for her to give birth.

The following day, Joy arrived at David Tanner's house in the early afternoon. It had occurred to her that Wendy and Grant were not going to be the only ones paying their respects to the fallen from the Great War and she had taken time out to spend two minutes silence in the garden. No doubt David Tanner would be remembering his brothers, too. She wondered if he had ever wished that he had died due to the injuries he had sustained. She had difficulty getting what his wife had told her out of her head.

There was no answer to Joy's knock at the front door, so she decided to go round the back to see if Patsy was in the kitchen.

The garden was deserted but for a cat sheltering from the cold wind under a bush. It lifted its head when it saw her and Rex before burying its nose in its fur whilst keeping one eye open.

Joy made for the kitchen door and knocked but no one called for her to come in. She tried the handle and the door opened. She tied Rex's leash to the leg of a chair and told him to be good. Then she left the kitchen and walked up the passageway to the foot of the stairs and called the girl's name.

There was no answer and she was about to retrace her steps when she heard the sound of a door opening. The next moment David Tanner appeared at the top of the stairs. His brown hair was tousled and even from this distance she thought he looked older than the last time she had seen him. He was wearing trousers and vest and his feet were bare.

'I'm sorry, Mr Tanner. Did I disturb you? It's Joy Bennett. I read about your loss in the *Echo*. I wanted to see how you and Patsy were doing and if there was anything I could do to help.'

'It's good of you to come,' he responded. 'If you could wait a moment while I put on the rest of my clothes, I'll be down in a minute. Patsy's out. Perhaps you could put the kettle on. The way the weather is you could probably do with a hot drink.'

Joy returned to the kitchen and put on the kettle. The room was colder than she remembered it being but perhaps that was because every time she had visited this house there had always been something cooking in the oven.

As soon as he entered the kitchen, David said, 'Let's go into the drawing room and drink our tea there.' He glanced at Rex and said, 'You can bring your dog.'

She thanked him and followed him into the drawing room. He waved her to a seat by the fire and sat on the sofa. Rex stretched out at her feet.

'I'm sorry you had to find out about Rose from the newspaper but as you can imagine it's been a bit grim since it happened,' said David.

'Please don't worry about it. I'm just sorry that you had to go through such a dreadful time,' said Joy.

He hesitated. 'It wasn't an accident, you know. I should have considered the possibility that she might take too many tablets. The birth process had been horrific and she so wanted the child. It was a reminder of him, you see.' He paused and looked wretched. 'I should never have married Rose. She was so pretty and I'd been in love with her for a while but thought there was no hope for me. She was in love with my eldest brother, and then when he was killed and I survived, she turned to me. I couldn't not marry her.'

Joy could feel his pain. 'You don't have to tell me all this,' she said in a low voice.

'I feel like you'll understand. You've been through bad times yourself. Things weren't right for us from the start but I had the business and could support her. I tried to make the marriage work but in the end I couldn't give her what she wanted.'

'I lost the man I loved in the war. Then I married a man I didn't love. I was fond of Robbie but I would have been content to have continued as his housekeeper if my mother hadn't died.' She took a deep breath. 'Still, life has a habit of throwing up the unexpected. Now I have a responsibility that I can't cast aside. I'm wondering how I'll cope bringing up a child on my own.'

'I'm sure you will,' said David. 'You appear to be a very capable woman to me, Mrs Bennett. Rose wasn't. Not her fault. Her mother always favoured her brothers and treated her as if she didn't have a brain in her head. I'll say no more on that score but it does lead me in to telling you about Patsy. I'll be selling this house. I just hope that you'll agree when I tell you that I've tried to do my best by her.'

'So what have you planned for Patsy?'

David reached for his cup. 'I don't know if she has mentioned to you that Rose's mother lives in Seaforth with her grandchildren and her foster son. Trouble is, Mrs Smith is getting too old to manage the house and the children. I have suggested that a young all-purpose maid who is good with children might be a temporary answer to the problem.'

'How old are the children?'

'Nelson is ten and Helen is eight. It's a matter of Patsy looking after them before and straight after school and during the holidays. Her wages will be paid from a trust fund that the children's father set up before he left to join his ship at the beginning of the war. He was in the Royal Navy.' David paused. 'I hope you agree with me that it is a position that Patsy could fill?'

'Yes. This foster son. How old is he?'

'Twenty. He's an apprentice ship's fitter. Patsy has already met him a couple of times. You can trust Greg Molyneux to treat Patsy with respect. Of course, when the old lady dies other arrangements will have to be made.'

Joy sighed. 'The war really has upset so many children's lives.'

'Indeed. That's why I wanted to see Patsy settled before going any further with my own plans.'

She was curious about his plans. 'Will you be moving to a smaller house?'

'I don't plan to look for another one yet. For ages I've been wanting to visit the spot where my brothers died. It's over ten years since the Battle of the Somme and it seems to me that now is the right time to make that journey.'

'I see.'

'After that I'm considering going to America. I have a client in New York. At least, he was my father's client when he lived in Liverpool. Now he would like to see me to discuss his affairs. Letters aren't always satisfactory.'

'Couldn't he come over to Liverpool to see you?' asked Joy.

David smiled and, getting up, put some more coal on the fire. 'He seems extremely reluctant to do so and, as I'd like to get away for a while, then I'm prepared to comply with his request.'

'So you're going to France and then New York,' she said as an idea struck her.

He stared at her. 'Is there something about my going there that gives you cause for thought?'

Joy wondered if it would be in terribly bad taste to discuss with him Brendan O'Hara and the shares in the silver mine that he had sold to Robbie. 'Yes, but...'

'There's an expression on your face that makes me think you've something on your mind that you want to say to me but are dithering about it,' said David.

Joy took a deep breath. 'It's just that if you're going to New York, I wonder if you could do something for me? Of course, if you don't have the time I understand. It's a lot to ask of you. I have mentioned my dilemma in a letter to a family member who lives in New York with her American husband but I haven't heard from her about it.'

'What is it you would like me to do?' asked David.

'There's a woman, a Mrs McIntyre. She's Brendan O'Hara's sister and lives in New York.' Joy paused and added hastily. 'I understand if you want me to go no further.'

David frowned. 'I can understand your reluctance to talk about O'Hara to me but you've roused my curiosity and I haven't forgotten that he was an old friend of Mr Bennett. What is your problem?'

'O'Hara sold my husband shares in a silver mine in America but I can't find the share certificate and neither do I know the name of the mine or its exact location. I guess without the certificate I mightn't have a leg to stand on when it comes to claiming any money for them. On the other hand, the situation at the time was unusual in that O'Hara and Robbie both died suddenly within days of each other. Your wife told me that she believed that the mine was out west. I know that it was worked by some of O'Hara's male kin. Hopefully Mrs McIntyre would know their address and the situation of the mine. The trouble is I don't know her address.'

David looked serious. 'Is there a lot of money involved?'

'Yes! Robbie sold all his previous wife's property and used the capital to buy the shares. I own the house I live in and its furnishings but he left little else.'

David was silent.

'I'm sorry. I really shouldn't be bothering you with all this. I can't even pay you a fee unless I get the money back.'

David waved her words away. 'I'm prepared to help you if I can. I presume you don't have any idea what happened to the documents? You don't think O'Hara conned your husband into handing over a stack of money and there is no mine? That Rose lied about that?'

Joy shook her head and told him about Grant's trip to Ireland. David could not conceal his interest. 'So Irish miners went out west to try and make their fortune. I've always enjoyed Westerns. Now *The Twisted Trail*...'

'Mary Pickford was in that,' said Joy.

David grinned. 'See, we have something in common. I'd enjoy going out west.'

'You can't possibly mean that you'd go out there if you discovered the location of the mine?'

'I'm certainly prepared to do so,' he replied. 'I'm in need of a good, long break and I'd like to see the country for myself. Once I've sorted everything out here, then I'll take off.'

Warmth flooded through Joy and her eyes glowed as she looked at him. 'You really are kind. I can't thank you enough.'

'I haven't got there yet,' warned David, returning her smile. 'And I might come back empty-handed.'

'I'll give you Tilly and Don's address in New York and you can call on them. They might be able to help you.'

'That could be useful,' said David. 'Now would you like more tea? This has gone cold.'

'I'll go and make a fresh pot, shall I?' offered Joy.

'Thanks. Then maybe Patsy will be back by the time we've drunk it and we'll know how she got on.'

'I do hope things work out for her,' said Joy fervently. 'Then I'll have one less person to worry about.' But having said that she knew that she would be praying for David Tanner whilst he was away.

Chapter Twenty-Four

The wind was blowing in from the Irish Sea when Patsy left the train at Seaforth Sands terminal. It fluttered tendrils of her light-brown hair against her small ears and chilled her cheeks. She took a deep breath of the fresh salty air before descending the steps on the landward side. This time, Mr Tanner had written down precise instructions for her to find the house. There were several roads she had to look out for before she reached her destination – in particular, Seaforth, Elm and Gladstone. She crossed the road towards the Caradoc Public House and put her best foot forwards.

Some twenty-five minutes later, Patsy reached her destination. She pushed open the gate and walked up the short path to the front door. Lifting a dolphin-shaped knocker, she banged it hard.

The door opened immediately as if someone had been watching out for her. A woman, who was as wide as she was tall, stood there, scrutinising Patsy in her navy-blue skirt and navy-blue woollen coat. 'You the girl who used to be at the Seamen's Orphanage?' she snapped.

'Yes! I'm Patsy Doyle,' she replied with a sinking heart.

'Then get inside.' The woman seized hold of Patsy's arm and dragged her into the vestibule. 'There's no time to waste. Yer might as well get started right away, so I can be off.'

Patsy shrugged herself free. 'Do you mind not handling me like that. You're not Mrs Smith, I take it?'

'Am I heck! I'm Mrs Robinson. I was the old lady's char but I told the lad I couldn't put up with her or the kids anymore. I'm glad to wash me hands of this place. The kids are playing out back when they should be at school but they all got up late, didn't they?' She brushed past Patsy and waddled to the gate.

'But Mrs Smith hasn't seen my references. I mightn't suit,' called Patsy.

'You'll do her, all right. Beggars can't be choosers,' called the woman over her shoulder.

'But-but where is Mrs Smith?'

'Upstairs, messing about, going on about Mister Rodney.' The woman paused in the gateway. 'She's going a bit balmy just like the children's mother, so you'd better prepare yourself for that.'

'What do you mean?'

'The children's mother wasted away, didn't she, half mad with grief,' replied the woman with ghoulish pleasure. 'There's too many ghosts here, but then the children will tell you about it soon enough. Good luck, girl!' She hurried away.

Patsy wondered just what kind of household had she come to?

The stained-glass-windowed vestibule door stood ajar, so she pushed it further open before closing the front door and stepping into a small square hall. On her right was a flight of stairs and ahead was a lobby. All was quiet but for the ticking of a grandmother clock on the wall facing her at the end of the lobby.

She took two paces forward and saw that there were two doors to her left. A black and white cat suddenly shot round the corner at the end of the hall, swerved on the parquet floor and went through the farthest doorway. The animal so startled her that her heart seemed to jump in her chest. She reached out a hand to steady herself against a dingy brown-painted wall. Should she shout up the stairs for Mrs Smith or should she find the children first?

She decided on the latter and walked along the lobby and round a corner and came into a room. There was a sofa, as well as a table and chairs and a dresser holding crockery. A sash window on the left looked out over a strip of yard with the dried remains of some plant tangled round a trestle against a wall.

Suddenly she heard voices and hurried towards the open door at the other end of the room. She came out into what was obviously the kitchen for there was a black-leaded range, shelves and cupboards and a scrubbed table, as well as a gas stove. A door leading outside stood ajar. No wonder it was cold in here. She could hear a boy's taunting voice and a girl's shrill one.

Patsy went outside but had to walk past a couple of adjoining outhouses before she was able to see the children. The sun came out from behind a cloud and for a moment dazzled Patsy. Then it went in again and a few spots of rain fell. She blinked and saw a girl tied to a tree. A boy held what looked like a hatchet and he appeared to be trying to saw through one of the girl's fair plaits.

'Grenville, stop that or I'll tie you to a tree, boy, and shoot arrows at you,' said a quavering voice from above.

'I'm not Grenville, Grandma,' yelled the boy, throwing back his head and gazing up at the house. 'You're confusing me with Dad again.'

'Am I? Who are you, then?' asked the invisible owner of the voice.

'Nelson, your grandson.'

Silence. Then the voice said, 'I'm coming down, and if you haven't untied Rose by then, I'm going to lock you in the hole.'

'Let's get out of here, Helen,' said the boy, taking a penknife from his trouser pocket. 'I'm not going in there again.'

He was about to begin sawing through the rope when Patsy hurried forward. 'Hoy, don't cut it!'

The boy whirled round. 'Who the hell are you?'

'I'm Patsy Doyle and don't you be swearing at me, my lad. Give me that knife!' She reached out for it but he put the knife behind his back.

'It's mine. It was Dad's and nobody is going to take it away from me. I suppose you've come to try us out. Well, I'll tell you now. We don't want you.'

'I can't say I'm keen on you right now but I'm here so I might as well see what your grandmother has to say about this job.'

'She'll have forgotten you're coming, so you might as well go away.'

'Not yet I'm not,' said Patsy. 'Now, give me that knife.'

'What about me?' yelled Helen.

Patsy turned and went over to her. 'Brothers! What would you do with them?' she said in a friendly voice.

The girl gazed at her from narrowed eyes. 'What did you say your name was?'

'Patsy Doyle. Your Uncle David sent me.' She looked at the knots in the rope and shook her head. 'No wonder your brother's only way of dealing with this is to cut it. He's made a right mess of tying you up. He could do with joining the Scouts.'

'Don't you criticise my brother! It's not your place,' said Helen, sticking out her tongue.

Patsy acted like lightning and seized hold of the tongue. 'That is not polite!' The girl struggled to speak and her eyes were furious. 'I hope you weren't thinking of giving me further cheek because I'll not stand for any lip from a kid, whoever you are.' Patsy removed her hand and, taking a handkerchief from her handbag, wiped her fingers on the white lawn cotton.

'I'm a Red Indian squaw and if I had the hatchet I'd scalp you,' hissed the girl.

'Not if I get my hands on the hatchet first,' said Patsy.

'I'm not old enough for the Scouts,' said Nelson, sitting on a bench and toying with his penknife.

'You could be a Cub. It would keep you out of mischief,' said Patsy, giving him her full attention.

He shrugged and ran the blade of the knife across his palm. 'Have you brothers?'

'Three.'

'Have you a dad?'

'He was lost at sea.'

'Ours was torpedoed.'

'Hey! What about me?' cried Helen. 'I'm still tied to this tree.'

'So you are,' said Patsy mildly.

'Well, aren't you going to free me?'

'Only if you ask me nicely.'

The girl rolled her eyes and muttered something indistinct.

'Can't hear you,' said Patsy, going over to the tree.

'Will you untie me, please?'

'It'll be my pleasure.' Patsy set to work on the knots as there was no way she was going to waste a good length of rope. But as soon as the girl was free, she kicked Patsy in the shins. 'You, little…' Patsy seized hold of her plait and put her other hand round her waist and lifted her off her feet. 'I think we need to speak to your grandmother about your manners.'

'Let me go!' cried the girl, struggling to get free. 'Don't tell Grandma! I'll be good.'

'Yes, let her go!' shouted Nelson, getting up from the bench and coming towards them with the penknife.

Patsy swore beneath her breath, lowered his sister to the ground and grabbed his wrist as he lunged towards her. He struggled within her grasp but she would not let him go until he dropped the knife.

The next moment Patsy found herself under attack from his sister again. 'You've no right to hurt my brother!' she screamed.

'I'm not doing anything of the sort,' said Patsy, grabbing hold of her by a plait. 'Now stop it the pair of you! Why are you behaving like this? I didn't come to hurt you.'

'Uncle Greg taught me to defend myself,' said Nelson, tilting his chin. 'I was getting bullied at school because of my name.'

'Yet you bully your sister by tying her to a tree when he's not here?'

'It was only a game. I wouldn't really have cut off her plait,' sighed Nelson, bending and picking up his penknife. 'Although she would like it bobbed, wouldn't you, Helen?'

The girl nodded. 'But Grandma might tan the hide off him… and here she comes,' she hissed.

Patsy glanced towards the house and saw an elderly woman in pastel shades of trailing chiffon standing a few yards away. Just looking at her clad in such impractical garments in November caused Patsy to shiver. 'Are you Mrs Smith?' she asked.

The old woman did not answer but screwed up her face. 'Who are you?'

'I'm Patsy Doyle. Mr Tanner has sent me here to see if I'll suit for the position as all-purpose maid and to help with the children.'

The old woman's expression altered. 'If Mr Tanner sent you, then you'll suit me. He knows what's what. What did you say your name was?'

'Patsy Doyle.'

'Then come inside, Patsy Doyle. I'm at my wits' end with these children. My husband thinks looking after children is easy. Men, they have no idea. He foisted Frank Molyneux's brat on me after he died in an accident. His wife was already dead. As if I didn't have enough with my three. Although, I don't know where Rodney's gone. He said he would be back soon but he's been gone ages.'

'Uncle Rodney is a sailor like Dad was,' whispered Nelson out of the side of his mouth.

The old woman glared at him. 'Did I ask you to speak, boy?'

'No, Grandma.' Some of the colour had ebbed from Nelson's face and he appeared to brace himself as if for a blow.

Patsy said hastily, 'He was just explaining to me who Rodney is.'

'Why?' The old woman's faded blue eyes fastened on her. 'You know who Rodney is. He's my son.'

'Yes, Mrs Smith. I've gathered that,' said Patsy. 'Can I make a suggestion? Can we go inside? You're not dressed for outdoors.'

'Don't you be telling me what I should wear!' The old woman's mouth worked and she came closer so that she was only inches away from Patsy and peered into her face. 'It's Joan, isn't it?'

'No, madam. My name is Patsy Doyle and Mr Tanner has sent me to help with the children,' she said loudly.

Mrs Smith's face lit up. 'Mr Tanner, such a nice man. He has three sons, you know?'

Patsy realised Mrs Smith's mind really was in a muddle because she was getting her Mr Tanner confused with his father. 'Shall we go inside, madam? You don't want to catch a chill, do you?'

'I suppose you're right.' Mrs Smith's wizened hand caught hold of one of the trailing lengths of chiffon and drew it round an arm.

Then with an unsteady gait she made for one of the outhouses and went inside.

'That's the lavatory,' said Nelson, putting his penknife in his trouser pocket. 'Grandma is losing her marbles. I think she's always been a bit mad, myself. Come on, Helen, let's go and wash our hands and make a sandwich. It must be time for lunch.' Without another word he headed towards the house.

Helen looked up at Patsy, who thought she could see traces of her Aunt Rose in her small heart-shaped face. 'It's true. Uncle Greg blames Uncle Rodney never coming back for the way she is.' The girl turned away and hurried after her brother.

Patsy decided to wait for Mrs Smith to come out of the lavatory. She recalled that when David Tanner had gone to America it had been in search of this Rodney. It was obvious from what the children had said that he had not been found.

A shivering Mrs Smith emerged from the lavatory. Patsy gazed at her and felt sad. 'Are you OK, Mrs Smith?' When she did not answer, Patsy added, 'Shall we go inside?'

'Whatever you want to do.' The old woman hugged herself. 'I'm cold.'

Patsy put an arm about her shoulders. 'I'll make us a cup of tea.'

'Is that a promise?' asked Mrs Smith, gazing at her.

'Yes.'

A shadow flittered across the old woman's face. 'You're not Rose.'

'No. I'm Patsy.'

She looked bewildered. 'I don't know a Patsy.'

'Mr Tanner sent me to help you.'

'Such a good man, but why do men waste their time in wars?' said Mrs Smith. 'I don't know where Rodney is. Do you know?'

'No,' said Patsy, ushering her in the direction of the house.

'Rose hates Rodney. She haunts the place and I can't get rid of her.'

Patsy felt a tingling in the back of her neck. The last thing she wanted was Rose's ghost flittering about the house. 'What do you mean haunts the place?'

Uncertainty flickered in the old woman's eyes. 'I don't know. Sometimes I see my daughter and sometimes I don't. Do you know where Rodney is?'

Patsy decided to steer her thoughts in another direction. 'I've met Greg.'

'Greg is a little imp and I've had to give him a few whacks to get him to behave. Wait until his father comes in and I'll tell him what's what.'

Patsy decided that perhaps the best thing to do was ask no more questions. She would wait until Greg arrived home and then she would discuss the situation with him.

Once inside she settled the old woman near the fire and made her a cup of tea. The children were in the kitchen spreading jam on bread when Patsy heard the sound of an engine.

Minutes later Greg entered the room.

'You've come!' His relief was obvious.

'Yes. And am I pleased to see you, sir!' she exclaimed.

'Sir!' He laughed. 'It's not me that's hiring you, Patsy Doyle, so you can dispense with the *sir.* If you stay, and I hope you will, then your wages will be paid from a trust set up by the children's father.' He removed his helmet. 'I hope the old woman hasn't given you too much trouble?'

The children who had wandered into the morning room now reappeared. 'Uncle Greg!'

He frowned. 'What are you two doing here? Why aren't you at school?'

'We overslept and Grandma didn't wake us,' said Nelson.

'Well, I hope you've behaved yourself for Miss Doyle.'

The children glanced at Patsy and she read in their faces what they wanted her to say. 'We're only just getting to know each other. I doubt that they are going to be my main problem. Mrs Smith is more confused than I imagined.'

Greg looked grim. 'Her condition is hard to describe to someone who isn't living with it. I hope what you've experienced so far has not put you off accepting this position. We desperately need someone like yourself here.'

'So Mr Tanner told me,' said Patsy. 'But I didn't expect Mrs Smith to be living in the past quite so much.'

'I know it's confusing but at least she's harmless,' said Greg swiftly. 'She's not going to hurt you.'

'She said that she had whacked you.'

'That was when I was a kid!'

'But she's living in the past. I cannot put up with violence,' said Patsy firmly. 'My uncle was a violent man.'

'I wouldn't expect it of you,' said Greg, looking worried. 'I swear, Miss Doyle, that if she were to hurt you or the children, then I'd have to speak to David about having her put away. It's not what I want to do despite all her faults. As an apprentice ship's fitter, I appreciate my home. Besides, I couldn't leave the children.'

'Of course, I understand that,' said Patsy, feeling reassured by his words.

'Do say you'll stay, Miss Doyle.' he pleaded.

'She threatened to put Nelson in some hole.'

'That's all she can do now – threaten. Honestly, she's not strong enough to back up her words with action. Once she was but she's only a shadow of her old self now.'

'OK! I'll take your word for it.'

Greg smiled. 'Thanks.'

His smile caused her heart to flutter. 'For a trial period,' she said sensibly.

He looked disappointed. 'Thanks. I appreciate you doing so.' He paused. 'Is there anything else bothering you? Being the family solicitor David will sort out your wages and I'll make sure you have money for anything you need to buy that isn't delivered. It's a waste of time giving money to the old woman. You're really needed here, Miss Doyle.'

Patsy liked being needed especially when it was Greg speaking those words to her. The chores would be no trouble but handling the old lady and the children would be far from easy. The upside of the job would be that she would see more of this man. There was something else that made the job appealing and that was living close to the sea. She quite fancied daily walks on the sands to blow the cobwebs away.

'When do you want me to start?' she asked.

'Immediately, of course.'

'You mean right now?'

'Yes.' His smile faded. 'Do you have trouble with that?'

'No, but you'll have to square it with Mr Tanner. There's also the question of my belongings,' said Patsy.

'You write a note for David and I'll deliver it this evening and collect your stuff. Follow me and I'll show you where there's pen and paper.'

He led the way into a room where there was a three-piece suite and shelves full of books and a writing bureau. No sooner had she finished writing her letter and had handed it to Greg than she heard Helen's high-pitched voice.

'Expect me to be late for supper,' he said, pocketing the note.

'Where will I sleep?' asked Patsy.

'The only vacant bedroom is Rodney's. The kids will show you where it is.'

'But what if he were to show up?' asked Patsy.

Greg grinned. 'Doubtful, whatever the kids and the old woman might believe.' He breezed out of the room which felt suddenly very empty to Patsy.

She took a deep breath and told herself that she needed to check on the old woman. She discovered Mrs Smith had fallen asleep and, leaving her snoring gently, she followed the chatter of voices and found the children in the morning room. There was no sign of Greg so she presumed that he'd returned to work already.

'So what would you like to do for the rest of the afternoon?' asked Patsy. 'Tomorrow you'll go to school.'

She thought they looked relieved. 'You're staying, then, and looking after us and Grandma?' asked Nelson.

'Unless something happens to make me change my mind,' replied Patsy. 'Perhaps your grandmother would like to go for a walk with us.'

'Maybe she will and maybe she won't,' said Helen cautiously. 'Depends on her mood and the weather.'

The three of them gazed out of the window but the slight shower had fizzled out. 'We can wrap up warm. The fresh air will do us all good.' Patsy thought that if she took the children to the beach and ran the legs off them it would tire them out and she would have less trouble getting them to bed.

'Have you got a mummy?' asked Helen out of the blue.

Patsy shook her head. 'I'm an orphan.'

'So are we,' sighed the girl. 'I was very sad when my mummy died. She coughed up blood and went to join Daddy in Heaven.'

Her brother shifted uncomfortably on his chair. 'She doesn't really remember it happening,' he said gruffly.

'It's very sad but you have to put it behind you,' said Patsy, remembering those words being said to her on several occasions about her own parents' deaths. She knew it was easier said than done.

'I was angry,' said Nelson, his face darkening. 'I smashed a cup and a plate and Grandma was very cross. She hit me with her slipper. Did you want to smash things when your mother died?'

'Yes. But I think we've had enough of such talk. We all need cheering up, not being made miserable. Go and put on your outdoor things.'

Helen opened her mouth as if to protest but a look from her brother silenced her. Patsy washed the few dishes while the children were getting ready.

Helen entered the kitchen, tying the bobbles on her hat beneath her chin. 'I've just remembered that Grandma doesn't like us playing on the beach.'

Patsy ignored the remark. 'Have you a ball?'

'No. The last one broke a window and Grandma said that we could not have another one,' said Nelson.

'And what did your Uncle Greg say?'

Nelson grinned. 'He keeps one hidden for when he and I go out together on our own and have a kick around on the beach.'

'I'd like two balls,' said Helen forlornly.

Patsy said no more but was determined to rectify the situation. There was an expanse of garden wall that was perfect for playing two balls and she reckoned that would keep Helen happily occupied for ages when out of school.

She went to check up on Mrs Smith and found her sitting with her eyes open, gazing out on the street. 'Mrs Smith, I'm just going to take the children for a walk, would you like to come?'

The old woman's head slowly turned and she stared at Patsy. 'Who are you?'

'I'm Patsy Doyle. We met earlier. I've come to live here and help you out.'

'I don't remember anyone of that name. Let me have a closer look at you.'

Patsy knelt in front of her and the old woman peered into her face. 'You're my cousin, Joan. I remember you now. I'm glad you've come. As long as you're a real help and don't flirt with the boys.'

Patsy rolled her eyes and decided to let this case of mistaken identity pass. 'I'm glad you're glad. So what do you want to do?'

'I'll just sit here and look through the window. Will you bring me some sweets?'

'Any particular kind of sweets?' asked Patsy, thinking she had a couple of pennies in her pocket and certain the children would be happy to guide her to the nearest sweet shop.

'Toffees,' replied Mrs Smith.

'Okey dokey!'

Patsy felt much more cheerful as she ushered the children out of the house. They had brightened up when she had mentioned toffees.

The tide was out and the sands seemed to stretch for miles. As Patsy gazed across the sea she could scarcely discern the hills of Wales through the mist that was coming down over the water. But if she turned her head she could still make out the Wirral coastline. She took a deep breath of fresh air. Sand, sea and sky. There was so much space here. Her spirits rose and she had an urge to run and run. She expected the children to want to do the same and gave them the go ahead.

Nelson took off across the sands. Helen dragged her hand free and went after him. A relieved Patsy followed them, thinking how different this position was going to be from her last two. It was for certain that she was going to miss Mr Tanner but having Greg around would make up for his absence.

Patsy was not to see Greg again for hours. She had to cope with explaining to Mrs Smith who she was all over again and being told that she was her cousin Joan. She was also asked why didn't she call her Violet.

After supper Patsy supervised the children in washing their faces and hands and made a jug of cocoa. She had Helen point out to her the bedrooms and discovered that Rodney's room was between those of the two children. Violet's was at the front of the house and Greg's was at the rear. She had a quick peek inside the room allotted to her and thought it appeared slightly overcrowded but she decided to have a proper look later.

It was a while since Patsy had needed to comb the hair of a girl of Helen's age. For a moment she was reminded of the twins and how different their lives were to that of her new charge. Helen was a bit of a wriggler and Patsy had to grip her head firmly and tell her to keep still.

'I can't help but wriggle. You're hurting me,' complained the girl.

'That's because you keep pulling away,' said Patsy, reaching for a comb to use instead of the hairbrush. 'You've knots. What you need is a good bob. Then you wouldn't have half the trouble looking after your hair.'

'I told you earlier that Grandma won't let me have it cut. Can you put rags in?' asked Helen, twisting beneath Patsy's hand.

'Of course I can.'

'Good. I'd like you to do them tonight and for Sunday School.'

'OK!' Patsy combed her fingers through Helen's waist-length hair. 'Where are your rags?'

The girl got up and hurried over to a chest of drawers and removed two handfuls of different coloured strips of cloth and skipped back with them. Patsy proceeded to twist the strips through hanks of hair and tie them off. When she had finished, she lifted Helen in front of the mirror so she could gaze at her reflection. 'How do you fancy going out like that?' she said.

The girl turned her head with its stiff clumps of bound hair. 'I look daft and I bet I could knock my brother out if I swing my head in his face.'

'You might poke his eye out, so don't you do anything of the sort,' warned Patsy. 'I remember my sister, Kathleen, hitting our brother, Micky, in the face. All hell broke loose and it ended up with Mam knocking their heads together.'

'Do you miss your mother? What's it like having a sister? Is it better than having a big brother?' asked Helen, gazing at her from big blue eyes.

'I've never had a big brother, so I wouldn't know,' said Patsy. 'Now, you hop into bed while I go and see what Nelson is up to.' She waited until the girl was settled before leaving the room.

Patsy frowned as she stood outside the door. She noticed there was a skylight on the landing but at this time of year it was not much help in brightening up the dimly lit space. The single gaslight sent shadows flittering around the walls and ceiling. No wonder the old woman had mentioned ghosts. Patsy thought about Rose and how she had once lived here. When she heard footsteps, she jumped. Then she saw Nelson coming up the stairs.

'You can help me with something... have I got the right bedroom here?' She opened the central door. 'It's full of stuff.'

His eyes gleamed in the gaslight. 'Grandma doesn't allow us in there but we sneak in occasionally. She said that there were too many valuable relics that we might damage and if we touched anything we would be cursed.'

Patsy stared at him in disbelief. 'You're kidding me.'

'The cat got in and took a bite out of one of the masks. It was dead the next day.'

Patsy felt a tingling at the back of her neck. 'Coincidence,' she said.

'Haven't you ever heard of the mummy's curse? Read in the newspapers about Tutankhamun's tomb being discovered and the deaths that followed? The curse was quoted in the newspaper – *They who enter this sacred tomb shall swift be visited by wings of death,*' he recited in a hollow voice. Then he added thoughtfully, 'Doom would have been a better word than death because it rhymes with tomb.'

'Go to bed,' she said, shooing him into his bedroom, and she opened the door of the one next to it. From a pocket she took a box of matches and lit the gas lamp above the bed and turned the flame as high as it would go. She scrambled off the bed, guessing the mattress was a feather one and the sumptuous bedcover was possibly silk. It was extremely vibrant, being red, purple and orange. There was a washstand made of bamboo and the bowl and jug were of pottery and decorated with exotic-looking birds. She caught her reflection in a mirror, along with that of masks and pottery figures.

She moved some sheets and blankets onto a chair and whipped off the bedcover. She unfolded a sheet and began to make up the bed. Afterwards she checked on Violet. She found her in the kitchen washing the dishes all over again. Patsy resisted saying that she had already done that. Instead she asked, 'Would you like a cup of cocoa?'

The old woman peered at her. 'Is that you, Joan?'

Patsy did not bother trying to explain. 'Yes. Cocoa?'

'That would be nice. Have you asked the others?'

'They've had theirs.' Patsy put the kettle on and wondered when Greg would be back. She hoped he hadn't had an accident on that motorbike of his as there were often reports of such things happening.

She had just poured out the cocoa when she heard the sound of an engine and then someone whistling 'Pack up Your Troubles'. It had to be him. Her spirits lifted and she was aware that Mrs Smith had cocked her head to one side as if she was also listening to the tune.

The door opened and Greg appeared, carrying a Gladstone bag. 'Hello, Miss Doyle. Is that cocoa I can smell?'

'Yes, sir, and your supper is in the oven. Are those my things you have there?'

'Yes. Clothes, a pair of boots and slippers, some books and a writing pad and a pen, as well as a carving of a dolphin.'

Patsy almost hugged him for remembering her precious dolphin. 'Thanks! You gave Mr Tanner my note?'

'Of course. He said to tell you that he'd had a visit from Mrs Bennett and he also gave me this.' He delved into the pocket of his trousers and took out an envelope. 'He said it's a bonus for all your good work.'

Patsy opened the envelope and removed three pound notes. 'How kind of him,' she gasped. 'He really is a lovely man. He mustn't have minded my staying here and not working out my notice.'

'He's relieved. David's been really concerned about us all.'

'I had that impression when he suggested I come here,' said Patsy, pocketing the money. 'I must write and thank him. Did he say why Mrs Bennett was there? Was it to see me?'

'Yes, but it seems she had a good talk to Mr Tanner about something that was bothering her and he's going to try and sort it out for her. He's going to America,' said Greg, pouring cocoa into a mug for himself. He glanced at the old woman. 'You all right?'

Mrs Smith nodded her head several times. 'I wondered where you'd been. Have you seen Rodney?'

'Not today. He's gone away on one of his trips, remember,' said Greg smoothly. He picked up a tea towel and went over to the oven and took out his supper.

'You're not going away, though, are you?'

'No, but Mr Tanner is and he says you're not to worry.' She nodded but her expression was vague. 'I think I'll go to bed now you're in.'

'You do that. Do you need any help?'

'No, I'll be all right. Up the stairs and I turn that way,' she said, indicating with her left hand and then shuffling out of the kitchen.

Patsy looked at Greg. 'You said Mr Tanner was going to America. What about his planned visit to the war graves?'

'He's still going there but he has a client in America who wants to discuss a few things with him.'

'That's interesting.' Patsy picked up her Gladstone bag. 'I'll go up to my room, although I must admit it gives me the willies. I suppose I'll get used to it. Nelson told me there's a curse on one of the masks.'

Greg grinned. 'He's having you on but if you're worried about it we could exchange bedrooms.'

She hesitated. 'I don't want to put you to any trouble.'

'It's no trouble but I'll tell you now that mine is smaller than Rodney's but less crowded.'

'That sounds OK.' She smiled. 'I like cosy. If you tell me where the bedding is, I'll change the sheets. I've put clean ones on Rodney's already.'

Greg said, 'If you wait until I've finished supper I'll take your bag up to my room.'

'Thanks, I do appreciate you doing this. I hope you don't think I'm daft but those masks and figures are a bit scary.'

'Rosie was always scathing about them. She couldn't understand Rodney's fascination for what she called the ugly and pagan. She was made up when his letters stopped coming.'

'Do you think he could be dead?' asked Patsy.

'I think it's likely. He was what you'd call a rover. He lived to travel. When you've lived in this house as long as I have you get sick of hearing his name.'

Patsy sympathised with him. Already she'd had enough of Rodney.

Soon after they went upstairs. Patsy stood hesitantly in the doorway of Greg's bedroom and watched him begin to strip off his bed. Fresh bedding was piled on top of a chest of drawers.

'I didn't intend to put you to all this trouble,' she said. 'I could have done that but let me make up the bed.'

He glanced her way. 'OK. But I am used to looking after myself. I'll get these out of your way and then empty the drawers and wardrobe. If you don't mind I'll leave my books and everything else until tomorrow.'

'Of course. I don't want to inconvenience you,' said Patsy hastily, glancing at the bookshelf. 'You've lots of books.'

He smiled. 'Most are second-hand bought from shop libraries getting rid of them at the end of winter. I can't afford new very often but having said that I do like holding a brand-new book. Pick one out if you need help getting to sleep.'

Perhaps she would scan the titles of his books once he had gone. They were bound to tell her something more about him and she would read one of them if she had time. She offered to help him carry stuff to the other bedroom but he told her that he could manage.

'You go to bed. It must have been a tiring day for you.'

She agreed that it had been and wished him goodnight.

As she made up the bed, she hoped that Greg had truly not minded changing rooms with her. He was another, like Mr Tanner, in that he seemed to accept her for the person she was and not just the domestic. Still, she must not read into Greg's actions anything other than gratitude for her being here.

She undressed and turned out the gaslight before opening the curtains and gazing down at the darkened garden with its outhouses. She presumed the one that was not the lavatory was a wash house. She turned away and climbed into bed. As she lay there it gave her a strange feeling, thinking about Greg having slept here. She yawned and was asleep in minutes to dream that he was defending her, from a ghostly figure, with a spear that he had taken from Rodney's bedroom wall.

Chapter Twenty-Five

It was not the rain beating against her bedroom window that caused Patsy to stir on a Sunday morning a month later but the rapturous noise of church bells. She threw back the bedcovers and tumbled out of bed. She washed in cold water and dressed in haste and rushed downstairs. Helen was in the morning room, sitting at the table crunching on grape-nuts smothered in sugar and milk.

'What time is this to be getting up?' asked the girl.

'Don't speak with your mouth full,' said Patsy automatically. 'What time is it?'

'You should have looked at the grandmother clock. Although, it might have stopped again because Uncle Greg forgets to wind it up because it was always Grandma who did it.'

'Is your grandmother still in bed?'

'Probably. Did you remember to get her salt fish and put it in soak last night?' asked Helen.

Patsy nodded. She and the children were used to each other now and relaxed in the other's company. She went over to the stove and drained the water from the pan in which she had placed the salt fish. Then she filled it with fresh water and put it on the stove. Normally she would have set about clearing out the grates but Greg had been there before her and done the job and lit the fires. It wouldn't be the first time either, because she had overslept last week after being disturbed in the night by Violet Smith wandering around.

'Have you seen your Uncle Greg this morning?' she asked.

'Yes. He's gone for a walk with Nelson along the sands.'

223

'In the rain!'

'He likes the rain.'

'So do I, when I'm dressed for it and it's not freezing cold.' Patsy paused. 'Did he mention whether he'd had breakfast?'

'No, but if he had, then you'd still be able to smell the bacon,' pointed out Helen.

Patsy smiled. 'You're right. I'd best get everything ready for when he comes back. He's bound to be starving after all that exercise.'

'I think they're both daft.'

Diplomatically Patsy remained silent but she agreed, although she was getting used to Greg's liking for exercise in the fresh air. Sometimes he ran along the front and at other times he and Nelson took a ball out and had a kick around. She and Greg were also getting used to living under the same roof, although they spent little time on their own. She respected him for the way he coped with the children. He seldom raised his voice to them, and if he did need to issue warnings about their behaviour and threaten punishment, he stuck to what he said. As for the old woman, he must get exasperated with her at times, but he did not lose his temper with her either, or persist in correcting her which would only have resulted in her getting even more muddled.

As soon as the salt fish was cooked, Patsy put it on a plate with a knob of butter and a couple of slices of bread. Then, having made a pot of tea, she put all on a tray and carried it upstairs. She knocked on the door and a quavering voice told her to come in. She went inside and noticed that the curtains were open and the old woman was sitting up in bed, looking at what appeared to be a map with a magnifying glass.

'Breakfast,' called Patsy in a cheerful voice.

The old woman did not immediately look up but continued to move her finger along the map as she peered through the glass. Then she stopped and made a mark on it. 'I can smell salt fish,' she said, looking up at Patsy. 'Is it Sunday?'

'Yes. It's not a very nice day.'

'No. But it's warm in bed.'

Patsy agreed, placing the tray on the bedside table. 'That's a really pretty bed jacket you're wearing.'

'Thank you.' The old woman smiled and stroked a pink satin sleeve. 'It was a present from an admirer. My sister wants it but I said she couldn't have it because it was specially made for me.'

'Some people are really clever. My sister's good with her needle. She works in a clothes shop in Chester.'

'Chester? Where's that?'

'The other side of the Mersey close to the River Dee.'

'Rodney's ship sailed up the Mersey. When did we last see him?' She looked bewildered.

Patsy removed the map and the magnifying glass and placed the tray on the old woman's lap. 'It must have been a while ago. Is there anything more you want me to do for you?'

'No. Here's my Rodney,' said Mrs Smith, pointing out a photograph on the bedside cupboard the other side of the bed. 'He's a good-looking lad, isn't he?'

Patsy glanced at a photograph and agreed that Rodney was as handsome as his mother believed him to be. In reality she considered him no Adonis but he had a cheeky smile. She was on her way out of the room when Mrs Smith said, 'Is your bed comfortable? Do you get a good night's sleep?'

'As long as there are no bumps in the night.'

'I've seen a ghost.'

'So you've told me but I've yet to see it myself,' said Patsy.

'Well, they don't talk to everyone.'

Patsy agreed and left her to eat her breakfast.

When she reached the kitchen she found Greg and Nelson hanging their mackintoshes on the backs of chairs in front of the fire.

'You're both soaked,' she said, dismayed. 'I hope you don't catch your deaths.' She fussed around them, taking their caps and placing them on the top of the fireguard. 'What made you go out in such weather? Go and change your clothes while I make your breakfast.'

'Yes, miss,' said Greg, grinning. 'I'll tell you why we went out. There was a ship I wanted Nelson to see heading for the bar. It was the first one I ever worked on and I haven't seen her since she was launched.'

Patsy said, 'Did you ever go to sea?'

'Only the once and I was seasick. But even the best sailors can suffer from seasickness. Admiral Nelson did, but I decided that me and the sea weren't compatible.' Greg rubbed his cold hands together and turned to Nelson. 'Come on, kid, let's go upstairs and get out of these wet clothes.'

Nelson said gloomily, 'I wouldn't have minded getting wet if we'd seen the ship properly but it just loomed out of the mist for hardly any time at all and then vanished, just like the *Marie Celeste.*' On those words he walked out of the kitchen.

'Unfortunately that's true,' said Greg ruefully. 'It would have made a good scene in a film. You all right there?'

She nodded. 'You're going to have to decide what you want us to eat for Christmas and put in an order.'

Greg looked relieved. 'Am I right in assuming that by asking me that question you're planning on staying for Christmas? You've been here just over a month. Is that a long enough trial to have made up your mind you can put up with us?'

Patsy smiled. 'I think so.'

'Great.' He winked at her before following Nelson out of the room.

Patsy hummed to herself as she got on with cooking his breakfast. Despite the problems that she felt were bound to arise in the future with a confused old woman, two orphaned children and being attracted to the only man in the house, all felt right with her world. When she had the chance she would pen some Christmas letters to Joy, Kathleen, Jimmy and the twins, as well as Tilly. She felt certain that all would be interested to know how she was getting on in her new job.

Chapter Twenty-Six

Joy stretched out her legs towards the blazing fire and sighed with contentment. Since the miners had all gone back to work, coal was now plentiful and the cost of a hundredweight had slumped to only tuppence more than it had been in April.

Wendy lifted her eyes from the newspaper and smiled across at her. 'D'you want to hear the latest on the missing novelist, Mrs Christie?'

'Yes, go on,' said Joy, closing her eyes. 'It'll be something else to write about in my next letter to Tilly.'

'They have an aeroplane out looking for her as well as hounds searching on the ground.'

'Perhaps I'll wait until they find her before writing to Tilly.' Joy struggled to sit up straight but her bulk made it difficult as the baby was due in four weeks' time.

Wendy glanced at her. 'You're not worrying about Mr Tanner, are you? We don't even know if he's set sail for America yet. He could still be in France. Miserable weather for it if he's visiting the battlefields right now.'

'I gave him Tilly and Don's address in New York,' said Joy. 'If he does get in touch with them, Tilly is bound to write and let me know what she thinks of him and how they got on. By the way, I had a Christmas card and letter from Patsy. It's nice that cards have come back into fashion again.'

'How is she?'

'She can cope with the work and the children in her new job but by the sound of it the old woman is likely to get worse. Patsy will be spending Christmas there.'

'So she won't be seeing the twins and Jimmy?'

'Probably not but Christmas, generally, is a bit special in the Seamen's Orphanage with treats provided by the Friends and I don't doubt they'll put on some kind of entertainment. A panto-mime perhaps.'

'So will you be going over to Chester?' asked Wendy.

'No. Too close to my confinement. I thought I'd ask Miss Parker next door to come and eat with us.' She cocked an eye at Wendy. 'Of course, you, Grant and Elspeth might have other ideas. You might want to spend the day with your family.'

'You're my family as well,' said Wendy, smiling at her. 'And I don't think you should be standing over a hot stove on Christmas Day but let someone else do the cooking. I think it will be easier for our family to cope with our first Christmas without Uncle Robbie if we're all together.'

Joy was not sure about that but she did not want to upset Wendy by saying so. She would have preferred a quiet Christmas without Rita ready to pick her up on anything she might say that she considered out of place.

As it turned out Elspeth had other plans for Christmas and surprisingly they involved Rita. 'We Scots don't make as much fuss about Christmas as you Sassenachs do,' Grant's sister told Joy. 'But I have been asked to go and stay with my cousins up in Scotland for a holiday and they suggested I bring a friend. I know Grant and Wendy don't want to leave you alone, so I've asked Rita if she'd like to go with me. She's agreed, saying she would have found Christmas and New Year upsetting with her brother not being here.' She paused to wipe an eye. 'Besides, she said it's time her children took some of the load off her shoulders and looked after the shop for a few days while she has a break.'

Joy was delighted with the arrangement and looked forward to a reasonably quiet Christmas. As for Miss Parker next door, when Joy went round to see her, she closed the door in Joy's face and mumbled something indistinct. Joy could only presume she was going a bit senile and told herself that she must keep a closer eye on her.

Christmas Day passed pleasantly enough, although there were moments when tears threatened. Particularly when Peter played the piano as Robbie had done the Christmas before and they sang carols. Joy was glad when the day was over.

Two weeks' later her waters broke and she was delivered of a boy after five hours of intense labour. When she held her tiny son in her arms she knew that the pain and discomfort had all been worth it. She felt extremely emotional and wept that her baby would never know his father or grandparents.

When Wendy saw him for the first time her face softened. 'I want one of those. He's so perfect and has lovely thick hair just like Uncle Robbie.'

'Except it's black,' said Joy, wrapping a lock of her son's hair around her finger.

'Well, Mam will tell you that Uncle Robbie didn't always have silver hair.' Wendy smiled as she sat on the edge of the bed. 'What are you going to call him?'

'Robert, of course,' said Joy.

Tears glistened in Wendy's eyes and she leant forward and kissed Joy's cheek. 'Mam will be so glad. Is there anything you need before I go and tell her the good news?'

'I think I'll just lie here and savour the fact that I'm still alive, and so is my baby, and I can plan his christening,' said Joy.

Wendy gave her another hug. 'Prepare to be spoilt. I've telephoned Grant at the office and he says that he'll be home early.'

'Good.' Joy smiled. 'Be a love and telephone Hanny for me. As soon as I'm up and about, I'll make time to write to everyone and tell them the good news and invite them to the christening.'

'Who are you going to have for godparents?' asked Wendy.

'You and Grant and Hanny and Freddie,' said Joy positively. 'I know Rita will probably think I should ask her to be a godmother but I want Robert to have young godparents if anything should happen to me.'

'Don't talk like that,' said Wendy swiftly. 'You'll live to be a hundred.'

'Gosh, that is ancient,' responded Joy, laughing. 'Now go and do what I asked, there's a love.'

Wendy danced out of the bedroom, singing 'Rock a Bye Baby on the Tree Tops'. Joy lay back with her child in her arms and rubbed her chin gently on her son's head and thanked God all over again for a safe delivery.

The christening was arranged for the first Sunday in February after Joy had been churched and, to her relief, Rita, who had called in to see her nephew when he was only a few hours old, did not have a face as miserable as a wet Whit Sunday as Joy had feared. She bought Robert a lovely layette in blue and white and placed a half-crown in his hand. Joy thanked her, and, shortly after, the pair of them took the boy to visit Robbie's grave in Anfield Cemetery and placed flowers there. The christening had been a family affair but Joy did not forget to write and let people know that Robbie's son had made his appearance and was the spitting image of his father.

—

'Mrs Bennett's had her baby!' Patsy's grey eyes shone as she looked up from the letter that had arrived ten minutes ago.

'Who is Mrs Bennett?' asked Violet from her position in front of the fire.

'A lovely woman. Mr Tanner has met her. He called her a paragon,' said Patsy, forgetting that the old woman would have problems making sense of all this information.

'I don't know what you're talking about.' Violet stared into the fire. 'Where's Rodney?'

Patsy chose to ignore that question. Instead she read Joy's letter again. The baby was six weeks old now and had been christened last week. Robert was a bonny baby and extremely good-tempered. Patsy decided that she must visit Joy. She would buy the baby a present but first she would need to arrange her half day off when someone could keep their eye on Violet. Patsy preferred a weekday when the shops were open in town but that would mean asking one of the neighbours. If no one was willing, then it would have to be a Sunday when Greg would be off work. She was reluctant to do that because she thought he deserved to have a proper day off rather than having full responsibility for the old woman and the children.

Fortunately their next-door neighbour agreed to keep Violet company and all Patsy had to do was to square it with Greg.

'That's fine by me,' he said. 'Will you be back in time for the children getting in from school?'

Patsy nodded. 'I'll make sure I am. If I set out about ten as I've agreed with next door, then I should have plenty of time to get into Liverpool, go round the shops and pay Joy a visit. It's just a pity I missed the sales last month but I might still treat myself to something with some of Mr Tanner's money.'

Greg smiled. 'You enjoy yourself, kid. You need some time to yourself. I'm grateful for the free time you've given me by coming to work here.' He kissed her cheek and left the house.

Patsy placed the back of her hand to the spot his lips had touched and sighed, feeling all warm inside. Then she told herself sternly that it was not much of a kiss and she'd be best forgetting it.

She thought about Christmas and that she should really have found time to see Jimmy and the twins. She had received hand-made Christmas cards from them which had pleased her. She had also received a parcel from Kathy containing a pair of cotton camiknickers trimmed with pink ribbon and lace. Patsy had immediately put them away in a bottom drawer, considering that they were far too light and pretty to wear for winter everyday wear. There had been a postcard from her brother, Mick. It had come all the way from Cape Town and reassured her to his wellbeing. He was enjoying life at sea and seeing different parts of the world. But now she needed to think about what she should buy for baby Robert. She was really looking forward to seeing Joy and wondered if she had heard from Mr Tanner.

Joy looked up at the sky as she pegged out nappies and hoped that the rain would hold off. There was a nice breeze so with a bit of luck the washing should dry in a couple of hours. As she walked up the garden with the empty basket on her hip, she paused to gaze down at Robert in his pram. She could only catch a glimpse of the tip of his tiny nose and the sweep of his dark eyelashes on his cheeks because he was swathed in blankets. Her heart swelled with love. Never had she thought when she had decided that she did not want a child that, one day, her own son would wrap himself round her heart so completely. It was frightening. How would she bear it if she were ever to lose him?

She went inside the kitchen with Rex trotting at her heels and picked up the letter from the table. It was from Tilly, congratulating her on the birth of Robert but also informing her that she and Don had had the pleasure of entertaining David Tanner.

> *What a pleasant man he is and he speaks highly of you. We had a very interesting and extensive talk about the battlefields in France. He and Don really got their heads together with them both having been there during the war. He and little Ronnie also took to each other. He would make a good father but made no mention of the death of his wife and baby, so we did not do so either. Instead we talked about you and Robert. He was pleased to hear your news and I'm sure will send you his congratulations himself. He has had some luck with tracing Brendan O'Hara's sister and I'm sure he'll tell you about that, too, and that he'll be heading west to Utah.*

Joy's spirits lifted. She looked forward to hearing from David Tanner. Maybe she would receive a letter any day now. She began to slice vegetables for a nourishing soup, humming as she did so. She was still thinking of David when she was roused from her reverie by a knock on the kitchen door. A voice she recognised asked if she could come in.

Immediately Joy rushed over to the door. 'Patsy! I was wondering when I would see you. How are things in the new job?'

'I'm coping!' Patsy beamed at her. 'What a time I've had getting here. It's panto week and the students are out in force collecting money for the hospitals and up to all kinds of stunts.'

'I did hear that they had kidnapped someone from the Adelphi Hotel and were holding him to ransom,' said Joy.

'I suppose it's all for a good cause.' Patsy paused. 'You do look well. Thinner but it suits you. I hope that gorgeous little boy outside isn't running you into the ground? I had a peek at him. What lovely eyelashes! He's going to slay all the girls when he grows up.'

Joy smiled. 'I don't want to even think that far ahead. I want to enjoy every moment of his development.' She seized Patsy by the shoulders. 'You look well, too, love. It must be all the sea breezes in Seaforth.'

'At this time of year they might bring colour to my cheeks but they also freeze your socks off.'

'Sit over here by the fire,' said Joy, ushering her to a chair. 'I've just received a letter from Tilly and she mentions Mr Tanner.'

'Is he OK?' asked Patsy. 'We haven't heard from him. I admit I do have a soft spot for Mr Tanner and worry that he's lonely.'

'He's fine, according to Tilly. He and Don had a long chat about the battlefields in France.'

Patsy sighed. 'I would love to see Tilly again. I suppose I'll just have to carry on making do with her letters and hearing about her when Mr Tanner comes home. Did he say whether he would be home soon?'

'No, he's not coming home yet but heading west.'

Patsy looked thoughtful. 'I wonder if he's searching for Rodney Smith.'

'I don't know about that but I do know he's on a mission for me,' said Joy, smiling. 'I'm looking forward to hearing about his adventures when he returns to Liverpool.'

Patsy gave her a keen look but kept quiet. They brought each other up to date with their latest news and Patsy asked Joy had she heard anything from her family in Chester about Kathleen.

'Nothing for you to worry about. She seems to be getting on OK over there, although I don't think it's news to you that she and Flora rub each other up the wrong way.'

Patsy grimaced. 'I hope our Kathy isn't getting too cocky. She can be, you know. She might forget that she's the hired help. I don't want her getting slung out on her ear.'

'I can't see that happening,' said Joy seriously. 'I think Alice would miss her if she was to leave. Kathy is the assistant that she wanted.'

'Anyone mentioned anything about her and fellas?'

'I doubt your sister has much time for flirting,' said Joy tactfully, deciding not to mention what Flora had ranted about last summer.

'Good,' said Patsy, relieved. 'When the weather gets better I'll see if I can take the kids to Chester for a day out.' She reached for her bag. 'I bought something for the baby. I hope it fits.' She handed the package over.

Joy opened it to reveal a baby outfit in primrose and white with several baby bunnies embroidered on the yoke. 'Now, that is nice and clean-looking and he should grow into by Easter and still get plenty of wear out of it during the summer.' She smiled across at Patsy. 'You really shouldn't be spending the little money you get on presents but I do appreciate it.'

Patsy flushed with pleasure. 'I enjoyed buying something for the baby.' She paused. 'I've heard from our Mick, so he hasn't forgotten me. I hope he thought on and sent postcards to the others, too.'

Joy smiled. 'Perhaps you'd like me to visit the orphanage and check on Jimmy and the twins this Saturday and ask if they've heard from Mick. It's easy enough for me to do so being so close.'

Patsy thanked her. 'I'd like to have seen them now, but what with it being a weekday, I wouldn't be allowed.'

'Don't worry. I'll do it.'

Patsy thanked her and soon after she had to leave to get to Seaforth in time for the children coming home from school.

That evening Joy was having supper with Wendy and Grant and she told them about Patsy's visit and their conversation. Wendy immediately said something that sent a chill through Joy.

'You haven't been reading the newspaper, have you? You're best staying away from the orphanage and people in general for that matter. There's a lot of flu around and the *Echo* says that Liverpool has the highest rate of five-year-old children being affected. The death rate is rising. You can't risk catching it yourself and passing it on to Robert. The young and the elderly are the most vulnerable but anyone can catch it.'

'Oh my goodness! I'm glad you told me,' said Joy, sick with fright. 'What can I do to protect Robert?'

'Whatever you do don't let anyone breathe over him and definitely no kissing, even from us,' said Wendy. 'The flu can spread like wildfire. I just hope that Patsy hasn't brought it here from those two children in her charge.'

Joy went deathly pale. 'Don't say that.'

'Did she nurse him?'

'No. He was in his pram. She did have a peek at him.'

'Did she seem all right?'

'As fit as a fiddle.'

Wendy relaxed. 'Then there's probably no need to worry. Just you keep him away from people. Best if you both stay in. Any shopping you need I can deal with it.'

'What about you catching it?' asked Joy. 'And what about old Miss Parker next door? I was going to check up on her.'

'I'll do that,' said Wendy. 'And I'll keep my distance from both you and Robert just in case she should be carrying anything. Although, she seldom goes out, does she?'

'No.' Joy was thoughtful. 'Perhaps you should make sure that your mouth and nose are covered by a scarf, so you don't catch anything.'

Wendy thought that was a good idea and decided to do exactly that and not to get too close to people. She did call on Miss Parker but did not get an answer. Even when she went round the back and tried the kitchen door she found it locked. She returned to the house, wearing a worried expression. 'I don't know whether she's just not answering or too ill to get to the door,' she said to Grant and Joy.

He suggested that she should try again tomorrow.

But when tomorrow came, Wendy forgot all about Miss Parker because word came via her sister that their mother had gone down with the flu. 'I could do with your help in the shop,' said Minnie. 'Either that or you can nurse Mam.'

Wendy looked at Grant. 'I'm not sure which is the better of two evils. I could catch it from Mam and bring it back here or catch it from someone in the shop.'

Grant's expression was dour. 'If you work in the shop you'll be mixing with all sorts as you've done in the past.'

'But I never even caught the common cold then,' said Wendy. 'Perhaps I'm one of those people who just don't succumb to infections.'

'You can't take chances,' said Grant. 'If you decide to nurse your mother, then you're going to have to wear a mask of sorts. The way these diseases spread must have something to do with people coughing and sneezing all over the place. It must fly through the air right up our noses or into our mouths. If you can stop that, then hopefully you'll be OK and Joy will allow you back into the house. I want you home at night but we'd have to make sure you didn't bump into Joy and Robert.'

Wendy's eyes flew wide. 'What about Elspeth? She's friendly with Mam. One of us is going to have to warn Joy.'

'Leave it to me,' said Grant.

Joy took the news that the flu might have already crept sneakily into her home as to be expected. She panicked. 'What am I going to do?'

'Joy, you're normally a sensible woman so stay calm,' ordered Grant.

'But I'm not sensible where Robert is concerned,' she wailed.

'You're not going to help him if you start acting hysterical. Keep him away from any risk and that's all you can do,' said Grant.

Joy nodded and resisted reminding him about how many people had died of influenza just after the war. She must heed Grant's words and hope and pray that they would not succumb to this terrible disease.

It came as quite a shock when Rita died. Elspeth was the most distraught of them all. Their friendship had been an unlikely one but they had become friends since Wendy and Grant's wedding.

'I never thought Mam would succumb to it,' said Wendy in a shaky voice to Joy. 'She always seemed the sort to survive.'

'I know what you mean,' said Joy, wanting to hug her but scared she just might be infectious. 'Her manner could frighten people off, so we all thought that she could do that with the flu.'

A funeral was arranged, but before it could take place, a white-faced Wendy surprised Joy by arriving in the kitchen and placing a brown envelope on the table. 'You'll never guess what's in that,' she said.

'What?' asked Joy.

'Uncle Robbie's shares. Mam must have found it when she was rooting in your sideboard the day he died.' Wendy looked stricken. 'I don't want to believe she could do this. She knew how important these shares were to you and must have been aware of Uncle Robbie investing in the mine before we were. It has to be pure spite that she did this to you.'

Joy opened the envelope and gazed at the sheets of paper. 'I thought she'd forgiven me when Robert was born. Maybe she just forgot about it.'

'How can you make excuses for her?' asked Wendy in a trembling voice.

'I don't want to be angry with her. What's the point? She's dead now,' murmured Joy.

Tears glistened in Wendy's eyes but she blinked them back. 'You're nicer than I am. What will you do? Will you inform Mr Tanner?'

'I can inform Tilly. She might know where he is,' said Joy, thinking how disappointed she was that she had not heard from him.

There was a typewritten letter enclosed with the certificate and she put both back in the envelope and placed it on the dresser. 'I'll have a proper look at those later. There's more important things to think about right now.'

'The funeral,' said Wendy. 'It's probably best if you stay at home. You can't risk catching the flu from someone else.'

That evening, after Joy had put Robert to bed, she opened the brown envelope and discovered that the silver mine was definitely in Utah. Joy decided to waste no time in writing to Tilly, informing her and hoping that David Tanner would get in touch with her.

–

It was to be well into March before the numbers of those who had died from the flu began to fall. At its height, a hundred and thirty-three people a week died in Liverpool alone. The fact that it was getting close to the anniversary of Robbie's death made it all the more difficult for the family to cope with that period in their lives but at least they could be thankful that little Robert did not catch the flu.

Elspeth did succumb to what appeared at first to be that dreaded disease but her symptoms were not so severe that she needed to take to her bed. But she was depressed during the month that followed Rita's death and made the decision to leave

Liverpool. Her cousins in Scotland were willing to have her live with them for an indefinite period.

Joy decided that, once the first anniversary of Robbie's death was passed, then she would put all the ills and misery of winter behind her and look forward to the spring.

It was when she was cutting daffodils in the garden for the house that she told herself that she must remember to check up on Miss Parker again that week. She had looked pale and drawn last time she had seen her but had not allowed Joy into the house. She wasted no time in going round and knocking next door. Receiving no answer she went round to the back of the house. The door was locked and she came to the decision that she would watch out for the bobby on the beat and tell him that she was a bit worried about Miss Parker.

When he hovered into view, Joy hurried out to speak to him. He listened attentively and then went with her to the back of the house and forced an entry. Joy waited outside. It was not long before he emerged from the house and she could tell from his face that it was as she had feared. The old woman was dead. He used Joy's telephone to send for an ambulance and then left to wait next door until it arrived.

Joy wondered what would happen to the house. No doubt they would discover that in the months to come. In the meantime she determined to enjoy spring and summer now that her fears for her son's safety had abated. There was also the comfort of knowing the share certificate had been found.

In the days that followed she hoped each morning to discover a letter from David Tanner on her doormat but she heard only from Tilly, expressing her relief that the share certificate had been found and saying that she'd had no news from David Tanner.

Joy did not know what to do about it all and in the end knew the best thing to do would be to put it out of her mind and concentrate on something else. She decided that with Elspeth gone she would advertise for a couple more lodgers and broached the subject with Wendy.

'It's your house, Aunt Joy,' she said. 'You must do what you think is best.'

With that assurance, Joy went ahead with her plan and placed an advertisement in the Liverpool *Echo*.

Chapter Twenty-Seven

Joy was amazed by the swift response her advertisement brought during the week that followed. Fortunately her would-be lodgers did not all arrive at the same time. Showing the first woman around proved a waste of time because she was not prepared to share the bathroom and lavatory when she heard that there was a man living in the house. This despite Joy explaining that he had a wife and was perfectly respectable.

Her next visitor was an elderly man, newly widowed and wanting three meals a day included in the price she was asking for the room. She turned him down. The second woman, a Mrs Sanderson, was a widow in her thirties with a boy of ten. She had two jobs, one cleaning a couple of offices during the evenings and also as a part-time waitress from eleven till two during the day. Joy took an immediate liking to her because she told her frankly that the reason they'd had to leave their last lodgings was because her son had inherited his father's fiddle and needed to practise to get a decent tune out of it. Joy offered her not only a large bedroom overlooking the garden but also the use of the outhouse where the boy could play his music in peace. She felt that Robbie would have approved of her actions.

It was not until the Friday that another man called at the house. He appeared to be in his late forties and told her that his name was William Donavan. One of his eyelids twitched and instantly Joy diagnosed nerve trouble as a result of the war. She could only offer him the smallest bedroom at the top of the house but he expressed his gratitude. She wondered if his situation was desperate but at least could reassure him that, although the room might be small, it did receive some sun all the year round.

She asked for a month's rent in advance and both Mrs Sanderson and Mr Donavan handed over the sum without hesitation. As they were not to have the use of the kitchen, she seriously considered cooking breakfast for them. It was what her mother had done when she had taken in lodgers, and that was in addition to offering Sunday lunch for a little extra money, but she decided to wait and see how they all got on.

'So what do you know about your new lodgers?' asked Wendy shortly after she arrived home on the day Mr Donavan moved in.

'Not a lot,' replied Joy. 'I gave in to my gut feelings.'

Grant shook his head when he heard what Joy had done and said she should have checked their credentials but she stuck by her decision. 'I remember Mother telling me that my grandmother took in my father when he was newly arrived from Scotland and she was a widow with a daughter.'

'So your father married the daughter of the house,' said Wendy.

'Yes. Mother was a few years older than Dah and a strong-minded woman. Poor Mr Donavan has obviously suffered from shell shock in my opinion because his eyelid twitches.'

'Poor man,' said Wendy. 'I wonder what his occupation is.'

'He was able to pay a month's rent in advance and his clothes are serviceable, if not the best quality, so he obviously isn't on his uppers.'

'At least if he goes out every morning and doesn't come in until evening that'll go some way to proving he has a regular job,' said Grant.

'At least I don't need to be a detective to work out that Mr Donavan does have Irish blood with a name like his,' said Joy. 'I'm just relieved to be having some extra money coming in, although it's not easy living with strangers, and truthfully, if I didn't need to, then I wouldn't have let out the rooms. Fingers crossed it all works out.'

In the weeks that followed, Joy's lodgers appeared to be settling in without any difficulty. Mr Donavan left the house most mornings about six, without taking breakfast, and arrived back about three. Some days he went out about ten and came home at nine in the evening. When Grant asked him what he did for a living, he answered that he worked in the kitchen of a hotel and had his meals there.

'Truthfully, Joy, I thought he seemed vaguely familiar but I can't remember where I've seen him before.'

'Does it matter?' asked Joy.

'I suppose not but for my own satisfaction I'd like to place him.'

Joy could understand that but did not think it was anything to worry about.

Mrs Sanderson asked Joy would she be prepared to go halfy-halfy with a small two-ringed gas cooker that she could have in her room. Joy agreed. After six weeks she offered a cooked Sunday lunch to both her new lodgers for an extra sixpence a week. Mr Donavan accepted her offer but Mrs Sanderson declined. Once the weather improved, she and her son had started to go out on Sunday.

Joy had still had no news from David Tanner and she was getting impatient. But at least William Donavan was being of help and offered to chop some of the logs into kindling for her. She liked him the better for it.

A week later she caught him whittling with a sharp blade at a piece of wood. It was taking on what looked like an interesting shape but he would not tell her what it was going to be. He only smiled and told her it was a surprise. Then he asked her how long the house next door had been empty and who owned it.

'A Mr Parker used to live there but he disappeared a few years ago. There was a scandal attached to his name and no one knows where he went afterwards. Until quite recently, the house was occupied by an elderly relative of his who died. I'm surprised a *For Sale* notice hasn't gone up yet. Naturally, I'll be interested to see who buys it. Someone who'll be a good neighbour, I hope.'

'I agree that you can't have too many good neighbours,' said Mr Donavan. 'Ones who'll give you a helping hand and keep an eye on the place when you go away.'

A few days later, when Joy was doing some gardening, she thought she heard noise coming from next door. She took a bucket and placed it upside down by the fence. Climbing up on it, she peered over into next door's garden. She caught a glimpse of a man walking up and down and his gait seemed vaguely familiar, as did the back of his head. When the man turned round, she saw that it was a sunburnt David Tanner.

'My goodness! Mr Tanner!' she exclaimed.

David glanced up and his lean features showed no surprise. 'Mrs Bennett, I was coming to visit you.'

'Why didn't you write to me?' she blurted out. 'And what are you doing in that garden?'

'I've been having a look round the house and now I'm looking at the garden and have come to the conclusion both need a lot of work.'

Joy could not help but think that he must be considering buying the property. 'But how did you hear about it being empty? I haven't seen it advertised in the *Echo*. When did you arrive back in England?'

'Only a couple of days ago. This house belongs to one of my clients,' said David.

One of his clients! Joy slipped and let out a cry as she fell off the bucket.

'Mrs Bennett!' shouted David.

Joy could only groan for she had narrowly missed landing on a rose bush but she had caught her hand on a thorny branch and it hurt like billy-o. She was struggling to get up when David appeared beside her. He dragged her upright and asked if she was all right.

'No, I'm not,' she said, wincing as she gazed at her hand.

'That must really hurt.' David took hold of her wrist and carefully drew out a couple of thorns that had ripped the skin at the side of her hand.

'I feel a bit faint,' she whispered and sagged against him.

David hastily put an arm around her waist. 'Here, let me help you inside.'

She allowed him to half carry her towards the house and all the time the thought was buzzing in her head that he could not possibly be Leonard Parker's solicitor.

David glanced at the sleeping baby in the pram and then at Joy's shuttered face as he helped her up the step and into the kitchen. He lowered her into a chair and then carefully went down on one knee so their faces were on a level. 'Are you feeling better now?'

Her eyes opened and gazed into his with a puzzled expression. 'Frankly no. My hand is still hurting but what's really bothering me is your saying that you have a client who owns next door. Why did you never mention that to me?'

'I saw no need. Mr Parker was a client of my father. I inherited him when I took over the business but it was only late last year that he got in touch with me.' David got up from his knee with difficulty and pulled up a chair and sat opposite her.

Joy could not take her eyes from his lean serious face. 'We are talking about Leonard Parker?'

'Yes.'

She drew in her breath with a hiss. 'Do you know that *he* is a thief and a murderer?'

David's expression was wary. 'Allegedly.'

'Allegedly!' She could not ignore the pain in her hand any longer and stood up and went over to the sink. 'I don't want to believe that you're involved with him.'

'I'm not here to talk about him,' said David, an edge to his voice. 'But about your shares.'

'You never wrote to me and you didn't even respond to the information I sent to Tilly, so why should I now think that my shares are important to you?' She felt angry, hurt and disappointed.

'I knew nothing about your letter until I returned to New York and saw Don and Tilly again,' he explained. 'The discovery of the share certificate was the best news you could have given me. When I arrived in Utah it was to discover that Mrs McIntyre was dead.'

'Dead!' Joy turned the tap on too far and cold water gushed out onto her damaged hand, causing her to yelp.

'Are you all right?' asked David, getting to his feet.

'Yes!' she snapped.

'I don't believe you. That hand is sore and I feel it is my fault.'

'Of course it's your fault. You gave me a shock turning up in next door's garden and informing me that Leonard Parker is a client of yours.' She gritted her teeth against the pain. 'And then to blurt out that Mrs McIntyre was dead...'

'Let's not discuss Parker but what I decided to do when I heard that the share certificate had been found.'

'Is it due to client confidentiality that you won't discuss him?' asked Joy. 'I don't think you know the kind of man you're dealing with.'

David's tanned features tightened. 'I find that remark insulting. I can't understand why you are letting yourself get all worked up about Leonard Parker. He didn't steal from you or hurt any of your relatives, did he?'

The colour rose in Joy's cheeks. 'That might be true but—'

'It was Parker who gave me Mrs McIntyre's address in Utah.'

Joy's jaw dropped. 'You mean he knew her?'

'Yes! He'd bought shares in the mine from her.'

'I can't believe it!' Joy realised the tap was still running and hastily turned it off. 'How did Mrs McIntyre die? Perhaps he had something to do with it?'

'I can't see how he could when he was thousands of miles away,' said David with asperity. 'The mining office in Utah was torched and she died in the fire. Most of the paperwork was destroyed. Her cousins were not prepared to accept my word about O'Hara having received money from your husband without proof.' His grey eyes were steely. 'I explained the situation but, although they were sympathetic, they stuck to their guns. You can imagine how I felt but I couldn't blame them for behaving like businessmen. Mining is a tough business with a lot of money to be made or lost. The work takes place in a harsh terrain and it made me appreciate the early pioneers and their courage even more.'

'*The Covered Wagon* and *The Iron Horse*,' said Joy automatically.

David nodded. 'The coming of the railway made a tremendous difference. People are still prepared to emigrate westwards. I liked the country but I haven't got the stomach to live there.' He paused. 'Now, are you prepared to listen to what I did, once I knew the share certificate was found?'

Joy took a clean dishcloth from a drawer and stared at him as she carefully dried her hand. She could not help but be fascinated by what he had said so far but was still disturbed that he was Parker's solicitor. 'Go on.'

'I wrote to them suggesting that when next one of their representatives comes to England they see the certificate for themselves. I was not prepared to let it out of our possession.'

Joy could see the sense in that but wondered when and if one of their representatives would bother coming to England if they already had their money. 'The letter enclosed with the certificate has O'Hara's signature on it. They just want to hold on to the money,' she said.

'I wouldn't deny it,' said David. 'But with the certificate found they'll have to return your investment to you. Either that or you hang on to those shares. As your solicitor, I would certainly advise you to consider keeping some of them.'

'I didn't know you were my solicitor. I told you that I couldn't afford to pay you a fee.'

'I never asked for one. I was prepared to help you because you were in a difficult situation and also a friend to Patsy. I could put the certificate and letter in the office safe. If your husband had involved his solicitor, then I doubt they'd have gone missing.'

Joy thought it was for certain that Rita would never have got her hands on them. 'I wouldn't argue with what you say.'

'The shares are valuable and ownership will need to be transferred to you. You'll also have to produce proof you are Robbie's widow.'

Joy decided she needed to think more about David Tanner being her solicitor. As much as she was attracted to him, she did not like the idea of sharing him with Leonard Parker, amongst others. But there was information she still needed. 'When you say the shares are valuable, how much money are we talking about?'

'I can't name a definite sum. Values of shares can go up and down. What I can tell you is that your shares could be worth a lot more in the future so it would be worth your while holding on to them.'

'But I could do with the money now. I've taken in a couple of extra lodgers to boost my income but it's not an ideal situation.'

He frowned. 'Did you vet these lodgers?'

The muscles of Joy's face tightened. 'You're as bad as Grant. He said I should have looked into their backgrounds. I believe that I'm a good judge of character, the same as you. Besides, I haven't anything to steal if you're hinting they could be thieves.'

'OK! Never mind that right now,' said David, leaning forward. 'I saw the site of the mine. The seams of silver near the surface have all been worked but there are seams deeper below the surface which require specialist equipment to extract it. But there's also a possibility that there's a vein of another important metal on the land owned by the company.'

She could not conceal her interest. 'What is it? Gold?'

He smiled. 'No. It's pitchblende which is a source of uranium.'

Joy frowned. 'I haven't heard of it. What's so important about it?'

'Uranium contains radium which is radioactive. It was discovered not so long ago by a married couple, Pierre and Marie Curie, that cancer can be treated with radium.'

Joy remembered her father's suffering and her expression altered. 'I do remember mention of it, and if one day it could really cure cancer, then I'd like to have a part in helping with that cure. I nursed my father when he had cancer.'

'I don't know all the details and I should imagine it's purely in the experimental stages. I haven't had the opportunity to look into it at any depth. But by the sound of it, I reckon there could be a great demand for it in the future if it does do the trick.' David was watching her face. 'But, of course, if you need the money I could buy your shares. You could name your price.'

Joy's brown eyes held his gaze steady. 'Explain how shares work to me.'

'When there's a profit during the year you'll receive dividends from your shares.'

'So I don't have to sell them to have an income?'

'No. But it all depends on whether the company makes a profit.'

Joy thought about that and guessed that Robbie's intention had been to provide her with an ongoing income. Then she thought of Robert and suddenly it struck her that, if she hung on to the shares, once they were transferred she could leave them to him. 'I think I'll hang on to them and one day they'll be my son's. He'll be able to think of them as his inheritance from the father he never knew.'

There was a hint of pain in David's smile. 'I think that's a good idea. If you'll fetch the certificate and letter I'll put it in the office safe for you.'

Joy made no move to do as he suggested. 'I still have difficulty dealing with the idea that you also represent Leonard Parker. I suppose you didn't read your father's case notes about him?'

David frowned. 'There are no case notes in my father's files. Parker told me about the accusations himself. He said that he was never taken to court because the police had no evidence of his being involved in the crime some believe he committed. He says he's innocent.'

Joy raised a hand and then let it drop and said wearily, 'He's only giving you his version of the truth. He disappeared before the police could catch him. They raided the house next door but he ran away. He's a thief and a murderer.'

'Allegedly,' said David sharply.

'I don't know how you can defend him! He buried the man he murdered in our garden.'

'He said that was an accident and he panicked.'

Joy made a humphing noise. 'What I can't understand is how he could still own the house, once it was known he was a criminal.'

David said patiently, 'He was never convicted, so his slate is clean. Haven't you ever heard of being innocent until proven guilty?'

'Of course I have! But surely the fact that he ran away is convincing evidence of his guilt?'

'It could also be proof that being an innocent man he panicked.'

A sharp laugh escaped Joy. 'He panicked all right. How can you represent him?'

'You make it sound as if I'm about to defend him in a murder trial in the high court!' said David, exasperated. 'But I have to admit that you've given me some cause to doubt him now.'

'Good!' Joy was relieved. 'I know he can be totally convincing.' She put on the kettle. 'Cup of tea?'

'Thanks.'

'Would you like something to eat?'

'If it's a slice of your home-made cake, I wouldn't say no.' David watched her as she moved around the kitchen from stove to table to cupboard.

She glanced at him and thought he looked fed up and tired. Impulsively she said, 'I'm sorry. You must hate me for bringing all this up when you put in so much time trying to help me.'

David's expression changed. 'I don't hate you. I'm only involved with Parker in as much as I'm dealing with the sale of the house next door. After that our connection will end naturally.'

Joy nodded. 'I do appreciate all that you've done. I wish I could pay you a fee.'

David shook his head. 'There's no need for that. I did it for you as a friend.'

Joy placed a slice of cake on a plate besides his cup and saucer. 'Thank you. Maybe leaving money invested for Robert's future might prove a mistake but I'm touching wood and keeping my fingers crossed.'

David was silent as he drank his tea and ate his cake. 'If you need to increase your income have you ever thought of hiring yourself out as a part-time caterer?'

Joy smiled. 'You've been listening to Patsy too much but I'll bear in mind what you've said, Mr Tanner.'

Before either could say anything further there came a whimper and the sound of the pram being joggled. Joy went outside and reappeared a few moments later with Robert balanced on her hip. He was sucking his fist and stared at the man from thickly lashed brown eyes. David returned his regard and Joy would have had to be blind not to recognise the yearning in the man's eyes as he looked at her child. She felt deeply sympathetic towards him.

'Is he like his father?' asked David.

'I never knew Robbie when he was young, but yes, he has his hair and the occasional expression. Sadly his sister, Rita, died earlier this year. She was someone who could have talked to Robert about what his father was like when he was just a lad.'

'What a shame.' From a pocket David took out his wallet and extracted a banknote. Reaching for Robert's free hand he rolled up the note and placed it in his fist.

Joy felt embarrassed. 'There's really no need for you to feel that you have to give him anything.'

David frowned. 'Don't spoil my pleasure.'

'In that case Robert says thank you,' said Joy.

David gazed at her from unfathomable eyes. 'I can see this young man is hungry. Time for me to leave.'

Before she could prevent him, he left.

Joy gazed after him, remembering the little that Rose Tanner had said about the war injuries that had caused his impotence, and felt a surge of anger towards the dead woman. Then she sighed and removed the banknote from Robert's fist. Her eyes widened when she saw it was a five-pound note. Riches! It would buy her son a decent pair of shoes once he started walking, and more. Maybe there might even be enough over to go into his piggy bank. Her mother had always said that it was never too early to start saving. Thank you, David.

Chapter Twenty-Eight

'Come on, kids! Come on, Patsy!' Greg hurried them out of the house to the passageway at the bottom of the garden where his motorbike and the sidecar he had borrowed were parked. Helen was still sleepy because it was only five o'clock in the morning but a total solar eclipse was expected and it would only last a brief time. They were leaving Mrs Smith asleep in bed.

Patsy was aware of a rush of excitement as she helped Helen into the sidecar. She strapped on the leather helmet Greg had handed her before accepting his assistance to climb onto the pillion seat.

'You're going to have to cling on to me,' he ordered. 'Don't want you sliding off backwards as we start off.'

'Yes, sir! I hope we get there in time,' said Patsy.

'The roads are bound to be busy,' warned Greg. He was about to draw down his goggles but paused to look up at the early summer sky. For days there had been discussions about whether they'd get a clear view or whether cloud would obscure the eclipse. But even if that happened, it was still going to be really eerie because it was expected that day would be turned into night for a few short seconds as the moon's shadow obliterated the sun. He was glad to be sharing it with Patsy and would have preferred it if they could have had this time alone. But he had to consider the kids and, besides, how often did an eclipse come along?

The engine roared into life, shattering the peace of the garden. With a whirr of wings several pigeons flew into the air.

Patsy clasped her hands firmly together against Greg's chest as he guided the vehicle out into the road. She was filled with happiness. They made their way to Little Crosby, a village of sandstone cottages with pretty gardens, and then went along country lanes until eventually they came out further along the Liverpool-Southport Road. It was really thrilling, roaring along the road with the hedgerows flying by so early that June morning. Patsy was aware that this was one of those moments in life which she would always associate with having an excellent excuse to snuggle up close to Greg. She was determined to enjoy herself. It was just a pity it was a weekday because otherwise they could have spent the rest of the day in Southport.

There were already crowds of people and motors parked near the sand dunes and on the beach when they arrived at their destination. Without too much difficulty Greg managed to find a place to park his vehicle that would give them an unobstructed view of the shortly expected eclipse.

Helen was shivering, but whether that was excitement or due to the chill of early morning, Patsy was unsure. Unfortunately there was a fair amount of cloud about but as she hugged the girl close, watching the sky and half listening to Greg talking to Nelson about what was about to happen, she thought how patient he was with the children. He understood about a child's need for trust and to feel secure. Their need, in particular, for a father figure. She considered the difficulties so many widows would have bringing up their children single-handed. She thought of her own tragic mother and father, only to be interrupted by a cry of, 'Here it comes!'

Greg reached out and gripped Patsy's free hand and she moved a fraction closer to him as the sky began to darken. It was really eerie as shadows began to cross the landscape and then darkness fell and there was a hush. She held her breath as she thrilled to feel the clasp of his fingers around hers at the sight of this natural phenomenon. But it did not last very long. It grew light and Nelson and Helen let out a cheer.

Greg and Patsy laughed. 'Quite a way to come for such a brief experience but worth it,' she said.

'In olden days they would have said it forewarned the people that the end of the world was nigh,' said Greg in a hollow voice.

'It makes you wonder who you'd like to spend those last minutes with if it was the end of the world,' mused Patsy.

'And doing just what?' asked Greg, gazing into her eyes.

Then he pressed his lips against hers just for a brief moment. Yet it was long enough to leave her lips tingling and to send a thrill through her. She did not know how to react and he must have realised that because he squeezed her hand and then released it. 'Come on, we're going to have to make a move if we don't want the old woman waking up before we get back.'

She agreed.

On the return journey Patsy clung to him on the back of the motorbike, not for the first time wondering what to make of his actions. Could she read anything of his intentions into that short kiss? Was there a future for them together? Despite his saying that first day last November that he did not pay her wages, she still felt at times that he was her boss and superior to her. How could there possibly be marriage in his mind? What would happen when the old woman died? She no longer talked as much as she used to do and was becoming incontinent which was a real bind. Rodney figured less and less in what she did have to say. It was as if she was forgetting more and more all that she had known. Patsy knew that the time was coming when a decision was going to have to be made concerning Violet Smith.

That decision was to be made sooner than Patsy had thought. They arrived back at the house to discover that the old woman was not in her bed. They searched the house from top to bottom and the outhouses, too, without any success. It was a harassed-looking Greg who made the decision for them to split up and comb the nearby streets, even going as far as the army barracks. This needed to be done before the roads became really busy with people going to work.

They had no success.

Helen suggested to Patsy that they try the beach.

'But she never went on the sands,' said Patsy.

'She used to go sometimes before you came,' said Nelson. 'She was looking for Rodney's ship.'

Patsy and Greg exchanged looks. 'But she scarcely mentions Rodney these days,' said Patsy. 'I reckon she could have gone to the shops for toffees. Perhaps I should go and look for her while you go to work, Greg.'

Greg shook his head. 'I'm not going anywhere until we find her. But the kids can get ready and go to school.'

'No,' cried Helen, tugging on his arm. 'I want to help find her.'

'OK! We all carry on looking for her. I suppose the more pairs of eyes we have the better,' he said.

'We should enlist the neighbours,' said Patsy.

'I didn't consider them,' said Greg, his eyes lightening.

'And what about the police?' asked Nelson. 'They find missing persons.'

It was decided that Patsy would alert the neighbours and Greg go to the police station.

'Me and Helen will go to the beach,' said Nelson.

'No,' said Greg, frowning. 'I'm not certain if the tide is coming in or going out and I'd rather not risk you getting trapped on a sandbank or in one of the gullies. I'd feel happier if you were in school.'

Nelson groaned. 'But we'll miss all the excitement.'

Greg gave him an exasperated look. 'Just do as you're told and take Helen with you.'

Nelson succumbed but he was obviously not happy about it.

With the children on their way to school and the neighbours alerted and the police informed, Greg and Patsy set out for the beach, looking in certain shops on the way.

Greg and Patsy walked in a parallel line several yards from each other, looking this way and that as their eyes scanned the expanse of beach. The tide was going out and there were pools of water in the ridged sand. Greg had chosen to walk nearest to the sea and it was he who spotted the old woman first. He shouted to Patsy and began to run. She followed him and, as she drew closer, realised that Violet was in real difficulties. She was up to her thighs in soft, wet sand. Even as Patsy watched, she saw her topple over onto her face. The girl let out a cry but by then Greg had almost reached the old woman.

He plunged in to the sand up to his ankles and then his knees and halfway up to his thighs before he managed to grab hold of the old woman's shoulder and heave her upright. She flayed her arms about and then fell against him. For a moment Patsy was convinced that he was in danger of falling backwards himself with her on top of him. But with an enormous amount of effort he managed to keep his balance. Then Patsy reached the edge of what she saw was blackened oozing mud and sand.

'Don't come any closer!' warned Greg. 'Just see if you can reach out and grab hold of her arm if I push her towards you.'

Patsy's heart was pounding as she attempted to do what he asked. Stretching out as far as she was able, she managed to seize hold of Violet's wrist. She pulled with all her might and the old woman screamed but Patsy did not let go. With Greg pushing and Patsy pulling, they managed to get her onto firmer ground. Once there, she lay muttering and moaning on the sand.

Patsy turned to Greg and held out her hand but he could not reach it unless he stretched himself out on the surface of the treacherous patch. If he did that she feared he might sink into it. 'Wait, wait,' she cried, removing the belt from her frock.

She flung an end towards him. He seized hold of it and, with Patsy heaving on one end, managed to drag himself out. Panting, he knelt with his hands on his knees gazing at her. 'Thanks,' he managed to say at last.

'Are you OK?' she asked anxiously.

'I've felt better.' He gave her a lopsided grin. 'We make a good team.'

She gave a relieved smile. 'Do you want to rest or shall we start making tracks right away? You'll need a bath and a change and so will she.'

They both looked down at Violet and between them they lifted her to her feet. She was smeared in mud and sand and smelt terribly.

'Let's get her home,' said Greg with a sigh.

They wasted no time in doing so, and by the time they reached the house, Patsy was almost as filthy as the other two. They went in the back way. 'I'll fill the boiler in the wash house,' said Patsy, 'and once the water is hot enough I'll take down the bath from the wall and fill it.'

'You'll do nothing of the sort,' said Greg, staying her hand. 'I'm going to have to strip off in the wash house. If you'll fetch my other set of working clothes and place them outside the door that'll be a help. I'll sluice myself down in the sink in there and then I'll lift down the bath before going to work. Hopefully, the boss will accept my excuse for being late or I'll lose a day's pay.'

Patsy hurried to do what he asked, thinking she would have been happier if he'd been able to stay off work but she understood that he could not afford to do so. She seated the old woman down on a bench in the garden and told her to stay put. Then Patsy removed her sandy shoes, washed her hands in the kitchen sink and went upstairs to fetch Greg's clothing. She shuddered when she thought about the danger he had put himself in by rescuing the old woman and realised just how much he meant to her.

She dumped his clothes outside the washroom door and told him that they were there before turning towards Violet. She had curled herself up on the bench and her eyes were closed but she was moaning softly. Patsy fetched a cushion and, placing a cloth over it, slid it gently beneath her cheek. Then she went and informed her next-door neighbour that they had found the old woman. Then she went back through the house into the garden.

A few moments later Greg emerged from the wash house. He was buttoning a sleeve. 'Will you be all right with her?' he asked.

Patsy nodded. 'Once I've given her a bath, she'll probably sleep the rest of the morning and perhaps even into the afternoon.'

'Well, don't you overdo it,' he warned. 'Don't be worrying about the housework. You have a rest. I'll slip into the police station on the way to work and tell them we've found her.'

'OK,' said Patsy.

Greg squeezed her shoulder. 'You're the best. See you later.'

'Sure. You don't go working too hard either.'

They smiled at each other and she stood watching him wheel out his motorbike. Once she heard the engine start she went into the wash house and set about filling the boiler. By the time she had bathed Violet and got her into clean clothes and rubbed her scanty grey hair dry, they were both ready for a rest. Patsy made tea and settled the old woman in a chair in the front room and, collecting a book from the bookcase, she settled herself where she could keep an eye on her charge, only to find the words on the page running together after a short while, and gradually she drifted off.

The noise of breaking crockery roused her and she forced open her eyes to see Violet on the floor. Patsy tried to rouse her but although she was still breathing she did not stir. For a moment Patsy could not decide what to do but eventually she left her and hurried to the corner shop. She explained what had happened and asked if she could use their telephone to call the doctor.

By the time the doctor arrived Violet had passed away. Patsy could only clench her fists and pray that this would be the last time for a long, long time that she would witness the end of someone's life.

Greg did not seem surprised when Patsy told him that the old woman was dead. As for the children, they accepted it without fuss. They just wanted to know whether their grandma would go to Heaven. Greg made arrangements the following morning to see the undertaker and vicar and arrange the funeral. Then he got in touch with David at his office and told him what had happened. He told Greg that he would call round that evening.

–

The children were playing out in the street when David arrived. Neither Greg nor Patsy saw any reason for keeping them in after they had been at school all day. Helen was whipping a top along the pavement while Nelson was playing rounders with some lads and lasses of his own age. Greg was tinkering with his motorbike and Patsy was making supper. Suddenly she heard voices in the lobby and recognised Greg's and David Tanner's.

'It's time you were rid of that contraption,' said David. 'They're bloody dangerous. You don't want to be the next one to go.'

'You're right,' said Greg, surprising Patsy. 'I'm going to sell it, and when I've saved up a bit more money and I'm out of my time and on journeyman's wages, I'm going to buy a little motor. It's bloody miserable in winter when you're out in the elements.'

'I'm glad to hear you're coming to your senses at last,' said David. 'So when's the funeral to be?'

Greg told him and asked would he be able to attend.

'Of course. But before then there are matters you need to be aware of before you start making any plans. By the way, how's Patsy?'

'She's a treasure. She's bearing up well considering she was there when my foster mother collapsed.'

Foster mother! Patsy wondered if she had misheard what he said but even so she felt herself glowing at Greg's compliment.

'I know Patsy's worth,' said David. 'But she is only seventeen and she can't stay here with just you and the kids in the circumstances.'

'I know what you're going to say but I don't want her to leave and neither do the kids,' said Greg.

'I understand that and that's why I'm going to suggest that I come and live here for a while,' said David.

'You mean you'd act as a chaperone,' drawled Greg.

'If that's how you like to put it. I just thought it would make life easier for all of us. I'm in the process of buying the house next door to Patsy's friend, Mrs Bennett, as an investment.'

'I see. When do you expect to move in?'

'Not for months. There's a lot of alterations I want doing to turn the place into three apartments,' he replied. 'One for myself and the other two for rental. I intend carrying out some of the work myself.'

'Well, you're welcome to stay here,' said Greg. 'What about the house? I presume it'll come to the kids.'

'Wrong,' said David. 'I tried to persuade your foster mother to alter her will in their favour about two years ago but she refused and left everything to Rodney and made him their guardian.'

Greg swore. 'But surely he must be dead, not to have been in touch?'

'Not all men who go missing want to be found,' said David. 'But for the children's sake we need to sort this out. Anyway, I've thought of hiring a private detective to try and find him. I can't do it myself, although I did have a try.'

'Have you anyone in mind?' asked Greg.

'As it happens I do,' said David, a smile in his voice.

Patsy wondered if he could possibly be talking about Grant Simpson. But David was talking again.

'In the meantime, Greg, you'll carry on as you've been doing. I plan to contribute to the housekeeping kitty and I'll pay Patsy an extra five shillings a week.'

'I'll speak to Patsy and ask her to prepare the bedroom for you.'

Patsy prepared to act as if she did not know anything about what had just been said, but despite the trauma of the last couple of days, her heart was singing.

—

It was not until a fortnight after the funeral that Greg said to Patsy, 'How d'you fancy going to the Regent tomorrow night?'

There was an expression in his eyes that gave her a lovely feeling. 'Do you mean take the children?' she asked with an air of innocence.

He took her hand and drew her towards him. 'You know I don't. I was thinking just you and me.'

'I'd like that,' said Patsy with a faint smile. She felt on a different footing with him since she had discovered he was not related to Violet Smith but was her foster son. 'D'you think Mr Tanner will be prepared to look after the children?'

'I'm sure he will.'

'In that case I accept,' said Patsy.

Almost immediately she began to wonder what to wear. It was a shame she had not had time to visit Chester and see her sister. She could have asked her to make her a couple of summer dresses. Maybe when the school holidays broke up she would take Jimmy and the twins, as well as Nelson and Helen, over there.

Later she checked that week's *Crosby Herald* to see what film was showing at the Regent. From the write-up in the newspaper *Ella Cinders* sounded a bit of all right. Much to her satisfaction Greg arranged with David to keep an eye on Nelson and Helen which proved to her more than anything that her former employer was in favour of Greg and herself having fun together.

The film was as enjoyable as Patsy expected. The heroine, Ella, who wanted to get into films, was chased by an escaped lion into a Hollywood studio and pleaded to the crew to save her. Her appeals to them were so heartrending that they hired her as an actress and she met her actor hero. The story was amusing and romantic and all ended happily. Greg held Patsy's hand throughout most of the film and she felt really happy.

As they strolled home, discussing the film, she was hoping for a goodnight kiss. She was not disappointed despite its brevity due to David still being up and about. She accepted that she and Greg needed to act sensibly. Besides, what would happen to their relationship if the children's uncle did come home? He might sell the house and take the children away. Where would she and Greg live then? And the children, how would they feel about being separated from them?

Patsy pulled herself up short. What was she doing worrying about the future? She could not depend, this early in her relationship with Greg, on it ending in a proposal of marriage with him prepared to have Jimmy and the twins living with them as well. Perhaps it was wiser not to think too much but to be content with Greg's companionship and to enjoy life in the present.

Chapter Twenty-Nine

'I can't believe you're doing this,' said Joy crossly, gazing up at David as he looked over the neighbouring fence at her. Rex barked at him. 'Shush, Rex,' she hissed. 'Don't wake Robert!' She seized him by the collar and shut him in the outhouse before resuming her conversation.

'What is it you find unacceptable about my actions? It seemed the sensible thing for me to buy this house and turn it into three apartments.'

'I'm not just talking about you buying the house from *that man* but about your having hired Grant to go to America in search of this Rodney Smith. He could be away for ages.'

'Possibly,' said David cautiously. 'What do you suggest? That I hire Wendy as well? How long have they been married?'

'Nearly a year and no sign of a baby yet,' sighed Joy. 'And I wasn't suggesting that you fork out more money.'

'It's not me that's paying but his mother's estate. I gather from Grant that Wendy hasn't had an easy life and apparently he lost his parents at a young age and was brought up by relatives. Perhaps they can both go and play detective,' said David. 'Of course, you will miss them but you'll have me coming and going next door to keep your eye on,' he said straight-faced.

'I've better things to do with my time,' said Joy, kneeling down to dig up a couple of lettuces, hoping to conceal a blush.

He scrutinised her rising colour with interest. 'I'm not saying you haven't a busy life. But putting that aside, let's talk about the share certificate and letter. They really should be somewhere safe, not just stuck in a drawer somewhere.'

'I haven't stuck them in a drawer,' she said indignantly. 'I sleep with them under my pillow.'

He slowly shook his head. 'Not clever. It's one of the first places a burglar would look. There and under the mattress.'

'But I'd wake up if a burglar tried that on,' she cried. 'Anyway, I can't see what good they'd do a burglar if I haven't made money from them. I think you're just trying to frighten me into accepting you as my solicitor.'

There was a long silence and she could not resist looking up at him. He looked furious. 'That's not true, but if you don't want me as your solicitor, I would suggest that you get yourself another one. What about the one who dealt with your husband's affairs?'

Joy shook her head. 'If Robbie didn't trust him enough to entrust them to him, I don't see why I should.'

'Fair enough. But if you're not prepared to let them out of your possession, then I suggest you get yourself a wall safe.'

'I'm not made of money. Anyway, have you heard anything from Brendan O'Hara's cousins?'

'No. I'd write to them again if I were your solicitor but seeing as I'm not I suggest you write to them yourself. I'll give you their address.'

'Thanks,' said Joy.

'I'm glad to help you.' He vanished.

Joy gazed moodily at the spot where David's head had been a moment ago and knew that the sensible thing would be to accept his offer of help but she did not feel sensible where he was concerned. She found him far too attractive and was struggling against allowing him to play a bigger part in her life. What she would like was to wander around the house next door with him and to hear his plans to turn it into three apartments. No doubt any lodgers he took in could expect more in the way of luxury than she could offer.

'There you are.'

Joy jumped at the sound of David's voice and turned to see him standing in her garden, holding a scrap of paper out to her.

'The address,' he added.

'Thank you.' She took the paper from him and placed it in a pocket. After a moment's hesitation she asked him would he like a cup of tea.

'Only if you've baked a cake today.'

She could not prevent a smile. 'I've made scones. Just don't wake Robert as you pass his pram.' She led the way to the house.

'I had a look at him just a minute ago,' said David, limping after her. 'He looks bigger than last time I saw him.'

'Of course he's bigger! It's over a month since you last saw him. He now has four teeth and I'm going to start weaning him and get him onto a bottle and solids.'

David followed her inside the kitchen. There was a mouth-watering smell of fresh baking. He liked this kitchen because of its homeliness.

Joy placed the lettuces on the draining board. 'Sit down and rest your leg,' she said.

'There's nothing much wrong with my leg.'

'I thought you injured it during the war.' She glanced at him and saw that the muscles of his face were tense and she could have kicked herself for mentioning it.

'I'd rather not talk about it.'

'OK! So these apartments, what are they going to be like?'

'My plan is to have an apartment on each floor with a wash-basin in all the bedrooms and a proper kitchen. I aim to put in a bathroom and a separate lavatory on two of the floors. There isn't room on the top floor for that but I'll expect a smaller rent for that apartment.'

Joy stared at him enviously. 'I wish I had the money for another bathroom and lavatory. If my lodgers were to hear what you're doing they'll desert me and move in with you.'

David said casually, 'I heard that you provided Mr Donavan with Sunday dinner and a pud.'

'That's true.'

'So when Grant and Wendy leave, then, you and Mr Donavan will be dining alone.'

Joy shot him a startled look. 'I haven't had time to think about that.'

'Thinking about it now, do you have any qualms?'

'Is there any reason why I should? He's always behaved politely.'

'But he might behave differently when Grant and Wendy aren't there,' suggested David. 'The way to a man's heart and all that.'

Joy raised her eyebrows. 'If you think I've my eye on Mr Donavan, you're very much mistaken.'

David said hastily, 'I would have thought the shoe would be on the other foot and that he would be setting his cap at you.'

'Nonsense!' Then a mischievous light came into her eyes and she went over to the mantelshelf and took from it a wooden dog. 'Although he did make this for me.'

David took the carving from her and turned it over between his hands. 'It's good. It's the kind of thing men do when they have time on their hands or for therapy.'

'I believe he suffered from shell shock but he seems content enough living here,' said Joy.

'He's found a haven here, you mean,' said David, almost enviously.

'I think so.' She took the carving from him and replaced it on the mantelshelf. 'The war destroyed so many lives. I don't talk about the war to him, though.'

'That's sensible of you. Those who weren't there can't possibly understand the horror of it.'

Joy felt a rush of sympathy and wanted to hug him. Instead, she only said, 'I hope my son never has to go and fight. It's my prayer.'

'I would have thought after all that happened to you that you'd have stopped believing in God.'

She gave him a faint smile. 'I'm not certain of the kind of God I believe in anymore but Jesus Christ, now, I respect his teachings and wish I could live up to them.' Joy was aware that he was staring at her with an odd expression and her cheeks burnt. 'Sorry, I've embarrassed you. I don't generally waffle on about religion.'

David stretched out his legs. 'I've given up on the old man in the sky, myself, but I'd like to believe that we go on in some form or other.'

'My previous employer was a medium and she certainly did,' said Joy, making the tea. 'Shall we change the subject? Did you get to see Their Majesties at all when they visited Liverpool?'

'Yes. I caught sight of them when they arrived at the town hall for lunch with the Lord Mayor,' said David. 'Did you?'

'Unfortunately no. I believe the streets were decorated with banners displaying the red rose of Lancaster and there were thousands of people cheering and waving the union flag.'

'Patsy and Greg were in the crowd when the king opened the Gladstone dock complex. It's going to make a tremendous difference to the size of the ships that can dock in the Mersey.'

Joy remembered how she had so wanted to see Buckingham Palace and Their Majesties. Why was it she had not made the effort to see them here in Liverpool? She could have taken Robert, so that when he was a man he could say that he had seen the king, but she supposed it was the thought of standing for a couple of hours or more, holding her son in her arms, that had put her off.

She thought about how she could do with some help with him and the house.

'How is Patsy getting on now the old lady has died? I know you're lodging there but what will happen when you move in next door?'

'You're wondering about Greg.' David took a buttered scone. 'And I can understand why, so I'll bring him along with me sometime and you can meet him.'

Joy was pleased. 'I'll keep you to that and don't forget and give Patsy my best wishes; I feel like I haven't seen her for ages.'

'I'll tell her,' said David. 'But I have a feeling that her next outing will be a visit to Chester.'

'To see her sister, Kathy, no doubt,' said Joy.

'I believe she's planning on taking not only the twins and Jimmy but my niece and nephew as well.'

'Five children! Managing one is enough for me. Still, no doubt Patsy will cope,' said Joy.

Chapter Thirty

'Keep up, Helen,' called Patsy, heading down the covered walkway towards the landing stage at the Pier Head with a twin clinging to each hand.

'Do we really have to go all the way to Chester?' panted Helen.

Nelson and Jimmy had gone on ahead but Patsy now realised the other girl was having trouble keeping up. 'What's wrong with you? You're not generally this slow. We're going to miss the ferry if you don't get a move on.'

'I've got a stitch and I feel sick. I think I'm coming down with something. Why couldn't we have gone to Southport? It's nearer.'

'Nearer for you but my sister doesn't live there,' said Patsy. 'Grab Mary's hand and we'll all run together.'

'I don't feel like running,' complained Helen.

'Don't be a whinge,' said Maureen, seizing Helen's arm. 'Let's pretend we're being blown by the wind. That's what we do in lessons sometimes – wahoo!'

Maureen ran with Helen, and spreading their arms, they tore down the last few yards and burst out into the sunlit landing stage. The Birkenhead boat was already in and passengers were making their way on board. The girls teetered to a stop as they were about to collide into Jimmy and Nelson.

Patsy read the boys' lips and guessed what they were saying to their sisters was far from complimentary. She told them to try to get seats on the upper deck, so they could watch the ships go by. She thought how it would have been all the better if Greg was with them. Even so, since David had come to stay, he often volunteered to spend time with the children, so she and Greg could go out together. They talked of their childhood and their family background, of films and music, even discussed having dancing lessons.

David and Joy were also a topic of conversation. What Patsy did not discuss with Greg was the plan close to her heart of providing a home for Jimmy and the twins. It could be a stumbling block to them ever marrying if Greg saw it as his duty to continue caring for Nelson and Helen if Rodney Smith was not found. He might think they could not possibly cope with five children.

Patsy dragged her thoughts away from Greg to her sister instead. Even today, it was unlikely they would be able to spend much time together. But Patsy was looking forward to seeing Alice's shop and hearing all about her sister's doings.

The ferry crossing passed without any disasters. This despite Maureen having to be dragged back from hanging too far over the rail a couple of times. It was a relief to pile onto the train at Birkenhead that would take them to Chester.

The journey could have been a real ordeal, keeping the children under control, if it had not been for the novelty of travelling by train and Patsy had brought a bag of sweets as a reward for good behaviour. Even so it was with a lift of the heart that she shepherded the children off the train and led them down into the city. She asked the first policeman she spotted the way to Foregate Street.

If Patsy was honest with herself she would have admitted to feeling more than a little apprehensive about turning up at Alice Bennett's shop with five children in tow. Perhaps she should have written to say she was coming. Suddenly, she spotted several soldiers and wondered if there was a barracks nearby. In Seaforth the barracks was about a ten-minute walk away from the house on the landward side. She hoped that Kathy would not be taken in by any men in uniform.

They arrived at the shop and Patsy paused so she could gaze at the display in the window of what must be the latest in bathing costumes. The green and white creation was knitted and all in one piece. She wondered if it was her sister's work and could not help admiring her daring. The ensemble consisted of costume, towelling robe, rubber shoes and a rubber bag and was arranged against a backdrop of water that was an incredible turquoise blue.

'Does madam like what she sees?' enquired a familiar voice.

Patsy glanced up from beneath the shallow brim of her pink cloche hat and said, 'Madam does but cannot afford it. Hello, Kathy, am I to take it that this costume is all your work?'

Kathleen's mouth fell open and then she collected herself. 'Patsy, what are you doing here?'

'I came to see you. Brought the kids, thinking you might like to see us.' Patsy waved her arms over the heads of the children. 'The ones you don't recognise are my two charges, Nelson and Helen.'

Kathleen said, 'Hello, you two. Sorry, but you won't all be able to come into the shop. You should have thought before bringing them all here, our Patsy.'

'I did! I was thinking you'd be having a lunch break and would be able to spend it with us. You could take us down to that river you mentioned in your Christmas card.'

Kathleen groaned. 'Gosh, is it that long ago since I've been in touch? I'd like to do that, Patsy, but by the time we get there, it'll be almost time for me to come back.'

Before Patsy could say anything in way of reply, a woman came out of the shop, carrying a cream-coloured paper shopping bag by its string handles. She was followed by Alice who immediately recognised Patsy.

'Hello, Patsy! I presume you've come to see your sister?'

'Yes, but I see it's a bad time. You're both busy in the shop.'

Alice smiled. 'Not that busy that I wouldn't allow Kathy to take some time off to spend time with you.' She turned to her assistant. 'Take them to the house and give them something to eat. You can prepare the vegetables for this evening while you're there. Be back by two.'

'Yes, Mrs Bennett,' said Kathleen, forcing a smile. 'Thank you.'

She began to lead the way.

'Gosh, you've changed,' said Patsy. 'If anyone had asked you to prepare the vegetables in the past you'd have had a face on you.'

'That's because Mrs Bennett has been good to me,' said Kathleen.

'What about Flora? Is she still getting up your nose?'

Kathleen shrugged. 'She'd be better if she had a job. It gives you pride in yourself. It would be even better if she left home. That's what really makes you grow up.'

'I had to grow up before I left home,' said Patsy seriously.

'But you had no choice,' said Kathleen. 'If we'd had a different mother and a dad who'd been home, think how different our lives would have been.'

'Don't you think I've thought about that a hundred times?' said Patsy.

'A girl needs a father,' said Kathleen. 'One who can give her some idea what a husband should be like. She also needs a mother who shows her how a woman should treat a man to get the best out of him. Mrs Bennett knows just how to twist Mr Bennett round her finger to get what she wants. But she also knows to make a fuss of him.'

Mary said, 'I don't need a mam and dad, I just want to live with our Patsy.'

Kathleen rolled her eyes. 'I'm glad to hear it because I've no intention of taking you on. I have plans and I don't need hangers-on.'

Patsy said exasperatedly, 'Well, you've made that clear.'

Kathleen smiled. 'No need to get in a twist. You've known for ages how I feel. I'll take you through the park that's named after the Grosvenors; the top nob is the Duke of Westminster. He's to Chester what Lord Derby is to Liverpool. Pots of money. He gave the land to the people of Chester to use as a park for their recreation.'

'Fancy you knowing that,' said Jimmy.

'I like this place so I'm interested,' said Kathleen. 'I'm doing something I like and Mrs Bennett encourages me to think for meself and have the courage of me convictions. You still want to be an engine driver?'

'Yes, but I don't think it's going to be easy,' he said gloomily.

'You stick by your guns,' said Kathleen, 'you never know what's round the corner.'

Patsy said, 'I was wondering if you could make me a couple of frocks. Say by the end of the month.'

Kathleen's eyebrows shot up. 'That's short notice. Is it for something special?'

'I want to make more of myself.'

'Who are you trying to impress?'

'None of your business.'

Kathleen grinned. 'It wouldn't be Greg, the dark-haired one with the blue eyes and the motorbike?'

'I'm saying nothing. Will you do it?'

'Make you a couple of frocks? Of course. If it weren't for you buying me that second-hand frock and us being invited to the wedding and Mrs Bennett spotting my embroidery, then I wouldn't be here now. As well as that I never repaid you the fare to get here,' said Kathleen. 'I'll take your measurements when we reach the house.'

Patsy was surprised and pleased by her sister's reaction and told her so. It was pleasant strolling through the park and the two sisters discussed colours, fabric and style as the children ran ahead. Patsy had told them to stop when they reached the river and they did as instructed. It really was as lovely as her sister had told her. The sun sparkled on the surface of the water and from a bandstand came the sound of brass instruments being played.

Kathleen led the way to Queens Park footbridge and stopped them all halfway to gaze down at the trippers in their rowing boats. The others piled up alongside her. Suddenly Kathleen said, 'There's Chris Davies. I wonder what he's doing fishing on a working day.' She looked at Jimmy. 'This could be a heaven-sent opportunity. He works in the railway engineering yard and his dad is an engine driver. Would you like to meet Chris?'

'Too right, I would,' he said eagerly.

'You don't think he's skiving, do you?' whispered Patsy. 'Because if so, then he won't want you letting on to him.'

Kathleen said, 'Don't be daft, Patsy! He's not going to be skiving if he's in full view of anyone crossing the bridge.'

'True,' said Patsy. 'I wasn't thinking.'

They all trailed after Kathleen down the other side of the bridge and along the riverbank. Patsy and the children stopped a few yards away from Chris but Kathleen went right up to him.

Without looking up, he said, 'Before you ask… I dropped a wrench on my foot. I've broken a couple of toes and can't be doing with standing in the workshop for long.'

'Poor you,' said Kathleen in a caressing voice, kneeling on the bank beside him. 'How did you get here if you're having trouble with your foot?'

He flashed her a grin. 'Ma and one of my brothers brought me on a handcart. She said the fresh air would do me good.'

'Do you think you'll catch any fish?'

'Doesn't matter if I do or not. It's dead peaceful sitting here and watching the world go by.'

Patsy gave Jimmy a little shove. 'Go and ask Chris about what his father does,' she whispered.

Jimmy drew closer to Kathleen and nudged her. She nodded. 'Chris, this is my brother, Jimmy. He's mad about train engines and he'll be looking for a job in a few months. Do you think your father could help him get started?'

Chris glanced up at Jimmy. 'He'll need a bit more muscle on him and it's a tough apprenticeship. You start in the engineering yard helping to clean the engines and crack coal. It can take fifteen years before you're considered good enough to drive an engine unsupervised.'

'I'm not scared of hard work,' said Jimmy, squaring his shoulders. 'Could you tell me more about what I'd have to do?'

'Sure. Sit down.'

Kathleen bent over Chris and brushed her lips against his cheek. 'You're not a bad bloke.'

Chris reddened. 'Get away with you, girlie.'

Nelson moved closer. 'How about fishing?'

Chris looked at him. 'What about it?'

'Never done it.'

Chris sighed and handed over the hand line. Kathleen and Patsy exchanged looks and winked. Then Patsy took a package from her shopping bag and placed it on the grass. 'Your butties are in there, lads. Behave yourselves and don't go falling in the river.'

Nelson and Jimmy nodded absently without looking up. Kathleen led the way to Victoria Crescent. Patsy decided not to bombard her with questions about Chris. If Kathy was set on having a future in the clothing industry, then she was not going to get silly over him. Kathleen had a key and opened the front door. She led them through the house to the kitchen and was about to fling open the door to the garden when she heard laughter coming from the drawing room. She exchanged looks with her sister. 'Best go and look,' said Kathleen.

Patsy accompanied her.

Kathleen flung open the drawing room door with a 'What's going on in here?'

Flora was sitting on the sofa with a young man stretched out on it with his head in her lap. Her face turned rosy when she saw them. 'What are you doing here, Kathy? Why aren't you at the shop?'

'Your mother sent me here. I'm sure she'd be shocked to see what you're up to,' said Kathleen.

Flora dug her elbow in the young man's shoulder and hissed, 'Get up!' He did not move instantly and she poked him again before turning to Kathleen and ordering her out.

'I'll move, Miss Flora,' said Kathleen, 'once he's gone.'

The young man eyed Kathleen with interest. 'Who are you?'

'None of your business,' she answered sharply. 'Get yourself out of here.'

'You've no right to speak to my guest like that,' said Flora, her cheeks even redder than a few moments ago.

'Don't worry about it, Flossy,' said the young man 'I probably won't see you at the rally. You'll have to find yourself someone else.' He left through the french windows.

'Now see what you've done!' cried Flora, enraged and almost in tears. 'It's taken me weeks to get him interested in our cause and now you've gone and spoilt it all.'

'What cause is that, Miss Flora?' asked Kathleen politely.

'None of your bloody business. No doubt you'll tell Mum what you saw and that will be an end to it.' Flora folded her arms and walked over to the open french windows and stared out.

'I'm not a clat-tailed tit whatever you might think of me,' said Kathleen. 'But you're certainly looking for trouble bringing young men into the house when there's no one here to hear you if you were to cry for help. Besides, he's far too old for you.'

'And you'd know about that,' yelled Flora, 'making eyes at my father.' She stormed out into the garden.

Patsy stared at her sister. 'What was all that about?'

Kathleen shrugged. 'It was true that when I first came here I really fussed over Mr Bennett but I soon realised I was making an exhibition of myself and all I really wanted was for him to like me and to treat me with respect. I've got that now because I'm prepared to work and do what Mrs Bennett tells me. But Flora's spoilt and jealous of me. She's not prepared to work and really doesn't know what she wants to do. She's supposed to be studying for some exam not entertaining the opposite sex.'

'You're right about that,' said Patsy. 'Hopefully she will have learnt her lesson with us coming in on her.'

'I really like Mr and Mrs Bennett and I don't want them upset.' Kathleen sighed. 'Right, let's go and get something to eat.'

Patsy and the girls left an hour later with Kathleen after the latter had taken her sister's measurements. They fetched the boys from the riverbank. Kathleen exchanged a few words with Chris Davies before heading for the bridge. There was a parting of the ways outside the shop and money exchanged hands. Kathleen promised to do her best to have the two dresses for her sister ready within the month.

'I'll bring them over,' she called.

Patsy raised a hand in acknowledgement and, gathering her flock together, headed towards the railway station. She hoped the children had found their day as interesting as she had done. At least they had all got on all right together which was promising. The memory of what Flora and Kathleen had said to each other remained with her and she was curious about what might be the outcome of that scene back at the Bennetts' house.

-

It was to be August before Patsy had a visit from her sister.

Kathleen placed a brown-paper parcel on the dining room table. 'There are your dresses. I hope all goes well with the boyfriend?'

Patsy smiled and began to unwrap the parcel. 'So how are things in Chester?'

'Big kerfuffle at the Bennett household. A couple of days after you left Flora went off without telling her mam and dad where she was going. They were frantic with worry.'

Patsy's hands paused in their task. 'I presume she's been found. Was she on her own or was she with someone?'

'She's not saying anything in front of me but she keeps crying. Mr and Mrs Bennett were at their wits' end with her. You wouldn't believe it, would you? She has a home and parents you and I would have died for when we were kids but she's unhappy.'

'So what's going to happen?' Just like her sister Patsy could not understand Flora's actions.

'They're going to get her out of the way for a while.' Kathleen paused 'You know where they're going to send her?'

'Where?'

'To stay with Joy Bennett.'

For a moment Patsy did not say anything and then she smiled. 'Now, Kath, there's a real example of families helping each other. She won't get her own way with Joy and at least she'll be company for her with Wendy and Grant being away.'

'I think the idea is that she helps take care of Joy's little boy. He'll soon be getting to that age when he's a handful.' Kathleen added grudgingly, 'Flora's quite good with kids. I've seen her with her younger brother, the Kirks' little boy and the Moran twins and she knows how to entertain them and keep them in order.'

'Well, that's a tick in her favour,' said Patsy.

'She was right miserable, though, when she was leaving.' Kathleen grinned. 'My life is going to be a lot easier without her around. So are you going to try these frocks on? You want to knock Greg dead when he sees you dressed fashionable for a change, don't you?'

Patsy smiled. 'I'd rather have him alive.'

The frocks fitted perfectly and, as Patsy did a twirl for her sister, she could not help remembering that evening when Mrs Tanner had come in from the sales and made her alter one of the dresses for the dance competition. It was over eighteen months ago now but seemed longer. At least David Tanner seemed to be much more content and Patsy wondered if that could have anything to do with him seeing more of Joy Bennett. She thought of Flora and hoped she would not get in the way of any love affair that might develop between them.

Chapter Thirty-One

'There's been an explosion in that new tunnel they're building under the Mersey. What d'you think of this here tunnel they're digging?'

David looked up from sawing a log and at the man gazing over the fence. 'It's a huge undertaking but will be worth it when it's done,' he said. 'It will save a lot of congestion down by the docks.'

The man nodded. 'It's been bad down there as long as I can remember. But with more motor lorries and cars on the road using the tunnel once it's finished, it'll mean less ferry boats and that'll put men out of work.'

'That's progress for you,' said David, taking a breather. 'Once upon a time houses were lit with candles or oil lamps. Now we've gas and electricity.'

'Mrs Bennett has electricity but not on the top floor where I live.' He paused. 'Will you be paying to have electricity put in?'

'Yes. With winter on its way, I'm thinking of having electric fires in several of the rooms.' David resumed his sawing, only to be interrupted again.

'That's a smashing lot of wood you've got there.'

David paused. 'I had to cut a tree down. It was growing too close to the house and a client of mine advised me to have it chopped down and the roots dug up. They could cause trouble with the drains, you see.'

'Makes sense. But the wood, now, will you be using all of it or could you spare some odd little lengths?'

David eased his back and flexed his fingers. 'Sure. But if you were thinking of using them for firewood you'd need to dry them out first. You could ask Mrs Bennett if she would like some logs to store for use in the new year.'

The man smiled. 'Sure, I'll ask her.'

'You must be Mr Donavan. I like your carving of Rex. It's a good likeness. You've talent.'

'It's not bad,' said Donavan, looking pleased. 'So can you spare me any odd bits of wood?'

'Why don't you come round and choose your own? You'll know what you want.'

William's craggy face lit up and then he vanished.

David remembered that he had a few bottles of beer in the kitchen and, as the weather was unseasonably mild for autumn and he had worked up a sweat, he decided to break open a couple. He went into the kitchen and soon heard a man's heavy tread outside. He called Donavan in and introduced himself. 'I'm David Tanner.'

Donavan shook his hand vigorously. 'I've heard about you. You're a solicitor and you bought the house off the rogue who beat it to America.'

'So Mrs Bennett told you that.' David would rather that Joy had not spoken to this man about what he considered a private matter.

'Not in so many words,' Donavan surprised him by saying. 'When I first came here, she mentioned about there being a bit of scandal attached to the owner of the house next door but it was Grant Simpson who told me the rest before he went off to America in search of that missing relative of yours.'

David was relieved to know that he had misjudged Joy. 'The problem arises when people don't want to be found.'

'That's true enough,' Donavan said heavily. 'I could tell you something about such men and give you reasons why they choose to disappear. Mind you, if I were this – Rodney Smith, is it?' David nodded and Donavan continued. 'If I were him and discovered that I had a house and money left to me, I'd get myself found pretty damn quick. As it is...' he shrugged. 'There's always a price to pay if one decides to go missing because a man has to give up some things he would rather not.'

Donavan's words intrigued David. 'Beer, Mr Donavan?'

His face lit up. 'I wouldn't say no. Can I have a look at the wood first, if you don't mind?'

'Help yourself,' said David, and left him to it.

When David went outside he found the other man sitting on one of the logs, his fingers searching a twisted length of branch. He glanced up. 'Can I have this?'

'Sure. Take what you want.'

Donavan thanked him and placed the branch across his lap and reached for the bottle David held out to him. 'When are you hoping to move in?'

'Depends on how the work goes. Besides, I'm needed where I am at the moment, so I'm not in a rush.'

'Good luck to you,' said Donavan, raising his glass.

They drank in silence until roused by a robin foraging in the soil and then flying off with a worm dangling from its beak.

'That's the way to get a meal,' said Donavan, pointing at the bird. 'I used to be a ship's cook. Bloody hard work.'

'I thought you'd been in the trenches,' said David.

'No, sailor. I now work in a hotel kitchen,' said Donavan. 'Still bloody hard work but at least the floor doesn't shift.'

'Is that what made you give up the sea?'

'That and the war.' Donavan drained the bottle and placed it on the ground. 'The war did for a lot of bloody things.' His expression was moody and his eyelid twitched.

David asked, 'Another beer?'

'Thanks.'

David went inside and when he came out found Donavan still sitting on the log, gazing into space. He nudged his shoulder and Donavan started.

'You OK?' asked David.

'Just remembering.' He took the bottle.

David was not as surprised by the bleakness in his eyes as some might be. 'Your war a bad one?'

'You could say that, although some things had gone bad before then. Only I didn't realise it straight away.' He lifted the bottle to his mouth and drank.

'Am I right in guessing you were born in Ireland?'

'That's right,' said Donavan, nodding jerkily. 'Only a kid when Ma and Pa brought us over here. We moved in with Pa's brother near Scotty Road but I got into bad company, so the long and short of it was that I ended up on a training ship for delinquent boys and became a sailor. I learnt my lesson and kept my nose clean after that.'

'So were you on the Atlantic run during the war?'

Donavan's hand trembled and his eyelid quivered. 'Torpedoed once,' he said hoarsely. 'All that I went through and then when I got home I found her—' He stopped abruptly and gulped down the rest of the beer.

'Sorry,' said David in a low voice. 'I shouldn't have pried.'

'It's OK. You weren't to know. How was your war? I notice you've got a limp.'

David's throat tightened but he forced himself to answer the question. 'I was a dispatch rider and a fuel tank exploded beneath me.'

'Bloody hell! That must have been nasty!' Donavan stared at him with pity in his eyes.

David took a mouthful of beer. 'Rather not go into details of my injuries. Sufficient to say that at least I didn't land on my head. You'd be surprised at how many motorcyclists were killed by head injuries during the war.' David managed a smile. 'At least we're both here to tell the tale.'

Donavan opened his mouth as if to say something else but just then Joy called out his name. 'Mr Donavan! Mr Donavan, where are you? Dinner's on the table.'

'He's here, Mrs Bennett,' shouted David.

'Where's here?' asked Joy.

'I think you know. The other side of the fence.'

'So you're there, Mr Tanner,' said Joy.

'Yes. I think this is me speaking.'

'Smart Alec,' he heard her mutter.

He grinned. 'I heard that.'

Donavan smiled and held out a hand. 'Thanks for the beer and for the wood. I look forward to us being neighbours.'

David took his hand. 'Interesting meeting you.'

—

'So, Mr Donavan, what were you doing next door?' asked Joy, pulling out a chair for him at the table.

'Getting wood,' he said succinctly.

'You mean for your carving?'

'That's right. You might have noticed that Mr Tanner had need to cut down a tree. Too close to the house,' said Donavan, reaching for the tureen of potatoes.

'Did you go inside?'

'No. We sat outside and had a couple of beers.'

Joy heard a low sound and shot a glance at Flora who was spooning carrots on to her plate. There was a disapproving expression on her face. Joy wondered for how much longer she could put up with the girl. Strange, how she could look so like Tilly at that age but be so different. Both had stunning red-gold hair and lovely features with green eyes and Cupid's bow mouth. Joy remembered a time when Flora had not always been so discontented and disapproving. Otherwise, she would not have agreed to have her stay whilst Wendy and Grant were away.

'Can I ask what you were talking about if you were there long enough to drink beer with him?' asked Joy.

'We talked about the war,' said Donavan. 'Now, that's something you two ladies wouldn't be interested in.'

'I don't see why not,' said Flora, taking Joy by surprise. 'It affected us as much as you, Mr Donavan. My father was horribly disfigured. I'll never forget the shock it gave me when he returned home. Like most men he chose to hide the truth. If only he'd have been honest it would not have affected us so badly at the time.'

283

'Ah well, Miss Bennett, women can be just as deceitful towards their menfolk,' growled Donavan.

'That's true,' said Joy, thinking of Rose Tanner.

'It was an unnecessary war,' said Flora in a tight voice.

Joy saw Donavan flinch. 'Enough, Flora!' Her voice was sharp. Flora looked mutinous but she said no more.

Joy wanted to apologise for the girl's words but decided to let it go. Although Flora could be sulky and disapproving, she was adept at handling Robert and for that reason alone Joy was prepared to continue to put up with her until Wendy and Grant returned. Joy glanced at her son who was sitting in his feeding chair, eating a Farley's rusk and dropping bits to Rex who was stretched out at the foot of it.

'Oh, to be like that little fella,' said Donavan, his eyes following hers. 'Not a cross word passes his lips and he has a smile for everyone.' He chucked the baby under his chin. Robert chuckled and hit the man's arm with the rusk.

'Don't do that, Robert,' said Joy, seizing a dishcloth and wiping the smear of food from Donavan's sleeve.

'It's nothing to worry about, Mrs Bennett,' he said. 'Children will be children. I remember—' He stopped abruptly and gave his attention once more to his dinner plate.

'What is it you remember?' asked Joy curiously.

'A girlie enjoying a sugar butty.' Donavan pushed back his chair and with a muttered 'Excuse me' he left the room.

'Now, how's that for bad manners?' said Flora. 'He hasn't finished his dinner.'

'Shut up, Flora!' Joy got up from the table and went after him, only to hear the front door slam.

She returned to the dining room. 'That man has sadness in his past, Flora. He could have lost his daughter. Maybe an only daughter after his wife died in childbirth,' she murmured.

'You don't know that,' said Flora.

'No, because he's not a man to talk about himself.'

'He obviously talked to Mr Tanner but then he's a man.'

'Don't state the obvious,' said Joy, going over to the sideboard and pouring herself a glass of sherry.

'Aren't I getting offered any sherry?' asked Flora.

'No. You're under age.'

'I've been in a pub and wasn't thrown out.'

Joy stared at her hard. 'That isn't something to boast about. No doubt that young man you ran off with took you there. Well, be glad that he doesn't know where you are now. He could have ruined you and you're still too blind to see it.'

Flora said passionately, 'It's obvious that you have never really been in love!'

'Don't talk nonsense, Flora!' Joy sipped her sherry.

'You would say that. You're as bad as Mummy,' said Flora, dropping her knife and fork onto her plate with a clatter. 'I'm going outside. I need some fresh air.' She opened the french windows and went into the garden.

Joy wondered whether to just leave her to sulk but decided instead to follow her. She found Flora stood in the middle of the garden, her shoulders heaving. 'He's not worth all this heartache, love,' said Joy.

'I know,' said Flora in a choking voice.

'You realise that, then, good!'

'I wrote to him and told him where I was staying. I thought he would come and take me away.' The words were punctuated by sobs. 'He didn't even answer my letter. I thought maybe it had gone missing so I wrote him another one but still he didn't write or come. It's as if I've ceased to exist for him.'

'I don't remember you posting any letters.'

'I crept out when everyone was in bed. I thought that dog was going to give me away but he just gave a low growl because he doesn't like me.'

'You haven't given him a chance to like you. Dogs sense when people don't like them,' said Joy.

'You believe that?' asked Flora, wiping her face with a handkerchief.

'Yes.' Joy sighed. 'Do you want to go back home? I suppose if you've come to your senses, then there's little point in you staying here.'

Flora faced her. 'I don't want to go back home. Kathy is the daughter Mummy wants, not me.'

'That's not true,' said Joy firmly. 'But you can't say that your behaviour has helped the situation. It's obvious that staying on at school hasn't been right for you and neither is working in the shop. What is it you want to do?'

A sigh escaped Flora. 'I don't know. I like children.'

'You'd like to have your own babies?'

'Oh, I love babies but one doesn't have to have them immediately these days. Have you ever read Marie Stopes' work on women's rights, married life and family planning, Aunt Joy?'

'No. I take it that you have?'

Flora said hastily, 'Of course not, but I have heard a lot about her and she's out to help women.'

Joy did not believe her. 'You're too young to get married, anyway.'

'I know. But I could try and get a job over here. I promise I'll behave myself from now on.'

'Really,' said Joy, smiling. 'If you do stay, then you're going to have to be nice to Mr Donavan. He was obviously upset earlier.'

'I know. Do you really think he had a daughter and lost her?'

'It's possible,' said Joy.

'And his wife to childbirth? I'm not sure about that, Aunt Joy, because he became angry and said that some women were deceivers.'

'Well, it's true they are.'

Flora slipped her hand through Joy's arm. 'So can I stay?'

'I suppose so,' said Joy, 'if you really mean it about getting a job. A part-time one would do, so that you can still help me with Robert and the housework.'

They went inside the house.

Joy was seeing to the dishes when there was a knock at the kitchen door. 'Mrs Bennett, are you there?'

'Of course I'm here.' Joy turned from the sink and stared at David as he stood in the doorway.

'I couldn't help but overhear your conversation earlier with your young relative,' he said, wiping his boots on the mat. 'Is she here?'

'You mean Flora?'

'Yes. I'd like to help the girl.'

Joy gazed into his serious grey eyes. 'That's really kind of you but in what way can you help?'

'I can give her a part-time job in my office. She'll be starting off as little more than a glorified tea girl but she'll gain experience and earn a little money.'

'Is there no end to your generosity, Mr Tanner?' Impulsively, Joy reached up and brushed her lips against his cheek. 'I'll call her and you can ask her yourself.' She turned away and left the room.

She returned with Flora holding Robert by both hands as he toddled before her. 'Good God! He's walking,' said David. 'How old is he now?'

'Ten months,' said Joy.

'Incredible how swiftly the time has gone.' He turned his attention to Flora. 'Nice to meet you, Flora. I was just wondering if you'd like a job?'

'A job!' Flora glanced at Joy.

'This is Mr Tanner who'll be moving in next door,' she said. 'He's suggested that you might like to go and work in his office part-time.'

'I accept,' said Flora immediately. 'When do I start? And where will I live when Wendy and Grant come home?'

David laughed. 'I'm sure you and Joy will be able to sort that out, young lady, when they do.'

Joy had a sudden sinking feeling in her stomach as she looked at the two of them. Surely the lovely Flora was not going to bewitch David? She prayed that she was mistaken because she just could not bear it if he made a fool of himself over the girl.

Chapter Thirty-Two

Joy was sitting at the dining room table making paper chains to decorate the house for Christmas when she heard a knocking on the french window. She turned her head and, to her surprise, saw a face pressed against the darkened window. She could scarcely believe her eyes when she recognised Wendy. Joy dropped the paste brush in the jar and rushed to unlock the door.

'About time you came home,' she cried happily, flinging her arms about her niece. 'I was starting to believe that you would stay the other side of the Atlantic for ever.'

A glowing Wendy returned her hug. 'No, Aunt Joy, I had to come home and besides I would never have stayed away for Christmas. I was beginning to panic but then Grant said *Just one last island*.'

Joy brought her inside into the warmth and over to the fire. 'What do you mean by that? Where's Grant? Did you find the man?'

'Yes! We followed I don't know how many leads without success but wherever we went Grant visited the local newspaper office and paid for an article to be enclosed with all the necessary information about the search, hoping that if Rodney Smith did not see it, then someone who'd been in contact with him might, and then get in touch. Grant put a little footnote asking them to telephone or write to the newspaper with information.'

'So where was he?' asked Joy, her eyes wide with interest.

'On a yacht in the West Indies,' said Wendy.

'No-o!' breathed Joy.

'It's true!' Wendy chuckled. 'He lived and worked in Florida for a few years, then he bought a yacht and set sail around the islands. Apparently he kept meaning to write home but as time passed and he married a Jamaican woman he just didn't get round to it.'

Joy shook her head. 'He's really thoughtless, isn't he? So he's married a Jamaican woman.'

'Yes. So in a way you can understand his reasoning for staying away. I'd say Tabitha probably has white blood in her somewhere. But from what I've heard about his mother, she would never have approved of her. Tabitha's pretty and wears brightly coloured dresses. As for the children—'

Joy gasped. 'How many children does he have?'

'Three. The little girl is so cute with curly hair tied up with bright-yellow ribbons.' Wendy smiled. 'Grant and I decided we'd be happy with a girl just as much as a boy.'

'You mean...?'

'Yes!' Wendy's eyes shone. 'Going away did the trick. Grant and I are having a baby.'

'That's wonderful! Look, why don't you sit down? You must be exhausted after all this travelling.' Joy pressed Wendy into a chair.

'No. But the voyage home was a bit of a trial.'

'But you're OK?' Joy asked anxiously.

'I'm fine. The baby's due in summer.'

Joy smiled. 'A much better time of year to be getting up in the night.'

Wendy gave a mock groan.

'This calls for a celebratory drink,' said Joy.

She poured out two sherries and gave one to Wendy. 'So how did you eventually find Rodney Smith?'

'He takes tourists out fishing on his boat and one of them happened to be a native of one of the towns we visited. They'd read the article and remembered his name.'

'So is he coming home?'

'Grant said he mentioned something about the British weather at this time of year.' Wendy grimaced. 'You can't blame the man. He gave Grant a letter to give to David.'

'I wonder what's in it,' mused Joy.

A silence fell.

Wendy cleared her throat. 'Aunt Joy, Grant and I have decided we need somewhere a bit bigger. I'm sorry but we're thinking of moving into one of David's apartments.'

Joy said, 'Is David aware of what you're planning?'

'He should be by now. Grant went straight to David's office with it being not far from the Pier Head.'

'Well, I hope all goes well for you both. Congratulations!' Joy raised her glass. 'I'm so glad about the baby and relieved that you're not moving far away.'

Wendy looked relieved. 'I'm so happy you feel like that, Aunt Joy. Hopefully we'll be able to move in right away.'

'That should please Flora,' said Joy dryly.

'Where is Flora?' Wendy glanced about her as if expecting the girl to pop out from behind a chair.

Joy explained about the part-time job. 'Anyway, it's wonderful to have you home and in time for Christmas. Not that I'm planning on being here.'

Wendy's face fell. 'But we've brought presents and you weren't to open them until Christmas. I suppose you're going to Chester?'

Joy nodded. 'I did spend last Christmas here with you.'

They both fell silent, remembering the sadness of that occasion. This Christmas there would be two faces missing. 'We'll have to visit the graves,' said Joy.

Wendy nodded. Joy guessed that, although there would be sadness at Christmas, it would not dim the glad news that if all went well there would be a baby to spoil next year.

Wendy wiped her eyes. 'What about Mr Donavan? Do you know what he's doing for Christmas?'

'He might be working in the hotel over the festive season,' said Joy. 'And Mrs Sanderson and her son will be spending it with family, I should imagine.'

'The same as David Tanner, no doubt,' said Wendy. 'It could be the last Christmas the children and Greg Molyneux and Patsy have in the house in Seaforth.'

'It's sad when it's been the children's home all their lives,' said Joy. 'I wonder what Patsy and that young man will do? I've yet to meet him.'

Wendy stretched her legs out to the fire. 'I guess you will sooner or later. He's bound to visit next door.'

'I've only seen David in passing in the last few weeks,' sighed Joy. 'Even so I've knitted him a pair of warm socks for Christmas. I thought I'd ask Flora to pass them on to him with a card.'

'Do you think she enjoys working in his office?'

Joy shrugged. 'She hasn't complained.'

'He's long-suffering is David Tanner. When you think what he put up with that wife of his. There's not many like him around, Aunt Joy.' Wendy gave her a hard stare.

'What's that look supposed to mean?' asked Joy, raising her eyebrows. 'I know David Tanner is a really nice man. What do you want me to do about it?'

'I'm not saying you should do anything,' said Wendy hastily, getting up. 'But I was thinking how fortunate I am to be married when I'm living in a country where there's probably almost twice as many women as there are men.'

'I guess that comment is supposed to make me think,' said Joy, feeling exasperated with her niece. 'Well, my thought is that being part of a couple is not always as easy as people imagine it to be.'

'I think most married couples soon become aware of that, Aunt Joy.' Wendy went over to her and kissed her. 'Have you the key to our room?'

Joy went and fetched it. 'Flora should be home in an hour or so,' she warned.

'Hopefully I'll be out of there by then,' said Wendy. 'Grant is sorting out our luggage. See you later.'

–

Flora entered the kitchen where Joy was preparing their evening meal and stopped to draw off her gloves and place them on the table. 'I've news,' she said.

'If it's that Wendy and Grant are back, I know,' said Joy.

Flora scowled. 'Damn! I had a feeling you might. I bet you don't know that they're moving in to one of the apartments next door?'

'So it's for definite, is it?' said Joy.

Flora took off her coat and flung it on the back of a chair. 'Well, you don't know everything, Aunt Joy. I bet Wendy didn't tell you that Mr Tanner wants Grant Simpson to keep an eye on Mr Donavan. What do you think of that?'

Joy was startled. 'What on earth for? He's got a nerve. Mr Donavan is my lodger, not his. He's got no right to spy on him.'

Flora stared at her uneasily. 'But he must have his reasons. I mean, why should he suddenly do this?'

'I don't know,' said Joy grimly. 'But I'm going to find out.'

Flora looked alarmed. 'You're not going to ask Mr Tanner? He'll sack me if he knows I've been speaking out of turn about confidential information.'

Joy was silent a moment. 'I'll ask Grant.'

'You really think he'll tell you?'

'No,' said Joy with a sigh. 'He'll say it's confidential.'

'I wish I'd kept my mouth shut now,' said Flora gloomily.

'So do I,' said Joy. 'I'll be wondering now over Christmas what this is all about.' She paused and came to a decision.

'I've knitted David a pair of socks; you can give them to him when you go into the office. I probably won't see him before Christmas now, with us going to Chester.' She was glad of an excuse to avoid seeing him. It hurt to think that he could have Mr Donavan followed without consulting her.

Chapter Thirty-Three

'I'm glad Uncle Rodney isn't coming home for Christmas,' said Helen, gazing up at Patsy. 'Aren't you?'

'Yes. But to be honest, I never thought he would be here because I believed he was dead,' said Patsy, putting the finishing touches to the Christmas tree.

'When he does come, do you think he'll take us to Jamaica?' asked Nelson.

'I don't want to go. He can't make us, can he?' Helen's voice was anxious.

Patsy swallowed a sigh and wished the children would drop the subject of their uncle. Ever since David had told them the news that Rodney had been found, Helen and Nelson had been unable to stop talking about their aunt and uncle and cousins. They had insisted on Greg getting out their grandmother's old atlas and pointing out Jamaica. Nelson had noted that it was pink, so it was part of the British Empire.

'You haven't answered my question,' said Nelson.

'It's not definite that he will come here. He just wants the money from the house.' Patsy felt angry every time she thought of him depriving the children of a home.

'It's not fair,' said Nelson. 'Grandma should have left us some of her money and not given it all to him.'

'Uncle Rodney hasn't even sent us Christmas presents,' said Helen.

'It doesn't matter,' said a familiar voice behind them.

Patsy turned and smiled her relief at David and Greg. They were loaded up with bulging shopping bags.

'I didn't hear you come in. Been doing some last-minute shopping?' There was a lilt in her voice.

'We knew the butcher was delivering an enormous piece of pork,' said David, 'but I couldn't turn down a turkey from a client or a bottle of port, for that matter.' He placed one of the heavy bags on the floor and smiled at the three of them.

Patsy looked at Greg. 'And what extras have you bought?'

'Nuts, tangerines, apples and lots of other goodies,' he answered, grinning. 'They were being sold off from a handcart along the dock road seeing as how it's Christmas Eve. I felt sorry for the woman standing there getting soaked in this weather.'

Patsy thought how different he was from the children's real uncle in Jamaica. She took the shopping bag from him and picked up the one on the floor. 'I'll put these in the kitchen.'

'What about presents, Uncle Greg, Uncle David?' asked Helen, jumping up and down with excitement.

Patsy paused in the doorway.

David winked at her. 'That depends on whether Uncle Greg and I get a good report of your behaviour from Patsy.'

'But I have been good,' said Helen. 'Honestly. And I'd like to hang up a stocking as well. The girls at school hang up stockings. They said Father Christmas would come and fill it with all sorts of things if I'm good.'

'There's no such person as Father Christmas, that's what Grandma told us,' said Nelson, fiddling with a toy trumpet on the Christmas tree.

'But the girls at school say there is, so there!' Helen stuck out her tongue at him.

'Enough of that or else,' warned David. 'Why don't you both hang up stockings from the mantelpiece in here before you go to bed and see if there's anything in them in the morning? I have a pair that Mrs Bennett knitted me. They're long and woolly and they were only passed on to me today by Flora at the office.'

'So what are Joy and Flora doing for Christmas?' asked Patsy.

'They're spending it with the family in Chester,' replied David. 'I'm glad that Grant and Wendy will be next door to keep their eye on things. It's a busy time for burglars.'

'You don't really believe that Joy's house or yours could be burgled?' asked Patsy.

David shrugged. 'It's always best to take precautions. Anyway, I'm sure everything will be OK.'

She hoped he was right and said as much to Greg when he followed her into the kitchen.

'He's just concerned that there's only Mr Donavan in Mrs Bennett's house while she and Flora are over in Chester.'

'But Mr Donavan has lived there for ages,' said Patsy. 'If he can't be trusted, surely Joy would have realised that by now?'

'Let's forget about them and think about us,' said Greg.

'OK! What's on your mind? You generally say the right things to comfort me,' said Patsy, smiling up at him.

'Now you sound like the Patsy I respect and love,' said Greg, drawing her towards him.

Patsy melted in his arms and looked up at him with shining eyes. 'Do you really love me?'

'Of course I love you,' said Greg, nuzzling her neck. 'What do you think I've been up to this last six months? I want to marry you.'

'You're serious? You're not messing about?'

His eyes twinkled. 'Am I one for messing about? I'd call us going to the flicks and cuddling on the back row, as well as going dancing, seriously walking out. I reckon we have to start making decisions about our future now we know this house is definitely being sold.'

'I think Rodney Smith is an extremely selfish man,' said Patsy fiercely.

'I wouldn't argue with you,' said Greg, nibbling her ear. 'I don't think he gives a hoot about Nelson and Helen. I don't know how much is in the trust their father set up for them but David will and he'll know if it's enough to feed and clothe them if we find a place of our own. I'd willingly have them living with us if you're in favour.'

Patsy's heart was beating fast. 'Is this a marriage proposal?'

'Of course. I'd marry you tomorrow if I could,' said Greg, caressing the outline of her breast with a finger.

The breath caught in Patsy's throat. 'I read in the *Echo* that Christmas Day is losing popularity with couples as a wedding day.'

Greg laughed. 'I didn't think we could get married that quickly.'

'Good, because I'd need to think about it.'

His laugh faded. 'What is there to think about?'

'Plenty!' She eased herself away from him. 'Right now I need to put the pork in the oven and make the stuffing for the turkey.'

Greg said wryly, 'Now, that's what I call evading the question. You're not scared of marriage, are you? I mean us sleeping together as man and wife?'

Patsy's cheeks burnt. 'I enjoy you holding me. I enjoy your kissing and caressing me but as for the rest how can I say if-if I've never…' Her voice trailed off and it was a minute or so before she said, 'What about my family?'

Greg stared at her. 'What do you mean *What about my family?*'

Patsy had to consider carefully how to answer his question. 'When I left the orphanage, I always had it in mind that one day I would provide a home for the twins and Jimmy, as well as my brother Mick when he made landfall. It's a lot to ask a man to take on someone else's relatives.'

Greg said slowly, 'Why have you never mentioned this to me before?'

'You've never asked me to marry you before.' Patsy clasped her hands together in front of her. 'I never intended marrying young.'

'Neither did I – or taking on five children,' he said roughly.

'And we could have babies of our own,' gulped Patsy. 'More mouths to feed and bodies to clothe. It's a big decision.'

Frowning, Greg wandered over to the window and gazed out at the bare trellis attached to the grimy whitewashed wall. He must paint it soon, he thought absently. He remembered the sweet peas were in flower when he had taken Patsy and the kids to see the eclipse and how much he had wanted to be alone with her. He took a deep breath. 'I still want to marry you. You know, I've never met any of your family even though you've talked about them a lot. Thinking about them now, surely it won't be long before Jimmy is working? As for your brother, Mick – if he were ever to favour us with his company, then his being a sailor means it would only be for short periods every now and again. Hopefully we can persuade him to help support your twin sisters.'

Patsy doubted Mick could help for a while as he was younger than her and would not be earning much. Even so she felt a surge of love for Greg for even considering taking on so many children. She put her arms round his waist. 'I love you. I so want us to be together and to be a family.'

Greg said, 'I can't say I'm passionate about the idea of starting married life with five youngsters to look after because I'd rather it was just the two of us. But if that's the way it has to be, then I'll give it a go. But first we have to find somewhere to live.'

Patsy agreed. 'Perhaps it'll take some time before the house gets sold. I'm sure David will agree to us living here until then.'

Greg nodded. 'But the day isn't far off when David leaves here to move into the house next door to Joy Bennett. If we want to be together we'll have to get married soon.' Greg kissed her and then reluctantly let go of her hands.

'Now, I've work to do,' Patsy said brightly. 'And no doubt so have you and David once the children are in bed.'

Greg hesitated and then, brushing his lips against hers, murmured, 'I was going to give you your present this evening but I'll wait until tomorrow.'

'What is it?'

'Surprise.' He sauntered out of the kitchen, whistling 'O Come All Ye Faithful'.

They woke the following morning to a white Christmas but it was not snow but just a layer of hailstones and they melted once the sun eventually made an appearance. Helen was cock-a-hoop when she discovered the stocking she had hung up was bulging with presents: a rag doll, a colouring book and box of paints, a skipping rope, a small jigsaw, sweets, a tangerine, a couple of nuts and a florin.

'See, see,' she crowed to Nelson. 'I told you there was a Father Christmas.'

He glanced over to a smiling David and grinned. 'OK. I accept there's a Father Christmas.' And he began to drag out his gifts.

There were more presents to open and Helen declared her best present to be the doll's house that was David's special gift. Patsy waited until after breakfast when she and Greg were alone before handing him his gift.

'It's not very exciting,' she said, 'but done with love.'

He unwrapped the socks, gloves and scarf she had knitted him.

He thanked and kissed her. 'I'll love wearing these because you made them for me.' From his pocket he produced a small square box.

Patsy stared at it with a rush of delight. She supposed that, after his proposal last evening, she might have expected this. He flicked open the box and took out a ring. It was a ruby with a diamond each side. 'Well, Patsy, love, are you still prepared to marry me?'

'Yes.' Patsy held out her left hand and he pushed the ring onto her third finger. She gazed at it with tears in her eyes. 'No one has ever bought me anything so lovely.' She flung her arms around him and kissed him.

David entered the kitchen as they were still in a clinch. 'Should I leave?' he asked, raising an eyebrow.

They drew apart and smiled at him. 'We've just got engaged,' said Greg.

David smiled. 'Congratulations!' He shook Greg's hand and kissed Patsy. 'I'm sure you'll suit each other very well. When is the wedding to be?'

'That's yet to be decided,' said Greg. 'There're a lot of things to sort out.'

David nodded. 'Well, don't wait too long.'

Chapter Thirty-Four

'I've news to tell you,' said Flora, entering the kitchen in a rush. The door slammed behind her. 'Gosh, it's freezing out there.'

Joy glanced up from the stove. Flora's cheeks were flushed with the wind and she looked lovely. 'What news is that?'

'Patsy Doyle is engaged.' Flora removed her hat and placed it on the kitchen table before kissing Robert's dark curls. He was in his playpen and trying to climb up the wooden bars.

Joy put down the wooden spoon and lowered the gas. 'I suppose David Tanner told you that.'

'Who else?' Flora shrugged off her coat and hung it up. Then she sat down and eased off her shoes and held out her stockinged feet to the fire. 'He thought you'd like to know.'

Joy was exasperated that she should learn the news through Flora. 'Of course I'd like to know but why couldn't he tell me himself? Or why couldn't Patsy visit and tell me?'

Flora looked surprised. 'I suppose he thought you'd get the news quicker if it was passed on through me. I mean, it's not as if you're related to Patsy.'

'No, but…' Joy hesitated. 'He could have popped in here and told me. I presume she's engaged to Greg Molyneux.'

'That's him. Have you met him?' Flora yawned and leant back in the chair.

'No.' Joy was wondering what David was thinking about allowing Patsy to get engaged to that young man when she was not even eighteen. 'Will Mr Tanner be working next door this weekend?'

'Supposed to be. In fact I'm sure he said that he would definitely be doing so. He's now behind with the painting and wallpapering of his apartment.'

'You seem to know a lot about it,' said Joy, still feeling irritable with the girl.

Flora smiled. 'That's because I ask, Aunt Joy. I like to know what people are doing.'

'But he doesn't have to tell you.'

Flora toyed with a lock of red–gold hair. 'No, but I have a way with me and men can't help themselves.'

'You really do have a high opinion of yourself, young lady. I hope you're not flirting with him?'

Flora opened her eyes wide. 'Me, flirt with the boss? He's at least fifteen years older than me.'

'About that.'

'I suppose Daddy would consider him much too old for me,' said Flora with a mischievous glance at Joy. 'But on the other hand he's not short of money, so would be a good catch.'

'You're being silly. I think we've said enough about Mr Tanner.' As she dished out their meal, Joy made up her mind to visit next door on New Year's Eve, which was a Saturday, and have a word with David.

But on New Year's Eve, Robert was getting another tooth, so Joy did not go anywhere but spent the midnight hour walking the floor with him, aware of the hooting of ships' sirens and church bells welcoming in nineteen-twenty-eight. She felt tired the following morning but at least Robert's tooth came through. So just before dinner time, while Flora took Robert for a walk in the park, Joy called next door in the hope of seeing David.

As it was, a tall, dark, young and handsome stranger opened the door with a paintbrush in hand. 'Can I help you?' he asked in a friendly voice.

'I've come to see Mr Tanner.'

The young man looked apologetic. 'I'm sorry but he's not here. He slipped on the ice and has broken his ankle.'

Joy's disappointment was intense. 'When did that happen?'

'Yesterday morning on his way here.'

'Poor David. Is he in much pain?'

'He's putting on a brave face and is mad with himself for what happened.' He hesitated. 'Are you Mrs Bennett?'

'Yes. I'm Joy Bennett.'

'Greg Molyneux.' He made to offer his hand but then withdrew it. 'Sorry. I've paint on both hands.'

Joy liked not only the look of him but also the fact that he had obviously offered to take David's place and carry on with the work here on his day off. 'So you're Patsy's fiancé. I'm very fond of her and I hope you'll both be very happy.'

He looked pleased. 'Thank you, Mrs Bennett. I'll tell Patsy I saw you. She'd have come with me but she wasn't prepared to leave David to the children's mercy just yet.'

Joy hesitated. 'How are the children?'

Greg frowned. 'Unsettled. The house has to be sold and they've lived there since they were born. Rodney's their legal guardian but I'm of the opinion he'll settle for me and Patsy to look after the children.'

'You and Patsy? That's a big responsibility for someone of your age.'

'I know. But they know me.'

Joy was about to say *What about David? Isn't he their uncle by marriage?*

'Patsy also has it in mind that she should provide a home for Jimmy and the twins,' said Greg, with a lack of emotion that did not deceive her.

'It's far too much for you both to take on when you're so young yourselves,' said Joy firmly.

'We're both aware of that, but what else can we do?' said Greg with a shrug.

'I'm sure there must be something,' said Joy. 'You can't cope with this on your own. You have no family, I take it?'

'No. Mr Smith and my father were in business together when my father was killed in an accident in the factory and that's why he took me into his own home.'

'Does David Tanner know this?'

'I've never discussed it with him.'

'I see,' said Joy, making up her mind. 'I presume he won't be going into the office for the next few weeks?'

'No. He'll be working from home.'

Joy smiled. 'It's been a pleasure talking to you, Mr Molyneux.'

'And you, too, Mrs Bennett,' he said, returning her smile.

She was halfway down the path when he called out, 'You didn't say what you wanted to see David about. Perhaps I can take a message to him?'

'That's kind of you but I'd rather speak to him face-to-face. It's business, you see, although, perhaps you can tell him to expect a visit from me. I presume he'll be staying put for a while?'

'Yes.'

Joy waved and returned home.

She told Flora about David Tanner's accident. The girl was dismayed, wondering how it would affect her position at the office. Donavan was sharing dinner with them and Joy wondered if Grant had kept an eye on him during the last week and whether he would continue to do so. She hoped that her lodger was unaware that he was being followed. She wondered what it was that David knew about him that she didn't.

The weather was so bad during the next few days that Joy changed her mind about venturing as far as Seaforth. She had planned to take Robert with her, certain that Patsy would like to see him. But as gales continued to batter the west coast she decided to leave him in Wendy's safe hands one day and set out for Seaforth.

–

'Do you think Joy Bennett will come today?' asked David, swinging into the kitchen on crutches.

'Perhaps,' said Patsy, thinking he had asked that question every day. At least his accident had served one good purpose and that was it had delayed the house being put up for sale.

At that moment the door knocker sounded. They looked at each other. 'Will I go or you?' asked Patsy.

He swung himself out of the kitchen and headed for the front door. Leaning on his crutches, he opened first the vestibule and then the front door. With a catch of the heart he gazed down at a flushed and wild-haired Joy.

'Hello, Mr Tanner,' she said, sounding breathless. 'Can I come in? It's still blowing a gale out here.'

'Of course,' he said politely. 'I've been expecting you for days.'

'Sorry. It's been the weather.' Her heart sank, thinking that he sounded cross with her.

'Come this way.'

She followed him into a room where a log fire burnt. 'Oh, lovely!' She put down her handbag and pulled off her gloves and held her hands out to the fire. 'I was blown here once I left the train.' She forced herself to make light conversation. 'What would you do with this weather?'

'Move to the Caribbean?' suggested David.

His reply surprised her. 'I presume that's a reference to your wife's brother? I'm surprised you can't do something legal to stop him taking the children's home from them. Although, it's not only theirs, is it, but Greg Molyneux's as well? It seems unfair that Rodney Smith gets it all and they get nothing. Especially when you know that young man stuck it out here with his foster mother, when she was going senile.'

David frowned. 'Is that what you came for – to tear a strip off me because you believe I'm doing nothing to help them?'

Joy was taken aback. 'Of course not!' She gazed at him and smiled hesitantly. 'I came to give you this and ask you to help me get the money.' She took an envelope from her handbag and held it out to him. 'I've heard nothing from those in charge of the company, so I've changed my mind about leaving the money invested in the mine. If you'll represent me and can get it for me, you can have a tenth of it.'

David took the envelope from her and waved her to a chair. He eased himself down into the opposite one and set aside his crutches.

'How are you?' she asked, taking off her damp coat. 'I'm sorry about your fall.'

He sighed. 'Damn fool thing to do. But never mind that. I'm OK. I'm more interested to know what made you change your mind about accepting my help.'

'I was wrong to be prejudiced against you because of Parker.'

David's face lit up. 'Thanks. I appreciate your trust in me.'

'I was thinking that I could also give a tenth of the money to Patsy and Greg for a deposit on this house. Perhaps they could afford to buy it then.'

'You'd do that for two young people who aren't related to you when you need the money yourself?' He shook his head as if he could scarcely believe it.

Joy gave a twisted smile. 'I knew you'd think I was daft. I had another crazy thought when Greg told me that his father was once in business with Mr Smith. I did wonder if the latter might have diddled Greg out of money that should have come to him. I thought Mr Smith could have felt guilty and that's why he took Greg into his own home.'

David said, 'It is something I've considered since looking through some old files in the office but it's too late now to do anything about it.'

'What a shame!' She sighed. 'I thought you might think I'm one of those people who are suspicious of other people's motives and I confess I am a bit.'

'It pays to not always take things at their face value,' said David, placing the envelope on the arm of the chair.

There was a knock on the door. 'Come in, Patsy,' he called.

She entered the room and smiled at Joy. 'Hello, Mrs Bennett. It's lovely to see you. Here, give me your coat and hat to put in the kitchen to dry out.'

'Thanks.' She handed the garments to Patsy. 'Congratulations, love, on your engagement. He seems a very nice young man. We had an interesting chat.'

Patsy looked pleased. 'Greg told me about meeting you. Cup of tea?'

'Not just yet,' said David.

'Okey-doke!' She left the room.

'So where were we?' asked Joy.

'You were talking about ways of giving Patsy, Greg and the children a helping hand,' said David. 'I'll tell you what I've done so far.'

Joy looked at him expectantly. 'Go on.'

'I've written to Rodney and told him just how well Greg and Patsy cared for his mother and that they are planning to get married and are prepared to foster Nelson and Helen. I suggested that he might consider selling the house to Greg at a price below its market value.'

Joy was pleased. 'If he agrees, that proves he's not the selfish person I've thought him so far.'

David frowned. 'You have to realise, Joy, that Rodney looks upon this money as a real windfall. You never knew his mother but she was not an easy woman to live with and demanded a lot from him. Eventually he decided to stay away for good. Now he has a family and, not only does he want to build a modest house for them, but to do some essential repairs on his boat.'

'I understand what you're saying but it seems unfair that he's prepared to take it all and leave the children with nothing.'

'Is that what Greg told you?' asked David.

'No. I'm just presuming that's the case.'

'Well, you're mistaken. The children's father left them money in a trust fund and Rodney has asked me to dispose of everything in the house, including the contents of his room, as I see fit. I'm to give the proceeds to the children and Greg.'

'Well, that's a good start but surely you won't get rid of all the furniture because they'll need it. And Greg still needs money for a deposit.'

David smiled. 'I'm certain we'll be able to raise a useful sum when we get rid of all Rodney's paraphernalia. I reckon there're a few valuable artefacts amongst the collection. I have a client who is an auctioneer. I'm going to bring him in to have a look at the stuff.' He paused. 'So you see, however well meaning and generous your offer is, I don't think it's necessary. Even so, I'll still write to the mining company and hopefully they'll respond favourably. But if you need the money desperately, I'm prepared to buy your shares.'

Joy was touched by his generosity. 'I do appreciate your offer but let's wait and see what they have to say. As for the rest of what you've told me, it looks like Patsy and Greg won't have to wait long to get married. I do still think that their taking on the children is a lot at their age.'

'I do have a plan that would enable Patsy and Greg to have regular breaks from caring for them,' said David hesitantly, 'but for that I need a woman's help. Yours would be much appreciated – that's if you felt able to take it on? Of course, I would pay you.'

Joy felt a real pleasure that he should want to involve her in his life. 'What do you have in mind?'

'I've decided not to rent out the top floor of the house, so the children can come and stay with me on a regular basis. Say every other weekend and sometimes during the school holidays. I'm no cook, so I wondered if you'd take on the job of preparing meals for us. Maybe, during the school holidays the pair of us could take them and Robert out on trips.'

'I think it's kind of you to have given so much thought to enabling Greg and Patsy to have some time to themselves,' said Joy. 'But you're forgetting Patsy's twin sisters and Jimmy.'

David's expression was comical. 'I had forgotten about them! Although, surely Jimmy will be working by then?'

'Yes.' Joy's eyes danced. 'You wouldn't have been so blasé about taking so many children out for the day if you had remembered them. How used to children are you, David?'

He said ruefully, 'Not as much as I'd like to be. I enjoy Nelson and Helen's company. Yet I knew to have them for hours on my own wouldn't be easy and that's when I thought of you.'

Joy felt a sudden rush of love for him. 'I'd say for a widower to take on just two children on his own is a real challenge. I'd be happy to take on Patsy's sisters. But I do think you need to speak to Patsy and Greg first.'

'Right! I can see my plan needs more thought,' he said.

'Of course, for outings it would be easier if we used the motor,' she said thoughtfully.

He looked puzzled and then alarmed. 'What motor?'

'The motor I had forgotten about because it's in the outhouse at the bottom of the garden,' said Joy, her eyes alight. 'It belonged to Robbie.'

'Not keen on vehicles with engines,' said David, fidgeting with the envelope Joy had given to him.

Joy recalled what Rose had told her about his wartime injuries and did not push him to explain further. Yet to have the use of the car with so many children would be a godsend. 'I can drive. I just need a bit of practice and we could take off with the children to Blackpool or Southport. Children love going to fairs and both those places have fairs.'

'Let me think about it,' said David.

'OK,' said Joy.

There was a silence.

Then she remembered the other reason why she had wanted to see him. 'There's something else I want to ask you.'

'You look annoyed. What have I done wrong now?'

'Why have you hired Grant to keep an eye on Mr Donavan?'

'I can't believe Grant or Wendy told you that,' he said.

'No. Flora told me.'

David was exasperated. 'I made a mistake taking on that young lady. She lacks discretion. What did she tell you?'

'Only that you wanted Grant to watch Donavan. He is my lodger, and if you're suspicious of him for some reason, then I'd like to know why.'

He hesitated. 'I'm just curious about him. I can tell you now that Grant's report was an eye-opener.'

'In what way?'

'Donavan had gone back and forth to work without fail and without being seen with any suspicious characters. But there were several things Grant found interesting in his behaviour. He went to a certain street near Scotland Road, stared at a house for a long time and then the following day he went back and knocked on a couple of doors and spoke to a couple of women. Since then he has visited Walton Cemetery and has stood outside the Seamen's Orphanage just gazing up at it several times.'

Joy was puzzled. 'I don't understand.'

'No, neither did I, until I recalled my conversation with him when I mentioned Rodney going missing. You know what Donavan said?'

'No, tell me.'

'That he could give me several reasons why a man might disappear and not want to be found.' David leant back in his chair and stared at Joy.

'You're saying Mr Donavan is such a man?'

'Yes. He's a seaman, who's lost someone, most probably a wife, and it's possible he believes he has a son or daughter or even several children in the orphanage.'

'So you're suggesting that he went to the cemetery to visit his wife's grave after being away for several years?'

'It's a definite possibility.'

'Was there a headstone?'

'No. But it had a small stone with a number on it, so Grant is busy trying to find out who is buried there,' said David.

'I presume Donavan hasn't actually called in at the orphanage,' said Joy.

'Not as far as we know. In my opinion he's reliving the past and is undecided about what to do. How do you disappear and then come back without creating more hurt to those to whom you mattered?'

'Do you mean he deliberately turned his back on his family and perhaps arranged his own death?'

'It's a possibility. Has he ever mentioned children to you?' asked David.

Joy thought about that question long and hard. 'Yes! When Robert was eating a rusk he said something about a little girlie. He got upset and went out. I thought his daughter must have died.'

'What if the daughter hadn't died and he felt he could not face her? Can you remember anything else that might relate to a wife or child?'

Joy felt all of a tremble and found herself clasping and unclasping her hands as she tried to recall her conversations with Donavan. Suddenly she remembered one last November. 'We were talking about the war and I got the impression he'd come home and found his wife…' She stopped and her jaw dropped.

'Yes, Joy,' said David, leaning forward and taking both her restless hands in his own and stilling them.

'That she had been carrying on with another man,' she said in a low voice.

They stared at each other and David was about to speak when they were disturbed by a rat-tat-tat on the drawing room door. 'Tea and cake?' asked Patsy.

'Damn!' said David beneath his breath, freeing Joy's hands.

All a tremble Joy stood up and went and opened the door. She took the tray and was about to close the door when she remembered her manners.

'Thanks, Patsy. This cake looks lovely.'

'The proof is in the tasting,' said Patsy, smiling. 'I thought you'd like chocolate.'

'It was my favourite as a little girl.'

'Lucky you,' said Patsy with a wry smile. 'I had to make do with a sugar butty.'

'Now, those I don't remember. Jam, yes, but not sugar…' Joy's voice trailed off.

There was a silence except for the crackling of a log on the fire.

'You look like you've seen a ghost,' said Patsy, peering into her face. 'I remember the old woman saying she'd seen a ghost here.'

'There's no ghosts here, Patsy,' said David. 'But you do look pale, Joy. Are you all right?'

Joy forced a smile. 'Just sick with hunger. I can't wait to taste this cake.' She carried the tray over to the occasional table and put it down. 'I was just thinking, Patsy, that you'll be eighteen in March. I'd like to throw a birthday party for you at my house. I'm sure Kathy would be able to come and some of the family from Chester. I could fetch the twins and Jimmy from the orphanage and everyone here could be invited. What do you say?'

A delighted smile broke out over Patsy's face. 'What can I say? I've never had a party thrown for me in my life! Yes, please.'

It was not until Patsy had left the room that David turned to Joy. 'When did you decide that you wanted to throw Patsy a birthday party?' he demanded.

Joy said, 'A moment ago.' She filled her teacup and then looked at David. 'A thought occurred to me but you might consider it potty.'

'Go on.'

'That Donavan could be Patsy's father.' Joy sounded calm but inside her stomach was churning.

David was silent for several moments. 'Will you pour the tea, please?'

'I knew you'd think I was being silly.'

'I don't think you're being silly but I think you should have given some more consideration to the idea before deciding to give Patsy a birthday party at your house. I can guess what caused you to make that decision. Bring him face-to-face with Patsy and see what happens.'

Joy stiffened. 'Obviously you think it's a bad idea.'

'If Donavan is Patsy's father, then he's taken on a new identity. He obviously doesn't want to be recognised.'

'Then why return to Liverpool? If he wanted his family to believe he was lost at sea, then he should have remained lost,' said Joy firmly. 'Patsy loved her father.'

'I don't doubt it,' said David. 'But having loved him, how is she going to feel knowing that he isn't dead but turned his back on her and the rest of the family, leaving them to fend for themselves? No, Joy, if Donavan is Doyle, then it's up to him to decide whether to make himself known to them. He'd be taking a chance on being rejected.'

'If we're to judge him by his recent behaviour, then he obviously has regrets and would like to see his children. We've heard about the kind of woman his wife was and perhaps he just couldn't cope anymore?'

David's face hardened. 'I don't find that a good enough excuse for his behaviour. If I had a daughter like Patsy I couldn't desert her.'

Joy agreed and added, 'But Patsy is the forgiving sort. You're the same. You forgave your wife and took her back.'

'Only for the sake of her unborn child,' he rasped. 'I'd stopped loving her a long time ago but I was prepared to father the child and I was upset when he was stillborn.'

Joy believed him. 'So what am I to do about the party? I can't retract my words. You saw how pleased Patsy was with the idea.'

'I know.' David stared into the fire. 'I think you'd best time the party for when Donavan's out of the way. She doesn't have to know of our suspicions. She has a home here. Greg will take care of her, so what use is a father to her now?'

Chapter Thirty-Five

It was St Patrick's day and Joy was praying that Patsy's eighteenth birthday would be one that the girl would remember with pleasure. Once David's ankle was out of plaster, Joy had seen him several times when he had visited next door. He had spoken to Patsy and Greg about the children and they were truly pleased at the idea of having some time to themselves.

Joy had asked her brother Freddie to check over the car to make certain it was still roadworthy in the hope that she could persuade David to go out on trips. He had already had his furniture taken out of store and moved into place. He would not take up residence until after Patsy and Greg's wedding which was arranged for Whit Saturday. David had heard from Rodney who had agreed to drop the asking price of the house by fifty pounds.

Joy was on edge, uncertain whether Donavan – or Doyle, if it was him – would walk in on the party. He had been coming and going at different times lately. One little bit of proof – if it could be called that – to add to the little they knew was the carved wooden dolphin that David remembered packing for Patsy when she had moved to Seaforth. He had asked her about it and she had told him that her father had carved it.

'Not definite proof,' David had said to Joy. 'But how many seamen fathers have you heard about who whittle away at wood and make such perfect little models?'

'None,' she had replied.

'What are you thinking about, Aunt Joy?' asked Flora, coming into the kitchen. 'You look miles away.'

Joy was not about to reveal her thoughts to anyone, other than David. 'Have you finished the flowers?' she asked. 'We've still loads to do and I don't want you skiving off.'

'You're saying that just because you think I'm annoyed you're giving this party for Patsy Doyle. Well, I've nothing against her. It's you I'm worried about, Aunt Joy,' Flora said solemnly. 'You haven't been yourself lately. I've even been wondering if you're in love.'

'Don't be silly,' said Joy brusquely. 'I'm too old to fall in love.'

'I don't believe that. I've noticed the way you look at David Tanner when you think nobody is watching and he's the same with you.'

'You're imagining it. He'll never ask me to marry him.' Joy was convinced that, however deep David's feelings were for her, the rejection and pain he had suffered during his previous marriage meant he would not allow himself to believe that a different kind of woman would accept him as he was because she loved him.

'But it's leap year, Aunt Joy,' said Flora. 'You could ask him.'

Joy's heart seemed to flip over and she was aware that the girl was watching her. 'Don't look at me like that! We've work to do,' she said sharply.

'Where's the birthday cake?' asked Flora.

'In a safe place where Robert can't get to it.'

'Makes sense.' Flora gazed fondly at Robert who was now over a year old. He was running a wooden engine along the floor that Mr Donavan had made. 'He is clever with his hands is Mr Donavan,' she said.

'Yes, very talented,' said Joy. She could no longer behave normally with him and felt certain he must have noticed.

'I was telling Mr Donavan about today's party,' said Flora.

'You didn't!'

'I did. What's wrong with that?' said Flora, looking affronted. 'Is it supposed to be some kind of secret? If so nobody has told me.'

'No, but…' Why hadn't she thought of casually telling Flora not to mention the party to him?

Flora's green eyes narrowed like a cat's. 'What's up? You look guilty.'

'What on earth have I got to be guilty about?' protested Joy. 'Did you say who the party was for?'

'I told him it was for Greg's fiancée as he's seen him around when he was helping decorate next door.'

'He didn't ask her name?'

'No, but he did ask why we were having the party here?'

'So what did you say?' asked Joy, her body tense.

'I told him it was because Patsy was an orphan and she'd lived here for a while with her brothers and sisters until they'd had to go into the Seamen's Orphanage.'

Joy groaned inwardly. 'What did he say to that?'

'He asked me where Patsy lived.'

'You didn't tell him!' cried Joy.

'Yes, why not?' protested Flora. 'He said that he'd like to give her a birthday card, because having listened to Greg talk about her, he felt he knew her.'

Joy was startled into saying, 'He certainly blooming does. It must be him!'

'Who must be him?' asked Flora, looking puzzled.

Joy did not answer but went to the telephone and asked for a call to be put through to David's office. When she came off the telephone she told Flora she was going to have to leave her to do the sandwiches, as well as look after Robert, because an emergency had come up and she had to go out.

–

Patsy was humming 'The Boy I Love is up in the Gallery' as she took Helen's party clothes out of the chest of drawers. She was looking forward to the party and was grateful to Joy for arranging the event. She would have a chance to see all the work that Greg and David had done in the house. Useful experience for when they could start work decorating this house, she thought with a happy sigh.

Having sorted out Helen's clothes, Patsy went into her own bedroom and opened the wardrobe and gazed at the frocks hanging there. She took out the one she had bought in the January sales. There was a sudden bang, bang, bang of the door knocker and she ran downstairs to answer its summons. She opened the door and her eyes widened in surprise at the sight of her sister. 'What are you doing here, Kath? I thought you'd be going straight to Joy Bennett's.'

'I thought I'd come here first with your birthday present,' said Kathleen, smiling. 'It's something to wear.'

Patsy was thrilled. 'If it's anything like what you've got on, I'll be made up. Is what you're wearing the latest fashion?'

'Would I wear anything else?'

Patsy stared at Kathleen in admiration. Gone was the simple shift dress of a few months' ago and in its place was a navy-blue figure-hugging frock with embroidery round the neck and sleeves; a red velvet rose was pinned at the waist. As for the hem, it went up and down like a wave with one catching only the odd glimpse of a knee when she did a twirl. 'You look stunning!' exclaimed Patsy.

Kathleen winked. 'That's the kind of effect I'm looking for and all I can say about what you're wearing is that I have made you something better.' She held out a parcel. 'I hope you like it.'

'Thanks!' Patsy's eyes sparkled. 'Come on in.'

Kathleen closed the door. 'I've also got good news for you about our Jimmy.'

'What's that?'

'Chris Davies's dad has arranged it so Jimmy can work in the railway engineering yard. He'll be starting right at the bottom but, as he's dead keen and is prepared to roll up his sleeves and do what he's told, then I'm sure he'll cope with the hard work.'

Patsy let out a whoop and would have danced with her sister up the lobby if Kathleen had not warded her off. 'That's great news!' Then she paused. 'But that means he'll have to find digs in Chester.'

'It also means that you and Greg won't have him living with you. Don't say I don't think about you! Mr Davies has found him digs. He'll be staying with a widow woman who lost her son in the war. She'll probably spoil him soft.'

Patsy went to hug her sister again but Kathleen warded her off once more. 'None of that. You'll crush me rose. Now open your present.'

Patsy led the way into the dining room and removed the string and wrapping paper. She gasped. The dress was of pink embossed satin with a white fur cowl neckline. There was plenty of material in the skirt and it came in at the waist and had three-quarter sleeves. 'It's lovely!' There were tears in Patsy's eyes.

'I thought, the way the weather's been mad so far this year, that you needed a bit of fur,' said Kathleen. 'Are you going to put it on so we can see how it fits?'

'Of course I am,' said Patsy, almost jumping up and down with delight.

The pair of them went upstairs and Patsy changed into the party dress. When she saw herself in the mirror she was thrilled. 'I look so fine. You wouldn't believe I was just an all-purpose maid.'

'You're nothing of the sort. Housekeeper more like and soon you'll be Mrs Molyneux.'

Patsy smiled. 'I can't believe everything has turned out so well. As for the dress, thanks so much, Kath. I feel great in it.'

'It's a perfect fit if I say it myself.' Kathleen gave a satisfied smile.

'Clever you,' said Patsy.

'Aren't I just?' said Kathleen, chuckling. 'So when will we be leaving for the party?'

Patsy gave a little shiver of excitement. 'I've never been the centre of attraction. I'll call the kids in soon to get ready and, by then, Greg should be here.' The words were no sooner out of her mouth when she heard a banging on the front door. Who was it this time? She went to open it and Helen immediately darted past her into the house. 'What's up with you?' asked Patsy.

'There's a man asking where Mr Tanner lives,' panted Helen, her eyes wide with fear. 'Do you think it's Uncle Rodney come to take us away?'

Patsy frowned. 'I doubt it, love. Where is this man?'

'Talking to our Nelson. I thought I'd best get you.'

Patsy went outside and almost immediately saw Nelson standing near the lamp post, talking to a man in a navy-blue reefer jacket. The latter's head was cocked to one side and he was obviously listening intently to the boy. Patsy could not see his face clearly but there was something about the way he held his head that was familiar.

Suddenly he turned and looked in her direction. For a moment they just stared at each other. He reminded her of her father and she wondered if he could possibly be of some relation to him. Then he threw back his shoulders and jutted his chin and began to walk towards her with a slight rolling gait that she did recognise. Her heart began to pound. It couldn't be! Yet there was a grimness about his mouth that reminded her of the last time she had seen her father. He had stormed out of the house after another flaming row with her mother, saying that he might never come back.

He stopped a couple of feet away from her. 'It is you, Patsy,' he said, a look in his eyes that twisted her insides and made her want to cry. 'And looking all grown-up and so fine and ready for your birthday party.'

'How d'you know about that? Is it really you, Dad?'

'Yeah, girlie, it's me, your old dad.' There was a quiver in his voice and his eyelid was twitching. 'And I know about your party because I lodge with Mrs Bennett under the name of Donavan.'

Patsy's mouth fell open and for a moment she could not speak. This couldn't be real. 'I don't understand! Did you know we'd lived there? Why change your name? Where've you been all this time?'

'You'll probably hate me when I tell you. I lived in America for several years and I stayed away deliberately because I wanted a new start away from your mother and her men.'

Patsy felt as if she had been smacked in the face. 'Bu-but what about us kids? Didn't you care about us?' she cried.

He looked miserable and jammed his hands into his pockets. 'Of course I cared for you, Mick and Kathy. Jimmy, I wasn't sure whether he was mine or not. The twins definitely weren't,' he rasped.

'Even so, if you cared for those of us that were yours, then you wouldn't have let us believe you were dead!' A tear rolled down Patsy's cheek and then another. She felt cold and shivery and wrapped her arms around her. 'I mourned for you, Dad. We had a terrible life when you didn't come back. Why have you come now when everything is going well?'

'Because I couldn't bear the voice in my head telling me I was a rotten father any longer!' His eyes glistened with tears. 'So I came back to Liverpool. Only when I got here I was just too bloody selfish to want to live with your mother again and I thought you children would hate me and I don't blame you for doing so. It was just chance that I ended up at Mrs Bennett's place.'

'But-but weren't you washed overboard, then?' asked Patsy, trying to make sense of what he was telling her.

'Yeah, but I was rescued by a fishing boat off the coast of America. I was in a bit of a state and so one of the men took me into his home and he and his sister looked after me. I was out of me head for a while.'

Patsy wiped her eyes on the back of her hand. 'So you didn't plan to leave us when you left home?'

'Perhaps the thought was there, buried, only waiting to—'

'What's going on?' interrupted Kathleen, coming out onto the step to stand alongside her sister. 'You've been crying, our Patsy,' she said. 'Did this bloke upset you?' She glared at the man standing a few feet away.

'Aye, I did, girlie,' he said hoarsely. 'You must be Kathleen. I used to call you my little blonde beauty when you were only a tot.'

'You what?' Kathleen took a step closer to him and peered into his face. 'You look familiar. Who are you?'

'Kath, this is our dad! He didn't drown after all. He was rescued and lived in America and for a while he's been lodging with Joy Bennett.' Patsy's voice sounded raw.

Kathleen gasped. 'I don't get it! If he stayed away all this time what's he doing here now? Did he lose his memory or something? Forget that he had seven kids?'

'I didn't have seven kids last time I looked,' growled her father. 'Had another, did she, to another bloke?'

Patsy gulped. It was true what her father said but she did not like hearing it. 'Anthony was adopted. It broke my heart to see him go. If you'd been here, Dad, then—'

'No! You can't lay the blame for that on me, girlie. He wasn't mine.'

Patsy cried, 'I know that, Dad, but even so, if you'd been there, then Mam mightn't have been murdered by that swine of a brother of hers and…'

Her father's face turned white and his mouth worked but no words came out. Then he managed to say, 'I had heard but I'll not take responsibility for that either, girlie. I was a sailor and that meant I spent time away. If she'd been faithful to me, then things would have been different.'

'It wasn't our fault,' said Patsy in a hard voice.

'No, girlie, I know that.' His voice had sunk so low that the girls could barely hear him.

Patsy and her sister looked at each other. 'What's he doing here?' asked Kathleen, looking bewildered. 'What's he want of us? He wasn't here when I needed him.'

'I just wanted to have a look at you all and see how you'd turned out. If you need money, I can—'

'Money!' cried Patsy, twisting her hands together. 'We needed money years ago when you weren't here, not now! We've built lives for ourselves. We've managed without you, Dad.'

'What's going on? What are you doing here, Mr Donavan?' asked Greg.

Relief flooded through Patsy and she flung herself at her fiancé. He put his arms round her and hugged her to him. 'What's wrong, love?'

'I only came to wish her a happy birthday,' said Donavan, taking an envelope from his pocket. 'If you'll give this to her.'

'Whatever it is, I don't want it,' said Patsy in a muffled voice.

Her father forced the envelope into Greg's hand and then walked away. 'I don't understand,' said Greg. 'Why should he—?'

'He's our dad,' said Kathleen bitterly. 'He thinks he can come back and we'll welcome him with open arms.'

Patsy lifted her head and presented a ravaged face to Greg. 'How could he have deserted us when he knew what Mam was like?' Her head drooped on Greg's shoulder and she wept.

He half carried her into the house, followed by Kathleen and Nelson. Helen was sitting at the bottom of the stairs. 'Are we still going to the party?' she asked.

Patsy lifted her head. The last thing she was in the mood for was a party. 'Do you want to go, love?'

'Yes!'

There was a long silence while Patsy struggled with her emotions. 'Then we'll go.'

'Are you sure, love?' asked Greg.

'Our Kath has made me a new frock and I want to show it off.'

'Donavan could be there,' he said. 'And if he is—'

'He won't be! I think he got the message that we don't want him,' said Kathleen fiercely. 'Now, you kids, scoot and get ready.'

They were all prepared to leave when David and Joy arrived.

'What are you two doing here?' asked Greg. Then his eyes narrowed. 'Or can I guess?'

David stared at his set face. 'Patsy's father's been here, then?'

'He's my father, too, you know?' said Kathleen belligerently. 'And we've sent him away with a flea in his ear.'

Joy exchanged glances with David. 'Do you think he'll go back to the house?' she asked.

'Yes. I don't doubt he'll pack his things and leave.'

'Then, hopefully, he'll have gone by the time we arrive there,' said Patsy. 'Obviously you knew who he was and didn't tell me.'

'Not for certain,' said David, looking uncomfortable. He told the girls everything.

'So his conscience really was bothering him,' said Patsy, overcome by conflicting emotions.

'It sounds like it,' said Greg, his eyes on her drawn face.

'Perhaps he deserves a second chance,' said David.

'I'm not sure about that,' said Patsy.

'Me neither,' said Kathleen, linking her arm through her sister's. 'But let's get cracking and get to this party and see what happens.'

–

Flora entered the kitchen where Wendy was keeping an eye on Robert. 'I'm bothered,' said Flora. 'Mr Donavan's just come in and he looks in a bit of a state. He went straight upstairs and I can hear drawers being opened and shut. I want to know what's going on.'

'I'll come with you,' said Wendy without hesitation.

They hurried upstairs and knocked on his bedroom door. 'Mr Donavan!' called Wendy.

He opened the door and stared at them. 'You'll know soon enough so I might as well come clean. My real name is Mike Doyle. I'm Patsy and Kathleen's father. I'm leaving, so if you'll let me get on with me packing, I won't be bothering them or you anymore.'

'So you're not dead, then!' said Flora, flabbergasted.

'Obviously not,' murmured Wendy. 'What's the rush, Mr Doyle?'

'I made a mistake in coming back.' His voice trembled.

Flora hesitated and then slipped her arm through Mike's. 'Why don't you tell us all about it?' she said in a soothing voice.

He glanced at his Gladstone bag on the bed and his expression was uncertain. 'I want to be out of here before everyone arrives.'

'Oh, there's plenty of time,' said Wendy reassuringly.

Mike's eyelid flickered. 'They don't want me and I don't blame them for that.'

'Give them a chance to forgive you,' said Wendy.

'I don't deserve forgiving,' said Mike.

'Nobody is perfect, Mr Doyle,' said Flora. 'So where were you when you went missing?'

–

An hour or so later Mike was still sitting at the kitchen table, drinking tea and looking nervous. Wendy had departed with Robert in his pram to pick up Jimmy and the twins and he could hear voices outside. The door burst open and Patsy was the first inside, followed by her sister.

Kathleen stared at her father who was sitting with Flora and glowered at her. 'How dare you be so palsy-walsy with my father, Flora Bennett!' she cried.

'You're still here,' said Patsy, still unsure of her feelings towards her father. 'I thought you might have gone.'

'I would have, girlie, if it hadn't been for this young lady here,' said Mike, getting to his feet. 'It's time for me to leave. It's your birthday and I don't want to be in the way.'

Patsy met her father's eyes and it suddenly struck her that this was a moment to savour, despite everything that he had done wrong. Her father was alive! She might not always feel so forgiving and thankful but for the moment she did. 'My birthday celebration can wait, Dad. I want to hear everything.'

Mike's chest swelled and, for a moment, he could not speak. Then he launched into his tale, beginning with how wooden flotsam from a torpedoed ship had provided him with the means to stay afloat until the fishing boat had found him. At some point Grant arrived and he listened with the other adults but the children went out into the garden.

When her father had finished telling his tale, Patsy realised that her birthday had not been ruined after all. In fact, it occurred to her that he would be able to give her away at her wedding. It also struck her that she might need his permission to marry Greg. She mentioned the matter to her fiancé an hour or two later, during a waltz in Robbie's old music room.

For a moment Greg looked alarmed. 'I suppose I'm going to have to ask him, not that I like the idea,' he said frankly. 'He didn't take care of you the way a father should.'

Even so, Greg did broach the subject with Patsy's father. Mike seemed uncomfortable at his doing so. 'I like you, lad. Of course you have my permission to marry Patsy. I feel it's wrong that you have to ask. It's not as if I own her and she's proved that she can manage her affairs without me. I'm even considering going back to sea, so you have no need to bother about me.'

In some ways that was a relief to Greg because he felt that she might feel that she had to offer him a home with them.

'If you do that, Dad, then I hope you won't go until you give me away at our wedding,' said Patsy.

'Aye, girlie, I'll do that and be proud to be there,' he said humbly.

Epilogue

Whit Saturday, 1928

'So I can stop worrying about Patsy now, David,' said Joy, stepping back as the car drew away from the kerb with Greg and his bride inside.

'Yes, but are you sure about taking on the twins while they're away?' asked David.

Joy smiled. 'They're good with Robert. Anyway, what a question to ask me when you're having Nelson and Helen stay with you.'

'It does mean the four children will see each other every day.'

'It would probably be more convenient if we were all living together,' said Joy casually.

David stared at her rosy face. 'You can't be serious?'

'Well, it is leap year, so I wondered if you'd like to marry me?' she asked, toying with a tendril of soft brown hair.

David did not answer her immediately but drew her apart from the rest of the wedding party. 'I'm deeply appreciative, Joy, of your proposal but I can't marry you,' he said in a husky voice.

'Why?' she asked bluntly. 'I think we'll suit each other very well. I could see to all your needs, make cakes, sew buttons on your shirts…'

'You're talking about a convenient match like the one you made with Robbie.'

'No,' said Joy firmly. 'I love you and I'm all for us having plenty of cuddles. What I don't expect is the kind of loving that Patsy and Greg will share.'

He took her hand and squeezed it. 'I love you. I'd like to accept but there's something about me that you don't know and I'm too embarrassed to speak about it.' His expression was suddenly bleak.

Joy took a deep breath. 'I know about your war injuries, David. I know you can't have children. Rose blurted it out that day I went to your house. I think she was trying to justify her behaviour.' Joy lifted his hand to her lips and kissed the backs of his fingers. 'I'm so sorry. I understand how much it matters to you, but there's so much more in life that we can share together.'

Tears filled his eyes. 'You've known all this time and—!'

Joy swiftly kissed him. 'So what's your answer? If it's no again, then I'll carry on asking you all this leap year until you're fed up with me.'

'Then it'll have to be yes because I can't ever imagine myself getting fed up with you, Joy of my life,' he replied, hugging her tightly.